TENTH BOOMER

A Brian Latimer Mystery Novel

I0657292

Richard Neil
Author

RNC SERVICES
Publisher

RNC Services, Publisher
P.O. Box 463
Rancho, Mirage, CA 92270

TENTH BOOMER. Copyright 2014 by Richard N. Crauthers
ISBN 978-0-615-32683-2

RNC Services' books may be purchased for educational, business, or sales promotional use. For information please write: Special Markets Department, RNC Services Publishers, P.O. Box 463, Rancho Mirage, CA 92270.

First RNC Services printing: January 2014

Printed in the United States of America

Visit website www.RichardNeilAuthor.com

Library of Congress Cataloging-in-Publication Data
Number: 2011943732

DEDICATION PAGE

For the important people in my life

Richard, Darren, & Kathryn

**And by extension
Robin, Ryan, Benjamin, and John P**

TENTH BOOMER

A Brian Latimer Mystery Novel

PROLOGUE

Wednesday night, April 13
Santa Monica, California

Something had to be in the beer. But, that couldn't be. He had brought both bottles from the refrigerator, opened them himself, and gave one to his guest. The bottles came from the same carton. Then with fading, tunnel vision, his eyes focused on small tears on the labels, first on the bottle he held and then on the empty one sitting on the table in front of him. With effort, he squinted to see the label of his guest's empty bottle on the far end of the coffee table. It had no tear. He could not see the label on the bottle that his guest still held.

In spite of his growing suspicion, he felt an odd sense of relaxation, actually very mellow. He realized something affected his mind, his body. His visitor must have given him the same drug they had given their target last week.

He needed to escape, to get away before the drug took effect. He now knew the reason for this surprise visit by his guest. He could now answer that far away question for suggestions of who could be the *fall guy*.

"Wait. Wait a minute. What's going on here?" The words struggled from his mouth, slow, garbled. He gripped the couch arm to stand up to defend himself. "You son of a…"

He fell backwards into the couch's soft cushions. His consciousness sank deeper, as if slowly falling into a shadowy black hole.

"At least you're observant" The guest had watched his host stare at the small tears on his bottles, and then at his own full one. He set his full bottle on the coffee table and turned it so the label would face his host. "See, it has the same tear as yours. I just haven't drunk from it."

"And yes, it's the same stuff that I gave you to give our target last week. My, my, you're just not suspicious enough, or fast enough. You acted on your own too many times, too recklessly. You should have remembered that I am in control of our little joint venture. I tell you what to do. You became a liability, so I have to remove you from the equation." He taunted his victim and smiled as he rose from his chair to close the drapes.

As he closed the drapes, he examined the courtyard. It was empty. He pulled the drape cords slowly, noticing that the sun had nearly set. Had he faced the window while he sat, he could have seen what must have been a lovely sunset. The western sky was filled with purple and red colors. A developer could definitely build million dollar condos on this site.

His host continued to mumble, something about how he would beat his guest into a fucking pulp.

In a few moments, his host would fade completely. The drug in his beers will have done its job. Then, he would complete his next step for the evening. No fateful trip over the mountains this time. The second drug would guarantee the results he wanted.

But first, he leaned over his host and stared threatening into his eyes.

"I'd really like to snuff you out. You've caused me so many problems. You're not tough; you're just stupid." He pulled a throw pillow from the couch and held it near his host's face. "In your state, I could smother you, or strangle you. But alas, either method wouldn't fit in my plans. And you know how I like plans. You had your chance."

His host continued to fade.

The guest pulled a pair of latex gloves from his jacket pocket and slipped his hands into them. He also removed a small eyeglass-case from his pocket. It contained a syringe filled with heroin, enough to overdose a half dozen people. He wanted plenty to complete this job.

He repositioned his nearly asleep host on the couch into a comfortable position, not that it mattered. He stuffed a throw pillow awkwardly under his head, and stretched one leg along the length of the couch, the other on the coffee table. A little drama never hurts. People who overdose unintentionally usually do not lie in relaxed, napping positions. They settle into a least resistance position, like a heavy liquid.

He knocked the flip-flop from his host's foot that lay on the coffee table.

His host was a drug user, even sold a little on the side. A fact that would surprise no one. Although he did not use the heavy stuff that his guest would now give him.

The visitor injected all of the syringe's contents between his sleeping host's two larger toes. The autopsy naturally would discover the heroin in his system, but that could require a couple weeks or longer to determine. Drug users often used hidden locations on their bodies. After all, he worked in a corporate environment that sanctioned casual dress, so leaving obvious drug tracks in his arms was not permissible.

When he finished the injection, he patted his host's leg, as if affectionate, and sarcastically told him, "You just rest now."

After a couple minutes, his host took a few deep breaths and stopped breathing.

Now for the next step in the visitor's plan.

ONE

NINE DAYS EARLIER
Monday afternoon, April 4
Santa Monica, California

"No one in our department will lose their jobs." The well-dressed thirty-something high-achiever said to his subordinate.

"That's good news. The others will be glad to hear that." The young, blond surfer grinned and nodded as he absentmindedly twirled his pen with his fingers.

"Pass the word to the others in the department." The surfer's boss said while he shuffled papers on his desk. "Not that anyone in our department worried."

"True. Since our department makes most of the money for this company. Anything else?"

"No, that's it." Indicating the meeting was over.

The young man rose from his chair and anchored his pen in his shirt pocket. He closed his boss' office door as he left.

Arthur Allen Dexter worked because he needed money, at least in the beginning. But he preferred riding waves over work anytime. Sometimes he invented excuses to leave work early to surf, especially when the giant waves pounded the beach. The hours spent in the sun and on the waves kept him in shape, his skin tanned, his brown hair bleached. He was twenty-eight but behaved more like a carefree high school sophomore.

His parents pushed him to attend college. He attended California State University in Carson, a small suburb in the South Bay area of Los Angeles County. He graduated with barely passing grades. Fortunately, his intelligence enabled him to pass exams with little study, and poor class attendance.

After graduation, he took his current job with Leonard Construction in Santa Monica a few miles up the coast. The company built hi-rise commercial properties worldwide, maintaining their headquarters in Santa Monica since the company was founded.

Profits had suffered for the last two years. Leonard began a project to examine their expenses and staffing requirements. Rumors of a layoff had circulated among the staff for the past week. Management had decided to cut staff by ten percent this year. Layoff rumors were no longer rumors.

Art stopped by two of his colleagues' desks to tell them the news, and to pass the word to the others. In their small department, word would circulate quickly.

Instead of returning to his chair, he tossed his writing pad on his desk and headed to the stairwell. Sure-footed as a big horn ram, he bounded up the stairs two steps at a time. Because his car was in a repair shop, a co-worker Greg Larkin had agreed to give him a ride home. He wanted to talk Greg into leaving work early. He could have called, but then he would be at his desk and probably feel the need to work. Work must be avoided, his motto.

Greg worked about three rungs above Art on the corporate ladder, but the people in the two departments shared relaxed, congenial relationships.

As Art rounded the corner, taking a few long strides, he raised his hand to knock on Greg's office door. The office was empty. Art turned to leave, and almost bumped into Greg returning from a meeting with his boss, probably with the same news.

"Hello Art." Greg's voice sounded upbeat. His department had escaped the dreaded layoffs also.

"Hello Mr. Larkin." Art returned the greeting in a mock formal but cheerful voice as he followed Greg into his office. "I really appreciate your giving me a ride. But any chance, we could leave a little early? That rain beating on the windows is really depressing."

"But we work inside. There's no rain in here." Greg teased.

"But it hard not to notice, with all of these windows."

"I'm just teasing. Sure. I'm pretty much caught up. Month end is over. Besides, traffic will be a real bear going home in this rain." Looking outside his window, he could barely see the Los Angeles International Airport, almost invisible from the heavy rain.

"What's with this rain, anyway? It's a lot more than normal. Besides, it's not supposed to rain in Southern California – isn't there an old song about that?" Art was in his usual playful, mood. "Maybe we can stop by The Deck, on the beach for a drink. I'm buying. Maybe you'll miss some of the traffic over Topanga."

"Unlikely. In this rain, the traffic will probably be worse. But a quick drink sounds good. Maybe the rain will subside some. We can celebrate no layoffs, at least in our departments." Greg picked up his can of Diet Coke and sipped it. It tasted tepid, room temperature. Feeling a little guilty, "But some departments weren't so lucky. We probably know a few unfortunate souls in other departments."

"Yeah, you're right. It's not entirely good news." The surfer felt maybe he shouldn't gloat, at least not aloud."

"Wait a minute. Isn't The Deck a little past your neighborhood?"

"Yeah. But only a little. I like The Deck. Great happy hour snacks."

"Just one drink. Ok?"

"Ok."

"Ok." Greg still needed to tell his staff that layoffs would not happen this year in their department. And he needed to finish a couple other quick tasks.

"I told the guys on our staff on my way up here. Thanks for the ride. Gotta go." Art turned to leave.

"See you in the parking garage, third floor, half hour." Greg called to Art's back.

"Lucky you. Assigned parking. See you there." Art teased, and waved as he took swift strides to the stairwell.

Born in Ohio to blue collar, hard-working parents, Gregory Dawson Larkin developed a strong work ethic as a young man. At six years old, and the youngest of four boys, he, his brothers, and their parents moved to California thirty years ago. His parents sacrificed to help him and his brothers attend college.

Greg stood two inches under six feet, trim frame, but with a small belly forming. He paid for gym membership, but rarely had the time to use it. His full head of black hair showed some gray at the temples. He kept it short, almost a crew cut; otherwise it curled and looked unmanaged. He kept his face clean-shaven. Three months ago, the company established a casual dress policy. Greg removed the tie, rolled up the sleeves, but kept the dress slacks. He preferred a clean-cut, professional appearance.

When Greg arrived to his car, Art was leaning against it. Greg drove a five-year old Toyota Camry, low on looks, high on reliability. Greg rarely gave rides to colleagues or other adults. He offered weak apologies to his passengers about the kid's toys in the back. He gave Art the same insincere apology. Seeing his kids' toys in the back seat area warmed him inside. He loved his family.

Before he married, before the kids came, Greg drove a sporty vintage Triumph II, and he kept it in mint condition. He washed and waxed it more often than it needed. When his wife became pregnant with their first child, he replaced the Triumph with this much more practical used Camry. He now washed the Camry every six months if he had the time. In the future, after the kids finished college, he expected more time, and more money to own an upscale car, maybe another sports car.

He and Art left for the restaurant, a few miles up Pacific Coast Highway, or PCH as locals called it. The rain had subsided, but only a little.

Greg turned his Camry into a parking space in the self-park lot. The valet parking kiosk was closed. He preferred parking his own car, anyway. In nice weather, they would need the favor of the parking gods to find a space, even on Mondays. But this rain kept people away. Greg and Art opened their umbrellas and rushed to the restaurant.

The Deck at Sunset restaurant sat on the beach where the famous Sunset Boulevard ended at the Pacific Ocean. City side, broad wood planks, weathered from the sea air, or other artificial means, covered the walls. Customers entered from the side under a large blue canvass awning with *The Deck at Sunset* in white script, and through large wood and glass doors.

Under the canvas cover, they shook the rain off their umbrellas and themselves. Once inside, the warmth welcomed them. Southern California does not have cold weather compared with most states, but for people who live there, even cool weather, especially with rain, can feel cold.

11

On the beach-side, giant windows maximized the ocean views from any seat in the restaurant. Outside, a wide wooden deck ran the full length of the building and wrapped around it to connect with the front entrance. Employees had stacked chairs and tables to one side. No one would use them today.

Half walls defined the inside space, separating the foyer, the bar, and the dining areas. In a large tank, against one half wall, lobsters lay motionless or crawled slowly over each other. A large dark, high-polished wood bar sat in the middle of the room. It separated the main dining area from the bar seating area.

A pretty, thin hostess in a long black skirt stepped from behind her station and welcomed her new customers. Art told her that they were here only for drinks, and continued to the bar area, where they found a small table. The hostess returned to her station and resumed her conversation with one of the waitresses.

"Order me a scotch-and-water please? Do you know where the men's room is?" Greg laid his raincoat and umbrella on an empty chair.

"In the back, past the bar." Art pointed past Greg's shoulder.

Greg walked with a purpose in that direction.

A short skirted, again thin, waitress with straight shoulder length brunette hair, approached. "What can I get you?"

Art almost interrupted her, "a Chivas and water for my friend and a Bud Light for me, please."

"A man who knows what he wants. Always a good thing." The waitress smiled a toothy smile and left to collect the drinks.

Art laid his umbrella and raincoat on the same chair that Greg had used. The waitress returned after only a minute. The bartender had heard the order. She set the drinks on the table and returned to chat with the bartender. The bar had few patrons.

After a couple minutes, Greg returned.

"Restroom hand blow dryers never work like they're supposed to." Greg rubbed his hands together vigorously and on his shirt to dry and warm them. He sat in the remaining empty chair. "Stopping here was a good idea - just as long as we don't stay too long. Otherwise, traffic in this rain could still take two hours to get home."

"Relax, we'll be out of here in no time." Art swigged his beer.

"Just so we keep track of the time. I don't usually drink on Mondays. Actually rarely drink, period."

"Okay. Okay. Enough small talk. Let's talk about that important meeting that our bosses went to after lunch." Art knew Greg well enough he could ask. "We know about the limited layoffs. What else? Your boss always tells you more."

"What if the other topics are privileged, on a need-to-know basis?" Greg teased. "Didn't Chas tell you anything?"

"He was busy, but he did say that there was some sort of accounting error, or maybe some digital pilfering." Art persisted. "You're in accounting. You know more. Come on, tell me."

"Ok! Ok! I'll tell you. At least what I can. I can't tell you everything. You know that. As you know there's a big effort underway to cut expenses where they can. Well, we, in Accounting that is, have been investigating expenses. I noticed some irregularities in some of the bill payments. So, I brought it up to Larry's attention. And, those irregularities are not from accounting errors."

"Well, what? What about it?"

"So, they're hiring a computer-systems-accounting expert to help resolve the problem." Greg stirred his drink with his finger and tasted it; a puzzled, distracted look skirted over his face.

"Chivas. The good stuff." Art teased.

"Oh. The good stuff." Gregg grinned. "Well, since you're buying."

"Yeah."

"There's a meeting tomorrow morning with the senior execs. I expect Chas will be there and I'm sure he'll tell you everything, afterward."

"He doesn't always tell me everything." Art prodded. "You'll probably be there, right?"

"Probably, since I discovered the discrepancies."

"Do you know who this forensics systems guy is?"

"No, no I don't." Greg drank more of his scotch.

Art continued his efforts to pump Greg for more information. Greg attempted to steer the conversation to small talk. But Art stubbornly returned the conversation to the details of the accounting problem.

The toothy waitress returned and asked if the men wanted more drinks.

"Yes." Art wanted to pump Greg for more information. Before Greg could protest, Art, with his finger, gestured an imaginary circle above their drinks. "Another round, please."

"Oh, alright." Greg grinned already feeling relaxed from his drink.

Feeling a little hungry, they visited the appetizer table. The restaurant provided a generous assortment of snacks for their drinking customers. Sunset Happy Hour, they called it. A few more patrons had arrived.

Greg selected a few shrimp and cocktail sauce. He planned dinner with his wife later. Art loaded his plate with tacos, salsa, and shrimp. No surfing today, so this would be his dinner.

They talked more. Art relented his efforts to pump Greg for more information. Small talk reigned. The toothy waitress returned.

"Wait, wait, look at the time. Art, come on, finish your drink. I need to get on the road. It's raining out, or have you forgotten?" Greg looked at the waitress and shook his head no. Then, to Art, he said. "I need to drop you off at your place and get over Topanga. It's nearly six. I need to call Alicia. It'll still take me a good hour to get home in this rain. It doesn't look like it's subsided much."

Art acquiesced with a nod and shrugged his shoulders. He gestured to the waitress for the check with mock writing in his palm, and then gobbled his last taco.

Greg reached for his wallet.

"No, no. I said I was buying." Art said, chugging the last of his beer.

The waitress brought the check. Art handed her a fifty and after a couple minutes, she returned with the change. Being a big tipper, Art gave her a twenty and thanked her. Her toothy smile grew even larger. Nearly a hundred percent tip.

Both men slipped on their raincoats, picked up their umbrellas, and headed for the parking lot.

Greg pulled out of the parking area onto PCH for the short distance to Art's place. He double-parked in front of Art's apartment complex. Art thanked him, and rushed up the steps to the covered stoop to his front door. The rain was steady, but not as heavy as earlier.

Greg completed a U-turn back to PCH. He looked at his gas gage. It registered a quarter tank, plenty for the trip home. Usually he kept his car's gas tank near full, but with the rain, he did not want to stop to fill it. Besides, he could buy cheaper gas near his home.

Only a few routes led through the Santa Monica Mountains from PCH into the San Fernando Valley, known as The Valley. Topanga Canyon and Malibu Canyon roads were the most frequently traveled routes. Most days Greg drove Topanga Canyon road home.

With the steady rain on the windshield outside, and the car's heater on high, Greg felt warmer. The drinks, the food, and the warm car felt soothing. He felt relaxed, tired, and even a little sleepy. He had only two drinks in a nearly two-hour period, so it should not affect his driving. He turned on the radio, pushed a preset button to soft rock, and settled into his seat for the ride home.

Greg thought about Art, and basically liked him. But they lived in two different worlds. Art liked to surf, and to party. Greg preferred home life with his wife and kids. On very rare occasions, he envied Art's carefree self-centered life, but mostly he thought it wasteful, unsatisfying. However, Greg did wish he worked in the Construction Projects Division. They received better pay and faster promotions. Even so, Greg liked his job. He just wanted promotions and healthy pay raises for a better life for his family.

The rain became heavier; it pelted the car's roof and windshield, raising the sound level to noisy. The rain sluiced over the windshield, distorting his view of the road like thick out-of-focus glasses. He switched the wipers to high speed, adding more noise inside the car. He turned off the radio. He wanted to focus on his driving. Topanga Canyon contained many curves, few passing lanes, and no streetlights, except for car lights in both directions. This time of the evening most cars headed one direction, toward The Valley, the same direction as Greg. He probably should not have stopped for the drinks, but it gave a nice break to his usual routine. The traffic had lessened.

To improve his alertness, Greg shook his head, forced a yawn, and squeezed his eyes shut and open. He reminded himself that he had had only the two drinks. And with food. And over a two hour period. He had slept well last night and had worked an atypical short day. He should not feel this sleepy. He massaged his jaw, stretched his neck, forced another wide yawn, and readjusted himself in his seat. Still, he felt sleepy.

An on-coming car honked and flicked its lights between high and low beams. Greg realized he had crossed into the oncoming lane; he swerved right, over corrected. He nearly hit the railing, swerved left, then swerved right again. The adrenaline surge woke him. But only for a minute.

A car followed him, its headlights flooding the inside of his car.

Another oncoming car honked its horn and blinked its lights too. Greg corrected his car back to his lane. He was just so sleepy. Perhaps he needed to pull into one of the few pullouts located along the route, and call someone. No way would he call Alicia, his wife and subject her to these conditions. He decided he would stop in the next one and rest a little. Just enough to wake-up.

Another oncoming car. More honking. More lights flashing. He was in the other lane again. What was wrong with him? He swerved a hard right. Overcorrected. Then, he countered with a sharp left. Too much. Another sharp right.

He hit the low metal railing, too late to swerve back left. He slammed his foot on the brakes. The car would not stop. It slid. His car blasted through the railing and became airborne, sailing over the cliff into the deep ravine below.

For just a moment quiet replaced the noise. Except for the windshield wipers in their futile attempt to thrash away the rain. He heard little sound. He realized the danger, the impending crash. If only he could wake-up. He tried desperately to shake his head, his mind awake. He should feel wide-awake, but did not. Fear overtook him. His heart pounded, trying to explode from his chest.

He thought of his family, Alicia, Annie, Kenny. He had to think their names. Their names made them more real. He could not leave them yet. This should not be happening.

Except for his pounding heart, he heard little. Then, he heard the sound of crunching metal. Then total silence engulfed Greg Larkin.

TWO

Tuesday Morning, April 5
Long Beach, California

Brian Joseph Latimer opened one eye, peeked at the bedside clock, and then opened the other. In three minutes, the radio alarm would play soft music on low volume. He preferred beginning his day with quiet music, instead of the jolting alarm buzz that most people used, as if preparing for a day of battle.

He rarely needed an external wake-up device. As a young man, he did, but that struggle ceased years ago. Somewhere along his forty plus years of work, he developed an effective internal clock. Few events altered his reliance on this internal time control, including travel, sleepless nights, different beds, and new time zones.

Another frustration, hotels provided small plastic clock radios that assaulted his senses with their grating buzz or clanging sounds. Sometimes, he packed his own clock, or used the front desk wake-up service. However, these so-called *services* used loud, obnoxious ring tones, and phony voice recordings. He disliked his urge to reply *thank you* to these devices.

Brian enjoyed listening to music for a few minutes before leaving a warm bed. Years ago, he would press the snooze button for a little more sleep, closing his eyes, but lie in a half-awake state.

Over time he had awakened to soft rock, light jazz, opera, and even country and western. Mostly, he liked stations that played 'the oldies', songs by Billy Joel, Cher, Elton John, and the Beatles. He liked the same music that he liked when he was a young man.

Brian believed that people listened to the music of their youth all their lives. In their fifties, their sixties, and even their eighties, they enjoyed the same music, the same entertainers. Older entertainers continued their popularity with their fans through the years, and often performed in retirement communities, such as Palm Springs, Miami, and Phoenix.

The first of the baby boomer generation had begun to retire. Brian's birth preceded this huge surge in American population by a couple years. This human bulge would influence American culture in their retirement years as they had all their lives. They would still demand their music, their entertainers.

Brian had one friend, not retired, but about the same age. With a successful small business, she had seen Neil Diamond twenty-six times, and would continue to buy the expensive front row seats every time he performed in or near the Los Angeles area.

Radio stations often referred to Brian's generation of favored music as *the oldies*. Nearing sixty, he had friends in their sixties and seventies. In denial about his own increasing age, he thought of them as the older ones, those who listened to Frank Sinatra, Tony Bennett, Ethel Merman, and Dean Martin. He resisted accepting that he was in their age bracket, admitting, when pressed, only that he stood in the lower end of the bracket.

He wondered if today's youth who listened to techno rock and hip-hop would continue to listen to the same music for the next thirty years. Would hip-hop really last that long? Would techno rock become *the oldies*?

He tossed the lightweight blanket and sheet aside, swung his legs over the side, and toed into his slippers. He donned a lightweight bathrobe over his pajamas. This April morning felt cool, but not as cold as it does in the mid-west. He liked Southern California's weather. He even liked the infrequent rain, including last night's. However, he, like most Southern Californians, did not like driving in it. The rain amplified their bad driving habits, resulting in rear-end crashes, fender benders, and traffic jams, causing traffic snarls, sometimes known as *sig* alerts.

Brian lived near the top floor of a high-rise in downtown Long Beach, California. The high-rise, known as the Spire by the Beach, rose over thirty stories and sat a few hundred yards from the Pacific Ocean. Each floor in the cylinder-shaped residential building contained eight pie shaped condos. The only exception, the top floor contained four pent-houses, bigger pieces of the pie. The best feature of the condos included floor-to-ceiling windows on all the outer walls. A balcony with wrought iron railings encircled each floor. Only small metal shields separated the balconies.

The location of the condo dictated the view. On the South and East sides, residents saw ocean and marina views. On the West and North sides, they enjoyed city light and mountain views. Brian loved his city lights view. At night, the lights extended as far as he could see. In the daytime, and on clear days, he could see the Hollywood sign in the Hollywood hills. He needed binoculars to read it, but he could see it.

Brian had lived in the condo for four years and never tired of the view. Sleepy as he was, he took a moment to savor the view. He opened the sliders, and inhaled his lungs full of the fresh air. The air smelled clean after last night's rain. This morning, he could see the Hollywood sign. Street sounds engulfed him, blaring horns, revving engines, the hiss of hydraulic brakes, and many indistinct voices from below.

Rain always cleared the smog in the LA area. Even though LA's smog problem had improved since the seventies and eighties, LA still had the dubious distinction of being one of the cities with the dirtiest air in the nation.

With fresh air in his lungs, he turned to his most favored ritual of the morning, his coffee. One of his pleasures as he has aged, involved sitting in a comfortable chair, with coffee mug in hand, for about twenty minutes, slowly waking as he started his day. Nearly every morning, he practiced this ritual. When he worked, he awoke thirty minutes early each day so he could enjoy his coffee, and a few minutes of quiet to prepare his mind, as well as his body for the day ahead.

Preparing coffee required little or no thought, only minimal consciousness. He filled the coffee maker with a half pot of water, then the filter, then a scoop of coffee. Sometimes he sprinkled a little cinnamon into the coffee grinds. He turned the machine on. While he waited the few minutes needed to brew the coffee, he retrieved the

Press-Telegram newspaper outside his front door. He leaned against the kitchen counter and read the headlines.

The coffee maker gurgled its final throes of brewing and beeped. He selected a mug from the cabinet, and poured hot coffee into it. He collected mugs from concerts, plays, and other performances that he attended and liked. The mugs pleasantly reminded him of the event. If he did not like the performance, he did not buy the mug. This morning he selected the 'Long Beach Playhouse' mug.

After pouring his mug of coffee, he moved to his favorite chair, a well-worn swivel rocker, sitting just inside the giant glass walls. He swiveled to enjoy the view of the city skylines and mountains that bathed in the morning sunlight. He liked this morning ritual.

During this ritual, Brian's mind wandered. He preferred pleasant thoughts, but worries often invaded. His first thought was pleasant. His friend Larry Davis called last week about a temporary consultant position that would last a few weeks, maybe longer. The work fit his skills as a computer forensics expert. Larry worked as a Chief Financial Officer in a corporation in Santa Monica. Someone had embezzled a large sum of money and Larry needed Brian's help to determine how the money was stolen.

Then, worry invaded his thoughts. He needed this job. He thought about his layoff six months ago, after working several years with the company. Usually he felt immune to layoffs but this time the company laid off twenty percent of its workforce, including his department. The layoff surprised him. For the last few years, he benefited the company in savings and efficiencies more than his salary.

Six months passed and he had no luck in his search for another job, until Larry called. For several weeks he felt depressed. He had known that older people experienced un-admitted discrimination in the job market. He now experienced that situation. Yet scientists wanted to extend the life span another twenty-five years. Giving everyone more time, along with more struggle finding employment.

Fortunately, his son had graduated college and was well employed. So now, he only worried about his son's happiness, and not his welfare.

But Brian's mother lived in a nursing home, and Social Security covered less than half of her expenses. He had some savings, but not nearly enough to pay them indefinitely. He loved his mother. His father had died when he was a kid. His mother supported the two of them, without complaining. Even now, a frail woman in her eighties, she supported him emotionally.

Another worry, he had saved little for his retirement. He desperately needed to work to save more, a lot more.

During most of his career, he rarely experienced difficulty in finding work. He possessed good technical skills and a strong work ethic. So this new state, called unemployment, deflated his sense of worth. He appreciated Larry's call. His depression lifted some. But worry sat in the back of his mind. In a month's time, he could be in the same position as now.

His internal clock alerted him to end his morning coffee ritual.

Brian had another twenty-minute ritual. Except for the last six months, he shaved, showered, and dressed following a set pattern. This ritual contributed to the waking process.

He flipped on the bathroom light, and turned on the hot water faucet. Leaning on the counter, he looked in the mirror at the lines in his face. He twisted his face muscles, and rubbed his beard growth and jaw with his hands. As he aged, he watched his body morph into that of an older man with extra weight around his middle and some sagging skin.

He never thought of himself as handsome, but liked his masculine looks, square jaw, muscular body structure, and even his salt-and-pepper hair when he had it. But now the neck skin sagged, the white hairs took ownership of his head, and even his chest hairs, the whites outnumbered the browns. He sucked in his gut, not bad, if only he could hold the pose. Unfortunately, he could not slow time's assault.

He would feel better after a shave and shower. He tested the running water; it was hot. He added some cool water, and pulled the basin stopper. As it filled, he opened the medicine cabinet (a misnomer since he kept no medicines there and set his toothpaste, shaving cream, razor, and deodorant in specific places around the basin. He began his second morning ritual.

Brian was fifty-nine, balding, and five-ten. When he was younger he fudged a little and told people he stood six feet tall. Usually they believed him. After all, who would force him against a wall and measure him. Now, he carried a paunch that stayed with him regardless of his attempts to exercise. Unable to see quick results, he felt little motivation to exercise. At times, he felt motivated to win the bulge battle, but his defiance level for the battle had lessened over the years.

As a younger man, he went to the gym three times a week. He joined friends for dinner and went to the bars on weekends. He stayed in shape. Those days did not seem that long ago. Even his John Wayne swagger had become more a march of a penguin. He tells himself that he subscribes to Bob Dylan's sage advice, *do not go gently into that good night*. Unfortunately, he listens less to these internal pep talks these days.

Brian finished his shower, sprayed Paco Rabanne cologne under his chin, and dressed for his first day of work in six months. He dressed professionally. He selected a clean, starched blue shirt, a conservative red power tie, and a dark blue suit. He pocketed his wallet, keys, and money.

Sensing the time, Brian moved faster. He emptied his coffee into the kitchen sink and racked the mug in the dishwasher. He poured a travel mug of coffee, and turned off the coffee maker. This morning he had a job.

With his brief case in one hand and his travel mug in the other, Brian left for work. Juggling the items he carried, he pressed the elevator call button. It opened with two neighbors standing inside. The three greeted each other and engaged in friendly small talk during the descent to the garage floors. They talked about the weather, living in Long Beach, and the upcoming Gran Prix race. Like Brian, they and most of the residents liked living in their hi-rise complex.

Brian exited the elevator onto his floor of the parking garage. The noisy preparations for the Long Beach Gran Prix race next weekend immediately demanded his attention. They were louder on this side of the building. The complex sat in the middle of this annual event. Over a hundred thousand people would descend on downtown Long Beach. He liked the excitement, the energy, the people watching, even if it complicated most activities, the parking, the entering and leaving the building, even going to the grocery store.

Celebrities as well as nationally known racecar drivers attended this race. Television crews taped, and showed the events on live, prime time television. Hotels filled their rooms. Solid booked restaurants turned customers away. On the weekend of the race, people often parked blocks away.

The condo complex provided prime viewing of the race, especially on the south and west sides. The balconies rose above the racetrack's eastern turn. Many residents hosted parties. Some rented their condos to companies to host large parties. For peace of mind some of the long-term residents simply left for the weekend.

The homeowner's association earned income from the event. They required passes to enter the building during the weekend. Each resident received two free passes and paid for additional passes. A large party could cost its host several dollars. The coming weekend would be a logistical nightmare.

Beginning on Friday, the noise from revving racing engines would require earplugs when standing on the balconies.

Brian unlocked his ten-year-old Ford Mustang, and laid his jacket and briefcase in the back seat. He idled his car at the garage's exit gate, and then slowly moved along an altered route to a different street, scraping his car's undercarriage twice. Workers had installed temporary fencing that blocked the normal exit that required exiting over traffic bumps, curbs, and street medians.

He drove through downtown Long Beach onto the 710 Freeway to the 405, also known as the San Diego Freeway. He was on his way to Santa Monica, to his first consulting job. He did not feel free of his worries, but he felt new hope.

THREE

Tuesday morning, April 5
Sherman Oaks, California

Wes Makelin, forty-three years old, single, and in good-shape, stepped out of the shower and quickly toweled himself dry. Using a hand blow dryer he finished drying his considerable body hair. He tore a paper towel from under the sink to remove the hairs that had collected in the shower drain, and tossed it in a nearby waste basket. He caught a deep breath, as if in a hurry, and sipped some coffee from his mug. It tasted tepid. He set the mug on the bathroom counter and told himself to remember to take it to the kitchen after dressing for work. Too often he would forget it. He returned to his bedroom to dress for work.

He often worked late, so on rare occasions, like this morning, he slept late. He defined late as an extra hour of sleep, and reduced traffic. He managed a high success rate for his cases, so his boss never micro-managed his work. Neither man believed punching a time clock solved cases.

He slipped on a pair of boxer briefs, catching his toe. He bounced on one leg a couple times before regaining his balance. He always wore a t-shirt, even in the summer. Otherwise, the body hair showed through his dress shirt, especially when he sweats. On those occasions, his colleagues would tease him about his gorilla body.

He selected a white shirt, gray slacks, and a stripped tie, which he believed gave him professional credibility. He dressed conservatively, with some style, for his job. Socks and shoes were last, this morning, the black ones.

He inspected himself in the mirror, checked his sideburns for symmetry and his eyebrows for any stray hairs. He rubbed his jaw. It felt a little like sandpaper already, but otherwise everything passed inspection.

Wes showed a beard shadow even though he shaved less than twenty minutes ago. Most men show after-five shadows, well, after five. His showed soon after shaving. Before special evening events, he shaved a second time.

He tucked and smoothed his shirt in his trousers. He aligned the shirt, belt buckle, and his pant's zipper. The military *gig* line. He adjusted his tie in the dresser mirror. Then he slipped his badge and cell phone onto the right side of his belt. He slipped on his shoulder holster with his revolver secured. Another look into the mirror, a twenty-first century cowboy, Wes grinned at his image.

Wes Makelin worked as a homicide detective with the Los Angeles County Sheriff's Department out of the Malibu San Fernando Valley station.

Wes began his career as a Sheriff's Deputy eighteen years ago. He started in the Patrol Division. Before that, he served in the US Navy, where he developed an appreciation for the work structure of military life. Know the rules, follow the rules, and keep personal life, personal. The Sheriff's Department offered a similar structure, and required similar behavior. Besides, being a Sheriff provided good public service.

The Department assigned him to the Malibu station serving mostly upscale neighborhoods. The station resides in the western part of the San Fernando Valley, dry and hot, especially in the summer, not near the cool, upscale city of Malibu, overlooking the Pacific Ocean. The station sits on five acres on Agoura Road, near the Ventura 101 Freeway that runs the length of the San Fernando Valley.

This Western section contains open land, mountains, and separates the warm valley from the nearby Oxnard-Ventura coastal communities.

The Sheriff's Department serves the fifteen million people who call LA County home. Most cities have their own police departments, but work with the Sheriff's staff on many cases. Other cities contract with the Sheriff's Department for their law enforcement.

Wes' work involves cases countywide.

While a deputy, Wes enrolled in classes at CSU Northridge located in the center of the San Fernando Valley. Juggling classes and work nearly exhausted him. After graduating, he passed the detective level exams on the first try and the Department promoted him to Detective, Homicide Division.

His supervisors recognized his abilities early. They quickly appreciated his analytical skills and his wolverine-like tenacity to solve a crime. His pay was good and with the overtime, he earned above average income.

With one last look into the mirror, Wes approved. He believed that if people perceive you as professional and successful, they treat you as such. They give you respect, ask few questions, and admire your achievements. They do not see your insecurities, or personality traits or thoughts you choose to hide.

He selected a dark blue blazer from the closet. He liked this blazer. It matched nearly every slack, shirt, and tie he owned. Even his grey and black underwear matched his jacket. He wore his jacket for most occasions. He hung the jacket on one arm, remembered his coffee mug, and headed downstairs.

Wes felt wide-awake. He had drunk two mugs of coffee, but filled a travel mug anyway and poured the remainder in the pot down the sink.

Preferring to work at the station, he rarely brought work home. He carried a small briefcase most places he traveled. It contained a notebook, pens, identification cards, a camera, and a digital voice recorder. In the car trunk, he kept a backpack containing other investigative supplies, latex gloves, paper and plastic bags, and other evidence gathering tools, but not to the extent that Crime Scene Units used.

Wes shut the door to his two-story townhouse in Sherman Oaks, not far from Ventura Boulevard. He tested the door. The lock was secure. Lush green plants surrounded the townhouses in the complex. Schefflera, bougainvillea, Lily of the Nile, and other plants lined the walkways and the perimeter of the courtyard.

The air smelled clean, thanks to last night's rain. The sun shone bright. In April, in LA, the temperature would rise to around eighty. He liked this time of year. Summer and fall seasons brought the unpleasant heat and smog.

Using another key, he opened the door to his two-car garage. He wished he had direct access from his townhouse. But in the San Fernando Valley, or anywhere in LA County, condos with direct garage access, and other premium features cost thousands of dollars more. Anyway, he liked his place, especially since housing prices nearly doubled in the last few years. As he entered, he used his elbow to press a button to open the garage door.

There it sat, the pride of his possessions, his champagne colored vintage Nissan 240 "Z". He spent too much for it. But he loved it. He normally lived life by a plan, practical, pragmatic. He never bought anything expensive without 'thinking about it' for a few days. He never took expensive vacations. He dressed well, but conservatively, and bought clothes on sale and off the rack. But this was his dream car, his "Z", with all the options. He bought it two years ago. He patted it affectionately on the hood.

Brian moved to the car sitting next to the Z, an unmarked Sheriff's four-door Chrysler sedan. The Department allowed him full use of the sedan. His job required frequent travel, during and outside so-called work hours. Department rules required using a Department vehicle for Department business. Traveling to the station morning and night to exchange his personal car for a Department vehicle wasted time.

He opened the car's back door, hung his blazer on a hook, and laid his briefcase in the back seat. He set his cell phone in its rack on the dash and coffee mug on the console. He backed out of the garage, stopped, and fastened his seat belt while the garage door closed.

Wes traveled the short distance to the Ventura freeway. Unlike most commuters on the LA freeway system, he headed west, away from the morning sun, away from downtown LA, away from most commuters.

His cell phone rang. Wes pushed a button on the cell phone rack so he could talk hands-free.

"Makelin, here."

"Makelin?" The Sheriff's dispatcher confirmed that he talked with Wes.

"Yes."

"Are you in a position to investigate an accident?" The dispatcher continued, almost without pause. "There's been an accident on Topanga Road; a car went over the side into the ravine. It probably happened sometime last night during that big rain storm. Your partner said you were coming in a little late today, and that the scene might be on your way."

"That it would be." Wes knew Topanga Road was a few miles further.

"Good. The caller told 911 Dispatch that there was a body in the vehicle. On Topanga, about three miles from PCH."

"Sure. Sure, I'll take it. Any other particulars?"

"Again, it's probably just an accident, but just in case it's more complicated. Patrol deputies are en route." The dispatcher answered.

Wes punched the disconnect button and continued west on the Ventura freeway to the Topanga exit.

FOUR

Tuesday Morning, April 5
Tarzana, California

At fifty-three, Karen Coffman felt comfortable with her life. She had enjoyed her youth, her travel to Europe and other parts of the world. She had married Benjamin, a wonderful man. On the less than positive side, she was short and always needed to lose a few pounds. But now she accepted herself as she was. She even let her gray hair show. She lived in a comfortable home in the hills of Tarzana California, dressed well, and used little make-up.

The only dark shadows in her life came from her husband's death four years ago. While returning home from work he died in a car accident on the Ventura Freeway, not far from the 405 interchange. He had worked late. A speeding drunk driver changed lanes carelessly and plowed into his car. He did not see the car in time to avoid it.

After his death, Karen's sister, Shirley, who lives in Tulsa Oklahoma, spent a few weeks with her to help her through her depression. Shirley too had lost her husband a few years before, and understood the pain Karen felt. Shirley managed the many funeral details and involved Karen only when needed. She answered the phone and carried the conversation when Karen's friends and acquaintances visited. She wrote thank you notes for the sympathy cards and flowers. She shopped for food and other needed items, and prepared the meals. At times she had to encourage Karen to eat.

To help ease the depression, Shirley reminded Karen of the fun times that she had shared with Benjamin. Together, they thumbed through photo albums, recounting the stories behind the photographs.

During those weeks, they relived other happy times, growing up on a farm in Oklahoma. They remembered walking barefoot on soft dirt roads, wiggling their toes in the warm sand, and wading in the cool water of a shallow creek. Only a year apart in age, they were best friends. They enjoyed other friends, even a couple boyfriends. But each was the other's best friend.

They finished college a year apart. Shirley married her high school sweetheart and stayed in Oklahoma. Karen developed a compelling sense of wanderlust and wanted to see the world. For this Oklahoma girl, California seemed like a good start. She found her first job in Los Angeles as a journalist with the LA Times, where she met Benjamin. He led a stable, predictable life as an accountant. He kept her grounded. Her sense of wanderlust no longer seemed important, so she switched to teaching journalism at the local junior college. She wanted job stability so she and Benjamin could raise children.

Sadly, their inability to have children left Karen depressed. But in time she accepted their fate and found purpose in mentoring students in her journalism classes.

After Benjamin's funeral, Shirley persuaded Karen to return to Tulsa with her and stay 'for as long as she wanted'. Her children were grown, so it would be the just the two of them, like old times. Karen accepted.

For a time they were little girls again enjoying the fresh Oklahoma air, taking day-trips to festivals in small Oklahoma towns, and cooking wonderful southern foods that their mother had taught them.

After a couple months, Karen wanted, needed some time alone, time to heal, time to accept Benjamin's death. She wanted to return home, to Tarzana. The great healer, time, reduced her depression and her optimism returned.

But occasionally, memories of his death would sink her into depression for a day or two. His picture, the display of his model cars, or one of his favorite shirts hanging in the closet would bring a comfort with the sadness.

After a few months passed, slowly pleasant memories replaced the sad ones. In time, she gave away his clothes, and boxed the model cars and gave them to her grand nephews. She kept the photo albums. Now, she could look at them with fondness and no longer feel the intense grief.

She and her husband had built a comfortable account of savings and investments. With the added life insurance money, she had more than enough to retire. She could pay her bills, travel, and enjoy dinner in restaurants with friends.

She renewed an interest with an old love – writing. She had written a few short stories in college, but her work as a teacher and a student advisor consumed most of her time. Consequently, her writing moved to the 'someday-I-will' list.

Two years ago, writing moved to the top of her to-do list. She reluctantly resigned her teaching job and approached her writing as a full time job. She wrote two mystery novels. A small fan base of readers had emerged, most of them in Southern California.

As with most writers, she hoped that her fan base would grow. She loved the process of writing, even when it frustrated her to find the right word, or the right metaphor.

Karen joined a writer's group based in LA to establish relationships with other writers, hone her writing skills, and focus on writing. The group met monthly in Santa Monica. Today she would attend one of their meetings.

In today's meeting, another published author, a well-known one, would speak on *Promoting Your Book*. An author had to promote his or her book, unless his or her name was John Grisham, James Rollins, or Anne Rice. She looked forward to hearing his ideas. Even with her own success, she felt a little star-struck, like a groupie and wanted his autograph. A copy of his book sat in her handbag in the seat beside her.

Karen looked over her shoulder, and backed her Camry out of her driveway.

Rather than the freeway, she chose to drive the scenic Topanga Canyon Road through the mountains to Santa Monica. The sparsely populated mountain wilderness contrasted sharply to the over-crowded Los Angeles and San Fernando Valley areas. She had driven this route many times, and never tired of the densely forested views, the oaks, the cottonwoods, and the pine trees. She could see a few houses almost hidden in the trees.

She passed the Will Geer outdoor amphitheater and the small mountain community of Fernwood. She planned to someday spend time in Fernwood, eat in one of the small cafes, or browse the shops sitting along the road, with the handmade woodcarvings, or colorful, tie-dyed t-shirts and comfortable women's clothing.

Although she understood that many people from LA lived in the area, she also understood that hippies from the sixties still lived here. My, they must be old. More comic than antiestablishment. She would not stop this time; otherwise she would arrive late for her meeting.

A few miles before the Pacific Ocean, just past one of the many switchbacks in the road, she noticed a missing section of roadside railing. The tear from its posts looked fresh. Her curiosity meter registered high. She slowed her Camry, and cautiously waited for an opening in the oncoming traffic, which was not heavy this time of day. She pulled into the graveled turnout area, which allowed room for only a few cars.

She parked, turned off the car's engine, and carried her keys with her. Steep mountains rose on both sides of the road and sloped downward creating a deep ravine that led to the enormous Pacific Ocean a few miles further.

Her curiosity meter still reading high, she approached the cliff's edge. Feeling a tinge of vertigo, she caught her breath to steel herself while she looked down the deep ravine.

Except for a few shrubs near the top, at the point of impact, a wide section of uprooted bushes and shrubs and scarred boulders continued down the hillside. Only a falling car or other heavy object could have created such a path as it fell. The overnight rain had washed the dirt and mud from the roots of the shrubs. She edged to her left to better see the bottom.

She saw a section of a mangled car near the bottom. She could not see the entire car, or anyone in it, but rational thinking, or perhaps her active imagination *saw* someone in the car, someone seriously hurt or dead.

She rushed back to her car for her cell phone. She struggled to open the passenger door, locked. She fumbled with her keys, found the right one, and unlocked the door. Her hands shaking, she retrieved her cell phone from her handbag. She dialed 911 for help.

"Someone went over a cliff on Topanga Road, about three miles from PCH. You need to send help right away." She tried to calm herself so her voice would not show the anxiety she felt. She just knew someone was in that car.

She described the accident location as best she could. The dispatcher assured her that help would arrive soon.

Away from the cliff's edge, Karen paced while she waited. Her low-heeled shoes made crunching sounds on the gravel. Intermittently she would stop pacing and stand close to the edge straining to see more of the car. Still convinced, she thought she could see someone in the car, just about. She dared not climb down into the ravine, too steep, too treacherous.

Karen wondered about the person in the car. If the person died, the family would hurt. Lives would change forever. Her creative mind explored the background that could have lead to this accident. What if it was not an accident? What if it was a suicide, or worse yet, foul play? She chastised herself for thinking it more than an accident. In her stories, it was ok to think the worst, but with real lives, it seemed sad, unfair. With effort, she stopped thinking of possible, fictional causes.

After about twenty minutes, it seemed longer, the ambulance and a fire truck arrived. The vehicles turned onto the gravel and parked on each side of Karen's car. They turned off their engines, and for a moment, quiet returned. Passing cars slowed as drivers strained their necks to see the roadside commotion.

Almost at once, two firemen and two paramedics jumped from their vehicles, slamming their doors. One of the paramedics and a fireman approached her, while the others retrieved gear from their vehicles.

"Are you the lady who called 911?" The paramedic asked.

"Yes. Let me show you." She walked to the edge of the hillside and pointed downhill. "The car apparently knocked out this railing, and went off there. You can see the car down there," Karen spoke matter-of-factly which belied the actual anxiety she felt.

"Have you seen any movement down there? Did you see the car go over the side?"

"No, no I didn't see the accident happen, and I haven't seen any movement. But I thought I could see someone in the car." Keeping her voice even, she added, "It had to have happened last night in the rain. You can see that the rain has washed most of the dirt off the shrubs and the gouging of the hillside.

"I'm sorry. Let me introduce myself. I'm Sharon Russell, Lead Paramedic with the LA County Fire Department." She smiled and offered her hand to Karen. She observed the formalities, but was eager to work the scene.

"I'm Karen Coffman." She shook the offered hand.

"And I'm Casey Stringer also with the LA Fire Department." He too smiled and offered his hand to Karen. He nodded to his colleague standing truck-side. "And that's my side-kick today, Jerry Presser."

"Pleased to meet you." Karen took Casey's hand, and nodded to Jerry.

"We need to hurry." Sharon prompted.

"Let's do it."

Casey fit the popular image of a firefighter, tall, fit, forty-ish, with some graying at the temples. He and his sidekick Jerry wore blue t-shirts with the fire department logo and bulky mustard colored canvass pants.

Sharon's image and demeanor focused on business. She wore her brown hair short. She wore a functional uniform of a beige, short-sleeve button-down shirt with the fire department logo. She wore dark brown pants with the shirt tucked into them. She looked people directly in the eye, functional, business-like.

Casey and Sharon tested the strength of the remaining railing and posts. They attached ropes and pulleys to a couple of the posts and slipped into harnesses. When all connections were secure, they rappelled down the side of the ravine. The distance was seventy or eighty feet, and steep.

They reached the car, near the bottom of the ravine, and discovered that someone was indeed there, crushed in the driver's seat. Extracting the body would prove difficult. The car was mangled around the driver. Casey would work with the Coroner to extract the body.

After Casey gave the ok that the scene was secure and safe for them to work. Sharon disconnected the ropes from her harness. She checked the victim. She checked for a pulse, but the body was cold, obviously dead; rigor mortis had set in. Sharon saw a little blood had run down the side of the victim's head but otherwise appeared drained of blood. The rain probably had washed away most of the blood during the night.

Sharon called the trauma center in Santa Monica General and relayed the information to them. A coroner's representative would need to examine the body and transport it to the county morgue. California requires the involvement of the County Coroner in cases of death from accidents or non-hospital settings.

The car had crushed on impact. The crash had pushed the front engine into the front seats, crushing the body. Windows had exploded from the car or were smashed with giant spider web cracks. The steering wheel had broken, and the column had impaled the driver. The body and car were compressed into a mass of human flesh and metal.

Casey and Sharon returned to road level to prepare for processing the scene.

"What is it like down there?" Karen hesitated to interfere with their work, but curiosity drove her.

"There is a body down there. We notified the Coroner's office and they'll send a representative." Sharon answered, more serious than before. She released herself from the ropes, leaving her harness attached. "The body can't be removed until the ME's reps process the scene and give the OK.

"I know it's too early to tell, but was it an accident?" Karen continued her questions.

"Probably, but we won't really know until after the autopsy." Sharon turned and directed her partner to retrieve more equipment. Then she, Sharon, and Casey descended the hillside to the crash site.

A tow truck arrived with its chains, towing straps and gears clanging as its tires growled to a stop, spraying gravel. The truck parked in the remaining space in the turnout. The obese driver wore a dirty, greasy uniform that he likely had worn the last three days. His belly hung over his pants, obscuring view of his buckle. He spoke in a loud, grating voice and displayed an attitude that what he wanted came first.

"Where's the car to tow?" He barked, working his cigar from one side of his mouth to the other, as he approached Karen and Jerry.

Jerry explained that the car could not be towed yet. The county Sheriff and Coroner would have to do their jobs and remove the body before towing the car.

In a huff, the driver waddled back to his truck and called his dispatcher. Swearing, he slammed the mouthpiece onto the dashboard. He paced beside his truck for a minute. His scarred, greasy, too-large-for-his-feet shoes flopped against the gravel as he returned to where Karen and Jerry were standing.

"I have to go do another job. I'll be back later." The gruff driver mumbled and turned without waiting for a response.

As Karen watched him leave, she felt glad such people were not a part of her world. Further, she would resist allowing them into her fictional world. They walked upright, but were questionably human.

On a practical side, she questioned that he could physically scale the cliff to chain the car to his truck's winch. But that problem was his. She returned her attention to the people working below. Questions swarmed in her head vying for order. She wanted answers.

FIVE

Tuesday Morning, April 5
Topanga Canyon Road, Santa Monica Mountains

An LA County Sheriff's cruiser swerved into the space vacated by the tow truck. Its tires sprayed gravel as it lurched to a stop. Two large, uniformed deputies exited the car, slamming the doors. They appeared bothered, probably not wanting to work a simple over-the-side-of-the-road accident, resenting the time, the paperwork.

The deputies approached Jerry, the younger fireman standing near the edge working with his counterparts in the ravine. Karen standing a few feet away approached them.

"I'm Sheriff's Deputy Webster; this is Deputy Rivera." The larger of the two deputies spoke.

"I'm Jerry Presser with the LA County Fire Department." The young fireman responded deferentially, feeling somewhat nervous speaking to law enforcement.

Jerry had worked with the fire department only a few months. He had graduated high school a couple years before, and liked the excitement of his new job. Built wiry, and barely meeting the height requirements, his enthusiasm easily compensated for any physical deficiencies.

"What can you tell me about this accident?" Deputy Webster placed his hands on his hips with a get-this-over-with attitude.

"The paramedic told me that a body was in the car below. She's already called the Medical Examiner's office." Jerry answered. "They're supposed to send someone right away. Casey or one of the paramedics could probably tell you more."

"Casey?"

"Yeah. Casey Stringer, my supervisor. He's the guy down there." Jerry waved to Casey for his attention.

Seeing the Sheriff's deputies from downside, Casey snapped the clasp attached to the hanging ropes onto his harness and rappelled up the cliff. He had dealt with law enforcement and other government types in his fifteen plus years with the fire department. So he could answer their questions with some authority.

The group at roadside waited for Casey to join them.

Officer Rivera joined the conversation. Facing Karen, "And you are?"

"Karen Coffman. I made the 911 call."

"Did you see the car go over the cliff?"

"No, no I didn't." Karen did not know how much background she should give. "I noticed the railing was missing, torn from the posts. It looked recent."

"You must be pretty observant to notice that."

"Actually, I am pretty observant." Karen said defensively, while reducing her tone to a matter-of-fact level.

"So you stopped to look."

"Yes."

"It's kinda hard to see the car from here..." Deputy Rivera growled skeptically.

"Yes. But I held onto one of the posts to brace myself. I thought I saw someone in the car." Karen fudged a little, but felt vindicated since the paramedic had already confirmed that a body was in the car. "So I called 911."

"Okay. Thanks." The officer relaxed, his voice friendlier.

Casey arrived topside, Jerry offered a helping hand, and Casey took it. He wiped his muddy shoes on the railing posts. Deputy Webster introduced himself and his partner. They asked a few questions, which Casey tried to answer.

Karen wanted to ask her own questions, but tightened her lips to stay quiet so the officials could do their jobs. However, she stayed near, and listened to learn what she could. She would ask her questions later.

Another car, a dark four-door Chrysler sedan, drove into the turnout across the road. The driver, a handsome man, probably in his early forties, pulled a jacket from his back seat. He slipped into the jacket, probably to hide the shoulder holster that he wore. He sported a heavy after-five beard shadow. He either worked all night, or was one of those men who shave more than once a day. He left his jacket unbuttoned, crossed the road, and approached the group.

"Hello, I'm Sheriff's Detective Wes Makelin, with the Malibu Station." He read the deputies' name badges. Although their names sounded familiar, he did not recognize either man. He nodded to the firemen and Karen.

Deputy Webster introduced himself to the newcomer. Then, in turn, the others, except Karen, introduced themselves.

"I'm a little surprised they sent you over this way. This being an accident and all." Deputy Webster challenged, as if there was no need for a detective's presence. He and his partner were quite capable to handle the situation.

"I was on my way to the station when the dispatcher called. So they gave me the assignment. The dispatcher understood a body was involved." Wes said. "And of course when there's a body, questions have to be answered."

"True." Deputy Webster agreed.

"And you are?" Wes offered his hand to Karen.

"Hello, I'm Karen Coffman. I called in the accident." Karen smiled and shook his hand.

"Sounds like you did a good thing."

"Thanks. But I understand that unfortunately, the driver was killed." Karen's voice sounded concerned. She faced Casey who could better update the detective.

"I guess I could probably update with the most information so far. Although we probably should wait for Sharon." Casey saw puzzled looks on their faces. "Sharon Russell, the lead paramedic. She's on her way up. Gary, her assistant, is the other guy down there."

The group turned as Sharon reached the top to join them. Jerry gave her a hand and pulled her the last step.

As another round of introductions started, a modified station wagon with dark tinted windows and a logo, Coroner of Los Angeles

County, pulled into the turnout behind Wes' car. Now both turnouts were filled. Two women exited the station wagon. They watched for a break in the traffic and joined the others at the cliff. They dressed alike, white shirts, blue trousers, and matching light windbreakers with the Coroner's logo on the front chest. The older woman, black, probably forty-five, and tall, wore her hair in a tight bun in the back. She led the way. The other woman, young, twenty, and Hispanic followed.

"I'm Carol Brover, Senior Rep from the LA County Coroner's. And this is my assistant Julie." Speaking clearly, she offered her hand to Deputy Webster, thinking he was the in-charge for the accident scene.

"I'm Sheriff's Deputy Webster. You probably want to start with Detective Makelin, here. He's the in-charge."

"Pleased to meet you Detective Makelin." Carol turned, smiled, and shook Wes' hand.

"Pleased to meet you." He responded.

The others introduced themselves.

"Well, seems like everyone is here." Wes grinned. He spoke casually but with authority, and nodded to Karen. "Ms. Coffman, here, made the 911 call that alerted all of us to this little event. I guess its best to start at the beginning. Mr. Stringer, Ms. Russell, why don't you two give us the status on what you've learned so far, since you probably know the most?"

Casey and Sharon recounted their activities since arriving on the scene. Some in the group asked questions. Of course no one could answer all questions until the coroner's reps completed their work and the autopsy and toxicology results become available later in the week, or even longer.

Everyone knew their roles to process the scene. Even Karen understood their roles from her research for her mystery stories.

Drivers on Topanga already slowed their cars, craning their necks to see the commotion on the side of the road. Wes asked the deputies to turn off the roof lights on their cruiser. He did not want a circus atmosphere anymore than necessary.

Wes recommended Karen move her car so Ms. Brover could move the Coroner's vehicle in place. They would need it in their work, most importantly transporting the body to the Coroner's facility. Karen asked if it would be all right to park her car across the road, behind

Detective Makelin's, so she could stay longer. She confessed her curiosity consumed her. Wes agreed.

The deputies stopped traffic to allow the vehicle exchange.

Carol and Julie pulled equipment, supplies, and clothes from their wagon. They slipped into dark blue coveralls, with the Coroner logo on the backs, over their office clothes. Wes rushed across the road to retrieve a pair of coveralls from his trunk for himself. He scrambled into them so he would not delay the work.

Casey and Jerry assisted the coroners' reps and Wes into harnesses and attached them to the ropes to scale the hillside. One by one they joined Gary at the crash site where everyone slipped on latex gloves.

"Other than checking for any sign of life, we haven't touched the body." Sharon stated clearly for everyone to hear.

"And we made sure the crash was safe, for you and for us." Casey added.

"Thanks. As you know, we need to take pictures, examine the body closely, and work a few other procedures." Carol offered a thin smile, slightly breaking her formal veneer. She stepped carefully to avoid the mud as much as she could.

"Sure thing," Casey and Sharon answered.

The steering column had impaled the body. The car's impact had crumpled the dashboard into the front seats. The seats, like sponges, were soaked with water. Puddles of water lay in small places that would hold it.

The seat belt still intact held the victim in place. Rigor mortis in the body indicated the man had died approximately twelve hours earlier. Maybe less, considering the cold, the rain, and overnight hours.

Julie took pictures from several angles, while Carol examined the body for cuts and abrasions. Their work involved identifying the body and the cause of death, other than the obvious.

Wes hovered, wanting to touch, to move items, but waited for Carol to finish her work first.

Carol searched for identification, and found a wallet in the victim's rear pocket. She handed it to Wes. Speaking clearly, Carol described her work as she processed the scene while Julie held a voice recorder to capture Carol's comments. .

Wes examined the contents of the wallet.

"According to his driver's license, his name is Gregory Larkin. He lives in Van Nuys, and is 33 years old." Wes read the information. He spoke in the present tense instead of past tense. It seemed more respectful. This victim lived only a few miles from his townhouse. "He has sixty-three dollars, a few credit cards, a couple ATM receipts, and a picture of a young mother with two kids. Probably his wife and kids." His voice took a grave tone. "This is tragic."

He dropped the wallet into a plastic bag that Julie held open.

He's wearing a wedding ring." Carol added as she continued her search. Julie continued to record the information. "A few small kids' toys are scattered in the back seat area."

Carol found a briefcase wedged tightly behind the driver's seat. She struggled to extract it and handed it to Wes. He set it on a small boulder and squatted to examine its contents. He found computer reports, pens, a calculator, notepads, some business cards and other contents common to accountants.

"He was a Director of General Accounting for Leonard Construction in Santa Monica." Wes read Larkin's business card. He closed the briefcase and handed it to Julie. He wrote a few entries in his own notebook. Wes and Carol continued to search. Julie continued to record the comments made while bagging and labeling the other items.

"Uh-oh." Carol found something. She held up a small vial that contained a small amount of white substance. "Not much in it, but enough for testing. He may have been doing drugs. That could certainly contribute to an accident. Of course, we'll have to verify it in the lab."

When Wes and Carol finished, they asked Casey and Sharon to help extract the body from the car. They disconnected the seat belt, and separated the seat back from the body. With effort they pulled the stiffened body from the steering wheel that had completely skewered the body. Meanwhile, Jerry lowered a portable gurney with a body bag down the cliff.

Because of the rigor mortis, fitting the body into the body bag and onto the gurney required effort, a struggle actually. After reaching topside, Carol and Julie loaded the body into their station wagon for transport.

Wes instructed the deputies to call the towing service again to tow the car to the impound garage. The coroner may want to investigate it further. He also asked them to remain at the scene until the car was towed. He thanked them for their help. Their attitudes had softened.

Casey and Jerry loaded the fire truck but would wait until the tow truck driver finished. The tow driver would likely need their help.

Sharon and her assistant, Gary packed their medical gear into the ambulance and left.

"Excuse me please," Karen approached Carol as she removed her coveralls. "May I ask you a couple of questions?"

"We're really very busy, ma'am. We need to take this body to the County Morgue." Carol sounded irritated. "We appreciate your civic mindedness for calling this into 911, but we really need to do our jobs."

"I understand and completely respect how busy you are," Karen persisted. "But please, just a couple questions, I really would appreciate it."

"OK please make it quick," Carol continued to help Julie finish packing their wagon.

Overhearing, Wes approached them.

"Maybe we both could satisfy your curiosity, especially since you were civic-minded enough to call this in." Wes joined the conversation, thinking he recognized the fifty-ish woman.

Wes removed his latex gloves, put them in a collection bag that Julie provided, and wiped the perspiration from his brow. He felt warm in his coveralls, so he removed them.

"As I said earlier, I'm Karen Coffman. What I didn't say was that I write mysteries. Sometimes I use real life situations as starting points." Karen had retrieved her identification cards from her purse and gave one to Wes, another to Carol. She hoped her credentials, as a writer would enable them to take her seriously. "I know this is a tragic, sad event. But I'd like to know more details if I could please."

"I thought I recognized your name. I really like your books, especially *The Comfort Zone*." Wes snapped his fingers and grinned, his interest level rising. To Carol, he added, "We have a celebrity here," returning to face Karen, "Ask away."

"I noticed that there were no skid marks on the asphalt. And the gravel did not show tire tracks from any attempt to stop. Of course the rain could have washed away some of that. Also, there are no new scars on the other railings, which should have been there if he had skidded along it before going over the side. In most accidents, I believe a driver would try to stop. Could it be that this wasn't an accident?" Karen began. "Is there anything you can tell me about the driver? I admit I tried listening to what you said, but I couldn't hear most of it. I know I seem nosy, but I am very curious."

Wes wrote in his notepad about the lack of skid marks and defensive marks on the remaining railing.

"Because I'm a fan, I can tell you some, but this will have to be off the record because we have several other procedures we have to finish, such as notifying the family. OK?" Wes asked. "So no talking with reporters."

"Agreed." Karen smiled and nodded.

Wes recounted some of the details regarding the deceased man, his age, where he lived, where he worked. He did not tell about the drugs that were found.

They talked more. Mostly Karen and Wes talked. He reminded her that he could get into trouble if she revealed any of this information to the media.

"Detective Makelin, sounds like you can handle this. So, if you don't mind, I need to take the body to the morgue." Carol interrupted.

"Sure. Oh, and Ms. Brover, thanks for your work. You do your job very professionally. My partner and I will contact the next-of-kin." Wes's voice took a serious turn. "That's never a pleasant task."

After Carol left, Wes and Karen talked a few more minutes. The deputies talked between themselves while they waited for the tow truck. Wes held up his badge to stop traffic so he and Karen could cross the street to their cars.

"Would you mind if I called you in a couple days for an update?" Karen asked as they separated to each one's car. "By the way, I'm pretty good with researching the Internet. Maybe I can help. Leonard Construction sounds familiar. Then, I can tell you what I learn."

"Sure. Any information could be helpful, although we have a pretty good technical support group for that kind of research. Just remember, I can't tell you everything. My bosses would give me a truck load of grief for involving a *civilian* in police business. Remember, we don't know whether this was an accident, a suicide, or worse yet, a homicide. We have to analyze the evidence." Wes liked being involved with a real writer, but knew he had to walk a fine line between his work and someone from the *public*.

"I understand. And thanks for any involvement that you can allow." She shook hands with Wes. Wes attached his siren lights to the roof so he could stop traffic to give Karen road access and to allow him to cross the road to return to the stationhouse.

By now, she had missed most of the writer's meeting and the speaker she wanted to hear, but could still arrive in time to chat with a few of her friends. She would join them for a drink. A glass of wine would relax her after the stressful morning. She would tell them about the accident, but not reveal too many details. She wanted to keep her word to Detective Makelin.

She speculated if the accident was really a suicide, or more interestingly, a homicide. She almost smiled at the what-if possibilities of a story. But with that thought, sadness swept over her. This death also meant a very real and terrible tragedy for a young family.

SIX

Tuesday morning, April 5
Santa Monica, California

Brian left the congested, snail crawl of traffic of the San Diego freeway onto the less crowded Santa Monica Freeway west-bound to Santa Monica. Brian dreaded the idea of working downtown LA. A twenty-mile commute from any direction required two plus hours each way. Added to an eight to ten hour workday could really age a guy. The exhausting work and travel routines left little time for social lives.

Living in the sprawling LA basin for thirty-five years, Brian had learned the freeway systems. During his first few years in LA, a Thomas Guide, the Southern California bible of maps, sat next to him on every car trip. Even as crowded as LA was, new development meant new streets, new addresses, and new editions. Global positioning systems, or GPS, and Internet mapping applications increasingly replaced the Guide. Now, smart phones with GPS and picture taking capability became the required accessory.

After a few minutes, a mile before the Lincoln exit, he saw the Leonard Construction headquarters building north of the freeway. A bronze tinted glass façade covered the twelve-story structure. It shined like a gold rectangle mountain against the blue cloudless Southern California sky. He imagined people working there, especially on the higher floors had terrific views of the Pacific Ocean, downtown LA, and the surrounding mountains.

He exited the Lincoln Boulevard off-ramp and drove the few blocks to the Leonard office campus. He parked in one of the two remaining visitor parking spaces.

From ground level, the shiny, bronze building soared higher than it appeared from the freeway. Large revolving glass doors dominated the building's entrance. They produced a heavy swoosh sound as Brian followed others through the glass doors. He inhaled a deep breath and walked tall as he went inside. The lobby soared two stories. Dark brown granite covered the floors and walls. To the right, sat a receptionist's desk of dark mahogany paneling.

Employees wearing laminated badges walked quickly through the lobby. Most headed to the bank of elevators just past the receptionist's desk. A few entered the smaller offices to the right and the left of the lobby. Most people took no notice of Brian as he approached the receptionist. Sitting behind the desk, an attractive middle-aged black woman gave him a broad smile. She wore a peach color silk blouse, a coordinated brown skirt, and matching lightweight jacket.

"Welcome to Leonard Construction, may I help you?" She leaned forward, her voice friendly.

"Yes, please. I'm Brian Latimer and I have an appointment with Lawrence Davis, in General Accounting." Brian returned her smile. He spoke clearly, hoping not too loudly. He noticed the nameplate on the desk, which read Carla Johnston. She presented a warm, welcoming impression to visitors.

"Very good, I'll call him and tell him you're here. Would you sign-in please?" She smiled again, turned the sign-in register toward Brian, and reached for her phone. After a moment, she spoke into the mouthpiece. "Hello, Liz. A Mr. Brian Latimer is here for his appointment with Larry."

Then to Brian, "Mr. Latimer, please have a seat, Liz Bowden, Mr. Davis' assistant, will be down in just a moment." Still smiling, she nodded to the nearby seating area, and handed him a visitor's badge. "Please wear this badge while you're in the building, and return it here when you leave. If you would please."

"Sure, be glad to." Brian attached the badge to his jacket and sat in the waiting area.

Yes, she was the right person for her job. Brian relaxed some.

While he waited, Brian watched the people entering the building.

Near the receptionist, standing a few feet behind her, a muscular, six-foot security guard leaned against the wall. In his early thirties, brown hair, in a military crew cut, and wearing a dark blue uniform, he watched the people enter the lobby. His earnest attitude and body language enforced a seriousness that complimented the receptionist's friendly, welcoming behavior. Apparently knowing many of the people by sight, he smiled, or nodded.   .

In less than five minutes, a lady in her forties, wearing a dark blue business suit and a robin's egg blue blouse, approached Brian, the only person sitting in the waiting area.

"Mr. Latimer, I'm Liz Bowden, Mr. Davis' assistant. Welcome to Leonard Construction. If you'll come with me, I'll take you to his office." She smiled and offered her hand to him. While friendly, she presented a more formal, professional behavior.

"Good to meet you." Brian rose, shook her hand, and followed her to the bank of elevators.

"I hope traffic wasn't too bad. I understand you live in Long Beach."

"It was heavy, but beginning to thin. An hour earlier, I'm sure it was very congested. And yes, I live in Long Beach, in a high rise, downtown."

"That sounds nice, cosmopolitan. You probably have a terrific view. As you will see, we have very nice views from here. Our offices are on the twelfth floor."

"I'm sure people enjoy working here, especially considering the views."

"We do."

The elevator bell sounded as its doors opened. Brian lifted his arm as if to hold the door open. Liz nodded, and thanked him as she stepped inside.

On the twelfth floor, they exited, and turned left. Another security guard sat behind an expensive cherry wood receptionist's desk. He smiled. His youthful handsomeness and friendly attitude contrasted with the seriousness of the guard in the lobby. Paneling, matching his desk lined the walls behind him. The same granite on the lobby floors covered these floors. Inch thick floor-to-ceiling glass doors on both sides finished the area. As Liz and Brian approached the glass doors, they heard a buzz, then an unlocking sound.

"Thank you, Sam." Liz said to the guard. Facing Brian, she added, "Later today we'll give you an employee access badge so you may come and go as you need. We'll need to take your picture for the badge. You'll have an office on the eleventh floor. The big meeting this morning is in the main conference room." She gestured to the glass doors the other direction.

The plushness of the twelfth floor mesmerized Brian for a moment. Executive success manifest itself in the thick hunter green carpeting, the rich, cherry wood paneling lining the walls, and the dark mahogany furniture. Expensive artwork hung on the walls or sat on pedestals with muted, spot lighting, adding to the richness. The noticeable quiet contrasted to the hyperactivity and noise in the downstairs lobby, and encouraged people to speak in hushed voices.

Liz rapped softly on Larry Davis' partly opened door. Larry rose from his chair as the two entered the room. Both men grinned as wide as their faces would allow. They shook hands and hugged each other. They had not seen each other for nearly ten years.

"It's so good to see you again, Brian. It's been so very long." Larry's voice rose, reflecting his excitement seeing an old friend.

"It's great to see you too, Larry. I was so glad to get your call last week, and not just for the consulting job. It's been too long."

"Way too long. Thanks Liz. Oh, Liz, any news about Greg?" Larry asked.

"No. He still doesn't answer his cell phone. It's really unlike him to not call. I'll call Alicia. I hesitate to call her, because I don't want her to worry."

"I understand. Please let me know as soon as he comes in." Larry nodded politely to Liz and returned his attention to Brian.

Liz left the room, pulling the door closed.

"Have a chair, have a chair. You look the same, good looking as ever." Larry turned the visitor chairs to face each other and sat in one. "We have a lot of catching up to do."

"We sure do. Now that I see you, I realize how much I've missed seeing you." Brian felt happy, very happy. He laid his jacket on a nearby chair and sat his briefcase on the floor next to his chair. "I've just let my life get too busy. My life has had its ups and downs since I left the corporate world six months ago. Or rather, it left me. The job market has been rough for the last several months."

"That it has. Maybe now that will change for the better." Larry became serious, but then his smile returned. " It sure is good to see you again."

Brian observed that Larry looked older, smooth top with only a trim of hair around the sides and a few more wrinkles around his eyes and mouth. He had not gained any weight. His friendly smile and youthful voice had not changed. He was still Larry, his friend. He would tease him about his hair loss later. Now, he was just glad to visit his old friend.

Brian's mind wandered for a moment.

In their thirties, Larry and Brian had met in a windowless West Hollywood bar in a decaying section on Santa Monica Boulevard.

In those years, bars, which catered to gay patrons, opened after dark, had side or back entrances. Instead of catchy names posted on bright neon signs on the front of the building, they used the street address, with little or no lighting. Passers-by would think the building closed, unoccupied. Nervous patrons entered by back doors to avoid detection by police, family, coworkers, or by anyone. Once inside, regulars could relax, knowing they were among friends, among their own kind.

On a warm August Saturday night, Brian went through the back door of the 1222 for his first time. The too loud music blasted his senses. Regardless, his nervousness and fear of discovery remained on his shoulders. Since he knew no one, he ordered a Bud, paid the bartender, and retreated to a dark corner. He felt himself shaking inside and hoped no one could sense his anxiety.

The 1222's walls were covered in dark, unpainted, worn boards. The type used in residential privacy fencing. Cheap posters of bikers or cowboys hung on two of the walls. Darkness nearly buried the room. Behind the bar, the lights under the shelves of liquor bottles highlighted their festive colors and shapes. A small task lamp, duct taped to the register provided light for counting customers' change.

Patrons worried about police raids, but knew they probably would not bother anyone as long as 'nothing was going on'. Stonewall patrons had rioted a few years earlier in New York City. Police hassled gays less frequently these days, especially in West Hollywood, California.

A slim, wiry man of average height sat at the bar, nursing a martini, his legs crossed, as only thin people can. He wore a hunter green polo shirt, a pair of Guess jeans, and brown loafers, not typical of the regular patrons, here.

He preferred a vodka martini but felt it reduced his sense of control, so in straight social events he drank watered-down scotch. He liked the Levi jean, plaid shirt look of masculine men, but preferred a more clean-cut, preppie look for himself.

He watched Brian enter and knew immediately that he was new, probably just 'coming out'. He smiled to himself because he had struggled with his own 'coming out' a few years earlier. Even now he was only 'out' when in a bar like this one or among friends. 'Coming out' is never easy. He watched the newcomer order his beer and move to the darkest wall behind him.

"Relax, it really gets easier in time." Larry swiveled on his bar stool to face the newcomer. He raised his martini in a simulated salute.

"Really?" After a second, Brian relaxed a little and returned the salute by lifting his beer. "How soon?"

Both men smiled. The simple greeting released some of Brian's anxiety.

"Come over here, have a seat. Let's talk." Larry patted the bar stool next to him. He offered his hand, "My name's Larry."

"I'm Brian. Good to meet you." He started to add his last name, but caught himself. People did not use their last names in these places. Even first names were often created. He pulled the stool a conversational distance and sat on it.

They shook hands. Men always shake hands.

"How are you tonight?"

"Fine, yourself?"

"Now we have the introductions out of the way. Do we talk about the usual? Do you live in LA? Where are you from? What kind of work do you do? The weather? Yada, Yada." Larry teased.

"I guess most conversations do cover those areas. What would we do without small talk?"

"True. Small talk does help grease the social gears, so to speak." Larry agreed. He turned his eyes upward as if reading from a checklist in his mind. "Ok, I'll go first. I've lived in LA for a little over ten years. I was born in Ohio and lived there until I moved here. I work as an accountant for a large bank in downtown LA. Your turn."

"Ok." Brian turned his eyes upward as if reading from the same imaginary checklist. "Lived here since I was ten. Born in Dallas Texas. I'm a computer programmer for a retail company in The Valley." He looked at Larry, then to finish the list. "Oh, and I love the weather."

"Ahh, the weather, I forgot. I like it too except for what the smog does to it. The bad smog can really ruin a day's sunshine, especially in the summer."

Brian pealed at his beer's label. Larry sipped his martini.

Larry began to feel a strong, mentoring feeling toward Brian. Although only a few years difference in their ages, he wanted to help Brian on this new road in his life. Their conversation soon took the tone of two friends talking over drinks, not two strangers meeting.

Larry recounted his 'coming out' process; he explained that he was, even now, closeted to the outside world, especially his work world. But here in the 1222, and with friends, he could relax, let-his-hair-down, so to speak. What little he had left anyway.

He enjoyed his work, except when the mostly male, mostly straight men would ridicule gay people. Like most people, he wanted a secure, financial future, which his career could give him. But sometimes he needed 'his' time, and the occasional roll-in-the-hay, as most men do. Even though he had never actually rolled in hay.

The bartender asked if they would like another round. Brian pulled his wallet from his pocket.

"No, no, I'll get this; you get the next. Ok?" Larry insisted as he pushed the money lying next to his drink to the bartender.

Brian talked about his marriage, and that he had a son. He began to open his feelings to Larry. He could never talk this freely to anyone, especially a stranger, but somehow Larry seemed different. Brian had to resist this new urge to keep talking. He bragged about his two-year-old son. He loved that boy and loved the time he spent with him. Brian did not tell Larry that he often wished he did not have these 'gay' feelings, thinking he could be a better father. He talked about his career, how it seemed secure, but without a lot of opportunities. Meanwhile he was content while he worked on the other issues in his life.

After that first meeting, they met a few times at the 1222; Larry became a good friend while Brian went through his divorce. They met at other bars and restaurants over the next few years. In time, they frequently went to dinner, dancing, and to the bars. After dinner or drinks, they developed a saying 'off to conquer' before hitting the next bar. Like most young gay men in those days, they focused on partying, and on sexual encounters, not unlike their straight counterparts.

But in the early eighties, AIDS reared its ugly head. Larry met someone and they became homebodies. Brian returned to the comfort of the 'closet'. He and Larry met for dinner less frequently, and eventually stopped seeing each other altogether.

"We definitely have to catch up. Why don't we meet tonight after work, especially since we both live in Long Beach? How about Amici's on Anaheim Street? I can't believe we live in the same city and not see each other." Larry proposed, leaning back in his chair, still grinning from the memories that flooded his mind.

"Sounds good to me. Do you still drink vodka martinis? I remember you could hold them better than most people." Brian added. "By the way, how's Peter?"

"I'll still have one now an then. Nothing like I could before. Life's a lot quieter now. Peter and I are both getting older, I admit under protest. He's doing very well." Larry felt a surge of energy from the memories and wanted to spend more time socializing. "Peter's retired full time now. He spends most of his time in our Palm Springs place. I go there most weekends."

"I assume you guys plan the live there full time when you retire."

"Yes, yes we do. In a couple more years, I'll be sixty-five. Then we'll sell the Long Beach place." Larry answered, and sat upright in his chair. "I wish we could talk some more, on a personal level. But unfortunately, we need to tackle this project. I want to tell you what I know before this ten o'clock meeting."

"Great. Tonight we talk old times. Now we talk work. I'd like to know as much as you can tell me before the meeting."

"Oh. By the way, Peter and I are having our thirtieth anniversary party next weekend. I really hope you can come."

"I'd love to. With bells on."

"I'll give you more details tonight at dinner. But first we really need to discuss this embezzlement situation." Larry changed topics. "Ok. Where do I start? Someone has embezzled a serious amount of money from Leonard Construction. We don't know how much yet. Worse, we don't know who is involved. My

Director of Accounting, Greg Larkin discovered these irregularities last week. I really wish he'd come in. It's not like him to be late."

Larry wiped the edges of his mouth with his thumb and index finger, leaned back in his chair, and laid his hands on his lap. "I need him in this meeting. He can fill you in on the technical details, later. In fact, you'll work with him mostly. Someone basically used the computer system to skim and divert money that Leonard pays its vendors. And Leonard pays a lot of money to a lot of vendors."

Larry gave more details. He identified people in the departments who could logically be involved. He added that hackers could be involved, since Leonard is a global company and uses a lot of high tech communications, including extensive use of the Internet.

"Only a hand-full of people knows about this. Maybe some of the same people will be in this meeting." Larry looked at his watch. "We probably should leave now. That'll give us time to make a bathroom stop. I need to check with Liz on Greg's status. I'm starting to worry."

Brian picked up his briefcase from the floor, stood, and slipped on his suit coat. Larry removed his jacket from the back of the door. Brian looked Larry in the eye and grinned.

"Off to conquer." As if on queue, both men chimed together, then laughed.

SEVEN

Tuesday, late morning, April 5
Santa Monica Mountains, Topanga Road

Wes easily found a space in the assigned area for Sheriff's vehicles. He retrieved his briefcase from behind the seat and locked the car. The mid-day sounds seemed inconsonant with this remote, quiet area of Southern California. Patrol cruisers' doors slammed shut, engines roared, and motorcycles sped from their parking spaces. Indistinct voices of officers and civilian employees filled the noontime air. An occasional wisecrack, a laugh, or mock get-out-of-my-way demand rose above the din. The sun shone bright, the temperature had risen, on its way into the eighties, a typical April day in the San Fernando Valley.

Wes walked through the employee entrance on the south side of the stationhouse. Once inside, the noise and hyperactivity of people escalated. A mostly male crowd of police, and civilian workers filled the building with a large bullpen in the center and offices around the perimeter. He joined in the mock wisecracking with a couple of the officers as he passed them.

People on too much caffeine hurried from desk to desk, surprisingly without bumping into each other. The station house chaos had its own rhythm, its own choreography. The mid-day activity danced in full swing. Only the public area in the front of the building where officers interacted with the public was quieter. Wes turned right from the bullpen area and walked to the detective's offices.

"Good morning Phyllis." Wes greeted his partner of four years as he laid his briefcase on top of his desk.

"Good afternoon, you mean, Wes. How are you?" Phyllis looked up from her work and smiled at him. "How did the little side trip for that accident on Topanga go?"

"Oh, I'm fine. And as for the accident, I'm not sure that it was just an accident."

"Oh. Go on." Phyllis, curious, laid down her pen and leaned back in her chair.

"Well, a few things don't add up. No attempt to stop the vehicle, just straight off the cliff. A suicide? But why would he wear a seatbelt?" Wes spoke his thoughts, almost in a stream of consciousness.

"It was raining, maybe it was just hard to see? Californians have trouble driving in the rain." Phyllis offered.

"True. But everything about him seemed like he lived a pretty good life. He worked as an accounting director for a construction company in Santa Monica. That usually pays pretty good, I think."

"And, he was a young family man. A few small kids' toys were in the backseat and on the floorboard. He had a picture of his wife and two toddlers in his wallet."

"That should make suicide less likely."

"True, but. But, we found a small vial of cocaine in his car."

"Ah, a chink in the profile." Phyllis nodded her head thinking. "Sounds more like an accident."

"Yeah. But an accident usually shows some attempt to stop. No banged up railing, just a missing section, and barreled over the cliff."

"True."

"The coroner rep expects they'll schedule an autopsy in a few days. I'll call them tomorrow. Maybe they can expedite them. Anyway, I'd like to be at the autopsy. My gut tells me there might be more to this."

"Well I have to admit, your investigation-by-gut technique usually works. Or is it simply years of accumulated experience?" She teased.

"My Gut technique is pretty reliable, isn't it?" Then Wes turned serious. "I need to notify the family. I dread doing that."

"Why don't you let the deputies notify them?" Phyllis asked.

"I think a personal visit from me would be better. Actually, I don't live to far from them. Besides, there's a slim chance that it may be more than an accident. I would need to interview the family anyway." Wes swiveled in his chair and faced Phyllis. "It'll be easier if there're two of us."

"Sure, I'll be glad to go."

"First I need to feed my addiction. Coffee, more coffee." Wes grabbed his mug and headed to the break room.

"I laid the folders for the Kenny case and the Harm case on your desk. I updated them this morning. After you review them, we can plan what to do next." Phyllis said to his back as he walked away.

People described Phyllis as average, average height, average weight, and average looks. She had a no nonsense approach to work that dictated her behavior, dress, and language. She walked with a purpose, and if not at her desk, carried case folders or writing pads.

She wore her dark brown hair short, in an easy-to-manage style, and wore little make-up. She considered applying makeup too time consuming and non-productive. She often wore turtleneck shirts under a blazer jacket, usually in public. She liked her professional look when wearing the jacket.

She had little time for overt feminine behaviors such as twirling her hair between her fingers or tossing her head to swing her hair seductively. When people saw her in social settings, they noticed she had dark good looks and strong feminine features, dark eyes, long eyelashes. Without the jacket, men immediately noticed her ample breasts. Phyllis could turn heads when she wanted.

After a few minutes reviewing the Kenny and Harm cases, checking his calendar, and e-mail, Wes prepared to leave. Phyllis stacked the folders on her desk, put them into a desk drawer, and locked her desk.

"Oh, I almost forgot. Guess who I met this morning? Actually she was the one who called in the accident."

"Now, how would I know that?" Phyllis accepted the playful challenge. "*Guess who* is just not enough information to go on."

"I met Karen Coffman." Wes said with pride.

"Oh. Ok. I'll bite. Who is Karen Coffman?"

"She's only one of the top selling, new and upcoming mystery writers in Southern California." Wes responded in disbelief. "Don't you read?

"Mostly the technical stuff." Phyllis grabbed her brief case. "Talk on."

Wes described his conversation and interaction with Ms. Coffman while they walked to the parking area. Phyllis smiled at Wes' obvious pleasure in meeting the writer.

Wes and Phyllis left the Ventura freeway at the White Oak exit that led through the Van Nuys area. He found the street, turned, and scanned the house numbers for the Larkin address.

The house sat among several other small two and three bedroom houses with single car garages. Built of wood siding and stucco with asphalt roofs, the starter houses varied in colors, but mostly white, and had limited landscaping. Narrow, cracked sidewalks lined both sides of the street, giving access to the equally plain walkways that lead to the front doors. Chain link fencing enclosed several of the front yards where a few small children played with their toys.

Wes parked, straightened his tie, and removed his blazer from the back seat. Phyllis brought her briefcase. Both inhaled a deep breath to brace for this difficult task.

The season's clean air, nice temperature, and blue sky could not remove the dread they felt. They had notified the next-of-kin only a few times in their careers. It was never easy.

Wes pressed the doorbell. The door opened. A gray haired man in his early sixties stood there.

"May I help you?" His voice was tired, his face filled with worry.

"Hello, I'm Deputy Wesley Makelin from the Sheriff's department. And this is Detective Hadley. Is this the Greg Larkin home?" Wes held his badge for the older man to see, and spoke softly, but with effort to speak the words respectfully.

"Yes he does; I'm his father." Weariness gave way to worry and fear spread across the older man's face. He now knew why the detectives were there. He groaned. "Oh God, something has happened to him, hasn't there?"

"May we come in, please?"

The senior Larkin opened the door further and motioned for them to enter. They stepped directly into a small living room. A short older woman in her late fifties and a younger woman in her late twenties joined them. Two small children, a boy about three, and a girl about five, clutched their mother's legs. They too sensed something wrong, and became quiet. Wes dreaded this moment.

"This is Alicia Larkin, my son's wife. And my wife, Ella."

Fear and hurt had spread over their faces.

Speaking to the younger woman, Wes said, "Mrs. Larkin, We're very sorry to inform you that your husband's body was found in a ravine off Topanga Road this morning." He looked in her eyes and switched to the older couple and back again to the younger woman. "His car had gone off the road during last night's rain."

The younger woman began moaning, sobbing. The tears began. She pulled her children closer to her as she sank onto the couch. The two children began to cry and hug their mother more. They obviously sensed the confusion and pain their mother felt.

The older woman began to cry as she leaned into her husband's arms. His body sagged, his eyes filled with tears. Both parents then moved to each side of the younger woman, to comfort her, and their grandchildren.

"I know it's little comfort, but he was wearing his seatbelt. He likely died on impact so he probably felt little or no pain. I'm so very sorry for your loss." Wes paused for a moment to give them some time.

Wes did not like the expression *sorry for your loss*. The words seemed so empty, so overused. They lost any meaning long ago, but people continued to use them, and yet in the most sad of human experiences. How do trite expressions ever give anyone comfort? For Wes, unfortunately, other words were unavailable, and if they were, they would probably be as inadequate.

Phyllis too lacked comforting words. Tears glazed over her eyes.

Wes avoided the details that could indicate suicide, or worse, homicide. Until the coroner finished the autopsy, and the labs returned the toxicology reports, those speculations, were just that, speculations. He would ask a few necessary questions and give this family time to grieve.

"The Coroner has taken Mr. Larkin's body to the LA County morgue in downtown LA. As you may or may not know, state law requires the Coroner to perform an autopsy on all accident victims. After the autopsy, you may have the remains sent to a funeral home."

"Again, I'm so very sorry for your loss." He used those empty, clichéd words again. He truly felt sad about Greg Larkin's death.

Phyllis removed a county death pamphlet from her brief case and handed it to Wes.

"This pamphlet should provide some of the answers to questions that you may have. It includes contact information you'll need to identify him, and later claim the body." Wes handed the pamphlet to the father.

The young mother was in such obvious pain. She continued to sob, holding her children, leaning into her mother-in-law. The grandmother whispered to her trying to comfort her and the children.

The pamphlet provided details on the disposition of the body, the timeline of law enforcement, the Coroner's procedures, and relevant phone numbers.

"Do you know if alcohol played a part in the accident?" The senior Larkin in obvious pain himself looked at Wes. "He had told Alicia that he was stopping for a drink with a colleague after work. Greg drank very little, so I know it shouldn't have been a problem, but still…"

"It's unlikely that alcohol was a problem, sir, but we'll have to wait until the toxicology results are in to be sure." Wes wished he had not said the first part of the sentence. But in the midst of such emotional pain, scripted words rarely fit. He wanted to comfort this grieving family.

"I… I want to see him. May I see him?" The younger woman managed to ask between sobs. She looked to Wes as she held her kids close to her.

"Yes, certainly." Wes responded quickly to her question. He pointed to the back of the pamphlet that the senior Larkin held. "There's a phone number you can call, and the address with a small map. It's in downtown LA."

"I'll take you there." The senior Larkin almost whispered to his daughter-in-law.

She slowly nodded.

"The children?" The grandmother asked, then added, "I, I want to, I need to go to."

"I want my kids with me."

"Honey, let's take it a step at a time." The father cautioned. "We'll be back as soon as we can. Let's be sure it's Greg. Let's adjust as we're able."

They whispered more among themselves. Trying to comfort each other as well as decide what they needed to do.

"If you have someone, a close friend, or neighbor. It might be better." Phyllis volunteered.

"You're right." The father said. "There are so many questions that we have. But now, we just need to adjust to this. Is there more you think we need to know?"

"Sir, you're going through a lot right now. Let me give you my card. If you have any questions, feel free to call me, either of us. We'll try to answer your questions. If not, we'll find someone who can." Wes handed his card to the senior Larkin. "In a few days we should know more."

Phyllis handed her card to him as well.

Wes had a brother and two sisters. His brother, Gerald, has two children. He knew how close they were to each other. If Gerald died, their family's pain would be unbearable. Wes' mother would cease to function. The same kind of pain this family now felt.

"If there is anyone I can call for you, I'll be glad to. Or if you need us to stay with you a while, we can do that. Otherwise, we'll leave to give you time alone." Wes offered, and added those words, "Again, I'm very sorry for your loss."

"Thanks for the words. But, no, I don't think there's anything you can do. We'll somehow get through this." Grief had consumed the senior Larkin. He now functioned in mechanical mode.

The senior Larkin escorted Wes to the door. They shook hands, again mechanical. Neither said anything further. Wes could not say the words of apology for their loss.

As Wes and Phyllis walked to their car, the mid-day California sun provided little warmth to ward away the sadness they both felt. Wes breathed deeply to lessen the tightness in his chest. It helped a little. He wanted to control his emotions, to reduce his stress, and to tackle the rest of his day. He knew the future would bring similar events, and silently he hoped there would be few. Wes could understand why detectives suffered mental breakdowns from these deep emotional interactions with grieving families.

"I agree with you. That may not have been just an accident." Phyllis expressed what they both thought, and opened her car door.

"A young man like that would drive very cautiously in rain. Those toxicology reports can't come soon enough." Wes slammed his door as a little vengeful anger edged into him.

EIGHT

Tuesday, late morning, April 5
Santa Monica, California

A high polished mahogany table, with twenty dark brown, overstuffed leather chairs dominated the center of the executive conference room. The same plush hunter green carpeting in the executive offices extended through this room. A floor-to-ceiling exterior glass wall provided more fantastic views of the Los Angeles skyline.

Two walls were painted a rich looking taupe. On one wall, a sixty-inch LCD screen for presentations hung above a shiny mahogany buffet table filled with food items. With the food, sat large urns of coffee, hot water, sodas, bottled water, and Lucite buckets of ice. Inverted china coffee cups, saucers, small plates, and glasses sat alongside. Silver trays containing an assortment of pastries, bagels, and cream cheese finished the available space.

A wide dark credenza sat against the other wall. On top of it sat two driftwood table lamps, stained to complement. Above the credenza hung a huge oil canvas of the headquarters building. Leonard built the structure ten years ago, and took pride in its design.

The inside wall of un-tinted plate glass allowed view of the small hallway with additional art, and doors to the restrooms and the break room with its expensive wood cabinetry.

Less noticeable were the technology features, speakers, cable plugs-ins, and recessed lighting. The special lighting illuminated work areas on the table and the artwork on the walls. Dimmers controlled the level of light depending on the meeting's purpose.

Larry and Brian poured themselves coffee. Brian felt a little odd drinking from china cups, instead of a large ceramic mug like those he used at home. Surprisingly, this coffee tasted no better.

Larry introduced Brian to Rob Carter, Vice President of Information Technology.

"Hello, Brian. It's good to meet you." Rob attempted to juggle his coffee and bagel to shake Brian's hand. Trim, early forties, dressed more casually than the others, he wore dark slacks and a button down plaid shirt, starched, expensive looking.

"It's good to meet you as well." Brian grinned appreciating Rob's awkward balancing act to observe civil protocol. "That's ok. We can shake hands later."

"I'll take you up on that. It's still good to meet you. I want you to know that my group will give you any help that you need."

"I appreciate that."

Bob faced Larry, "Larry, I understand that Greg isn't here for this meeting. I hope everything is alright."

"No he apparently won't be here. Liz talked with his wife a few minutes ago. She's frantic. She's tried calling almost anyone she could think of all night. His cell phone, the police, the hospitals." Larry explained to the small group that had gathered around him.

Looking at his watch and then to Brian, "Why don't we take a seat?" Larry gestured to chairs near the middle of the table. Others began sitting, moving chairs, giving themselves plenty of room since less than ten people would attend this meeting.

Daniel Post, Leonard Construction President and CEO, entered the room. He wore subtle, but noticeable signs of his success. He wore a Brooks Brothers suit; a Rolex watch peeked from under his sleeve, cuffed with expensive gold links. However, his tie choice, a bright colored Jerry Garcia one, departed from his CEO look. At 55, he enjoyed his achievements. He had worked hard in the construction industry, started his own company, and watched it grow over the last twenty-five years. His company went public ten years ago increasing his considerable wealth. He kept huge chunks of the stock for himself so he could control the company.

He kept his tough, no non-sense bulldog approach to business from his construction days. He dealt with projects and problems head-on. He worked hard and expected the same from his people, whether in the boardroom or at the construction site.

Judith, his administrative assistant followed him into the room and pulled one of the chairs beside the credenza. She opened her notepad and would record notes of the meeting.

"Good morning everyone." Daniel began in his usual get-right-to-it tone. "Before we begin discussing the reasons for this meeting, I see a new face who I presume is our new consultant."

Larry took his cue and nodded to Brian. "I would like to introduce Brian Latimer, a computer forensics expert. He has many years of detailed experience in computer systems, databases, and accounting. I've known him several years and know his work. I've hired him to assist us in investigating this issue."

Looking around the room, Larry continued, "We want to keep Brian's work quiet, and to limit who knows the real purpose of this investigation. So, ostensibly Brian's consulting work will be to improve the security and efficiency of our accounting systems.

"Since he will work in systems that affect your departments, I'd like you to introduce yourselves. Rob, why don't you start?" Larry swiveled his chair to his left, and looked past Brian.

"Brian." With a laugh, Rob nodded, and offered his hand. "Since we met at the buffet a moment ago, you already know me and my department. I guess we can shake hands now. I want to assure you again that you will receive complete cooperation and quick response from my people in anything you need. I'd just like to be kept informed."

Brian nodded. "Thank you Mr. Carter."

"Call me Rob, please." Another friendly laugh.

"Brian, we're pretty much on a first name basis around here. Rarely are we in a situation where we use last names." Daniel Post added. "Even I go by Daniel to most employees."

A soft laugh swept about the room.

Sitting beyond Rob Carter, at the end of the table, a man of about fifty and sporting a full head of graying hair spoke. "I'm Don Hovey, Executive Vice President of Human Resources. I'll assign one of my key people to help you. You'll be his first priority. If you have any questions, he can answer them, or if you need any personnel files, he can pull them for you. That way, fewer people will know what's being researched."

"Sounds good. I appreciate that. Good to meet you. Don." To far to reach for a handshake, Brian nodded, sat forward, and rested his arms on his chair arms.

"I'm Chas Erickson. Senior Director in Construction Projects. I'm sitting in for Donna Girardi, Vice President of Construction Projects. She's in Europe and not able to tell you herself, but she has directed us in Construction Projects to give you full cooperation as well. I just want you to know I'll give you any assistance you need. I'll be your primary contact in our division. I have access to all our data, and know our systems pretty well. So it'll not be a problem involving other people. So, call me anytime." Chas leaned forward, slid his card across the table, and smiled at Brian.

Taller than average, trim, broad shoulders, Erickson wore paisley suspenders over a blue shirt with a white collar, a small gold pin connected the collar's rounded corners under the tie. In his late thirties, he dressed for success, probably better than anyone else in the room, except for the CEO.

Brian took the card, thanked him, and smiled back. Others also slid their business cards to him.

"And I'm Jesse Dietz, head of Public Relations. If anyone has questions, especially if they're from the outside world, refer them to me, if you would please." He nodded to his left. "Stan here and I try to control the information that goes to the outside world. It keeps the information consistent, reduces the rumors, and helps insure positive publicity for the company."

Dietz appeared the same age as their CEO, Daniel, but less evidence of the success Daniel displayed. Shorter than his boss, his hair grayer, he wore a dark suit, wearing his jacket while most at the table had hung theirs on the backs of their chairs. Brian wondered if Dietz wore his jacket in his office.

"And I'm Stan Brothers. Legal Council for Leonard. Naturally, I'll be involved to protect Leonard's interests from a legal standpoint." Brothers sat next to Daniel, as if his right hand man.

Brothers barely smiled, not impolite, just formal. Tall, thinning hair, thin body, again the blue shirt with the button down collar, he sat straight in his chair. His pronounced, bent nose resembled an eagle's beak, a true legal eagle.

Daniel resumed control of the meeting. "Now that Brian knows us. I want to say that in my experience Larry doesn't make accounting mistakes. Even the external auditors have audited us for years and we've not had any problems." Daniel rested one arm on the table as if to challenge anyone to disagree. "Larry, how about a quick overview of our problem."

"Thanks. Normally, I have a lot of confidence in our accounting systems, their accuracy, and their security. However no system is perfect. Someone has apparently found a way around our internal controls. With Brian's help, we will find the cause and close the loophole. Unfortunately, we don't know the full extent of this problem, or how long it has been going on. Greg has identified about two million dollars going to strange accounts over the last eighteen months." Larry leaned forward in his chair.

"I was hoping Greg would be here. Liz is trying to track him down. It's very unlike him not to be here." Larry's face showed his worry. "Meanwhile we'll hope for the best, and proceed without him. Greg brought this missing money issue to my attention last week."

Over the years Larry's reputation for honesty and thoroughness had grown among the other executives. All knew Larry could control and account for business expenses better than anyone, and if there was a problem, he would resolve it.

"We found four, possibly five companies that we've paid good money to. These companies involve high dollar projects. In several of the payments, a small percentage of the payments were siphoned to strange accounts. We've put a hold on the payments until we can investigate each situation. Brian's abilities involve researching databases, accounting records, and the very technical details of security. We have to resolve this problem within two weeks. These companies won't like our slow payment of their invoices. "

Any questions?" Larry looked around the room at the worried faces.

"So, where do we start?" Someone asked.

"Let's give Brian a day or two, then we can re-meet." Larry answered.

"Larry will chair this project. This group will meet as needed. Judith," Daniel nodded to her sitting beside the credenza, "will contact you with the times and dates. I want this resolved before month's end. I like Larry's two-week timeframe. Does every one understand? So, Larry, Brian, what do you need from the people at this table?"

"Thanks Daniel. I'm going to give that question to Brian."

"Thanks, Larry." Brian felt some apprehension with all eyes on him. He had just met these people. He knew little about their systems, security, and people. But felt confident he could do this job. He inhaled deeply, but not loudly to relax, so his nervousness would not show in his voice. "Larry has already given me an overview of the accounting systems and the people. First I'll cover the systems with broad-brush strokes in a few hours. Then I'll dig deep into the nitty-gritty details over the next few days. I work fast. So I appreciate hearing your cooperation. Let's jump in."

Fingering his pen above his writing tablet, he faced Rob Carter. "I'll need to understand the computer system rules that control accesses to the databases. That includes identifying everyone who can access those databases. And, I will need access to those databases, not the ability to change the data, just to read it. "

"You got it." Rob re-affirmed. "Ralph Chung, in charge of network security. And Dean Horvath, our super techie, there's not much that he doesn't know about computers."

"Thanks." Brian wrote their names on his notepad.

Brian inhaled another deep breath, still hoping his anxiety did not show in his voice. He did not want to sound like a field marshal commanding his troops, but wanted quick action. He wanted; no he needed the full cooperation of these people.

"Larry will assign David Frazer to help me with the accounting side. And Chas, I'll need to work closely with you or whoever you assign to understand the Construction Projects side."

"That'll be me. You're on the top of my priority list." Chas sat forward eager to help.

"After this meeting, I will develop an action plan with specifics on what steps I'll take and anyone else I need to work with. I will…" Brian stopped mid-sentence, and looked through the glass door.

Liz stood outside the room. She motioned to Larry to join her.

"Please continue." Larry joined her in the hallway. He knew it had to be important. Otherwise, Liz would never interrupt an important meeting such as this.

Brian resumed speaking, "I'll give all of you the details that you want. For faster results, I suggest that I keep Larry current. Then he can set additional meetings as he chooses. Or if you want, group meetings, whatever you like."

"I'd like you to keep Larry current. That way you can focus on your work. He can pass what you learn along to me, Stan and whoever else we think needs to know."

"Sounds good." Brian liked this method better.

"Furthermore, as Larry said earlier, I want all of this kept quiet while we resolve it." Daniel looked about the room. "If any of this gets out, it could embarrass us, or affect our stock. It could get the attention of the SEC or worse, the IRS; none of which we want."

Through the glass, Brian could see Liz holding her hands over her face, appearing to cry. Larry hugged her for a moment. She lowered her hands to her sides, and seemed to regain her composure. She nodded her head to something Larry said and left. Larry returned inside the room. His face was pale, his eyes moist.

"Everyone, I have some very sad news. Liz just informed me that Greg was killed in a car accident last night going over Topanga Canyon." Larry paused a moment to regain his composure. He walked to his chair, and sat.

Like cold night air, a hush lay over the room as each reacted to the news. In seconds, the emotional heaviness replaced the business focus of the meeting. Most in the room knew and liked Greg. They had worked together, and had socialized at staff and company gatherings. They had become friends as well as colleagues.

"That is sad news." Daniel spoke after a moment. "Larry, do you need some time? We can continue this later."

"No, no Daniel. I just need a moment." Looking first at Daniel, then at the others, Larry said, "Although, if Brian has finished, I think we've covered just about everything for this first meeting. Brian and I will start this project this afternoon as planned."

"I think I've finished, Larry." Brian said softly, unsure of what to say, or how to say it.

No one else said anything, respecting Larry's feelings.

"I would like a little time to absorb what has happened. I need to meet with my staff. They'll take this pretty hard. We all will. As you may have seen, Liz is very broken up over Greg's death." Larry said, his voice shaky.

Everyone quietly pushed his chair from the table and just as quietly left the room. A few paused beside Larry, laying a hand on his shoulder, or shaking his hand, offering condolences. They knew Greg was like a son to him.

NINE

Tuesday, early afternoon, April 5
Santa Monica, California

After the meeting, Brian, Larry, and a few of the executives walked through the security common area to their offices. Their heels clicked against the granite floor. A few of the executives split to the bank of elevators to their offices on other floors.

On his way to the elevator, Chas turned to Larry and squeezed his shoulder, "Larry, I'm really sorry to hear the news about Greg. I really liked him. We'll all miss him. He has a nice young family, too. It's a painful loss for all of us."

"Thanks, Chas."

"Brian, again, I want you to know that I'll provide you all the information you need, at least about the Construction Projects division. When you're ready, I'll introduce you to Art Dexter, my operations accountant." Chas looked Brian in the eye and seemed sincere, even eager to cooperate in the investigation.

"Thank you Chas. Maybe we can meet later this afternoon. I want to meet with David Frazer first, and develop a skeletal action plan."

Walking to Larry's office, Brian spoke first. "Larry, I can work on the action plan alone for a while, if you'd like some time to yourself?"

"No, that's ok Brian."

As they approached Larry's office, they saw a young man and two women with Liz talking. The sadness seemed to saturate the air.

"Why don't we all just take a seat inside?" Larry gestured to his office, his face pale with sadness.

They filed inside. David closed the door. Brian pulled one of the chairs from the small conference table and sat to the side of the group. Liz, David, and Erica sat in the other chairs that Brian and Larry had occupied earlier. Larry stared out the window for a moment while he regained his composure.

Larry turned to face Liz as he slumped in his chair. "How's Alicia? The kids? What can we do to help them?"

"Naturally, she's very distraught." Liz was near tears as she spoke. "Greg's parents are there. Her parents live in Las Vegas. They should be there in a few hours."

"Is there anything we can do to help? Anything?" Larry asked, feeling helpless.

"If you don't mind, later, I'm going to go there to help if I can. I want to spend a little time with Alicia. She and I have become good friends. I love those two little ones." She attempted to smile, thinking of the two toddlers, but the sadness weighed too heavily.

"Yes, by all means, go. And if there's anything I can do?" Larry meant his words, but they felt inadequate, hollow. "Erica, would you please gather everyone on our staff into the accounting conference room. We need to tell them this horrible news. Although, they probably already know. I'll be there in a minute. I think we need to be together."

"Sure." Erica started to rise.

"Thanks" Oh, I'm sorry Brian." Larry caught himself. "This is David Frazer and Erica Montgomery. David. Erica. This is Brian Latimer, the consultant I told you about. Erica is the Admin Assistant on Eleven. She assists Greg and David and the others there. Or rather did assist Greg."

Brian shook hands with them.

With hazel eyes and dark brown hair, David Frazer looked eighteen but was twenty-eight. Shy of six feet by three inches, he had an athletic build, probably from tennis or swimming, but not football. He dressed professionally, gray trousers and a blue button-down shirt, no tie.

Erica Montgomery, a single mom of a cute two-year-old girl, carried a few extra pounds on her five foot two frame. Her husband had left her soon after the birth of their baby, but she had adjusted well. She enjoyed her life with her daughter, and enjoyed her work, which provided enough income to support her daughter.

"Brian, there's probably no real need for you to join us."

"I understand." Brian dipped his head slightly in respect, and added, "If you have an empty office somewhere, I can start outlining the action plan."

"That sounds good. David, please show Brian the empty office next to Greg's and then join us in the conference room." Back to Brian, "Just give us a half hour or so, is that ok?" Larry looked at his watch. "I'm sure some of the staff will want to talk about Greg's death."

"Sure." Brian followed David to the door, and turned back to Larry. "Larry, I want you to know that I'm really sorry to hear about Greg. I didn't know him, of course. But I can certainly tell by your reaction, and the reactions from the others, how all of you cared for him."

Brian genuinely shared their sadness.

"Thanks." Larry tried to smile.

After Brian and David left, Larry sat quietly in the silent room.

Larry sat for a while to regain his composure. He must be strong for his staff, his *family*. The meeting would feel more like a funeral, than a staff meeting. Larry's small department was family to him. He did not like corporations using the term 'family' to ingratiate employee loyalty, to engage their dedication and hard work. But when the bottom line suffered, *family* members became expendable.

The same corporations gave their top management millions of dollars as rewards or in separation agreements. A few of those millions could easily keep many employed and help hundreds of families, and really earn employee devotion and loyalty. Instead many executives viewed their companies as their own personal piggy banks.

As they approached the stairwell, "Brian, the stairs should be faster. I'll show you your office so you can settle in a little. It's only a couple floors down." With visible effort to control his quivering jaw, David attempted to keep his voice steady. "After our staff meets, I'll show you where the cafeteria, restroom facilities, and break rooms are, and we can begin our work."

"David," Brian looked him in the eyes. "Greg's death is a big shock, I understand if you need a little time. I'm sure Larry would understand if you took some time off to absorb all that's happened. I'm sure someone can point me in the direction of the cafeteria, and break rooms."

"No. That's all right. I'll be ok. Later, if I need the time, I'll talk to Larry." David escorted Brian down the stairwell to his temporary office. Then, he left to join the others.

Brian laid his briefcase on the desk. Two large windows filled the length of the small office. A functional laminate desk occupied the center of the room. A well-equipped computer workstation sat on a credenza, against the wall. A comfortable looking, ergonomic chair sat between the desk and workstation. A small conference table filled the rest of the office space. Through the windows, Brian could see much of the city of Los Angeles and the surrounding mountains, the same view Larry saw upstairs.

He could enjoy working here. He allowed himself a moment to enjoy the view before beginning the big task ahead.

He rummaged through the desk drawers and mentally inventoried their contents. He pressed the power-on button of his computer. While it booted, he took his notepad from his briefcase and reviewed his notes from the morning's meeting.

Then, he explored the computer's contents for the available software and accesses to digital files. Apparently Leonard Construction liked Microsoft Office software, specifically Word, Excel, PowerPoint, and Access. He inventoried other software for accounting, inventory, and sales applications. He liked that he had worked with most of them. His job would be easier.

For several minutes, he wrote detailed notes, and scripted an elementary action plan with steps and target dates. He would prioritize them later after discussion with Larry and David.

He heard a light rap on the opened door, and looked up. David stood there.

"Hi David." Brian smiled.

"Hi Brian." David, still somber, asked, "ready for lunch?"

"Yes, yes I am." Brian laid down his pen. "How is everyone? How are you doing?"

"Everyone took it pretty hard. There were tears, of course. A few will go home. A couple people took the news especially hard, so Larry is spending a little time with them. As for myself, I feel better now," David paused, "some. The news hurts but I'm adjusting. I think staying busy will help."

"I understand. Anytime you need or want some time alone, just tell me. Ok?"

"Thanks. I'll do that." David attempted a slight smile.

"Are you sure you want to go to lunch? I can manage."

"Yes, I'm sure. But maybe we could bring our lunches here and discuss the project. If that's alright with you?" David stared out the window a moment. "I often bring my lunch to my desk, for the quiet."

"Sounds good. Let's do that."

In the cafeteria, David pointed to the different food stations, a sandwich and deli bar, a make-your-own salad bar, and a hot food station that provided two or three main entrée choices. They met at the checkout stand, paid for their lunches, and returned to Brian's new office.

Sitting at the small conference table, they engaged in small talk for a few minutes while they ate. David explained the locations of the copy rooms, the break room with coffee and vending machines, and naturally the restrooms.

David explained that Erica and Liz would handle the administrative stuff – employee badge, parking decal, email accesses, phone directory, and the like. And that he would obtain all necessary system accesses from IT for Brian. Just provide a list.

David gave Brian a key to the office and said Erica and Liz had backup keys if needed. He told Brian that Larry had allocated this office solely to this project, essentially to Brian. Not even the janitor has a key. They were to shred all discarded documents, and set the containers, along with other waste outside the door.

When they finished eating, they bussed their dishes to the break room. The cafeteria people would pick them up later.

David then gave a brief overview of Leonard Construction, its offices and projects in the US, Germany, and Australia. He identified the major systems involved in the company business, the accounting, sales, inventory, and how all of them passed information among themselves. Then, like skirmishes in a military attack, he provided details of those systems in a rapid-fire delivery that would confuse most listeners. But Brian absorbed most everything David said. Many questions were asked and answered without skipping a beat. Both men were in their elements.

Pointing to an organization chart, David identified the key players, those who approved any contracts and any payments on those contracts. He knew his company and much of the technology it used. David took a deep breath. He relished this challenge, this escape.

"You've done this before." Brian grinned, impressed with David's knowledge and ability to communicate.

"Yeah." David smiled. "I like knowing my business."

A good partnership between the two men had begun.

"Next, let me describe the nature of the discrepancies that Greg and I identified. Greg worked on it more than I did. Basically supplier' invoices were altered for amounts six and seven percent above the original amount. When we paid the full invoice, that difference went to a different bank. Our system automatically pays the full amount of the invoice. Our reports only flag for research payments that are greater than that six or seven percent. The supplier gets what they expect. We think we've paid the proper amount in full. Collectively the dollar amounts really add up. So far, we've identified over two million dollars." David explained.

Nearly three hours had passed, and Brian needed to formulate an action plan for Larry. He and David concluded their meeting and would resume later. Also, Brian would identify steps related to IT security later.

Seeing the two men absorbed in their work, Larry knocked softly on the open door.

"Hi Brian, David."

"Hi, Larry." Both responded.

"How are you feeling? How are the others?" Brian leaned back in his chair, his voice genuine, caring.

"As expected, the staff took the news pretty hard, especially a couple of them. I gave them the option to take the afternoon off. As for myself, I feel better now. At least the initial shock has subsided somewhat. For a few minutes there, I just couldn't think. Talking with my people actually helped." Larry added, "David, if you'd like to go home, you're more than welcome to do that."

"I may later, but like I was telling Brian, I think working will help me. I feel like I'm going to be ok. I'm really going to miss Greg. I liked working with him, but we were also good friends. I'm sure there will be times when I'll want to be alone, but for now I'd like to stay busy."

"Well, ok. Whenever you want some time alone, just tell me. Ok?"

"Sure."

Larry took a deep breath. "Brian, you both were in such deep discussion that you've probably not had time to work on that action plan. Any chance, I'll be able to present it to Daniel this afternoon?" Larry switched to a business state of mind, his voice stronger.

"Actually, I had worked on it a little earlier, a preliminary one at least. David has been updating me on the operations here at Leonard."

Brian printed copies of his preliminary plan for the three of them to discuss. He began at the top of the plan. David and Larry inserted occasional comments.

"Great." Larry folded his arms across his chest. "I'd like to say that we three, with Liz as a close fourth, make up the primary team for this project. While we will know all of the details, I'll inform the others, especially Daniel." Larry unfolded his arms. "Brian, you'll find most of the people here at Leonard are very helpful. Just keep in mind that one of them, perhaps more, perpetuated this embezzlement, and may try to distract you."

Larry continued, "David knows our systems. Both he and Greg are…" Larry paused, his emotions affecting his thoughts, "… our key players in running this department. Of course with Greg's death, that work will fall onto David's shoulders, at least, until we can find a replacement for Greg. Speaking of work, are you two at a breaking point? David I need you to run a couple ad hoc reports for me."

"Sure. The Ledger Trials?"

"Yeah."

David left.

"Oh, Larry." Brian hesitated, changing the topic. "About tonight… we can cancel it if you like. You're probably not in any mood to socialize."

"No. No. Let's not cancel. I think it would be good to visit with an old friend. We can all get a good start tomorrow morning. Besides, a martini couldn't hurt."

"Still a martini man?" Brian grinned.

"Yeah." Larry tried to smile.

TEN

Tuesday afternoon, April 5
Santa Monica, California

After Brian met with Larry, David escorted him to Chas' office on the ninth floor. This floor matched the eleventh floor with its gray fabric walls, metal cubicles, and berber carpet. Only the cubicles against the building's walls had views. Overhead, fluorescent bulbs flooded this floor with bright, but comfortable light.

A few plants stood sentry along the narrow hallway, and motivational posters hung on the limited wall space, providing the only color. Small electronic devices emitting 'white noise' sat on the cubicle walls in a few locations. This 'white noise' muffled the employees' voices and the clicking of computer keyboards, giving some sense of quiet.

They approached the end of the floor where Chas' office sat among four other similar ones. In contrast to the rest of the floor, Chas' office contained expensive furniture similar to that on the Executive floor, dark cherry wood desks and cabinets, and a couple quality art pieces. Office décor obviously reflected the ranking within the company. Chas had some stature in the Leonard hierarchy.

One of the two secretaries outside Chas' office rose from her desk. The other looked up and smiled.

"Hi David. Chas is ready for you," she stepped from behind her desk to greet him.

"Hi Jean. This is Brian Latimer. He's working on this accounting project." David gestured to Brian. "Brian, this is Jean Martin, Chas's Administrative Assistant. You'll probably talk with her quite a bit during this project. And that is Carrie, Jean's assistant." David gave her a small wave.

Jean offered her hand. Brian took it. Carrie waved. Brian waved back.

Jean, in her mid-twenties, wore a fitted navy blue skirt and soft white blouse with a loosely tied collar. She worked as Chas' administrative assistant while she completed her senior year for a Business Administration degree. Chas liked projecting a top-notch image, so he hired Jean. She projected this image.

As they entered Chas' office, he rose from his desk and shook their hands. Just then, another man, in his twenties, joined them. Tanned, with sun-bleached hair, he looked uncomfortable in his off-the-rack suit. Unlike his boss, smart business fashion was not a priority.

"Brian, this is Art Dexter. Art, this is Brian Latimer." Chas gestured to the small conference table. "Let's have a seat. Would anyone like a soda, water, or anything?" Chas looked to his visitors. Everyone said no. "Well, Jean, I guess we're okay."

Jean closed the door behind her.

"I've briefed Brian on the accounting systems, including reports and operations. And to some degree, I covered the Construction Projects operations. But you'd be better at giving him the details." David laid his flow charts and a writing pad on the table.

Chas, like David, had an organization document, in a similar format, and containing much of the same information. Subsequent pages contained more details related to his division. It was obvious that both men were practiced using their documents to explain company operations to their superiors, auditors, and investors.

Chas explained the roles of the key people in his department, starting with his boss, Donna Girardi. For the next two hours, Chas covered his group's work. Who approved which vendor, who accessed which computer file, who reviewed which report, and the like. As they talked, Art retrieved examples of reports and forms from stacks in his office.

Brian wrote several notes on the handout and on his notepad. On the side of his notepad he listed follow-up points. He asked several questions and was satisfied with the answers, for the moment.

Chas closed his small handout, and laid it before him. "That's our operation. You're welcome to any of these reports, but you'll probably prefer looking at them online. I'd be very happy to show you how." He leaned back in his chair. "Any more questions?"

"This has been a good description of your operations. Thanks." Brian nodded his head, his mind saturated. He persevered, "Could we spend a little more time discussing the approval of vendors, of how vendors get on the master file?

"Sure." Chas re-opened his document.

"If I understand correctly, only accounting department people can actually update the master files – that would include Greg, David, and Jennifer Pounds."

"Yes," Chas responded. "In this department, Donna, Art, or I sign-off an approval form, a report, or will send an e-mail to them in urgent cases. They flip the switch that performs the update."

"Usually Jennifer enters the new vendor information, a new vendor, or a change to an existing vendor - such as a change of address – into the update program which runs nightly. The next day we can see an online report of those changes. Unfortunately we're often too busy to review that report every day." David added.

Chas continued. "Anyway, if there's a problem, or the amounts are out of range, the system tells us. We research the cause."

"How easy would it be to review some of these reports, online if possible?"

"Easy, we can show you. All of the reports for the last eighteen months are online. Further back, we'll have to ask IT to load history files, for up to ten years. Maybe more." Art spoke, one of the few times during the meeting.

"When you're ready, call me. Or if you can't reach me soon enough, call Art." Chas offered. "I'm sure between us and David, we can answer most of your questions."

David and Art nodded agreement.

"Tomorrow when we meet with Rob Carter, you can give him the list of the accesses you want. I'm sure he'll have them working within the hour. I can show you how to use the systems, which are fairly intuitive. You shouldn't have any problems. And then Chas or Art can help you with their systems."

"May I keep this handout?" Brian asked before placing it into his brief case. "It'll help me a lot understanding what we've discussed."

"Of course." Chas closed his folders and rose from his chair.

The others also stood, ending the meeting. The men shook hands.

Brian and David returned to the eleventh floor. They sat at Brian's conference table.

Brian leaned back in his chair. "I don't want to put you in an uncomfortable position of talking about your colleagues and friends. But someone is embezzling. The computers don't do this by themselves. Larry tells me I can trust you, as well as depend on your work."

"I appreciate that."

"But what can you tell me about Chas and Art?" Brian asked point blank, "On a personal level."

"That would be a little difficult."

"I know." Brian tried to reassure him. "But I'm good at keeping confidences."

"Well. Chas. He's smart, but a little aloof. He's the power base in that department. Everyone knows it, including Donna his boss. He has an MBA from the University of Southern California, and knows accounting, and his department inside and out. How much of IT, I don't know. He's polite, friendly, but..." David groped for the right words.

"That's alright. Remember, I keep confidences. Right now we're just talking."

"Chas is polite, friendly, but he seems a little phony. He smiles when he talks, but sometimes, his requests sound like commands. I like working with him to the extent that I like working with people who know what they're doing. It's just that, sometimes, he seems condescending. Does that make sense?" David looked to Brian for a sense of understanding. "Please don't tell anyone I said that."

"Yes, yes it does make sense. If anyone needs to know that, it'll be your decision. Okay?"

"Okay." David continued. "Chas lives in an expensive condo in Manhattan Beach. But he's ambitious and Donna probably pays him very well to keep him so he can afford a comfortable lifestyle. And I think his parents have a lot of money as well."

"Thanks."

"And as for Art, you should talk with Dean Horvath in IT. You'll meet him tomorrow. Both guys are surfer types. They both live near the beach."

"Thanks." Brian felt tired. "David, if you don't mind, I'm going to organize my thoughts and work on the action plan some more. Frankly, my mind is a little saturated. I need a break."

"Sure. I need to do some of my regular work, anyway." David left for his office.

Brian's mind really did feel saturated with information. He had been in meetings for well over eight hours with only the short break for lunch. He recognized that age slowed his endurance levels. The sixteen-hour days of steady, intense work were now a thing of the past. He needed to rest his mind a little, and organize his thoughts. At least now he had experience on his side, and could prioritize better than he could twenty years ago.

He closed the door, sat in his chair and stared out the window. He needed five quiet minutes or so to regain his focus. Also, he was a little hungry. He remembered he had a couple nutrition bars in his brief case. He retrieved one and ate it.

The time was now almost six. The sun would set soon. He liked the longer days of Daylight Savings Time, which started a couple weeks ago. He could not see the sunset from this side of the building, but it cast a golden glow on everything in the LA basin. Cars inching their way on the freeways mirrored back the sun's bright rays.

The five minutes of rest worked. Maybe the nutrition bar helped. He refocused on his work. He arranged his notes, the flow charts, and other papers on the desk in front of him. He pulled a stapler, a blank writing pad, and pencils from the drawer. He always felt that a little OCD, Obsessive Compulsive Disorder, never hurt anyone. It would serve him now. He pulled two chairs to each side, between his desk and computer workstation. He could then swivel his chair and work in 360 degrees.

He always thought more clearly when he converted handwritten notes to computer printed ones. Clear, easy-to-read notes jump-started his mind, allowing him to recall minute details from meetings, or what he had read. He especially liked using the table feature of his word processing software with a column reserved for unanswered questions, or further needed actions.

He liked flow-charting software. He could draw boxes and circles with names and notes inside them. He could draw lines from one to the other. He loved the graphical nature of this software. He would absorb and understand this company in short time.

ELEVEN

Tuesday evening, April 5
Long Beach, California

Brian looked at his watch, a quarter after seven. He needed to leave now to meet Larry by eight. Commuter traffic should lessen by this time, he hoped. Following his usual tendency, Brian had packed too many activities into his schedule. Although he sometimes arrived late for social events, he always arrived on time for business meetings. Fortunately, he performed his work well, and had an amiable personality, so others often overlooked his occasional tardiness.

But tonight was special, he wanted to arrive on time, mainly to renew his friendship with Larry. However, they would likely discuss business as well. He shredded the paper trash and set it outside his office, locked the door, and rushed to his car.

83

Traffic still inched its way along the 405 freeway. He would barely arrive on time.

Brian exited the Lakewood Boulevard turnoff to the Los Alamos Circle, or the roundabout, to the Pacific Coast Highway, then west to Redondo and down to Anaheim. A few years had passed since he had eaten at Amici's, a neighborhood bar and grill that catered to an older crowd. Brian ate in restaurants less frequently in the last six month. Eating at home saved money, and he needed to save as much as he could, at least until his consulting business became profitable.

Brian drove slowly by Amici's, looking for a space in the small parking lot. Full. Why did good, small restaurants always have such limited parking? He glanced at his watch. Two minutes before eight. His anxiety grew. When he found a space near the end of the block, he sighed, relieved. After two tries, he paralleled parked his car, grabbed his jacket from the back seat, and pushed the button to lock his doors. Several cars moved along the street, while people strolled on the sidewalks, looking in the store windows. Even on a Tuesday night, this section of Anaheim was busy.

The air smelled lightly unpleasant, an oil-based odor. Probably from the refinery located a few miles away. Although costal cities boasted cleaner air than most of the surrounding cities, they still contained a level of pollution. The LA basin contained far more industries than just the movie and tourism businesses.

Brian walked quickly to Amici's. The brown stucco building with two large windows faced the street. A small red, green, and white neon sign, which read *Amici's, an Italian Trattoria* hung in one window. On the side of the building, the double door entrance faced the small parking area. A half round canopy of the same Italian colors sheltered the doorway.

Brian pulled open the heavy aged wood door, and stepped into a small paneled anteroom. A second heavy door opened into a large dimly lit room with a small matre'd stand near the door. A large mahogany bar with brass inserts, a foot rest, and supports dominated the right side of the room. Small dining tables with white tablecloths and candles burning filled the center of the room. Comfortable looking booths lined the opposite side of the room. Patrons filled most of the tables and booths. Against the back wall, a pianist played soft jazz.

Brian saw Larry seated near the piano, a martini sat on the table in front of him. Each acknowledged the other. Brian motioned to the matre'd that he saw his party as he walked to where Larry sat. Rising from his chair, Larry greeted Brian.

"Made it!" Brian pulled in a deep breath of air and opened his arms to give his friend a hug.

They embraced, an old friends' embrace. The good part about being in a gay friendly bar-restaurant, they could hug each other without anyone reading anything into the behavior. No criticism, no ridicule.

"No, no. You're on time. Eight for dinner means around eight. Two minutes doesn't count. Besides, I arrived only a few minutes ago, myself."

"I'm glad we could meet now. I know we'll get busy and absorbed in work later, so socializing won't be easy." Brian laid his coat on the back of a nearby chair.

"It's really good to see you again. Driving here I started to get more excited about catching up with you. We hung out together so much in years past. How did we lose touch?" Larry asked reflectively.

Brian pulled in another deep breath. The waiter approached and asked Brian if he wanted a drink. He ordered a scotch and water, and pointed to Larry's martini as if to order another. Larry shook his head no.

"What? No Bud?" Larry teased.

"No. I've matured." Brian joked back.

"There's so much to catch up on. Our conversation this morning just wasn't enough. I want to know how you are. What you've been up to. How's your son? John, James, is it?"

"It's James. Well, Jimbo… I call him Jimbo. He's not crazy about the nickname, but dads get special leeway. Anyway, Jimbo graduated Long Beach State a couple years ago. Got a business degree. He works in Studio City for an insurance company." Brian laid his napkin in his lap and leaned back in his chair. His grin could not spread any wider. He liked bragging about his son.

"You sound proud, and you should be."

"I am. He's a great kid."

The waiter returned with Brian's drink. They paused their animated conversation, just enough to give the waiter time to set down the drink, and recite the specials for the evening. He left to give them a few minutes to decide.

"My mind is filled with so many questions. I want to know everything that's happened to you since we hung out together. So you still live in Long Beach, you had said."

"Yes. I still live in Long Beach, near the Virginia Country Club. We bought it sometime ago."

"Nice area."

"We like it." Larry smiled as he ran a finger around the rim of his martini glass. "Do you like living downtown? You live in the Spire by The Beach, right?

"Yes, yes I do. I have a great view of the LA basin. I love it, especially at night. I can't believe we both live in the same city and don't see each other. We should kick ourselves."

"We should. What's it been, ten years?"

"More like twelve."

They talked. They laughed. They enjoyed and shared the old, familiar memories that flooded their minds, and spilled into their conversation. They remembered times past, nights out on the town. They almost forgot they were in the restaurant to eat. For the moment, the twelve years dissolved, went away. They were thirty-five again, no longer two men approaching senior citizen status. They forgot about work for a while.

As they talked, Brian, in moments, saw signs of age in Larry's face. His behavior more subdued, more grown-up. And less hair. Although they had met in their thirties, they had often behaved as twenty-somethings. Life was different now. But tonight, they were old friends again.

The restaurant crowd contained mostly men in their forties, their fifties, even older. The sat casually, in suits, work clothes, and casual wear.

"Life really has changed a lot since we hung out in the 1222." Brian could almost read Larry's thoughts as they both wandered down memory lane.

"Sure has."

Crowds in the 1222 in the Eighties differed radically from those in Amici's tonight. Although some of these same men probably patronized the 1222 then. As younger men, they had more courage, more bravado. Actually their pelvic areas probably controlled more of their behavior than their brains. They followed the eternal quest, the eternal search for sex, which drove most young men, gay or straight.

Then, men in their fifties and sixties rarely went to the bars after work. Hell, in the eighties gay friendly bars often did not open until nine or ten, well after dark.

Young men could party, even on weekdays, but especially on weekends. They would recover the next morning, and manufacture some straight story for water cooler conversations. It was not fair, but life required living two lives. For most, business success required diligent use of the closet for their personal lives. Brian and Larry too maintained separate public and closeted lives.

On a late Friday night in June of 1982, Brian and Larry sat drinking in the 1222. More than thirty people sat or stood, drinking their beers, scotches, and a few martinis. They were considered a 'Levi and leather crowd. Most wore jeans, a couple wore leather vests, but a few wore slacks and polo shirts. They were Levi-leather friendly.

Brian wore his usual, Levi's, boots, and a lightweight plaid shirt. LA people never wore heavy, woolen plaid shirts. He had rolled his sleeves above his elbows. He liked the height that his boots added to his already six-foot frame. He wore his baseball cap with its rounded bill to show-off his eyes. He liked other men in jeans and plaid, especially if they had lots of chest hair, even though he too had a generous supply of his own.

Larry wore tan slacks and a pastel polo shirt. He felt more comfortable in slacks than jeans. Besides, some men liked a guy in slacks. Larry definitely enjoyed seeing and occasionally connecting with men in jeans, tank tops, and baseball caps.

They had been friends for about four years now. While Brian was Larry's type, their attitudes toward each other quickly shifted into friendship mode. They enjoyed talking, sharing each other's lives, worries, and successes.

The noise in the bar had increased during the evening, the conversations, and the loud rock music. Some men had to move their feet, wanted to dance. Others who talked had to lean into each other and speak into the other's ear to be heard.

Just after midnight, a loud commotion at the door interrupted the room's noise. The door swung open. Voices became quiet. The lights came on. Four of LA's finest had entered the room. They held their batons chest high and began pushing the patrons, at the same time yelling for them to clear out, to move outside. The patrons wanted to run, some left by the back door before the police reached them. Outside the back and front doors other policemen were waiting. As patrons went outside, the police lined them against the building.

Some patrons protested, but were pushed against the wall. The group became quiet, worried. They whispered amongst themselves. A couple men were near tears. They knew if they were arrested their lives would be in shambles. The police approached a few of the men, had them empty their pockets, and frisked them for drugs.

"Like what you feel?" A bold man asked as he was frisked.

"Shut up faggot." The man in blue demanded.

Inside, the police looked behind the bar, behind stacked cases of empty beer bottles, even in the bathrooms. Using their flashlights they read the alcohol and city licenses posted on the wall behind the cashier's station. The absence of music and the bright overhead lights removed the festive mood of the bar. It now seemed dirty, used, and unappealing.

After about an hour, the police told the men that it was ok to re-enter the building. A few, still visibly shaken, left. Most returned inside. Most had been through this police treatment before. It was harassment, clear and simple, for gay patrons and businesses. But there was not much that anyone could do. It was the Eighties.

Once inside, the bartender turned off the overhead lights, returned the music to its almost too loud state. After a few minutes, and drinking more beer, the mood returned to its earlier party state.

Brian's beer and Larry's martini sat where they had left them, before the interruption, the police harassment. The drinks were now tepid. They ordered another round, complained about the gay state of affairs and moved on in their conversation.

Brian shook his head to end the revelry. "I'm getting hungry. How about some dinner?" Brian felt his stomach churning. He had not eaten anything all afternoon, except for a nutrition bar.

"Sounds good to me."

They scanned their menus, quickly decided their choices, and laid their menus aside.

"We probably should discuss a little business. Since the work is such an important project. Ok?" Larry did not want to change to business, but work was necessary. "First I need to make a trip to the john."

"Sure, not a problem."

When Larry returned, the waiter approached and asked for their orders. Brian ordered a New York steak. As Larry ordered a whitefish entre, Brian thought he noticed a little white powder in one nostril. He had to be mistaken. There was no way that Larry was the kind of person who would use drugs. Larry squeezed his nose between his thumb and index finger. The white stuff was gone; Brian thought his mind played tricks on him. Probably, the flickering candles, the low lights. He just had to be mistaken.

"David and I discussed the systems for a couple hours. He's very good by the way. And after you and I met, David and I met with Chas Erickson and his assistant, Art Dexter, I believe his name is."

"Wait a minute, we can catch up on business the first thing in the morning. I feel my martini. Let's just have a good time. We're allowed some social time."

"I like that idea." Brian raised his scotch for a toast.

"Tell me about the consulting life, about your so-called *semi-retirement*." Larry twisted the word retirement.

They talked for several minutes, and ordered another round of drinks.

Twenty minutes later, the waiter brought their dinners. He asked if they wanted another round of drinks. Larry said yes. Larry excused himself for another trip to the bathroom. He joked about a small bladder.

The food looked and smelled great.

"This steak tastes better than sex." Brian joked.

"Especially at our age."

Being with a friend contributed to the high mood both felt. Their drinks also helped. Even while they ate, they recounted more stories from their past.

TWELVE

Wednesday morning, April 6
Santa Monica, California

"Good morning, Erica." Brian greeted her, his voice upbeat as he passed her desk to his office. "I need more coffee. My one addiction."

"Good morning, Brian. I'll get you some." Erica rose from her desk. "How are you this morning?"

"No, no. I'll get it. But thanks anyway. That was purely a statement on my part. I remember where the coffee room is. Would you like some?" Brian offered. "To answer your question, I feel good. Will feel even better, after more coffee."

"I'm fine. Thanks, but I just got mine. Oh, David is in his office if you need him. I'll bet your brain is a little saturated with all those meetings and paper work yesterday." Erica sipped her coffee and resumed checking her e-mails.

"That is true." Brian would not admit that he had a slight headache, maybe a little hung-over from last night's scotches. Age did allow some believability of small white lies. "You guys must get in early. I thought I'd be the early one."

"I come in early to beat the traffic. I live in the Valley, near Greg. Sometimes, he and I would car pool. Not always, because he works longer hours than I do…, did." She corrected herself. "He and David both come in early. They're just ambitious. I mean that in a nice way."

Brian laid his briefcase on his desk, turned on the computer to boot itself, and hung his jacket behind the door. Then he went for coffee.

"Good morning Brian, Did you have a good night last night?" David had heard him and Erica talking. "Looks like you're headed for the coffee room. I'll join you, if that's ok, I need another cup."

"Of course, please join me. To answer your question, I had a very good evening. Larry and I had a nice time catching up. Yourself?" Brian smiled back. He did not tell any specifics about his dinner with Larry. It would probably be better to keep outside friendships low-key for a while. "How are you?" Brian added. "I mean about Greg's death."

"I have my moments. But working definitely helps." David answered. "Do you need anything from me before we meet with the IT group?" David asked as they walked to the coffee room.

"I definitely need you there with me. I need to organize my thoughts. I worked last night, but I've slept since then." Brian grinned. He savored the aroma of the coffee as he poured it into their mugs. "I guess I'm taking the last cup from the pot. Is it the rule here that the guy who takes the last cup, has to refill the pot?"

"Yeah, that's the rule." David grinned, "But let me do it this time. That way you'll know where the filters and the coffee packets are."

As David prepared a fresh pot, they engaged in small talk, the traffic, the weather, and of course the great views from the office windows. David joked that the views were the top incentive to earn a promotion in the company. He pushed the brew button.

"I'll just finish checking my emails and reports. Then, I'll meet you in your office just before eight." David said as they returned to their offices.

With only a minute to spare, Brian and David arrived to Rob Carter's corner office on the fourth floor. His office was as plush as the offices on the twelfth floor, and the same size as Larry's. After all, he was the Vice-President of Information Technology, or IT.

For three decades, IT had become a critical component of corporate businesses. Even low level IT employees were treated with high respect, usually spelled m-o-n-e-y.

Like the twelfth floor, Carter's office contained dark, mahogany furniture and paneling, and floor to ceiling windows on two sides, which provided a terrific view of the Pacific Ocean to the west and all the way north to Malibu and the mountains.

Rob's administrative assistant saw them approach. She rose from her desk, greeted them, and knocked on Carter's door announcing their arrival.

Two other men sat at the mahogany conference table, a smaller version of the one in the Executive Conference Room. The two men rose from their seats. Rob walked around his desk, occupying the other half of the room, and shook hands with Brian and David. He gestured for them to sit, and took a chair himself.

The two men were young, early thirties at most. *Why were IT people so often young?* Brian asked himself. A lot of older people liked technology and knew evolving technologies. Granted, an older person could not pull all-nighter work sessions as they once could, but they could still design and produce reliable, problem-free results. He felt he had a better grasp of technology than most people half his age. He enjoyed technology.

"This is Dean Horvath. He is our computer and network specialist. He knows how our computers are wired in the minutest detail." Rob introduced the man closest to Brian.

"Hello, sir."

"Hello, good to meet you." Brian shook his hand. There was that word, *sir*, the one word that tells the listener he is a senior citizen, or nearly one. Or, maybe Dean meant it only as a form of respect. Brian chose the latter. Anyway, he would show this person that he knew IT too.

Dean's shock of dark brown hair did not contain one gray hair. Dean probably did not own a comb, but preferred the tussled style. He was thin, stood a few inches less than six feet, and wore baggy jeans, t-shirt, and sandals. He probably shunned comfort foods and ate only a vegan diet. He looked more like he was skipping school and heading for the beach than working in a corporate environment. Dean, in sharp contrast to his looks, knew computers. He was in charge of the corporate computer network. He knew and controlled all accesses to company computers and data. Brian expected to hear him use words like *dude, cool, and you-know.*

"And this is Ralph Chung. He sets the security rules that ensure that our systems are secure. He and Dean work closely together."

Ralph shook hands with Brian, patted David on the shoulder, and said hello. Ralph was head of Information Security, second only to Dean in his ability to access company data within and outside application systems. He was Dean's age, but differed in appearance and behavior. He dressed business casual, wearing brown slacks and a blue oxford button-down shirt, and sported a near buzz cut hairstyle. He too had absolutely no gray hair.

The five men sat around the conference table. Brian and David faced the window with the great view of the coastline. Brian would really have to focus on this meeting to avoid the visual distraction. Fortunately, this early in the morning meant little or no glare from the western sun. With little small talk, Rob introduced the topic of the meeting, that Brian's work was a form of an audit and that he was an outside consultant. Rob gave some background information on Brian and on Dean and Ralph.

Then came Brian's turn. Nodding toward David, Brian began, "Yesterday, David gave me a good overview of the accounting side of the systems from an internal accounting and department operations such as paying for goods, services, and supplies relative to major projects. Then we met with Chas Erickson and Art Dexter who expanded on their roles in the Construction Projects division." Brian did not give any indication of the embezzlement problem, but continued Rob's storyline of outside systems audit.

"Naturally, as with most company systems, IT plays a major role. Without IT, those systems would not work in today's world." Brian continued. "So we need information from you. Please tell me about how people get into those systems from a technology perspective. OK?"

"Ralph, why don't you begin?" Rob nodded to him.

"We take security very seriously here at Leonard Corp. We use a lot of technology to control access. Every access to every piece of data is traceable to a specific individual. We use individual passwords, and in some cases biometrics, namely thumbprints. By policy, we never share passwords, except in rare situations. Like the warehouse people use a locator system to find parts, they have no ability to change any data. While I say that, we try to achieve transparency, so our people can easily use our systems."

"We simply cannot have security so restrictive that a person cannot do their work. So somewhere between total security and easy access is our goal." Ralph provided a handout with summaries and discussion points that described how computer and data security worked in their technology environment.

Ralph also provided examples of security operations reports. IT people used most of the security reports. Ralph volunteered to work with Brian to identify the specific reports he needed. Dean would change the security system to allow Brian the access he needed.

After a few minutes, Rob excused himself to attend another meeting. He assured Brian full cooperation. Dean and Ralph nodded agreement. The remaining four men continued discussing security. All took notes, used a whiteboard attached to the wall, and asked many questions of each other. Except for a bathroom break, they focused on the task at hand.

After more than three hours, the men had identified the key master files, critical reports, and data logs that Brian needed. He especially had interest in online activity that could bypass security controls.

During the discussion, each man gained respect for the others' IT abilities. Brian concluded they deserved their positions, even Dean with his surfer type looks and behavior. And yes, he used the words *dude* and *cool* a few times, but took his work seriously. Ralph relaxed his reserved, starched-shirt image, and joined freely into the discussion.

"Before we wrap up this meeting, could we spend a few minutes talking about the people who access these computer files and reports?" Brian chose his words carefully. "I'm not trying to pry into people's lives, but I'd like to get an understanding of the people, for example, if someone is a stickler for reviewing reports, if they know computers enough to solve their own problems. Or even if someone would share their password. I've worked in companies where the manager hated computers and would delegate any computer-related work to an admin or some other subordinate, even down to reading and responding to his emails."

"Well, naturally Dean and I know our computer environment. While we like to think we do a thorough job, I think if you talk with

Rob or others in the company, you'll find they think positively of us."
Ralph spoke haltingly, not accustomed to self-praise.

"Brian asks everyone this question. I don't think he's out to hang
anyone. It's ok to talk." David offered his reassurance.

"Thanks, David. I just want to know if a control, a report is not
used, maybe a different method can be devised." Brian continued.

"I think most of the senior people we deal with in Accounting and
in Construction Projects are fairly knowledgeable about computers,
including Chas, Art, Larry, and of course David here. " Dean became
bolder as he felt more comfortable.

"And Greg." Ralph added. "I'm really sorry to hear about his
accident."

"He was a good man to work with." Dean added.

"When some of my Help Desk people work with them, they tell
me that those guys understand computers better than most." Dean
continued, "And they never call with easy, simple problems – they
usually solve those on their own."

"When I review access logs, I regularly see Chas and Larry access
their management reports, which shows they're probably thorough in
their jobs. I don't know anyone who would share their passwords."
Ralph added.

"Art and I are good buds. He's stayed late with us several times. I
think he just wants some of our pizza" Dean grinned. "We often order
pizza when we work late. It's on the company's dime. I know he
knows quite a bit about computers." Dean grinned.

The men continued to talk about the *people* aspect for a few
minutes, and then decided to close the meeting.

"This meeting has been helpful. Thank you, both of you. This
information will really help." Brian spoke sincerely. "As I review these
reports, I'll probably have more questions."

"We'll help you any way we can." Ralph assured.

"That we will." Dean echoed.

The men stacked and bundled their reports and notes. They again
shook hands and thanked each other and left with newly developed
respect.

"I don't know about you, but I'm kind of hungry. Would you like
to break for lunch now?" Brian asked David as they waited for an
elevator.

"Sounds good to me. I'm almost always hungry." David agreed. "But if you don't mind, I need to handle some personal business, so I'll bring my lunch back to my desk. So, if I could have twenty or thirty minutes to take care of that business? Then..."

"Not a problem. Take your time. In fact, in the past I frequently ate my lunch at my desk. Why don't we meet at, say one-thirty? That'll give me some time to absorb what I've learned. Maybe I can organize some of my thoughts." Brian walked toward his office, unlocked the door, and laid his briefcase on his desk.

David left for his cubicle.

When Brian returned to his office with his club sandwich, he spent a few minutes enjoying the view. He watched the planes queuing to land at LAX. He counted at least six planes in line to land. He also watched the always-busy traffic on the Santa Monica and San Diego freeways, two of the major freeway systems in LA. He could watch for an hour, but allowed himself only a few minutes. He had work to do.

As he finished his lunch, he organized his notes and reports into discrete piles on his desk and side chairs. He faced his computer, rested his hands on the keyboard, and transferred his thoughts onto the screen. Before David returned, he wanted to expand his action plan. And by mid-afternoon, he wanted a reliable, thorough plan he could present to Larry. He needed to work fast.

Brian fortunately knew his job. He knew IT and accounting. He had a strong ability to focus on key business functions. He felt confident he could identify the problems and the weaknesses in the system where the embezzlement could happen. The difficult part would be to identify the guilty party.

He would need to know the personalities of all the people involved, their financial, personal, and even their social situations. He would need to know their motivations. His experience had taught him that motivated people found creative, or simply available, ways to steal from a company. First he would answer the *how* question.

THIRTEEN

Wednesday Night, April 6
Studio City, California

Through the door, he heard the doorbell play a few bars from the William Tell overture. His mother Nancy had bought the chime several years before her death, three years ago. His father Eldon, now suffering from cancer, remained in the house and had changed little since her death.

Many thought, a few said, but never in her presence, that she was a trophy wife. She bore him two sons. A stay-at-home mom, she loved her role as wife and mother. The son, now visiting, had grown up here. He had felt close to his mother who had protected him, nurtured him. She called him her good son.

In the early years of their marriage, when their sons were young, the sounds of guests and dinner parties filled the house. The boys' friends often visited. Their sounds of play bounced off the walls. The smell of cookies or snacks wafted from the kitchen after school.

Unfortunately, like too many fathers, Eldon favored his older son because of his success in school sports. He showed his favoritism in subtle and obvious ways. For his older son, he always had a smile to outright bragging about him to friends. For his younger son, he complimented him, but the words sounded hollow, insincere.

He pushed the doorbell button again. The overture played again. The craftsman house was eighty years old, a big two-story structure with dark wood floors, doors, and wainscoting. Colorful, but tasteful oriental rugs lay in most rooms. Only the kitchen had been modernized with state-of-the-art appliances and lighting. The house no longer seemed as clean or as warm as when his mother was alive. Fresh flowers and vibrant green plants no longer decorated the house. Without her, he felt little attachment to this place.

But tragedy struck the family. The boys were fourteen and sixteen. A sleepy driver of a big rig slammed into the bus carrying the high school football team home from an out of town game. The older brother and two teammates were killed.

Both parents sank into depression which lasted for several years. The family became increasingly isolated. As Eldon advanced in age, his health deteriorated. He contracted prostate cancer, and later developed emphysema and heart disease. Nancy, so much younger, became his caretaker.

She took the lead role in the family, parenting her remaining son, managing the household, and handling the family investments. She developed her own financial skills, and grew the family fortunes.

Fortunately, their money allowed them the medical attention Eldon needed. Although they hired nurses, he expected his wife to attend to him, to be available. He considered it her duty. Somehow, she managed. After a few years, life seemed better. Her husband's health stabilized, did not improve, but stabilized. They lived comfortably in the quiet house.

The Good Son went to a nearby university and eventually earned an MBA. He found work in the LA area. He visited his parents often, mainly his mother.

Four years ago, his mother developed breast cancer. Within a few months the cancer metastasized spreading throughout her body, the liver, and the lungs. She died within the year. Before she died, she extracted from her son a promise to care for his father after her death. His mother had placed all of their assets into an irrevocable trust, with his father's signature, leaving all of their assets to her Good Son. The son fulfilled that promise, but deeply resented the responsibility.

During the passage of time and under the weight of his filial duties, he ceased thinking of himself as a good son and began thinking of himself as an alpha male.

In spite of the resentment he felt, he wanted his father's approval. He wanted to prove that he could succeed in his own right, earn his own fortune, from his own efforts. Why, couldn't his father understand and praise him as he had his older son.

As his father's health deteriorated, he wanted to put his father into an assisted care facility. But his father refused. So the son hired expensive round-the-clock nursing care for him. He would not sacrifice his life and time as his mother had. The old man's money covered the costs. Besides, now with inoperable cancer, the man would probably die soon.

He rang the doorbell again. In mid-chime, a middle-aged black woman in nurse's scrubs answered the door. He never called ahead. He could observe the results of the nursing care better if unannounced. Besides, where else could they be.

"Hello, sir. Please come in. How are you?" The nurse recognized him and opened the door wider. "I was in the back helping your father. It's been a while since you've visited. Unless, of course, you've been here when I've not been here."

"Hello Jenny. I'm good, thanks. But you're right; it has been a while since I've seen you. Although I was here a couple weeks ago. Faye was here then."

"Your father's watching TV in the den." She called the room by its original purpose, the family room den.

He could hear the sound from the TV, an episode of Law and Order, emanating from the back room.

"Thank you." He walked in front of her to the den, passing the formal dining room, around the back of the stairs.

She followed him, but stopped at the small alcove just outside the den. It served as a nurse's station, with a comfortable chair, a desk with nursing supplies, and monitoring equipment. A small TV, phone, and a couple magazines sat on the desk as well.

He entered the den where his father lay in an adjustable hospital bed. The den was a family room when his mother was alive. The dark plank wood floors showed wear but no longer had their high polish that his mother kept. In those years, before his older brother's death, family and guests visited, played board games, did homework, or watched TV.

But since her death, his father's health deteriorated further; the upstairs master bedroom was too inaccessible for his weakened condition. They removed some furniture from the den to place the adjustable bed in the center of the room where the big couch sat.

He appeared to have aged more each time his son visited. He had lost so much weight. His pale skin, sunken cheeks, and beard stubble gave him a sickly, near death appearance.

"Hello, Dad." The son greeted him with little emotion in his voice.

"Why, hello son. It's been awhile." His father cleared phlegm from his throat, the words slow and almost inaudible. "What's it been? Two, three months? I don't understand why you can't visit more often. You know I don't have a long time left for this world."

"Dad, it hasn't been that long. I was here a couple Saturdays ago." He said defensively. He determined to not allow his father to set him on a guilt trip.

Feeling chastened by his father, his resolve failed. He felt twelve again. All of his education and success gave him little strength, little standing with his father.

"Besides, I've been very busy at work. Working lots of hours. I want you to know that I expect another promotion in the next few months." He looked his father in the eye, but still felt twelve years old.

"Well, family is more important than work. You'll realize that, as you get older. You should visit more often." He ignored his son's pride.

Was his father so unaware of his past treatment of him? Had he forgotten that he showed little appreciation for his family? Except for his oldest son, the one who died more than twenty years ago. How could he sound so sincere now, so interested in family? Was he so unaware of the cruel words he had used, how he had treated his wife and youngest son?

"Yes, Dad. I know family is important. Have you been taking your medicines like you're supposed to?" He redirected the conversation.

He knew the nurses delivered the medicines and shots on schedule. Faye worked days. Jenny worked nights. A couple other nurses worked part time, on weekends, or on-call when Jenny or Faye was unable to work.

The nurses took good care of him. They were paid enough. His sheets were clean. He wore clean pajamas, and except for the beard stubble, appeared clean. He hated electric shavers and would rarely allow his nurses to shave him.

"Yeah, Jenny, here, and Faye too see to that. I don't have to remember anything. They serve some good meals too. But I usually don't feel up to eating them." Today, he appeared lucid, alert.

His father occasionally went into fugue states and correcting him never worked. Then, he would switch to the present, forgetting anything that was said during his fugue state. Sometimes, in those states, they would argue, which of course was useless. He learned, as others had, to play along in the old man's drama, which required switching their parts as necessary.

He and his father talked more. Their conversation ebbed and flowed. The Law and Order episode played too loud on the TV that hung on the wall. His father's attention frequently shifted between their conversation and the TV. During a lull in the conversation, the son wandered to the nearby wall of pictures to the right of the doorway, away from the TV.

The pictures chronicled their lives, at least when his mother was alive. Now, most pictures were of the older son, the dead son, in athletic poses from school sports. Only a couple pictures of the younger son remained, included in group photos. His father had told him that the pictures of his mother depressed him, so he stored them in the attic. If the boy wanted any, he was welcome to them.

"Dad, you have so many pictures of Jeff here. Why…" He left his question unfinished. Sometimes, he wanted to confront his father about why he favored his older brother. Why couldn't he appreciate his younger son's successes. But he just did not feel in the mood for the argument that always followed. What would it accomplish, besides his father was still absorbed in the TV.

Instead he said, "I need to go to the john."

"You know where it is." This time his father answered, his attention still on the TV.

101

In the hallway, just outside the bathroom, built into the wall was a cabinet with a small counter that divided two sets of glass doors, one above, one below. In years past, an old rotary dial phone probably sat there. The shelf and cabinets now contained medicines and medical supplies. Medicines were kept in these cabinets instead of the bathroom where the humidity could affect them.

He read the labels on some of the bottles. His father took medicines for his heart, pain, nausea, cholesterol, and sleep. So many prescriptions, and non-prescriptions, in the form of pills, capsules, powders, liquids. No wonder his father needed full time nurses. How can anyone, especially the sick person, remember? Also, on the shelves were cotton balls, a box of syringes, and other medical supplies. As part of his need to control, he knew the purpose of most of the medicines.

"Did everything come out alright?" His father attempted humor with an old joke when his son returned.

"Yeah, yeah it did." Go with the flow. Don't make an issue. Why point out the obvious? Another argument would follow. Why did old people behave so predictably?

He thought again of confronting his father about why he could not accept him as he had his older brother.

"Dad, do you need anything?"

"A cure for cancer?" Another weak attempt at humor.

He resumed watching TV with his father. The Law & Order episode ended and another began.

"Well, Dad, I need to get back home. It's getting late, and I have another full day tomorrow." He stood thinking they could talk another time.

"You just got here. You never stay for long. But I guess I understand."

"If you need anything just have the nurse call me."

"Yeah, yeah, I know. You'll get whatever I need. Your mother always said you were the good son. I just wish the good son would stay longer."

"Maybe next time, Dad, maybe next time." He leaned over the bed rail and kissed his father's forehead. Puzzled how he could feel both resentment and care for this old dying man, his father.

On his way to the front entry, he stopped in the alcove for a brief chat with Nurse Jenny. She laid the magazine she was reading on her desk and stood. While they talked about his father's condition, the squeaky dialog of the new episode of Law & Order played through the small plastic intercom speaker on her desk.

FOURTEEN

Wednesday Evening, April 6
Long Beach, California

Brian had worked late. After meeting with Larry, he spent more hours developing a thorough action plan with more specifics. After eight, he drove home requiring only forty minutes, probably the only advantage to working so late. In his condo, he, for a brief moment, appreciated the jeweled city lights view. He flipped on the kitchen lights, hung his jacket on the back of a dining chair, on his way to his office/bedroom. He thumbed through his mail, mostly unwanted junk mail, misleading mortgage offers, grocery ads, and other waste of paper. Why couldn't the Post Office give people the option to not receive such mail? He tossed the junk mail into a wastebasket.

The only piece of true mail was a bill from the nursing home where his mother lived. His answering machine flashed two messages. First, he opened the nursing home bill. In bold print the statement read past due. It listed the Social Security payments for the last couple months and then the current and past charges. He owed nearly seven thousand dollars, a major hurt to his budget. Unfortunately, he had few choices.

He could move his mother in with him. But he barely had enough room for himself, much less two people. Even so, he would have to hire assisted care services while he worked, once he finds work. He wished he had saved more for retirement, for a rainy day, and these were rainy days. He laid the invoice on the desk, and borrowed a thought from the movie, Gone with the Wind. He decided he would worry about it tomorrow.

Brian sucked in a lungful of air to reduce his tension, and pressed the listen button on the answering machine. He hoped the messages were good news, at least positive news.

The first message was from his son, Jimbo. Brian always called him Jimbo from the beginning. The name James just seemed too formal for the six and a half pounds of flailing limbs, and crying life form.

Jimbo wanted to meet for dinner. Maybe they could meet this weekend. They had not seen each other for a few weeks. He added that he had received a new job offer, and wanted his dad's input. He needed to decide soon.

Brian felt his chest bursting with pride for his son. Jimbo had graduated with an MBA a couple years ago. Brian helped with his finances during his education journey, but Jimbo had qualified for a couple scholarships, and had earned money with part-time jobs. Brian expected his son to achieve greater success than he had, and hoped he would do a better job preparing for retirement.

Brian resolved that he would never be a financial burden on his son. He paid his long-term care insurance premiums, kept his debts low, and had saved some for retirement. All seemed on-track until he lost his job six months ago. The unexpected loss ate into his savings.

He did not resent caring for his mother. She had certainly sacrificed to help him in his life. But he did feel the financial pressure.

Some news pundits referred to the baby boomer generation as the 'sandwich generation', caring for aging parents, and children. For many, including Brian, the term fit. But for several years, the term 'triple-decker' fit him more accurately, when including the limited savings. At least until Jimbo got his first full-time job.

Although retirement stared him in the face, he knew he would have to work several more years. But he felt competent that he could work, care for his mother, and save money. He was not alone. Studies showed that more boomers expected to work well into their so-called retirement years. What happened to the idea of reduced work, more leisure, and early retirement?

During the early high school years, Jimbo had become quiet, distant. Brian worried that he was losing his son, the most important person in his life. He worried that Jimbo could not, or would not accept what took him years to accept of himself, his homosexuality. He hoped that it was the natural inclination of high school kids to distance themselves from their parents, regardless of orientation.

But then, the stress, the distance disappeared. Jimbo called his dad frequently. He asked for advice about college and careers. Now, Brian just enjoyed having his son in his life. They liked spending time together, movies, burgers, and an occasional Dodger baseball game.

Brian would return his son's call shortly, thinking they would have to meet before the weekend, or afterwards. Brian planned to leave Saturday morning for Larry's anniversary party in Palm Springs.

The second message, from Ian Keller, one of Brian's few long time friends, that their poker game was Friday night. He, Ian, and three other friends played poker the second Friday of every month. Until a year ago, they met every Friday. But their lives had become more complex. One had married, another's wife had a problem with the frequency of game night, and another moved to Corona, about thirty miles northeast of Long Beach. So they grudgingly changed to a monthly schedule. Ian lived centrally to the others and acted as the un-official president-secretary-host.

Ian had called everyone to remind each person to attend, and to bring something, usually beer, chips, and something else to eat. Everyone brought more than needed. No one went hungry. Brian would not join them this time. He expected to work late Friday on his new consulting job. The group would understand.

Brian called both his son and Ian. Jimbo agreed Tuesday night would be better. Ian understood and congratulated Brian on his first consulting job.

Brian went to the kitchen to finish his after-work ritual. He retrieved a caffeine-free Diet Coke from the refrigerator, and picked up his jacket from the chair back on his way to the bedroom. He switched on a table lamp. He removed his wallet, keys, and change from his pockets and laid them on the dresser.

He stripped down to his underwear, and hung his slacks and jacket in the closet. He lived alone, so he spent most evenings in his briefs if the weather was reasonable. This evening would be no different. Even with the glass exterior walls, he theorized that anyone looking in the windows from twenty-six stories below would need powerful binoculars. Besides, anyone using binoculars probably had serious peeping tom issues. They could not see anything obscene even if the bulge in his briefs stretched the limits of the fabric.

Brian turned off the bedroom light, carried his soda to the glass slider, opened it, and stepped onto the balcony. He figured no one could see him on the dark balcony. After all, he technically was wearing clothes. Scanning the city lights relaxed him. He never tired of looking at them.

The cool evening air, the city sounds from the street below, and lights immediately engulfed his senses. He heard the sounds of car engines, horns, indiscernible voices, even the hum of an airplane in the sky. A metro bus' hydraulic brakes hissed to a stop for a passenger in front of the Long Beach Café below. Lights, thousands, no millions of them in every color twinkled below him and beyond. They filled his view into the far distance up the sides of the surrounding mountains. He enjoyed these lights, these sounds.

He thrust his thoughts of financial stress to a backroom in his mind, so he could enjoy the scene before him. Somehow his life, his lifestyle, was worth the effort to continue working. His worry and long work hours had taken its toll on his body, and on his attitude. But he would persevere a while longer.

He felt tired, and a little hungry. At his age now, he ate only light meals in the evening. Otherwise, he would not sleep well. He needed his best energy for the Leonard Construction project.

Feeling chilled, he scanned the lights of the LA basin one more time to savor the view, returned inside, and closed the slider. The city noises virtually ceased. The sliding glass doors provided an amazing insulation from the sounds of the outside world.

He would work a couple hours before watching some TV and going to bed. He wanted to produce results to enjoy success in his new consulting role.

FIFTEEN

Thursday morning, April 7
San Fernando Valley, California

Wes arrived to work a few minutes after Phyllis, as usual. They worked well together as partners, never competed. Wes relied on his instinctive Gut Technique and Phyllis counter-balanced with logic and procedure. They worked in a modified bullpen office configuration. Beige fabric half walls separated the three pairs of detectives. Enclosed small conference and interrogation rooms lined one nearby wall.

For Wes and Phyllis, mornings began with small talk, coffee, reading emails, coordinating online calendars, and updates on their cases.

"Ready for the Greg Larkin case?" Wes was eager to recount the details of his trip to yesterday's autopsy.

"Yes. Definitely." Phyllis stopped writing notes and laid down her pen. She looked across their cluttered desks at Wes.

"It pays to have friends at the Coroner's office." Wes bragged a little. "Harold rescheduled the autopsies and moved Larkin's a couple days ahead. He also pulled strings for some of the toxicology results."

"Go on. Don't keep me waiting." Phyllis grinned at his crowing.

"Learned a few things. One. Mr. Larkin is, was a very healthy individual. Two. The alcohol content was very low, point-zero-two, a fourth of the legal limit. Of course, the blood loss and the body being dead for twelve hours could have affected the number somewhat. And three. No drugs. No coke, no pot, nothing. So, as expected our young father was not a user, or at least had not used any in the last week." Wes shifted his bragging into lower gear as he related the details.

"So. Do we eliminate an accident as the cause?" Phyllis asked, and using her notes, she added the new points onto the chalkboard.

"I think so. At least for reasons of alcohol and drugs, and the rain by itself seems unlikely. Unless, it's some kind of car problem. Let's send the forensics guys to the impound garage to check out the car more." Wes added a note on his to-do list, with a large asterisk beside it.

"So, no drugs, and limited alcohol. So, it's logical that he should have been alert that early in the evening. I would think there would have been indication that he would have really tried to stop." Phyllis agreed, and drew arrows with question marks next to the points that no longer supported an accident. They would move those points into another column.

"Right, there were no skid marks, no sprayed gravel, and no scarring of the remaining railing. More reasons to eliminate an accident as a cause. Suicide, then?" Wes rubbed his jaw.

"But he wore seat belts. You don't wear seat belts if you're trying to kill yourself." Phyllis added a column with the header, *Suicide*. "Besides, suicide by car accident would be a rough way to die. Statistically, men use guns."

"Unless, he wanted his family to cash in on an insurance policy. Insurance companies generally don't pay on a suicide." Wes shook his head, no. "Besides, he could have just as easily crippled himself, and they would have been worse off. No I don't think suicide is logical."

"Another thing. Forensics called yesterday. It's a little odd, but they could not find any fingerprints on the coke bottle. I don't think a user would wipe the bottle clean after using it." Phyllis thought aloud. "And if he wanted to kill himself, why would he leave the coke bottle in his car? Just throw it out the window. Unless he didn't know it was there. Maybe it wasn't his bottle?"

"Are we talking homicide here?" Wes asked what both thought.

They talked further, brainstorming, restating, countering, supporting. They could not eliminate an accident completely, or even suicide. Wes' gut analysis technique resurfaced several times. He just knew they had a homicide case.

As they talked, Wes' phone rang. He answered.

"Detective Makelin, this is Karen Coffman. Do you have a minute?"

"Certainly, Ms Coffman. How are you?" Wes grinned at Phyllis and mouthed *gotta-take-this.*

"Oh, Detective, please call me Karen. I hope we have a good friendship started."

"Well, thank you. Karen. And please call me, Wes."

"Will do. Thanks. Wes, I hope you'll excuse my bothering you."

"Not a bother at all." Wes responded. "I think we can use your information gathering skills."

"That's good. I've already researched Leonard Construction. They have a website with lots of information on the company, its founder, their executive staff, and a few other people who work there." Karen jumped into what she had learned. "And I immediately recognized my friend Larry Davis. He works in the accounting area."

"That's interesting, because, our decedent works in accounting. What is your friend's last name, again?" Wes cautioned himself about releasing information. He wanted to talk more with Phyllis. They needed to update their boss.

"Davis, Larry Davis. In fact, I'm planning a trip to Palm Springs this week-end to his anniversary party."

Maybe Ms. Coffman would not be as much an outsider as he had thought, especially if this case is a homicide. Although he trusted his instincts about her, he decided to delay giving her more details until he thought further.

"Again, we have to be careful what we discuss." Wes re-emphasized that he had to limit what he told someone outside his office. "So, please understand if I seem to hold some information back."

"I understand. And I won't take offense." Karen tried to reassure him. "And I'll be open with you, regardless. If I see a point or line that's awkward to cross, with you, or with Larry, I'll back away from the situation. I don't want either of us to feel uncomfortable in this relationship."

"I appreciate that. I figure if we're both upfront, this can be a productive, cooperative even enjoyable effort."

"I'm glad." The smile in her voice returned. "If you like, I'll give you what I've learned so far, names, places, websites, and the like."

"Sure. Sounds good, thanks." Wes pulled a pen and pad from his desk drawer.

"Daniel Post founded Leonard Construction which is worth about ten billion dollars. My friend Larry started work there, I believe, about twelve years ago." Karen talked from her notes.

"Let me give you the Leonard website. It contains most of the information that I've collected." Karen gave Wes the URL, and added, "The site has an organization chart with more history and bios of the key people. It even has a page on the accounting department, with a brief bio on Larry."

Wes scribbled the URL for the website on his notepad.

"I found very little on Greg Larkin, just that he graduated from Cal Poly in San Luis Obispo ten years ago." Karen decided that she did not need to read her notes to Wes. "In fact, why don't I just send you my notes? I'll attach them to an email to you."

"Sure. You have my email address, don't you?"

"Yes, I do. It's on your business card that you gave me at the crash site."

"Ms., err, Karen, I'll call you tomorrow. We'll talk a little longer then." Wes needed time to analyze his information and decide what he could tell her. But he would give her a couple details. "We notified the Larkin family Tuesday afternoon. They're a young family with two small toddlers. It helped that his parents were already there. Naturally, he hadn't come home that night. As you'd expect, the family was frantic with worry. It was sad, seeing their grief."

"That must have been depressing."

"Yes. It's the one part of my job that I don't like."

"Talking with a victim's family has to be sad. Usually when I use real life as a starting point, I use the newspaper, or a magazine article. But in a case like this, it seems so much more personal, more real. It's hard not to feel emotional. As I learn more about the family, I may just need to step back." Karen reflected on her feelings.

Emotion also crept into Wes's voice. "Well, I need to take off here."

"Sure, I won't keep you. And Wes, thanks for talking with me."

"You're very welcome, Karen. Thanks for your help. I'm going to enjoy our conversations." Wes set the receiver in its cradle.

"I take it, that was that writer you met at the crash site."

"Yes. She was. She asked that I call her by her first name, Karen." Wes smiled, his buoyancy returning, feeling connected to someone special.

"Don't you think it's a little risky talking about a case with an outsider? You're usually the one who is such a stickler for keeping the details behind a block wall. Besides we have a Public Relations department to handle that." Phyllis cautioned him.

"Yes, yes, I know. But the PR guys work best with the media and curiosity seekers." Wes allowed nothing to dampen his excitement about personally knowing Karen. "But this is different, we can think of her as a confidential informant or an unpaid consultant. That could be a cool thing."

"Yeah. Yeah. You're just star-struck, a veritable groupie when it comes to writers."

"Just wait. Hear me out." Wes persisted. "I'm thinking she could be a confidential informant. It's a win-win situation. She wouldn't do the real investigation of course. Just some of the research, like on the Internet. Did I say she's handy with the Internet?"

"Keep talking."

"She has already found background information on the company and on some of the key players. She gave me some information already. That could relieve us for the more important work, like catch the criminals. How about that?" Wes wore his most convincing facial expression. "Besides, with our workload, we could use some help."

"Part of me says we should still require her to contact the Public Relations department" Then grinning, Phyllis said, "But, of course, they probably won't give any more information than they give the media. Even if they give any at all. But, I suppose, if we're careful--"

Wes grinned back at her. He had won her to his thinking.

"And we have to keep our boss in the loop." Phyllis continued.

"Of course. Of course." Wes grinned.

"Look at the time. It's almost eleven. I told you about my doctor's appointment at eleven-thirty. So I need to take off." Phyllis closed the case folders and slipped them into her desk drawer, reserved for her active files. She pulled her keys and handbag from a lower drawer, and slid her chair under her desk.

Wes' phone rang again. He answered.

"Hello Harold. You have news for me?" Wes held his hand over the mouthpiece. He mouthed to Phyllis, *the Coroner's office*.

"Wait, wait, let me write this down." Wes sat straight in his chair giving his full attention to the conversation. He scribbled on a notepad. "Just as I suspected."

After more of the cryptic one-sided conversation, Wes thanked Harold and hung up the phone. He looked directly at Phyllis.

"Larkin had a drug in his system after all. Rhohypnol, actually a Rohypnol-like drug, I can't pronounce the real name." Wes' face displayed some confusion. Would they have to rethink the suicide angle? "And after we thought he had a clean system."

"That's the date rape drug. Used on a guy? Must be something hidden about him." Phyllis laid her purse on her desk, and sat on the edge of Wes' desk. "But, didn't you say that the family seemed like a normal young suburban family?"

"That's right. Unless, Mr. Larkin wanted to do away with himself and didn't research his drugs enough. Maybe he knew the drug disappears over time. Only he didn't know that it didn't disappear in a dead body, which really doesn't metabolize much of anything." Wes speculated. "We need to start the investigation."

"That we do." Phyllis looked at her watch and hung her purse over her shoulder again. "But I have to keep this doctor's appointment, first. So, I have to get going, I'm already pushing it."

"I'll visit the family while you're at the doctor's. I can handle that myself. We can go to Leonard Construction together, maybe around three. Call me on my cell after you finish at the doctor's, so we can work out the logistics. I'll call the Larkin's and Leonard Construction to expect us." Wes dialed the Larkin home.

The memory of the first visit weighed on his mind. Maybe he should wait for Phyllis. Partners worked better in family grief situations. The possibility of suicide or even homicide would double the stress level for the family. If he waited for Phyllis, they would have to postpone the trip to Leonard Construction until tomorrow. No, he would go to the Larkin house alone.

The older Larkin answered the phone on the third ring. Wes could still hear the grief in his voice. Wes asked how the family was doing. He told Mr. Larkin, Senior, that he wanted to ask a few more questions and would prefer to ask them in person. Could he visit in half an hour? Mr. Larkin agreed.

In homicide cases, investigations followed similar paths in the beginning. The Sheriff's Department developed a Policies and Procedures manual for new employees to learn, and experienced staff to follow, hence the expression, *By The Book*, which Wes knew instinctively.

The Sheriff's Department Operations manual listed the basic procedures. Identify the COD, or Cause of Death. Collect and examine the evidence – clothing fibers, DNA, weapons, and a thousand other items. Interview families, friends, and colleagues. Sort that information and hopefully identify and arrest the culprit.

Although the investigations followed a straightforward process, blind alleys, false leads, and hundreds of other complexities slowed, or even halted an investigation. Unfortunately, nearly half of the crimes in LA County went unsolved. Documentation for those cases were stored in a cavernous basement below the station house. Smelling of decaying cardboard, dust, and stale air, the basement contained boxes, stacked to the ceiling, of cold case files, representing murderers and rapists uncaught, and families still grieving. The cases waited for an investigator's time, new evidence, or new technology for solutions.

Wes decided he'd call Larry Davis at Leonard Construction after he and Phyllis were ready to go to their offices. He packed his briefcase and hurried to his car. His questions collected into a mountain in his mind. He needed to write them down. Meanwhile, he would start with the Larkin family.

SIXTEEN

Thursday, late morning, April 7
Van Nuys, California

The emotional weight of last Tuesday's visit firmly imprinted the directions to the Larkin's home on Wes' mind. After parking, he entered through the chain link gate.

This time, maybe from subconscious avoidance for the task ahead, he noticed the cracks in the aged gray sidewalk that led to the forty-year old ranch house. It split the lawn into two nearly equal squares. On the left, a single large fruitless mulberry tree with its large vibrant green leaves, grew, probably planted when the house was built.

The front lawn indicated limited maintenance typical of busy young fathers. Retired men spent more time on their lawns. Recently planted pink vinca and bright red geranium flowers grew along the front of the house behind a row of brown scalloped concrete blocks. The landscape needed more plants and the grass could use some fertilizer. A few children's toys lay on the recently mowed lawn.

Wes closed the chain-link gate behind him. His sadness returned as he approached the front door. He rang the doorbell. The senior Larkin opened the door. He looked more tired, older than he did Tuesday.

"Hello, Detective Makelin. Come in." Mr. Larkin's voice, still filled with sadness, held the door open. The rest of the family stood expectantly in the middle of the living room.

"Mr. Larkin." Wes nodded respectfully. "I'm sorry to bother you again."

"I understand. Any news?" He sounded almost mechanical, but polite. He gestured to a nearby chair. "Would you like a seat?"

Wes sat in a nearby chair. The others sat on the couch, or stood as they gathered around Wes. The young mother sat nearest him. Another older couple had joined them. The senior Larkin introduced the two new people, Alicia's parents. The adults all looked so very tired, their eyes red from crying. Their grief weighed so heavy that their shoulders seemed stooped. Even the two toddlers appeared tired but restless. They were unlike other small children, usually full of energy, laughing, playing.

Wes struggled with what he would say first. He expected discussing the possibility of suicide or homicide would become unbearable for them. But he had to do his job. He had to ask the difficult questions. In most homicide cases, victims often knew their killers. Did this family know Greg's killer? As other investigators approached their work, he too would begin with the family, acquaintances, co-workers, and then others.

"As I said on the phone, I needed to meet with you again to discuss your husband's death." He did not use the word accident this time.

"We talked with the Coroner this morning." The senior Larkin spoke. "They said we couldn't have Greg's body until next week. The man on the other end of the line wouldn't say why. Just that we'd have to talk with you first."

"Please, tell us what's wrong. Something's just not right." The young Mrs. Larkin began to sob.

Her mother gave the little girl she held to her husband, and sat next to her daughter, hugging her.

"What the Coroner's office isn't at liberty to tell you anything until the final autopsy and toxicology results are in. I'm sorry, but I'll be direct. The initial lab results indicated the presence of a drug. Do you know if your husband used drugs?"

"No way." Greg's mother said, more in defense than surprise. The others agreed.

"Greg did not use drugs." Alicia said flatly. For a moment she stopped her sobbing.

"He never used drugs, not in high school, and I doubt he tried any in college." The senior Larkin crossed his arms, filled his chest with air, defending his son at the accusation. "Maybe, he drank a beer or a scotch once in a while, but that was pretty rare."

"I'm not accusing. I just have to ask. We need to find out how this drug got into his system." Wes tried to reassure them. He knew this was stressful. "The drug was something like Rohypnol." Wes did not tell them about the coke found in the car.

"What on earth is that?" Her mother asked.

"It's that date-rape drug." Her husband answered, bouncing his granddaughter gently in his arms.

"Date-rape? Why on earth…"

"It's a new drug that's like Rohypnol. Often it's used for medicinal purposes, for patients in pain. Did Mr. Larkin have any health problems that he'd need any pain medication? Any prescription medication?" Wes looked mostly to Alicia, the young mother.

"No. He didn't have any health problems. Maybe on occasion he'd take a couple ibuprophin for a headache" Her crying had subsided a little. "He kept pretty healthy. Worked out at the gym, sometimes."

"Can you tell me about his state of mind over the last few weeks? Did he seem depressed? Was anything bothering him?" Wes changed his line of questions.

They talked more about the young Larkin's mental state and his activities. He loved his family. His career was important to him, so he worked a lot of hours. But mostly his work was a means to provide a better life for his family. He spent most of his free time at home. He worked occasionally with woodcrafts in the garage. The tools and unfinished projects took most of the space in the garage, and required them to park their cars in the driveway or in the street. Greg Larkin seemed happy with his life.

Most of the young Larkin's family social life centered around visiting the grandparents, and attending events with his co-workers. Alicia explained that the company had social events three or four times a year. And the accounting department, being small, socialized more frequently, probably every month or so. A dinner with just the spouses, or backyard barbeques with the whole family.

117

Wes had already concluded that the death was not a simple rainy night accident. And the likelihood of suicide became less evident. Unless, there was something in his life outside the home and family, that would cause him to commit suicide. Usually, lonely, depressed people committed suicide, not happy, content young family men.

And murder. Why would someone murder a young family man? The man's lifestyle just did not fit a murder victim's profile. What in the young Larkin's life would result in his being murdered? Wes kept the conversation to generic fact gathering. The homicide suspicion would stay quiet until he gained more information

Wes asked if the junior Larkin had any enemies, someone who would want to hurt him. Again, the young Larkin did not appear to interact with people outside work and family. He had never talked of anyone who disliked him, and certainly of no one who would harm him.

After Wes had asked his questions, he thanked the family, and expressed his condolences again. He told them he would update them as he learned more. He asked if they still had his card. They did. He left.

Wes shut his car door and sat quietly for a minute. He needed a moment to adjust. In his years of law enforcement, he never grew accustomed to dealing with a family's grief. Solving this mystery, this puzzle, and finding the bad guy would lift his spirit. He had to solve this case.

Wes drew a long breath of air and started the car. He pulled his cell phone from his pocket and dialed Phyllis' number. Her doctor's appointment should be over. Maybe the trip to the Leonard Construction headquarters would reveal more information.

SEVENTEEN

Thursday afternoon, April 7
San Fernando Valley, California

"Detective Hadley, here." Phyllis answered on the second ring.

"Out of the doctor's?"

"Yeah. About two minutes ago. Walking to my car now."

"Want to grab some lunch before we head to Leonard Corp?" Wes started the car's engine. "I'm just leaving the Larkin place. Nothing unexpected. I'll fill you in when we meet."

"Sure. I am a little hungry. We'll probably be at Leonard Corp most of the afternoon anyway." Phyllis stood at her car's door, ready to unlock it.

"So, what do you feel like eating for lunch?"

"I'm open for suggestions."

"How about Cupid's hot dogs? It's in the neighborhood."

"A little spicy, aren't they.

"Yeah, I love 'em spicy. You know you can have them without the chili, don't you?"

119

"Ok, ok. I can handle them if you can." Phyllis started to open her car door. "I'm not far from there. Why don't I leave my car here and you pick me up."

"Will do. It's on the way. Shouldn't take more than fifteen minutes." Wes closed his cell phone.

Wes turned onto White Oak, then to Ventura Boulevard, to pick up Phyllis, then back a short distance to Cupid's, on Ventura, near Tampa Street.

Valley locals refer to Ventura Boulevard as The Boulevard. It runs for many miles along the length of the San Fernando Valley. People who live in the hilly South of the boulevard are generally considered upscale, rich. When meeting in a bar, a pursued woman sometimes asks 'do you live north or south of the boulevard? A south answer usually ends in a more successful evening for the pursuing man.

After Phyllis joined him, Wes drove to the nearby Cupid's.

A few Cupid's Hot Dog stands were located throughout the LA area. Barely more than food vendor kiosks, customers sat at three or four tables, or stood. Cupid's served the best known, the best tasting chilidogs in LA. They wrapped their dogs in double and triple sheets of paper to contain the grease. Very busy. Very successful. The after-bar-closing crowd also loved their chilidogs to counter the effects of the alcohol, or more probably as an excuse to eat comfort food.

Wes parked on the side street in a rare open space. He left his jacket in the car, but slipped his phone and a small notepad in his shirt pocket. They could see the car from Cupid's eating area.

The weather felt great. Wes closed his eyes and faced the sun to savor the warmth for just a moment. He wanted an hour of this weather, sitting in the sun. Winter' chilly temperature and overcast skies left last month and Spring's pleasant warmth and clean air had arrived. Summer's heat and smog would not return for another two months.

Each ordered two hot dogs, and a coke, one regular and one diet. Wes ordered extra chili. They waited while three people in hospital scrubs, students from a nearby nursing school, collected their food wrappers and containers and discarded them in the nearby trash bin. Not uncommon for the tables to be full during lunch and late night dining. Customers often stood while eating, setting their drinks wherever they could, sometimes on the ground. The busy boulevard traffic noise interfered with conversation, which was one of the costs for a good hot dog in LA.

Wes leaned forward so Phyllis could hear him. "Well, from talking with the family, it's hard to understand why he would kill himself. From their perspective, he seemed very happy. Loved doing things with his wife and kids. Liked his work. And as far as homicide, there are no known enemies. Both sets of parents were there. Unless he has another life that no one in the family knows about. Now, unless we learn something from the people at work..." Wes let the last word hang in the air for a moment. "They just don't seem like the kind of people that would hide something."

"Maybe we'll pick up some leads this afternoon from the people where he works. I'll call Debra in the White Collar Crimes unit, Technical Support. She can pull bank records, phone records, arrest records, the gamut." She bit into her hot dog and retrieved her cell phone. Laying her hot dog on an already greasy paper plate, she dialed Debra's number.

"While you call her, I'll call Larkin's supervisor, Larry Davis. Tell him we're on our way." Reading his notes, he pulled his cell phone from his shirt pocket and dialed the number. He shielded his other ear from the street noise with his free hand.

Wes normally did not give advance notice to anyone he planned to interview. He would arrive unannounced, not give the interviewee time to prepare answers, or worse leave. But working in Los Angeles, unexpected arrivals had drawbacks. Driving to Santa Monica could waste a lot of time if Mr. Davis was not there. He was after all an Executive VP and could be out of town. As Greg Larkin's supervisor, he very likely would plan an important role in this investigation. Expecting a secretary to answer, Wes paused a second when he heard Davis himself answer.

"Larry Davis here." Larry answered on the first ring.

"Oh, uh, Mr. Davis, I'm Detective Makelin from the LA County Sheriff's Department. I need to talk with you about the Greg Larkin case." A little surprised, Wes stuttered a little.

"Detective Makelin, hello. How may I help you?" Larry asked, his voice sounded cooperative. Then he added, "We're all in shock here, about Greg. That was such a terrible accident. We just can't believe what's happened."

"Actually, Detective Hadley, my partner, and I would like to talk with you in person. We would like to leave in a few minutes to your office, there in Santa Monica. We should arrive in about an hour. I know you're probably very busy, but we need to talk with you. Can you make yourself available?" Wes asked, trying to sound normal and authoritative in spite of the nearby traffic. He expected a yes answer, otherwise, he would use stronger language. He would see Larry Davis in an hour.

"Well, sure. Certainly. I'll do whatever I can to help." Larry volunteered. "Just tell the receptionist downstairs that I'm expecting you."

"Thanks, see you in about an hour." Wes closed his phone and returned it to his shirt pocket.

About the same time, Phyllis finished her conversation with Gina in Records. They finished their food, collected the food wrappings, and discarded them in the trash barrels. With smiles and small talk, other diners sat on the newly vacated benches, while an employee wiped the table, a cursory cleaning.

Wes and Phyllis returned to their car, fastened their seat belts, and joined the noontime traffic. In a courageous quick move, Wes, seizing a small break in traffic, crossed three lanes at one time. No simple feat this time of day. He wanted to catch the nearby Tampa onramp to the Ventura Freeway. They would follow it East to the San Diego Freeway. Both freeways were packed. The twenty-mile drive would easily consume the next hour, maybe more.

During the drive, they discussed the case, which included the facts, some gut-feelings, and possible causes. They often brainstormed the details of their cases, at least until they solved them. Sometimes, they simply let the details ferment in their minds.

Using his GPS system, Wes drove directly to the Leonard Corporation offices.

Wes pulled his car into the visitor's parking area. It was full. A few spaces ahead someone loaded a briefcase and suit jacket into the car's backseat. The driver smiled at Wes, but seemed to dawdle getting into his car. His smile seemed friendly, but could have been satisfaction from feeling in control. The unknown driver started the car's engine and slowly backed out of the space. This slow action frustrated Wes. Maybe, if he showed his badge, and yelled at the driver that he was on police business, the driver might exit the space faster.

They waited, parked, and entered Leonard Construction's huge lobby. Scanning the lobby, he and Phyllis appreciated its two story glass windows and expansive use of granite on the floors and walls. Granite may feel cold but it also says money, which has its own warmth.

A receptionist sat at a chest high desk to their right. A uniformed security guard leaned against the wall a few feet to her right. They approached the desk, identified themselves, and told her that Mr. Davis was expecting them.

"Yes, I know. We've been expecting you. I'll call Liz, his assistant. She'll be right down to escort you to his office. Here are your visitor's badges. And would you please sign our guest log?" Carla smiled and turned the logbook to face them.

"Thanks. Sure." Wes and Phyllis attached the visitor badges to their jackets and signed the guest log.

"You're welcome to have a seat. It'll be just a moment." Carla nodded to the chairs on her left as she dialed Liz's number.

In less than two minutes, Liz approached them, and introduced herself. She too was polite, but low key. As they walked to the bank of elevators, Liz commented that the entire department was saddened by Greg's death. Wes gave his condolences and explained that they needed to follow-up with a few questions. After they exited on the executive floor, a second security guard smiled at Liz and her guests as he buzzed them through the glass doors.

As they approached Larry's office, he saw them and rose from his desk. He shook hands with each of them as they introduced themselves. Larry gestured for the detectives to sit in the two visitor's chairs. Liz offered to bring coffee or sodas. Each declined.

"Mr. Davis, we appreciate your seeing us on such short notice. We know you're very busy." Wes said. Politeness never hurts.

"Not a problem. As I said on the phone, we're all shocked about Greg's death. It was such a tragic accident. Wasn't it?" Larry asked concerned about police involvement so quickly in an accidental death.

As if to answer the unspoken question, "In cases like this we want to act quickly, to resolve any issues that relate to the case. As you may or may not know, all deaths, not from natural causes, in Los Angeles County, must undergo an autopsy by the Coroner, and undergo a certain amount of investigation." Wes laid the premise for the meeting.

He continued, "The toxicology results aren't complete, but the initial results indicated a drug was in his system. While the drug did not cause the death directly, it most likely played a part. We want to determine very quickly whether the cause of his death was an accident, a suicide, or a homicide."

Larry sat, shocked, unable to speak.

EIGHTEEN

Thursday Afternoon, April 7
Santa Monica, California

"Oh my god." Larry gasped. His breathing halted for a moment. His heart skipped a beat. He felt as if someone had punched him in his solar plexus. "That's, that's so hard to believe. I had trouble believing he died in an accident, much less that he could have died from suicide, or worse, a homicide. Are you sure? Of course, you're sure, you're law enforcement."

"I'm sorry. I know it can be a shock to learn about the death of someone you know well." Wes sympathized. After a moment, he asked, "Please tell us a little about Mr. Larkin. His job here. His co-workers. Who he interacted with. Any problems with anyone?"

"And I can't believe suicide. Greg seemed very happy. Everyone liked him. Even those he didn't know well respected him." Larry continued reacting to the news. He dismissed suicide, but struggled with the idea of homicide. "Well... Greg was our Director of General Accounting. He's worked here for around ten years. He and David Frazer had responsibility for the company's accounting records. Greg worked the General Ledger and the Accounts Payable side, which of course paid all of the company's bills. And David, a Senior

Accountant, reported to Greg, but worked the Accounts Receivable side."

"I understand a little accounting, that it's complex, requires considerable expertise, and requires a lot of hours." Phyllis added.

"Yes, a lot of hours. Both Greg and David are CPA's and work fifty to sixty hours a week, most of them around month end. Trial Balance. P&L's. Balance Sheets. That sort of thing. "

"Could the hours, the stress have depressed him?" Wes asked.

"Greg certainly didn't seem depressed. Our work involves stress as well as hours, yes. But, he seemed to thrive on it. It's the nature of our business. Here at Leonard, we reward our people well. Both Greg and David have received good raises and promotions in the last few years. Greg said he was happy with his work, and liked the rewards. The raises were always a little better than he expected." Larry continued. "Besides, neither Greg nor David impresses me as particularly troubled with the stress."

"How about the stress on Greg's family life? His social life?"

"Both Greg and Alicia, his wife, would have preferred more time together, especially with their kids. But his success allowed her to be a stay-at-home mom. They liked that situation, and accepted the long hours." Greg interlaced his fingers, and leaned back in his chair, "They loved their two kids. And Greg's work success was the price they were willing to pay. They had goals of a successful future, the same goals that most young couples have, like buying a better home. And with Greg's skills and work ethic, they will reach those goals. Sooner than most people in my opinion." Larry added.

"As for his social life, I think most of it revolved around us here at work. We have a social event every three or four months for my division. Usually a picnic, or other family outing. More often a few of us, including Greg and David, would have dinner out with just the spouses or significant others. We'd have backyard barbeques with the kids." Larry looked to Wes, then to Phyllis, and back. "We spend so much time together at work, our association spills over into our private lives. We know each other's families very well."

"Sounds like a close knit work group. But in my experience, sometimes, there are stresses between the employees or their wives. Were there any conflicts, any confrontations within the group or with others in the company, or outside the company?" Wes pursued.

"Not really. Oh yeah sometimes during month-end close, people would become a little tense with pressure to deliver the numbers on time. But we usually delivered on time, and the tenseness would subside." Larry looked directly at Wes.

"Can you give us the names of the people in the other departments that Mr. Larkin worked with? We want to talk with them as well. His contacts, and the like." Phyllis looked over Larry's shoulder to sneak a quick look at the beautiful view of the LA basin. On the credenza, behind Larry, she saw a picture of him and an older gentleman. She would inquire about that later.

"Sure. Why don't I give you an organization chart and highlight the likely people involved?" Larry swiveled his chair and opened a file drawer in the polished cherry wood credenza behind him.

He pulled a five-page document from the files. It contained rectangle boxes, lines, names, titles, and phone numbers He laid it in front of Wes and Phyllis. They leaned forward as Larry pointed to the second row.

"We're a flat organization, mostly by function. As you can see, six of us report to our CEO and President, Daniel Post." He pointed to the top box with Daniel Post's name in it. "I have responsibility for the accounting functions." He turned the page to the accounting group with several more boxes with names inside. "At Greg's level, we deal mostly with the Construction Projects group, and of course Information Technology. We work with Marketing, Public Relations, and Legal groups only when circumstances require it."

Larry, as well as others in the organization, had used this document many times to explain the Leonard organization. He could read Wes' and Phyllis' reactions to the information, and gauged the level of detail he gave them. If they wanted, he could overload them with details.

"Sounds like you guys really stay busy. May I have this document?" Wes broke in. "We'd like to talk with some of these people. Anyone you can suggest to start with?"

"Sure. First, why don't I invite David to join us?" Larry pointed to David's and Greg's names on the chart and then reached for his phone. "He and Greg worked closely together."

"Sure."

"Okay." Larry dialed David and asked him to join them.

While they waited for David, Larry returned their attention to the organization chart. "In Construction Projects, Greg worked mostly with Art Dexter and his boss Chas Erickson. They both report to Donna Gerardi, Executive VP of Construction."

David knocked softly on the door and entered the room.

"David, this is Detective Makelin and Detective Hadley from the LA County Sheriff's Department. David Frazer. The detectives are investigating Greg's death..." Larry's voice trailed, not finishing his sentence. "Have a chair."

David shook hands with the detectives, and pulled a chair from the nearby conference table for himself.

"But it was an accident. Wasn't it? Did something..." Puzzled, David scrunched his brow.

"We're just following-up. We do this on all cases where death does not result from natural causes. We're waiting for additional autopsy and toxicology results which should be ready in a few more days." Wes did not reveal what he had told Mr. Davis.

"They were asking about Greg and the people he knew. I've already told them about our get-togethers. And since you probably know Greg and Alicia as well or better than I do, I thought you could help." Larry spoke in an uneven voice, still affected by the shocking news.

"Well, sure. I'll help if I can. I still can't believe he's gone." David's voice tone was young, helpful, but a little nervous.

"I know this is difficult for all of you. I understand that you worked closely together and were friends as well as colleagues. But anything you can tell us, or anybody you can point us to would really help." Phyllis looked directly at David.

"What kind of things. There's probably a lot I could say about Greg. He's... was... a good guy. Kinda like a big brother."

"The basics. Did he enjoy his work, his life? Who were his friends? Any problems with people?"

"Well, we are pretty close. I guess because we worked so many hours together. Greg and Alicia often invited me over for dinner or a barbeque. I'm not married. Like my parents, they made me feel welcome. I'm not much of a party person, as far as nightlife goes. And Alicia, well the kids and Greg were her life. She liked being a stay-at-home mom. But I don't think either had a lot of time for other people or activities. Although, she did belong to a Moms-and-Me group of other young mothers. They did daytime activities together with the kids and traded off babysitting. Greg worked so many hours. They seemed happy. " The loss of Greg crowded David's mind, but he tried to maintain focus and answer the detectives' questions. "Liz and Alicia were pretty close."

"Liz, your secretary?" Wes nodded toward the door.

"Actually, we refer to her as our Administrative Assistant." Larry corrected. "She does so much more than secretarial duties. This department couldn't survive without her."

"Sorry." Wes grimaced, he knew better.

"I'm sorry. I didn't mean anything by saying that. It's just that she's so important to us here." Larry apologized.

"I guess I'm just having trouble accepting his death." David continued, trying to explain. "As for people here at work… Because he liked technology, he spent time with the IT guys. They'd show him new features to some of our software, or how new software worked. You could talk with Dean Horvath in IT."

Wes wrote a note on his pad.

"As for work, Greg basically oversaw the company's books, and paid the company's expenses. Other than debt payments and utility payments, the Construction Projects Division generated most of the bills to pay. Well, then, of course, there is Payroll. Also a big budget item. But of course, Greg wouldn't have a lot of interaction with them, unless he had a problem with his check. Greg spent most of his time with the guys in Construction Projects, especially Art Dexter and Chas Erickson. Mostly they just talked about work. I didn't hear them talk about much else." David paused and looked to the detectives.

"Was there any stress between Greg and any of these men?" Wes asked.

"Never with the IT guys. Greg really liked learning what they knew. And I think they respected him for his interest. As for Art or Chas. Art's a surfer type, likes to party, but does his job, always eager to go to the beach. I think Greg would get frustrated with him sometimes, because Art could take too much time to review his numbers, and delay our closing at month-end. But I never saw anything that you could describe as a problem. And Chas, well he's super-thorough, always very business-like. He often would go over budget. But that really wasn't our issue. That would be between him and his boss." David looked to Larry for his approval.

"I'd have to agree with that assessment." Larry pointed to the organization chart where Chas and Art were listed. "Their phone numbers are there as well."

"We would like to talk with them." Wes looked at Phyllis. "Anything unusual happen on Monday, the date that Greg died?" Wes asked another question as he looked at Larry, and then David.

"No. Things had slowed a little. Month-end close had finished." Larry thought of the embezzlement and struggled with himself to keep it quiet. He relented and inhaled a deep breath. "I probably should add that last week Greg and David had identified a potentially serious problem in the accounting records – a possible embezzlement. We, the company, want to keep this quiet until we learn more, but…"

"An embezzlement that Mr. Larkin discovered...." Wes's *gut analysis technique* lifted its head. "Can you tell me more?"

"We don't know much yet. As I said, Greg and David had identified some irregularities. We've hired a computer forensics expert to help us research it, a Brian Latimer. Until last week, we thought no one could break into our accounting fortress, but apparently someone has. Brian's a bulldog when it comes to solving a computer systems problem. He won't let go until he solves it." Larry leaned forward with his elbows on his desk.

"Has he discovered anything, yet?" Wes asked.

"He only started Tuesday. He's talked with several people and has worked the databases some. He expects some serious results in the next week." Larry tapped his desk with his fingers. "As I said, the company wants to keep this quiet, but I can assure you that we will cooperate with you fully. I'll tell Daniel, our CEO about your investigation. I know he'll cooperate fully."

"We would appreciate that. In fact, we should meet with him as well." Wes wrote another entry on his notepad.

"To answer you question about Monday. You might want to talk with Art. Greg was giving him a ride home after work. Art's car was in an auto repair shop. Art might be able to tell you something." David answered the earlier question.

"We would like to start with Art and Chas if that's possible." Wes spoke politely and sat upright in his chair.

"Sure. I'll ask Liz to make an appointment with them. Ok?" Larry pushed the intercom button. "Do you want to meet with them at the same time? Also, I'll call Donna Gerardi, their boss, and tell her that you will need to speak with them."

"She's in Europe, right now" David reminded Larry.

"Oh that's right. But, I'll still keep her in the loop."

"Yes, we'd like to meet with both of them." Wes and Phyllis rose from their chairs.

David told the detectives that he would help where he could and returned to his office on the eleventh floor. Liz escorted the detectives to the small conference room to wait for Art and Chas.

NINETEEN

Thursday afternoon, April 7
Santa Monica, California

Liz escorted Wes and Phyllis to the small executive conference room. This smaller room allowed meetings for no more than four or five people. Although any of the executives' offices could easily accommodate ten or twelve people, they would choose to meet in this smaller room because it fostered an even playing field for those who attended. Of course, no one questioned power issues in the main conference room; the CEO controlled the use of that room.

This small room, a sixth the size of its brother, the executive conference room, was equally plush with expensive art hanging on the cherry wood walls. The outside wall of floor-to-ceiling glass allowed the same panoramic view of the LA basin.

"May I bring you coffee, or sodas?" Liz asked.

"Thanks, but no thanks." Wes responded. "But I would like to use the restroom, if I may."

"Certainly, I'll show you where they are. The break room is there also, in case you change your minds about coffee or sodas."

"I'll join you." Phyllis added taking advantage of the break.

Liz led them down the hall through the thick glass double doors to the other side of the executive floor.

"Right through here. "Liz opened a single glass door, but equally as thick and as tall, just past the security receptionist's area and pointed to the restrooms and break room. "As you can see the coffee room is there too, if you change your minds about the drinks. You'll find coffee, and sodas, juices, and bottled water in the refrigerator."

"Thanks." Wes carried his briefcase with him. Liz carried hers too.

Liz waited in the security foyer and chatted with the receptionist.

Wes did change his mind about the coffee and poured himself some in a beige ceramic mug with the Leonard Construction logo. Phyllis returned from the women's restroom and scanned the contents of the Sub-zero stainless steel refrigerator.

"Nice setup. A little better than the station house." Wes understated the obvious, noting the upscale features of the break room, with its dark wood cabinetry, indirect lighting, and granite countertops.

"Just a little." Phyllis contributed to the understatement. "Just look at these choices. Soda, tea, water, juices. Better than an AM/PM mini-mart." She selected a bottle of cranberry juice.

They returned to the security foyer and rejoined Liz. Wes held up his coffee mug and grinned. Liz returned the grin and escorted them to the meeting room again. As they laid their briefcases on the conference table, two young men approached and the older one knocked on the door. Liz and the detectives turned toward them.

"I understand you wanted to talk with us?" The older-by-a-few-years man asked.

Liz introduced the detectives to the newcomers, Charles Erickson and Arthur Dexter.

"If you need anything, I'll be at my desk." Liz smiled and closed the door for their privacy.

For a couple minutes, they engaged in small talk - the usual, the plush offices, the views, living in LA. They sat on the plush leather chairs around the conference table. Wes and Phyllis arranged legal pads with pens for easy access.

"We want to thank you both for meeting with us, especially on such short notice." Wes spoke with polite words, but any delay would have been unacceptable. "We need to ask a few questions to follow up on Greg Larkin's death. We're talking with all who may have worked with, or dealt with him. We understand that both of you worked with him."

"Yes, we did, just about every day. Especially around month-end." Chas nodded his head. "I didn't know that the police investigated accidents so thoroughly. Except of course at the accident scene."

"Actually, we're with the Sheriff's department." Wes corrected. "We investigate all deaths in LA County that happen outside the hospital, or from unnatural causes. Did either of you have any interaction with Mr. Larkin on the day of his death?"

"I don't think I worked with him any that day." Chas furrowed his brow and looked to Art.

Art shifted in his seat. "I did. We left work a little early for a change. About four, four-thirty, I think it was. He gave me a ride home. My car was in the repair shop. We stopped by The Deck for a couple drinks. The rain was pretty heavy. We hadn't *shot the bull* for a while, and Greg wanted to let some of the traffic die down. He lives in The Valley and normally takes Topanga home. So my place was on his way home."

"What kinds of things did you talk about?"

"Just work, the layoffs, the weather. Nothing important. Just to pass some time. We had a couple drinks, and ate some of their appetizers. You can almost make dinner out of their happy hour appetizers. Greg didn't eat much, said his wife would have dinner for him." Art spoke freely.

"Did Mr. Larkin seem worried about anything?" Wes asked as he jotted something on his note pad.

"Well…" Art looked at Chas as if for approval. "Initially, we were worried about layoffs. The big execs on the top floor held a meeting earlier that afternoon. Chas had told me some, but I was curious about what Greg's people had told him."

"Not a problem." Chas straightened his neck and shifted in his seat. "Let me add to that. Rumors had been flying around for a couple weeks about possible cuts in staffing. But our management wanted to assure us that wasn't going to happen."

"So they could stop the rumors." Phyllis concluded for Chas.

"Yes. But people in our two departments don't usually worry about layoffs, anyway. Our functions are just too critical to the company. I don't think that would have been a worry for Greg."

"Could Mr. Larkin have been worried about something else?" Phyllis asked. She and Wes already knew about the embezzlement, but wanted to hear what these two men knew.

"No. No I don't think so." Art answered. "At least not that night."

"We understand that sometimes, around the end of the month, stress between accounting and others could build up. As it relates to Mr. Larkin, what can you tell me about that?" Wes rubbed his jaw and leaned back in his chair.

"I wouldn't call it stress in the negative sense." Chas responded. "Sometimes, we didn't like the numbers and would require them to change something, or rerun the reports. Other times Greg would complain that we didn't get the numbers to them in time."

"Was it if particularly stressful between Mr. Larkin and anyone else, at that time."

"Wasn't his death an accident? Didn't his car go over the edge driving home in the rain?" Chas questioned the direction of the conversation. "These questions sound more like an investigation into something more than an accident."

"Let me ask the questions." Deciding that he over-reacted, Wes explained. "As I said earlier, we investigate all deaths that result from un-natural causes. We don't' know for certain that it was an accident. It's our job to investigate, Mr. Erickson."

"Sorry. I didn't mean anything by my question. I'm just curious." Chas twisted in his seat.

"Not a problem. I understand." Wes resumed his casual line of questioning. "Were there other people, who experienced difficulty with Mr. Larkin? Anyone who might want to hurt him? Inside or outside the company."

"I really don't know of anyone. Art worked with him more on a day-to-day basis." Chas looked to Art.

"I know Greg liked to maintain this clean-cut image, family man and all. But I think a part of him wanted to get away sometimes, to party." Art twisted uncomfortably in his seat. "I don't want to talk about anything negative, but…"

Hearing the verbal pause, Wes asked, "Could you expand on that a little?"

"I think he liked a little artificial stimulation, better times through chemistry. Know what I mean?"

"Not really. Why don't you tell me?" Wes prodded. He remembered the small amount of cocaine found in the car. But there was no coke in Larkin's system.

"Well, I think he liked to get high, used a little coke. Of course he didn't want anyone to know. He could get away with it. Him being married and all." Art stopped talking, acting as if he had said too much.

"I didn't know that. I can't believe Greg would do that." Chas swiveled in his chair and looked directly at Art. "Are you sure?"

"Yes, I'm sure. You'd be surprised how prevalent it is in the company." Art defended his statement.

"That's interesting." Phyllis wrote a note on her pad.

"Well, like I said, he didn't want anyone to know and had a good cover, family man that he was."

"About what time did he drop you off?" Phyllis leaned forward in her chair.

"We left The Deck a little after six, I think. It was still raining. He double parked, and I ran up the steps to my apartment."

Art never mentioned that he and Greg had discussed the accounting irregularity and the hiring of the computer forensics expert.

After a few more minutes of discussion, the detectives thanked the men and concluded the interview. Chas again reassured the detectives that his department would cooperate in any way they could. They exchanged business cards and shook hands. Chas and Art left.

Wes asked Liz to call the two IT guys that Larry had identified to meet with them. Liz knew that Larry had already given Rob Carter, Executive VP of IT, a heads-up about the detectives talking with his people. Liz wore her hands-free headphones, and pressed Ralph Chung's number. Ralph told her, he and Dean would be there in a couple minutes.

Moments later, Liz tapped on the partly closed door. The IT guys had arrived. Liz introduced them. Ralph, a smartly dressed Asian man wore pressed khaki slacks, polished shoes, and a starched button-down checked shirt. The other man, Dean, a Caucasian, with long, over-his-eyes hair wore un-pressed khakis, not wrinkled, but un-pressed, another surfer type.

Wes saw that both men possessed that indomitable energy and independent attitudes that often characterized young IT people. The world was theirs and they knew it. They eagerly shook hands with the detectives, took the chairs that Chas and Art had vacated.

"We appreciate your talking with us." Wes began. "To put you at ease, we have to follow up on all cases where the victim died of un-natural causes, in this case Mr. Larkin's. I understand that he liked working with you, that he liked all things computer. Whatever you can tell us will be helpful. Please tell us about your relationship with Mr. Larkin."

Although Wes tired of repeating his canned statement of why they investigate accidents at the beginning of every interview, he had long ago learned that when he used this statement, people relaxed, and answered questions more freely. He preferred questioning people individually, so he could compare stories for inconsistencies. But sometimes, especially in the beginning, the process went faster in small groups.

Wes and Phyllis asked the two IT guys the same open-ended questions they had asked Chas and Art. They received similar responses, but more positive. Both men liked and enjoyed working with Greg. They shared a common interest in computers and to some extent in accounting.

Only Art's reference to drugs was absent.

"We understand that Greg might have used recreational drugs. Do you know about that?" Wes alternately looked directly at each man to determine if body language would tell him anything.

"No." Ralph stated clearly.

"No way!" Dean sputtered. "Greg just wasn't that kind of guy. No way would he use drugs. He liked his job, the people here, and especially his family. I'm sorry but there's no way I believe that."

"I agree. There's no way he would use drugs. Where did you hear that?" Ralph asked in disbelief.

"I'm sorry, but I can't tell my source. But we needed to ask." Wes almost felt chastised, and asked. "It doesn't sound like Greg was the depressed type, either."

"No he wasn't. Like most of us, he wanted more money, more success. But he was getting that, here at Leonard." Dean brushed his long hair out of his eyes. He looked away. His eyes were moist. His respect for Greg showed.

"I'm curious. Another guy asked us similar questions a couple days ago." Ralph tilted his head and wondered if there was a connection.

"Oh." Wes curiosity spiked. "Who asked these questions?"

"Maybe I shouldn't be so curious. But a Brian Latimer is doing a special audit into the accounting systems. The company hired him a couple days ago."

Wes remembered that Larry Davis had talked about the computer forensics consultant they had hired to help investigate the possible embezzlement. Now his gut technique stirred. He now became convinced that Larkin's death was connected to the embezzlement. The company might want to think it's just coincidental. But in Wes' book, coincidences just do not happen.

After more discussion, Wes concluded that Greg was well liked and was probably pretty clean-cut. Only Art had said something negative. Wes would investigate Art further.

TWENTY

Thursday afternoon, April 7
Santa Monica, California

Liz saw the door to the small conference room open and heard the voices of Ralph and Dean offering their cooperation to the detectives. She tapped lightly on Larry's open door, and told him the detectives had finished. Larry stood at the door.

"Detective Makelin, Detective Hadley. May I speak with you for a moment?"

"Of course, please have a seat." Wes gestured to one of the empty chairs. He felt a little awkward behaving as if the room was his office.

"Well, I talked with Daniel Post, our CEO, about your investigation. I told him what you had said about the drug in Greg's system, and that I had mentioned the embezzlement to you. He too is now worried there might be a connection. We hope not, but just in case. Could you both join us in the executive conference room? We and a couple others would like to talk with you."

"Sure. Be glad to." Wes and Phyllis started collecting their papers and storing them in their briefcases.

"It'll take a couple minutes to gather everyone. I'll ask Liz to bring you to the conference room when everyone arrives." Larry left and asked Liz to call Daniel and the others to the meeting. They all were expecting her call.

In less than two minutes, Liz escorted the detectives to the executive conference room. The clicks of their heels on the travertine floors sounded loud as they passed through the security reception area.

In the conference room, the expensive artwork and furnishings in the room, and the outstanding views of Los Angeles captured their attention. The artwork looked like original pieces. They consciously avoided the views and focused their attention to the people sitting around the table.

"Detectives, I'd like you to meet our CEO Daniel Post, our company founder. Daniel, may I introduce you to Detective Makelin and Detective Hadley with the LA County Sheriff's Department." Larry gestured with his hand for the somewhat formal introduction.

"Good to meet you both." Daniel stood and shook hands with the detectives. He motioned to two chairs on his right. "Won't you have a seat, please?"

"Good to meet you sir." The detectives sat in the plush dark leather chairs.

Larry sat next to Brian, with their backs to the windows.

"Let me introduce you to the others here and then we'll get into the reasons we've asked you to join us. To your right is Stan Brothers from our Legal staff." Daniel introduced the others at the table, including Rob Carter, head of IT, Chas Erickson of Construction Projects, and Don Hovey, of HR. He finished with, "Next to Don is Brian Latimer, a computer forensics consultant we hired Tuesday to work with us."

Daniel added that Chas represented Donna Gerardi, head of the Construction Projects division. She is in Europe. Jesse Dietz, Public Relations, was out of the office today.

Daniel swiveled his chair to face Larry. "Larry, why don't you explain our situation?"

"Certainly, I'll just jump right into it to the details." Larry took a deep breath and looked directly at the detectives. "As I told you earlier, we believe we have an embezzlement in the company. Someone apparently is or was skimming large sums of money from the company. About two weeks ago, Greg uncovered the data that indicated the embezzlement. Now that we've learned his death might not have been an accident, we, Daniel, Stan and I, thought we should bring this situation to your attention."

"We want to cooperate fully with law enforcement, and we want to protect Leonard Construction's interest." Stan spoke and switched his eyes from the detectives, to Daniel, and back. "We in no way want to interfere with your investigation, but we must protect our image, and our stock value. An embezzlement situation could indicate that we don't protect the company's assets adequately. We hope we can achieve both."

"We understand. We want this investigation to go as smoothly as possible, and as quickly as possible. We're glad to hear about your cooperation. Investigations go smoother when all parties cooperate."

"Good. Rest assured you will have ours." Daniel smiled and leaned on the table. "So, can we talk about what you need from us?"

"We've talked with a few of your people. Mr. Davis, Mr. Erickson, and two IT people. They were all very cooperative." Wes nodded to Larry and Chas. He did not add that the questions were generic and not provocative. "We probably should talk with Mr. Latimer for starters. I understand we're asking some of the same questions. While your focus is on the embezzlement, ours is on Mr. Larkin's death. And since I don't believe in coincidences, I'm sure our work will overlap."

"I'm glad to participate, with Larry's, or rather Leonard Construction's approval." Brian sat forward in his chair.

"As I said earlier, we will cooperate. So yes, you're welcome to talk with Brian." Daniel ruled.

Larry shifted in his chair creating the squeak of fabric against leather. "I might add that Brian has an excellent background in computer systems and is certified in computer forensics. I've known him a long time and know the quality of his work. He started work here Tuesday, and is becoming familiar with our systems. I don't think he's had enough time to solve anything yet."

"I have completed a skeleton plan of action and some results." Brian cleared his throat and spoke as if one of the team. "I've identified key access areas and databases to research."

"I'd prefer that I be present. In fact, since Mr. Latimer works for us, I want to talk with him first." Stan, the legal eagle, interrupted. "We have proprietary interest in what he learns, specifically our costs, project bidding data, customers. If this information gets out, and our competitors learn it, it could hurt us."

"We have a real challenge here. We need to protect Leonard's proprietary interests and rights. But at the same time, we will cooperate with your investigation. I'm sure we can work this out." Daniel intermediated. "Detectives, do you have a problem with Stan joining in the process?"

"I'm sure we can work out the details." Wes agreed. He wanted to keep the relationship favorable. "As I said our focus is Mr. Larkin's death. If his death was an accident, or suicide, then our investigation closes."

"When I first heard of Greg's death, I felt a real loss. Like the passing of someone in my family." Larry looked at no one specifically, but expressed what weighed on his mind. "This morning, hearing that it wasn't a very tragic accident, worries me."

"I know, me too." Rob Carter added looking at Larry. "I really liked the young man."

"I just had the thought." As if a light came on, Larry sat up straight in his chair. "Detectives, if this was a homicide, does that mean that others of us might be in danger?"

"Its not been determined that it was a homicide, yet. As we said it could have been a suicide." Phyllis spoke, hesitated, then added, "The drug could have been self-administered."

"I can't believe that." Larry responded.

"Me neither." Another said.

"Greg just wasn't that kind of person. He loved his life too much. Besides, wouldn't he have chosen another way? One that it would look like an accident, a real accident. I mean, so his family could collect the insurance." Larry looked about the room.

"With suicide, his family wouldn't collect." Don Hovey, the Human Resources man added. "Our standard insurance for his level is a million dollars."

"That's a healthy amount of insurance." Wes looked at Don. "Who's the beneficiary?"

"His family. I've already started the paperwork." Don replied.

"Thanks."

Wes encouraged those at the table to talk about Greg. He stayed alert to comments that he would investigate individually later. They expressed some of his earlier thoughts. They gave their opinions and speculated about his death. They liked and respected him. None thought he was depressed, much less suicidal. No one knew anyone who disliked him. Only Art Dexter had given the negative comment earlier about drug use.

As the comments slowed, Wes returned the conversation to the embezzlement. As expected, companies often did not alert law enforcement, the public, and especially their stockholders about internal problems. They did not want the bad publicity. Many companies lost thousands, even millions of dollars, and the white-collar criminals often went unpunished, just fired, to avoid the publicity.

"How long before you think you'll have some information for us?" Phyllis asked Brian. She wrote notes on the comments, behaviors, and reactions of the people while Wes asked his questions.

"As I've said, I've talked with some of the key people in the affected divisions. David and I expect more specific information by tomorrow afternoon. First, we hope to answer the *how* question. Answering the *how much* will take a little longer. The hardest question, *who* will be more difficult. Although you're probably most interested in the *who*." Brian felt a little uncomfortable with the attention focused on him.

"Who is David?" Wes asked.

"The young man you met in my office earlier. David worked with Greg on the initial discovery of fraudulent data." Larry reminded Wes that David worked the Receivables side and Greg worked the General Ledger and Payables side of accounting.

"Right, right. I remember. Sorry."

"David knew of the discovery, but hadn't been involved in the details that Greg had found." Larry's leather chair squeaked again. He grinned. "Did I get the talking chair?"

A nervous laugh escaped from a few people. The atmosphere returned to serious.

"To answer your earlier question, Mr. Davis, about others in danger. It is a real concern." Wes' face turned very serious. "Homicide. If it was a homicide, and the embezzlement is related, some of you could be in danger. Meaning the person who committed the embezzlement, probably committed the homicide. I don't want to alarm all of you, but he, or she, could do it again."

Gasps of alarm spread about the room. They looked at each other, startled, not knowing what to say. The expressions of disbelief on their faces soon gave way to fear.

"Now, that is something to worry about." Daniel took another deep breath, worry showing on his face. He swiveled his chair to face the detectives directly. "What can we do?"

"Well, first, don't panic. This investigation is our first priority. The remaining toxicology results should be available in a few more days. When homicide is suspected, the lab increases the priority of the tests. Naturally, we will be here just about every day to solve this case.

"My advice. Be cautious. Use your security people to escort you to your cars. Know who's knocking on your doors at home. Just be more vigilant, more aware. Those steps can go a long way towards self-protection. If you suspect anything, or anything appears unusual or out of the ordinary, please call us." Wes pulled a few business cards from his briefcase and passed them around the table. He wanted to put their minds somewhat at ease. But they could be in danger, so caution, awareness would be important.

"Mr. Latimer, we will notify our White Collar Crimes unit. They have considerable expertise in computer forensics as well. Their problem is they are short staffed with a large caseload." Wes added. "They contract some of their computer forensics work to certified consultants, such as yourself."

"Sure. If I may add. I'm aware they use certified computer forensics experts. In fact I sent them my resume a couple months ago." Brian felt a twinge of excitement about working with law enforcement, another avenue for his fledging consulting business.

Brian felt somewhat conflicted and did not want to appear too eager in front of his current clients. He pushed his business cards across the table to Wes and Phyllis.

"As far as the embezzlement, that becomes more of an open question to the level of participation. Actually, you, Leonard Construction, will officially have to file charges that an embezzlement crime has been committed." Wes internally bet such a case existed, and hoped they would file the necessary charges.

"What do we need to do to file those charges?" Daniel asked, knowing that Stan Brothers would have an answer.

But Daniel was no longer as concerned with keeping the embezzlement quiet, as he was earlier. If his people were in danger, he wanted to protect them. He would deal with the stockholders and the public later. Besides, he owned most of the stock.

"We have to involve the District Attorney. I'll call them as soon as we leave this meeting. Mr. Brothers, I'm sure you'll be their primary contact." Wes looked from Daniel to Stan.

Daniel looked about the room for further questions or comments.

"I guess our open item from Tuesday, about notifying the authorities about the embezzlement, has essentially happened." Daniel added a little levity to relieve some of the tension in the air. "If no one has anything more to say, or if you detectives don't have anymore questions, I think we should adjourn this meeting." To Larry, he added, "Larry, continue working with Brian and these detectives, while keeping Stan and me in the loop."

"Will do."

"Well, have we done all we can in this meeting?" Daniel wanted to end the meeting. To Wes and Phyllis, he reaffirmed his cooperation. "We'll cooperate with you in anyway we can."

Several heads nodded agreement. People pushed themselves from the table, but did not leave. Wes and Phyllis rose from their seats, thanked the others for their cooperation, and shook hands with a few of them. Brian shook their hands and said he looked forward to working with them.

Larry caught Liz's eye through the thick glass walls and motioned for her to join them. He asked her to escort them to the small conference room near his office. Wes again thanked Larry for his cooperation and said they would contact him tomorrow. Phyllis concurred.

As Liz escorted them to the elevator bank to the downstairs lobby, Wes noticed that Larry Davis returned to the conference room instead of to his office, the other direction. Wes suspected the management team would continue to meet, probably to strategize their next steps.

Without the detectives, Daniel said, "I want to cooperate with the authorities, and we will. But I especially want our people to be safe and find this embezzler. Stan, Larry, come back with me to my office. I want to talk with Allen in Security. If we have to hire more security people, we will. I want our people to be safe.

"Larry, Brian. Find this embezzler. If you need more help, hire it. Work all the hours you need to. With that said, I still want us to keep the best interests of the company in mind. Larry, I'd like you to meet with Stan and me in the mornings and in the afternoons. We may not completely control the information that we pass to the authorities, but at least we'll know it."

Larry and Stan both nodded and agreed.

"We need to resolve this situation. I can't state that strongly enough. I know you're already busy, but we need to resolve this." Daniel was in his element as commander. "And Brian, we appreciate having you on board. We need the results that you gather as quickly as you can. Keep Larry informed. After meeting with Stan and me, Larry will update you on our positions. Please remember that you work for us and a lot of the information that you'll come across is proprietary. Remember the disclosure agreement you signed. Again, I want to be cooperative, but the company's interests are also important. Do we all understand? Are we on the same page?"

Daniel heard several yes's from the men.

"Now let's find this embezzler and killer." Daniel felt anger rise in him, that someone would dare steal his money and hurt his people. He gathered his thin brief, and left the room.

TWENTY ONE

Thursday evening, April 7
Santa Monica, California

After meeting with the Sheriff's detectives, Brian accompanied Larry to his office. They would continue to strategize the embezzlement investigation. With Greg's death now likely a murder, their work became far more urgent. Their timeframe jumped from a couple weeks of thorough and detailed professional research to reliable results in forty-eight hours. Meaning, find the embezzler, find the murderer. No miss-steps allowed. Every hour counted.

Brian's mind raced to deal with this turn in events. The project was no longer search for problems in computer systems, procedures, and reports. Solving the computer problem this time could mean solving a murder. He had little time for thorough planning. He must use his best analytical skills and work night and day if necessary.

As a young man, he often worked well past midnight, writing and testing computer programs. But now he was older, his body just could not endure the long hours as it once had. He still felt confident in his brainpower, just not in his physical endurance. He worked smarter now, more consistent. He ignored, or refused distractions.

"As I'm sure you're already thinking, this change in events will really require a lot of hard work, and fast." Larry said as he sat behind his desk.

"Yes, I do. I already have some ideas to change the action plan to expedite the work. May I assume that David can continue working the long hours with me?"

"Yes, of course. I'm sure you've already found that David is very cooperative in the long-hours department. Let's bring David up-to-speed." Larry reassured him as he reached for his phone, and pressed David's extension. "In fact, let's have Liz join us too. She can handle the logistics, appointments, and the like. She's very good at the administrative stuff. Besides, both of them need to know that Greg's death is possibly a homicide."

In less than a minute, David and Liz joined them around the small conference table. Larry informed David and Liz that Greg was likely murdered. David gasped, and sat silent for a moment. About to cry, Liz retrieved a box of tissues from Larry's credenza. Neither could believe what he told them. An accidental death was horrible enough. But murder. They lived normal lives, structured lives. Yes, car accidents happen, and people sometimes died. But those things never happen to them, not to one of their own. Those things happened on the bad side of town, where gangs lived, where poverty reduced people to an aggressive state, to an animal level.

After David and Liz regained some composure, the small group committed to resolve this crime, the words about Greg's death felt like a monstrous stranger invading their minds. Brian commended their resolve, but told them they could also be in danger. Greg's death likely resulted from his discovery of the embezzlement. They, David and Liz, should take precautions.

Brian listed the steps the detectives had recommended. Liz and David nodded they understood, but still determined to help where they could.

Tears forming around her eyes, Liz added that she did not care about the danger to herself. She felt enough difficulty adjusting to Greg's death. And poor Alicia, Liz wanted to help her and her two small children. David did not care about the personal danger either, but his chin quivered, still feeling the shock from the news.

"The detectives also believe that Greg's death is likely related to the embezzlement. I think we all do now. Management initially wanted to keep the embezzlement investigation quiet. But with Greg's death, keeping anything quiet will be impossible. But hopefully we can avoid alarming the employees." Larry cautioned.

"Larry, anyone who knows something about the embezzlement could be in danger. They need to know." Brian shifted in his chair. "Perhaps more security people are needed, to escort employees to their cars, and the like."

"Since we four know the most about the accounting systems and the missing money, we're at the top of the list." Liz almost whispered.

"I really don't think it's possible to keep this information about Greg's murder quiet. We're a small organization. Everyone knows everyone, work-wise. And many know each other outside the office. Several people know Greg and Alicia personally. You know they're calling Alicia. I'm sorry, but I think management would be expecting way too much to keep this news quiet." David had regained his composure.

"David, you're absolutely right." Larry scribbled a note on a nearby pad. "I'll bring this up with Dan. He needs to address this to the employees, and soon. Our grapevine is far too active to ignore this situation. We don't want rumors running rampant, and they will, if we aren't upfront with everyone about this."

Larry leaned back in his chair and tapped his fingers on his desk. He continued, "Maybe we're jumping to conclusions, here. The detectives did say that the autopsy and the toxicology results have not been completed. That Detective Makelin, he even alluded that Greg could have killed himself. But, there's no way that I can believe that."

David and Liz mumbled their disbelief.

Larry dialed the CEO's number. Judith, Daniel Post's admin assistant, answered. They spoke briefly.

"Judith said he'd call me right back." Larry bit his lower lip, thinking. "The more I think about this situation, the more I believe people need to know. If any of us are in danger, I think it's irresponsible of the company to not tell the employees."

"Otherwise, if something else happens, everyone will really be scarred and hate the company for not telling." Liz added.

"I agree, Liz. It's just how we tell them. And the information has to come from the top." Larry sat straighter in his chair.

"If the toxicology results came in soon, it could help with the company response." Brian added.

They sat in silence for a few minutes. The expressions on their faces alternated between worry, determination, and eagerness to resolve this embezzlement. Brian watched their composure return as their courage grew.

"David, Liz, give Brian all the assistance that he needs. David, assign you regular work to Michael and Brenda. I'll assume Greg's duties." Larry interlaced his fingers and leaned on the table. "We'll stay on top of this project. I'll keep Daniel in the loop. And we'll give the detectives all the help they want. If we need more resources, we'll get them. Brian, you're the project lead. I have confidence in you. I'm sure Daniel will return my call shortly. Brian, David, go solve this thing."

Liz returned to her desk outside Larry's office. Brian and David returned to the eleventh floor.

As a computer forensics expert, Brian had analyzed many computer accounting problems and solved the vast majority of them quickly. Almost as second nature, he could outline an action plan to focus on the cause of a problem. He liked having this ability. But this time, he realized his work could involve life and death.

"David, I really need your help." Brian sat at his small conference table. His mind raced, organizing his thoughts as quickly as he could.

Brian spoke his thoughts in a stream-of-consciousness, but logical. David sat in Brian's chair in front of the computer, and recorded those thoughts. Brian rattled topics to David about accounts, following the money, companies involved, banks, contractors, date/time stamps, and reports. The list seemed to never stop. But David followed, persevered, recording those thoughts with little difficulty.

Brian paced the small room as he listed the needed tasks for David. Brian wanted to find patterns in the data. Most white-collar crimes followed patterns. If a criminal escaped detection, they often repeated the same patterns, continuing the crime. Unless good internal controls were in place, most employees were often too busy to catch those people. People by nature trust their co-workers.

To the outsider, Brian and David's conversation would seem scattered, tangled, jumbled. But they would conquer this embezzlement.

After Brian and David finished detailing and recording their thoughts, they identified the sections they could attack now, without needing others. Brian called Dean in IT for access to three additional databases that he and David had identified. Dean gave him the access while on the phone. Another late night ahead.

Brian never drank caffeinated coffee in the evenings, but tonight he would. His body would hurt tomorrow, but the situation demanded results. And results only come from hard, long work.

TWENTY TWO

Thursday late afternoon, April 7
Santa Monica, California

Wes and Phyllis returned to their small temporary conference room.

"Well, it's after six. While I like these comfortable digs, I think we've done about all we can do here, for now. We need more information, a lot more. Maybe, we'll get some good detailed information from Mr. Latimer tomorrow. As far as phone records, court records, bank records, and any other outside information, we need to check with Debra. Why don't we start back?" Wes scanned the table and other surfaces in the room for any of their notes or documents.

"Sure. I am tired. I need a short break. After we're on the road, I'll check with Debra on the status of the reports she's running for us. I'll ask her to get our case on their calendar." Phyllis stretched her neck for some relief. "Do you think we can rely on this Brian Latimer?"

"Let's investigate him. He said he sent his resume to Debra. Knowing her, I bet she's already vetted him. We can also review his website. I bet his full resume is there. While you have Debra on the phone, ask her about him." Wes snapped the latches shut on his briefcase.

Phyllis dialed Debra on her cell phone.

152

"But… there is the negative side." Wes rolled the cylinder numbers on his briefcase to secure the lock. "He works for the company, so his first loyalty is probably to them. They could filter the information before passing it on to us. But, then again if Debra's group monitors his work closely, we should be ok. We can always bring them into the case if we need to."

"I know Debra's investigation involves extensive background checks on consultants, calling prior employers, checking education and certifications, that sort of thing. Her files should give us a good assessment of him." Phyllis changed her attention to the party on the other end of the line.

Wes and Phyllis approached Liz's desk and told her they were ready to leave. She escorted them downstairs to the lobby where they returned their visitor's badges. Wes loaded his briefcase into the car's backseat. After Liz clicked her seatbelt, she laid her briefcase on her lap. They would discuss the case on their trip to the station.

"How do you want to go home?" Wes pulled out of the Leonard Construction visitor parking. He drove toward the Santa Monica freeway.

"Let's take PCH, the scenic route. The 405 probably still resembles a parking lot with all the commuters headed to the valley." Phyllis settled into her seat. "If we go over Topanga, maybe we could stop by the accident scene, so I can see it. You've seen it, but I haven't. I know it's getting dark, but it'll help me visualize the site better."

"Fine with me." Wes snaked the car to the right-most lane to the West 10 Freeway onramp.

"It's not too much out of the way. Don't forget, you have to take me to my car, anyway."

"Oh, right. Will do."

They passed through the now lighted tunnel that led to the PCH. Behind them, eastward, lay the crowded cities of LA. Thirteen million people lived and worked in the LA basin, surrounded by mountain ranges, filled with dense housing, busy airports, and congested freeways.

On the other side of the tunnel, the six-lane freeway, narrow by LA standards, changes into a divided highway with fewer houses, quieter. The sun shines brighter. The driver, for a moment, forgets about LA's congestion. Southern California's best feature comes into view, namely the Pacific Ocean.

The Pacific Ocean gives Southern California its label of paradise. The blue-green water, the blue sky, and occasional clouds fill the visual world and uplift the spectator, even the depressed. The sunsets, with their reds and oranges mesmerize people. The constant waves play tag with the beach. The receding water erases footprints, and leaves small shells and sand crabs on the wet sand. Even in storms, when the angry waves pound the beach and reclaim some of the sand. People still use the word, beautiful.

Even hardened locals, who travel the PCH always sense the beauty of the coastline, and relax as they exit the tunnel and see the immensity of the ocean. People park their cars in the occasional turnout to walk down to the water's edge, just to enjoy the ocean, its affect on their senses. To not only see the ocean, but smell it, and feel its sea breezes.

Wes and Phyllis reacted no differently. After exiting the tunnel, silence settled over them as they absorbed the view. The sun had edged its way to the ocean's horizon. Dusk would soon settle over the coast.

"Someday, I want to park and really enjoy the view." Phyllis almost whispered, breaking the silence.

After a few miles, the six-lane divided highway narrowed into a four lane coastal highway. It followed the California coastline for several hundred miles to San Francisco. But here, especially from Santa Monica to Malibu, homes of the super-rich lined the beach and clung to the hillsides. Even though this scenic section of PCH had its own stop-and-go traffic, the view relaxed the senses.

Soon the change to Daylight Savings Time will give people more time to enjoy the beach and the sunsets after work. Many people paid the price of long commuter traffic to live in LA, but in return the ocean views provided a sense of regeneration.

"Nice, nice view, but back to business. What did you think about the meeting?" Wes settled into the left lane for the eight-mile drive to the Topanga exit.

"I thought it was informative. I liked that they talked freely. Even the legal guy Brothers didn't raise many objections. But he could still become restrictive when the results start coming in." Phyllis looked at Wes.

"Their being open about the embezzlement should help our investigation. I'm convinced there's a relationship between the embezzlement and Larkin's death. The toxicology results should confirm our suspicions. The person who committed the embezzlement murdered Larkin." Wes stated flatly.

"I tend to agree, telling us about the embezzlement shows cooperation. But let's keep an open mind." Phyllis sneaked a look beyond Wes at the ocean.

"Did you notice that they continued the meeting after we left? Cooperation or not, I'm sure the company comes first. The CEO and that legal eagle Brothers will see to that."

"Yes. But I think they're pretty scared right now. Especially since someone they know has been killed as a result. They know they could be in danger. I'm sure it's more than just money right now." Phyllis looked at the cars around her as they inched their way to Topanga.

Wes felt tired, but wanted to discuss the case. He knew Phyllis would write thorough notes while they traveled. He like the way she summarized their discussions. Living in a congested metropolitan city required spending a lot of time in the car. Like many other commuters, they worked while driving.

Wes looked into the rear-view mirror and to the cars around him while he drove, many of them expensive. Jaguars, Lexus', BMW's, and even a couple Rolls Royce's shared the road. A limousine, carrying a movie star, or a business mogul, with blackened windows, jockeyed for position with the other cars. And a few sad, unwashed older cars drove in the mix. Wes wondered if their drivers felt intimidated or were happy just sharing this part of *paradise*.

Housing crowded every inch of the private land between the ocean and the PCH. High fences and solid walls blocked the view into the houses. Beachside, the walls were likely all glass. Cars had little turn-around room between the housing and PCH. People paid millions of dollars to live in this crowded environment, and were happy for the privilege. Southern California was a great place to live for those with money.

"I think Art's our bad guy. I know. I know. I'm jumping to conclusions. But my gut tells me he's our guy." Wes scratched his beard stubble and talked about the case. "He was the last person to see Greg alive. And don't worry. I'll keep that opinion just between us as we investigate."

"Good. While I think your *gut technique* has some reliability, I don't want any early, unsupported conclusions to affect our investigation. It can, you know." Phyllis cautioned, stretched her legs and her eyes escaped from the ocean view to the landside of the highway. She trusted Wes' gut feelings, or GAT as they called it because he was often right. If Wes was a woman, they would call it intuition.

Many commercial buildings lined sections of the highway. Restaurants, bait, surf, and tourist shops occupied the storefronts. A few gas stations with their high prices posted provided fuel for the PCH travelers. No room to expand buildings on the highway, on either side, except maybe skyward. But the city would not allow that. It would block the view. Even Mother Nature could not get a permit to build anything.

"Lets talk about Greg. While suicide isn't completely out of the picture, it really looks like he's a homicide victim." Wes switched lanes.

"Greg's life seems pretty normal. But to keep an open mind, we need to ask ourselves if his life was really normal? After all, you did find cocaine in his car." Phyllis looked at Wes.

"But the coke we found wasn't in his system. It was another drug." Wes glanced quickly at Phyllis. "Besides, coke stays in the system for at least five days, so he hadn't used any in a week. A drug addict doesn't go without for a week, especially if he has some available."

Wes maneuvered the car to the rightmost lane. The Topanga exit lay ahead.

"I'm beginning to agree with you about Art. Let's put some pressure on him." Phyllis spoke her thoughts. "He is the only one in this scenario whose story doesn't fit. He mentioned Greg's drug use. Everyone else denied it. "

"Maybe he didn't know he had it. Greg, I mean." Wes' grinned at the obvious. "And why would he wipe the bottle clean of fingerprints, drop it on the floorboard, and forget about it? Was he trying to frame himself for something? With kid's toys on the backseat, I don't think he'd chance their finding it." Then Wes mocked, *"Hey Daddy, what's this?"*

"It had to be a plant." As if a light came on, Phyllis tilted her head, exploring Wes' comment. "That would be more evidence pointing to Art." Greg turned the car onto Topanga.

"Just too many questions, not enough answers. Which is good. That's why we have jobs." Phyllis teased to lighten the conversation.

"We have no way of proving who put the coke there, or even when it was put there."

"Yeah. Unfortunately." Wes slowed the car as he approached the section of Topanga where Topanga turned into a winding two-lane road over the mountains. "We do have a lot of questions to answer."

"What about the people in the meeting? Are any of them likely candidates?" Phyllis moved the conversation to other possibilities.

They discussed the people who attended the meeting as if completing a checklist. With each person, they considered the possibilities, the opportunities, and the motivations. Except for the legal guy and the CEO, only two divisions were represented in the meeting.

Of course the key players were in those two divisions, unless the embezzler was someone outside the organization. Their victim worked in one of the two divisions. They recognized that over one hundred people worked in the two divisions.

Phyllis held the company's organization chart handy as they discussed the individuals. They needed to narrow the number quickly. Maybe Brian Latimer would have some useful information tomorrow.

"I'm going to check my voicemail." Phyllis pulled her cell phone from her briefcase.

Phyllis checked her own voice mail. Debra had left a message. One of her technical assistants had run the reports.

"The reports are ready. This could be a late night." Phyllis unfastened her seatbelt, closed her briefcase and laid it on the backseat. She took a deep breath and refastened her seatbelt.

"Good. That way we can get a running start in the morning. I want to interrogate Art, and get an update from Brian. Maybe Debra can help us with some kind of embezzler profile." Wes did not like moving his current cases to hold status. But the first few days in any case were critical. They needed to act fast in the Larkin case.

TWENTY THREE

Thursday Night, April 7
Venice Beach, California

The man who now thought of himself as the alpha male parked on a side street in the Venice area near Pacific and South Venice. He removed his tie and laid it with his suit jacket in the back seat. He slipped on a navy blue windbreaker and baseball cap. He headed the short distance to Chuck's Bar, a small out-of-the-way neighborhood watering hole. The touristy Venice boardwalk ran along the beach a few blocks further south.

He walked briskly with his head down. He did not expect to encounter anyone he knew, but did not want to risk it. Less than those in small towns, people in LA seemed less aware of other people on sidewalks. There, they smiled at the passers-by, and said hello, uncommon in LA.

The sun had nearly set in the horizon. On this street, several restaurants and bars had outside patios, mostly empty on this cool April evening. Besides, today, midweek, most people focused on errands before returning home. On Fridays and weekends, crowds would gather on these patios, to drink a glass of wine, watch the sunset, and socialize.

He had agreed to meet with his associate at Chuck's Bar because no one would likely recognize them there. The bar was plain and ordinary, no outside patios. No plants in brass pots hung from the ceiling or sports memorabilia on the walls. Rarely did the trendy, upwardly mobile crowd drink here. They went elsewhere, to places on the beach, or places with better views. Patrons here consisted of retirees and other older people, with low to mid level incomes. They probably had moved into the neighborhood long before Venice became trendy, expensive.

In his illegal, but lucrative venture, the alpha male had amassed a large sum of money, which he stored in secret off shore accounts. As much or more, he liked beating the system. And manipulating other people provided a tasty icing.

He paid his partner a small share for his *services*. The partner referred to himself as an action-man, the kind of man who sees a problem and fixes it. The alpha allowed, even encouraged this self-deception, to a limit.

But recent events jammed the metaphorical wrench into their project's machinery. He would suspend the project for a while, just until the recent attention subsided. His action man would not like the news because he liked spending his money. He just needed persuasion.

The alpha male entered the dark bar. A jukebox sitting against the back wall played a song by Chicago. The air smelling of beer and old wood surrounded him. Decades old planks covered the walls. Vintage neon beer signs hung on the walls, collecting dust, probably new when they were hung there twenty years ago.

Patrons sat on the bar stools at the counter, at a few of the tables in the center, and in the high-back booths along the wall. Two waitresses served beer and mixed drinks. They served appetizers, the kind prepared in a microwave or from large plastic jars. The noise level was low in the half filled room. The man-of-action sat in a booth near the back, a half full mug of beer and a plate of buffalo wings sat in front of him. He was building a house of cards with square beer coasters. He had stacked them two levels. It fell. He began again.

Did the behavior indicate a lack of dexterity, or a simple mind? How did this action-man graduate from college?

"Have you been waiting long?" The alpha male asked, although he did not really care. His politeness was really part of his manipulation.

"Nah, this is my first beer." He grouped his remaining beer coasters into a single stack next to his beer.

A drink and appetizer menu board sat on the end of the table. Alongside, a small votive candle burned in its thick glass holder.

"Good selection. The bar, I mean. It's inconspicuous." The alpha male slumped forward as if he could reduce his visibility. He left his jacket and cap on for more anonymity.

"I know you wanted someplace quiet. But you know what they say about 'hiding in plain sight'. I've been here, maybe a couple times. I've never come with someone I know. The place is boring, mostly older types. And I doubt that you'd come here, or that anyone we know would. So I don't think we'll see anyone we know. Besides, with the noise, no body will overhear us talking." He leaned forward and took another Buffalo wing. Then, he resumed fingering the small stack of beer coasters.

"It seems a little quiet."

"Don't worry, it'll get louder."

A waitress interrupted. "What can I get you?"

The newcomer ordered a Samuel Adams, and gestured to his partner across the table. He thought he maybe should have ordered a mug instead of the trendy beer, less attention.

"Nah, I'm ok." He pointed to his half full mug, and shook his head.

"Coming right up." The waitress left.

The alpha male rhythmically tapped his fingers on the table before he spoke. He wanted his so-called partner's cooperation. But first, small talk was necessary. Small talk provided a certain level of comfort, agreeableness. Afterward, they would discuss this meeting's purpose.

They talked about the Venice area, the nearby Boardwalk, and living near the beach. Occasionally, they looked around to see if anyone was listening.

The waitress returned with the Samuel Adams. The two men paused talking for a few seconds. She asked if they wanted anything else. They said no. The alpha male paid her and wiped the top of the bottle with a napkin. The waitress pocketed the money and turned to help other customers. Management frowned on running a tab.

The alpha male decided enough small talk. They would not use anyone's name.

"Things didn't go as planned. It went a little farther than we had discussed. What happened?"

"He died in an accident. Plain and simple. That's what happens when you mix drugs and alcohol."

"But we'd agreed that you'd give only enough of the drug to cause an accident, to knock him out of commission for a few weeks."

"Yeah. Yeah. But I had to give him enough for it to work. What if he pulled off the side of the road and called someone? The pressure would really be on." He took a swig of beer.

"My point is, we have to stick to the plan."

"Sometimes, you have to improvise, given the circumstances."

"I don't care. You have to follow the plan as I tell you."

"Wait a minute. We're partners here. I know what I'm doing." The action-man sat straighter in his seat, bracing for an argument.

"But you've created some problems. It'll be harder to clean up the paper trails. Investigators will become involved. Deviating from the plan just creates problems." The alpha male tried reasoning. He had not come to his main point, the reason for this meeting.

"I think it works out better. He's eliminated from the picture. Otherwise he could still talk with the others and tell them what he knows. Besides, as I said, the police think it's an accident, another accident caused by Southern California rain." He sarcastically referred to the elements.

"Okay. What's done is done. We need to talk about what we do next."

"And, I added a little more to the picture."

"What? What do you mean?" The alpha caught his breath, now worried.

"I dropped a bottle of blow in between the seats."

"Blow? You mean coke?"

"Yeah. It'll damage his clean-cut image. More reason to explain why he had the accident." He restarted building his house of cards with the beer coasters.

"Damn it. They'll test for drugs. I sure hope he used some, and it was still in his system." He shook his head in disbelief. He just might explode himself. He had to quiet himself, or people would hear them.

"Listen. There's nothing to worry about. I did what would make the event work." He stopped building his house of coasters and glared across the table. "As I've said in the past, I'll take care of my side of this agreement. You take care of yours. Besides, you probably shouldn't know the details anyway. The less we know of each other's activities, the less we're likely to slip up."

"Ok, I'll let it drop for now. But sometime, in the future, we have to talk more about the details, and sticking to a plan."

"Okay. Okay."

"Now we need to talk about something else, about what we do next. As you know, there is this internal investigation." The alpha male leaned against the seatback. He wanted to avoid a confrontation, at least in public.

"What about it? Sounds like something in your area of expertise, something that you'd handle. Right?"

"Yeah. But to handle it, we need to put our little venture on hold for a while. Just a few months." His voice filled with command.

"By on-hold, do you mean no money coming in?" He stopped building his house of coasters.

"Yeah. Yeah, I do." He could see the anger again rise in his partner's eyes. "Now, calm down, hear me out." He had to stay in control. Maybe this partner would be a problem after all.

"I need a little time to clean the data transactions and files. Muddy the waters, so to speak. The investigation must not provide any clues, anything that would point to us. Maybe, however, it could point to someone else. Then, after some time, everything will blow over. Then, we can restart the venture. You've got to understand. We can't be careless." The alpha male could see his partner calming.

"Well, maybe."

"We have to put this project on hold. If this consultant is as good as they say he is, he could trace the money to us." He looked directly at his action man. "It has to be this way."

"I don't like it. But if it's not too long, I suppose I could handle it." He drank more of his beer. "We have a good thing going here. I'd like to keep it up."

"I know. I like it too. But if we're caught, everything comes to an end."

"Well if you say so. You're in charge."

Had he persuaded his action-man to cooperate? Good.

"But we do agree eliminating the one guy worked out after all. Right?" He almost sounded sincere. *Was he seriously asking for approval?*

"Maybe. What's done is done." He would not give his approval, yet.

They sat in silence for a while. The action-man ate more Buffalo wings and drank his beer. Alpha man tried a Buffalo wing, too spicy. He sipped his beer.

"Well, maybe eliminating someone else could help?" He grinned and started building his house of cards again.

"Yeah, right." The alpha said sarcastically. "And then the police would really see connections. You are kidding, right?"

"Yeah, I'm kidding." Still grinning, trying to add a second level to his coaster house. He liked pushing buttons.

"Besides, it won't hurt to lie low for a few months. I've been thinking that pointing the blame to someone else might be a good idea. Someone else takes the blame, and after some time, I, uh, we can restart the venture." He did not tell his action-man-partner that he might be the fall guy, especially with his recent uncooperative behavior.

"A few months? Maybe I could do something to help speed things along." His coaster house fell again. "Damn."

"I need some time to clean up some things. So let's just stay cool for a while."

"Okay. Okay. I'm with you. Just don't take too long." The partner liked the feeling of control.

More silence.

"I said I was kidding, but… What about the eliminating-someone-else idea? In addition to pointing to a fall guy."

Again worried, he set his Samuel Adams on the table, and looked away. *But could that be a possibility?* He took a deep breath. "Let me think about it."

"Oh." He cocked his head to one side. He had two stories in his coaster house. He started a third floor. The coaster house crashed. "Are you coming to my way of thinking?"

The new thought intrigued the alpha male. Eliminate someone else, and point the evidence to the fall guy. Maybe before the fall guy *fell*, he could eliminate the new target. He wouldn't get his hands dirty. It might work. *Where was his conscience? Ask someone who cares.*

He hated to admit that his partner might have a good idea, even a partially good one. He felt a little annoyed that this unthinking, knee-jerk reacting, and questionably educated man had the idea first. But he needed this muscle sitting across from him. He leaned back in his cushioned seat and rested his head.

He then leaned forward. "We have to plan carefully. Because if the plan doesn't work, then we'll be up shit creek. Let me think it through." He sipped his Samuel Adams beer. "We can talk later."

The waitress returned and asked if they wanted another round. Both declined, and said they would leave shortly. They decided to leave separately, as they had arrived. The partner finished the Buffalo wings, and gulped the remainder of his beer. He wiped his mouth on his shirtsleeve, and left. The alpha man waited a few minutes to finish his beer. The bar had become louder, now filled with patrons. He laid a five-dollar tip on the table and left.

Once outside, the street seemed quiet, at least compared with the noise inside. After he walked a block, his hearing returned, and the street noises became louder. He could hear the indistinct voices, the passing cars, brakes at the signal lights, and an occasional horn blast.

He thought about his partner, the so-called action man, and worried. He liked having a *servant*, someone to handle the dull work, the dirty work. In the beginning, he felt he could control him. His *servant* had limited needs, buying his friends drinks, using a few drugs, taking inexpensive trips, and just generally having extra money in his pocket. But lately, he had become less controllable, his ease with killing, and his short temper. This action man could become a problem.

TWENTY FOUR

Friday morning, April 8
Santa Monica, California

Brian arrived to the office early, six-thirty. He and David worked until almost midnight last night. He had slept just over four hours, and had skipped his morning coffee ritual. Instead he filled his travel mug with coffee and drank it while he drove. Opening the door to his office, he saw his reflection in the window, stepped closer, and could see the city lights extending into the distance, even up the mountainsides. Cars had already congested the freeways. A line of headlights snaked in one direction along the 405 freeway, tail lights in the other. A few planes, with only their lights visible, glided toward LAX.

He switched on the office's overhead lights. The recessed fluorescent lights flooded the room with unforgiving brightness. Even with coffee in his system, he felt sluggish. He needed more sleep. His body ached. He wanted more coffee.

Twenty years ago, he worked long hours with little consequence. But now lack of sleep assaulted his body and required two days to recuperate. Nevertheless, he had to focus on the work, to produce results. Ironically, this time it literally involved life-and-death.

For a fleeting moment, his constant worry about investing for retirement invaded his mind. He wished he had planned better. He shook his head with self-doubt. He was supposed to be a smart man. But a comfortable retirement seemed far away. But, he could not think about that now. He shook his head harder as if to free his mind of those thoughts. He needed to work. A good part of this project meant he was paid by the hour. But hours only count if he produces good results.

Brian switched on his computer to boot, and carried his mug to the break room for that coffee. When he returned, he clicked several commands on the keyboard. The screen displayed the reports from last night's work. He opened the reports, and wrote notes.

After a few minutes, the coffee took effect, his mind seemed clearer. Thoughts on retirement had moved into a backroom of his mind.

His analytical skills returned. He could hold four, five pieces of information in his mind at the same time - names, dates, amounts – while he toggled from one report to another, or from one database to another. Soon his work absorbed his full attention. He looked for patterns, and sequences in the data. He could split the screen's display so he could see two or three reports or data results at one time. Of course, at times, he had to squint to see the small displayed data.

He remembered the days when he would stack reports on a large table. Standing, he would move about the table to search for clues and patterns. With paper, he had to submit and resubmit computer jobs and wait a couple hours. Now with a few clicks of the mouse, and within a few minutes or even a few seconds, he saw results on the monitor. He loved the new technologies.

Later, a soft distant sound, a knock pulled his attention from his quiet cave of information.

"You didn't get much sleep either, I see." David stood there and grinned.

He appeared tired, but not as tired as Brian felt. David was young, and the young always recuperated quickly.

"I plan to go to Palm Springs tomorrow for part of the weekend. So, I thought I'd try to get an early start. My mind's a little fresher in the morning." Brian looked up from his computer and returned the smile. "Besides, I could say the same about you. You were here as late as I was."

"We must think alike." David crossed his arms in front of his chest. "I assume you're going to Larry's anniversary party."

"Yeah." Brian wondered if it was okay to mention his plans.

"I'd planned to go, but something came up with my parents. Sounds like it'll be a fun party. Lots of people."

"Yeah. I'm looking forward to it."

They commiserated briefly about their lack of sleep, tiredness, and workload. Before returning to their work, they agreed to meet before nine to update each other and then meet with Larry.

As David turned to leave, Larry joined them. He sat in a chair opposite Brian. With David listening, Brian gave a brief status of last night's work, and told Larry they'd have more organized information for him, around nine, if that was okay? It was.

"You're still coming to my anniversary party tomorrow, aren't you? I'd really like to have you there." Larry switched from business for a moment. "David, I wish you could come, too, but I understand."

"I am sorry." David pushed his hands into his pockets.

Brian felt relaxed with the topic change. "Wouldn't miss it. That's why I really want to accomplish as much as I can today. It'll probably be another long day. I figure if I leave by noon tomorrow, I'll make it in plenty of time."

"I know this project is serious, but I want this party. We've put a lot of planning into it. It's our anniversary after all, our thirtieth. I will just shut this embezzlement out of my mind for a couple days." Larry said with resolve in his voice. Then softly, he added, "Although Greg's death will stay on my mind."

Brian paused before saying, "That is special. Thirty years is a long time. For any relationship." Brian wanted add *gay or straight*, but still stood in the doorway of his closet.

"Well, guys, I plan to leave a little early this afternoon, if possible. I'd like to beat some of the traffic. Friday afternoons, traffic from LA to Palm Springs can take hours." Larry rose from his chair and smiled. "See you in a couple hours."

"Sounds good. David and I will be there."

David returned to his office. Brian swiveled his chair to face his computer screen.

Leaving Long Beach for the weekend had another benefit. He could escape the chaos of the Gran Prix festivities. The Gran Prix had lost some of its appeal for him over the last couple years. For the first few years he enjoyed the excitement, the people, even the roaring racecar engine noise. He did not mind the difficulty entering and leaving the building. As with many things, over time most experiences lose some of their appeal. A first ice cream cone can taste great, but the fourth one less so. The diminishing-returns rule.

Twenty minutes before nine, David joined Brian to strategize their meeting with Larry. Afterward, they walked the flight of stairs to his office, pausing at Liz's desk. She told them he was on the phone, but should finish any second. When he finished, Larry hung the receiver in its cradle and motioned for Brian and David to enter.

Liz asked if anyone wanted anything to drink. The three men declined. She closed the door for their privacy.

"We have some interesting results from last night, but as expected we still have more to research." Brian handed Larry a stapled copy of three summary sheets. "As you can see, we've divided the results into three areas."

"Page one identifies the accounts, companies, and dollar amounts involved, so far. As you can see, those amounts are already well over two million dollars."

"Page two identifies the security rules and times where it appears that someone has circumvented them. This is critical. During these times, someone turned off the security audit feature for a few minutes, then, turned it back on. We're searching databases to see if data was changed during those times. Early indication shows activity on those accounts, listed on page one."

"And page three identifies who has access to the data files. It will be difficult to tie these names, or any other names, to those data changes." Brian paused to allow his listeners to absorb the information.

"Let me explain further. The accounting system will automatically pay a bill that is no more than five percent of the expected amount. And, the system can split that payment, the right amount going to the vendor's bank, and the less than five-percent amount going to another account." Brian spoke in full caffeine mode.

"Turn back to page one. David has identified nine companies where split payments happened. More research into these payments and accounts will give us a clearer picture. We will need some legal help and law enforcement help to identify the owners of those bank accounts." Brian added.

"Now to page two again. I discovered that the security audit feature was disabled twenty-six times during the last six months." Brian explained. "The lapse times averaged five to ten minutes. So during those times, I checked the Vendor Master and Accounts Payable files. Both files were changed. And some of those changed transactions involved the same companies and bank accounts that David found in his work."

"I think I'm following you, but it's a little difficult. I'd forgotten how fast you can talk sometimes." Larry grinned, while trying to wrap his mind around this detailed information. "I certainly understand the system as it's normally used. But this technical security stuff confuses me a little."

"Sorry. I'll lighten up on the details, and stick to the more summary level. Because the perpetrator disabled security, we have to back into the details. I expect we'll have more results this afternoon.

"Now, page three. This list identifies the people who have approved access to the system. They naturally include people in your department - you, David, Greg, and two others. The list also includes six people in the Construction Projects Division, and five people in IT."

Brian continued. "The problem is – if someone is smart enough to disable the security system, they are probably smart enough to directly change master files. Meaning, you normally use an online form to enter data, the system uses that data and updates the files. Circumventing normal procedures, that person directly changes the files. No audit trail, no date-time stamp, and so on. Does that make sense?"

"That does make sense. I think I'm getting it." Larry smiled, pleased.

"And. To do those two activities requires a lot of IT smarts." Brian stood and paced in front of the window. "Is anyone on this list that smart, or do we have an outside hacker?"

"In my opinion, except for the IT guys, none of them." David said. "And those IT guys don't know a whole lot about accounting. So what do we do?"

"We have to allow that whoever did this could be someone outside the company." Larry shook his head in disbelief. "I can't believe one of these people, one of our people, did this."

"True. If none of these people have the level of IT skills I've just described. Then we'll have to look for an outside hacker." Brian shook his head, and pointed to page one. "We need to identify who owns those bank accounts."

"Well." Larry took a few breaths of air to release the tension that all the information had generated. "I'll update Daniel and Stan with what you've told me. Also, on a related note, I talked with Daniel last night about a statement to the employees regarding Greg's murder. That's so hard to say. About someone I know, someone I like. Anyway, Daniel agreed and said he, Stan, and Jesse would come up with something this morning."

Larry's phone rang. He could see in the display that the call came from an outside line. He answered. Talked briefly.

Larry returned the handset to its cradle. "That was Detective Makelin. He and his partner, Detective Hadley want to meet with us."

"Anything I can prepare for?" Brian asked, his voice curious.

"He wants to talk about the case of course. But he also wants to discuss your services, Brian. Looks like you'll have two employers, Leonard Construction and the Sheriff's Department. I personally don't have an issue, we're all interested in solving this problem."

Brian felt good that the authorities were interested in hiring him. He had actually sent them a resume two months ago.

"The detectives should be here in about an hour. Meanwhile, you guys continue with your analysis. We have a lot of questions to answer." Larry pressed Liz's intercom button. "Liz, Detective Makelin will be downstairs in about an hour. Would you escort them up here, please?"

Brian and David rose from their chairs and gathered their work-papers, reports and notes into their briefcases.

TWENTY FIVE

Friday afternoon, April 8
Santa Monica, California

"Brian, Larry, here. The detectives will arrive soon. A few more people want to participate in the meeting. Daniel. Stan. We want to talk some before they arrive. We're in the executive conference room. Could you join us please?"

"Sure, be right up." Brian left his papers sorted about the room. He packed his three page summary document into his briefcase, locked the office, and hurried upstairs.

The uniformed woman sitting behind the security desk buzzed him into the hallway to the conference room. Larry sat to Daniel's left, and Stan, the legal guy, sat on his right. The other two men were Dan Hovey, Human Resources, and Jesse Dietz, Public Relations.

"Thanks for coming, Brian. Have a seat." Daniel gestured to the empty chair, next to Larry, and skipped any small talk. "Two things. We need to discuss what information we pass on to the detectives? As you uncover information, we probably should filter any proprietary information. And what will be your relationship to the detectives? Stan has raised some concerns about both of these topics."

"We have to control what we tell the detectives." Stan almost interrupted, to press his concerns. "You're covering a lot of ground, very quickly. You're not only learning how we do business, you're seeing a lot of financial information, not only about Leonard's, but also about our suppliers' and customers. We go to great lengths to keep this information confidential. If our competitors learn any of this, it'd really affect our competitive advantage, our bottom line. We simply cannot have you freely handing over all you learn during this investigation. We don't know how they will protect the information."

Brian thought as Stan spoke. It was true, he had learned a lot about Leonard's business dealings, and their bottom line. "Stan, I hear you. Let me reassure you, all of you, that all the steps I take are the same steps any computer forensics analyst would follow, including those in the Sheriff's Department."

"That's my point. If they see everything you do, they'll see too much. That's risky." Stan insisted.

"But I can't get the results we need if I don't follow all the appropriate steps. That's the only way we're going to understand this embezzlement, and prove anything." Brian defended his work. "If we start to filter the information, they might not trust our work."

"I cannot sit by and allow all of this information to flow freely outside the company." Stan slapped the table.

"Another thing, if we filter, or even appear to filter this information, we could be seen as obstructing an investigation." Larry sided with Brian.

"We have rights, to protect our proprietary information. That is not obstructing an investigation." Stan glared at Larry.

"Maybe we could present the information, all of it, to them together?" Brian proposed.

"No, we still may need to keep some of it to ourselves." Stan was adamant.

"I'm sorry, but hiding information would be unethical. As a certified forensics analyst, I cannot simply hide information." Brian had looked forward to working with the Sheriff's Department. A real roadblock may have just blocked his path.

"That's what I'm afraid of; too much information can pass outside Leonard's control. This brings me to the second point. If you're working for us, how can you work for them too? Sounds a little like a conflict of interest to me." Stan had abandoned all sense of cooperation.

"It doesn't have to be a conflict of interest. If I do the same work, observe the same principles. And not hide any related information; my results can meet both needs, Leonard's and the Sheriff's." Brian tried logic, leaned on the table, and looked directly at Stan. "I'm confident that this can be done."

"I disagree." Stan said, still defiant.

"My loyalty is to Leonard. I can decline working with the Sheriff's Department, if you want. You hired me, so my loyalty is to Leonard." Brian sought a workable solution. "However, they will likely send in one of their own people…"

"Another forensics analyst consultant." Larry added rhetorically, making a point.

"Yes, another analyst who would repeat the same steps, delaying the work, and we'd have even less control over the information." Brian discouraged this second approach.

"Well, the embezzlement is our business. We solve our own problems."

"Wait a minute. This embezzlement has resulted in the death of one of our good people, and my friend, Greg Larkin. I won't sit here and agree to take the slow approach to solving this embezzlement." Larry almost shouted. "Back off, Stan."

"I…" Stan was speechless.

"Another thing, most employees see Brian as an auditor, reviewing the systems. He's already accepted by our people." Larry controlled their attention. "Law enforcement presence in all this would bring attention from the media and really alarm our employees. What about our image, then? Stan, I know Brian working for us and for law enforcement has its risks. But his way is the best course of action."

"Larry's right. And until law enforcement tells us what they want, we can only speculate." Daniel ended the confrontation. The detectives should be here in a few minutes. Let's take a break and cool down a little."

"I just want to emphasize that there are company proprietary concerns here." Stan started again.

"We know Stan." Daniel leaned forward. "I want to protect the company more than anyone. But, there could be serious personal risk to our people. That's unacceptable. It's no longer just a company financial or image issue."

The group recessed before the detectives arrived, talking in groups of two or three. When they reconvened, Liz knocked on the open door, and escorted the detectives into the room. As they entered, Larry shook hands with Detectives Makelin and Hadley. A new person, a woman, was with them.

"I don't believe we've met." Larry offered his hand. "I'm Larry Davis."

"This is Debra Becken. Ms Becken works in our forensics unit, the White Collar Crimes Division, or the WCC as we call it. She helps with the technical computer stuff."

"Yes, It's good to meet you." She took Larry's hand. Standing just over five feet, she was on the thin side. She wore her hair shoulder length, and berets kept the sides behind her ears. Thin metal, lightly tinted glasses shielded her hazel eyes. She wore a brown suit with a closed collar sage green blouse. Professional.

"Nice to meet you, Ms. Becken, or is it Detective Becken?"

"Ms. Becken, thank you."

"Actually, it's Dr. Becken. She's one of our very educated professional staff." Wes wanted the listeners to know her credentials.

"Let me introduce you to our CEO and company president, Daniel Post." Larry turned to face Daniel.

Daniel rose from his chair. The others gathered near, introduced themselves. Stan stayed in his chair, and nodded when Larry introduced him. Liz asked if the newcomers wanted anything from the break room. Yes, after more than an hour on the freeway, they requested a quick bathroom break.

Liz escorted them across the hall. Liz pointed the women to the women's restroom. When they returned, Liz invited them to select coffee, soda, or whatever they wanted from the break room. Wes selected a mug, filled it with coffee. Phyllis and Debra selected cranberry waters. They followed Liz back to the conference room.

"Won't you have a seat, please, and we can get started." Daniel half rose from his chair motioned to the chairs between him and Larry. Larry and Brian had shifted to chairs down the table.

"Sure, thanks." Wes said.

"We want to welcome you." Daniel began. "Now that we know each other. We have a couple things we want to talk about. We have some questions, and we hope you have answers for us. Otherwise, from our standpoint, we're open to topics. Would you like to start?"

"Sure, glad to." Wes looked about the room at the people around the table. "I don't want to alarm anyone, but I'll start with the latest info we have. We received the final results from toxicology. We're now definitely looking at Mr. Larkin's death as a homicide. It appears that someone definitely killed him."

A mini-tsunami of shock washed across the room. Several gasped, or uttered sounds of worry. Even Stan's wall of anger appeared to crumble. All eyes and strict attention turned to the detectives.

"We're convinced that it was a homicide." Wes restated himself. He would give more details, hoping to reduce the inevitable questions that would follow. "We talked with his family and with people here. The idea of Mr. Larkin committing suicide just doesn't fit."

"Is it likely that this person was someone who knew him. One of our people..." Thinking of the names on Brian's list, Larry's voice became weak as he realized the seriousness that engulfed him.

"Yes, the drug could have been given to him any time during the afternoon, in a drink, a soda, in drops on chewing gum." Wes opened his palms, gesturing the list could be long. "And, we believe his death is connected to the embezzlement. So the embezzlement is no longer just an internal problem. I know this information is alarming. But any of you could be at risk."

"I guess we can eliminate the idea that an outsider could have hacked into our systems." Larry voice still sounded weak.

"It reduces the likelihood of it." Brian added.

"This is alarming." Daniel, in his usual fix-the-problem approach, took-charge of the meeting. "We've got to catch this guy, meaning, we have to solve this embezzlement. But priority one, we have to protect our people. Let's talk about how."

"Yes, that's a good first priority. Until we catch this guy, you must be very careful - going to your cars, answering your doors, walking after dark. If he killed Mr. Larkin because of something he knew, you, especially those of you who know the same information, could be at risk." Wes inhaled a deep breath and paused for a moment. "You need to realize, that this is no longer just a case of skimming money from the company's coffers."

"We're beginning to think that." Don Hovey, the HR guy, spoke his thoughts aloud.

"Wait a minute, Wait a minute. You mean one of us could be the killer's next target?" Stan's fear overcame him, his earlier bravado gone.

"Can't you provide us protection?" Don asked, fear in his voice.

"We don't have the resources to provide you, all of you, round-the-clock protection. We expect to be here every day for a while. And certainly, if any of you see anything suspicious, call us. We'll alert the other law enforcement agencies – including the local police departments where you live."

"How can anyone protect us from someone spiking our drinks?" Someone ridiculed the futility of protection.

"We can beef up our own security, especially for those of you, close to the embezzlement." Daniel would use company resources to protect his people.

"You, know…" Larry spoke softly, paranoia creeping into his voice. "That also means that the perpetrator could very likely be one of our people."

"That's scary, very scary." Don echoed Larry's worry.

To ease the minds of those seated around the table, Wes answered their questions, sometimes answering the same question two and three times. They were visibly upset. He believed this information was like a double edge sword. On one side, it alarmed them to the point they would behave cautiously. On the other, they would cooperate and answer honestly.

"This is obviously no longer a lets-keep-the-embezzlement-quiet situation. We need to tell our people something. Jesse, Stan, we have that statement we worked on this morning. Let's modify it a little, and put it on our internal website. As I understand only our people can access it. Isn't that right Larry?" Daniel retook control of his meeting.

"Yes." Larry shook his head in the affirmative. "But once our people read it, then how do we control what they do with it?"

"It has a number to call with more questions, or if an employee just wants to talk about it. I'll have a couple people available just to deal with the questions." Jesse tapped the table with his fingers, thinking.

They talked more than an hour. The Leonard staff became calmer, more comfortable.

"Next, we need to discuss Brian's work as it relates to Leonard and to what he'll do for the Sheriff's department." Wes, Phyllis, and Debra were unaware of the earlier confrontation on this subject.

The group gave Stan a quick glance as they turned their attention to Wes.

"As you probably know, Brian's work is likely the same work that our WCC unit would do." Wes continued. "Debra, why don't you describe the working relationship with Brian that you would expect?"

"Thank you. We have a limited staff, and we're often overloaded with cases. So, we use certified forensic consultants, like Brian, on many cases. Brian had sent his resume to us a few months ago. We liked what we read." Facing Brian, Debra added, "We contacted your references, and they spoke very highly of you. We would have probably called you in a few weeks, anyway."

Debra continued. "The forensics steps that we perform are the usually the same steps that any competent, certified forensics expert would perform. Naturally, I, or one of my leads in the department, review the consultant's work, in detail. I want to emphasize that we require the same high standards of performance for the consultants that we expect of our people. Namely, the work must stand up in court." Debra spoke carefully and with authority that belied her petite and understated appearance .

"We look forward to working with Brian. Otherwise, we would have to use our own people or a consultant like Brian. Sometimes, we take only copies of files, reports, and databases. At other times, we take the physical computer equipment, or we may cordoned computer equipment and allow no access until we finish our work. Needless to say, any of these avenues would interrupt your work. And with our caseloads, that could take time." Debra paused allowing the impact of her words to sink into her listeners' minds. "Sharing Brian's work will reduce the interruption. My preliminary review of this project indicates this is probably the best route."

"Also. Although I expect to be satisfied with Brian's work, I will meet with him separately and talk with him frequently in the course of this case. Nothing secretive. Just technical stuff, computer commands, code review, query code, and the like. Maybe he and I could meet after this meeting?" Debra asked rhetorically.

"I'd like to say a couple of things about Brian." Larry wanted to praise Brian's abilities, just in case anyone doubted. "I've known Brian several years. We often hung out together in the early years. Over time, our careers led different paths, but we saw each other occasionally. I've read a few articles about him and have heard about his qualifications from other accounting colleagues. I've come to respect him professionally as well as appreciate his friendship. For this job, I thought of him, his competence, and his integrity. So I could present him to the others in this company, I asked Don, in HR, to get more background. Brian, I hope you don't take offense. I knew he was best for the job. I just wanted more ammo to convince the rest of you, so you wouldn't think I was just hiring a friend."

"Not a problem." Brian grinned at Larry.

"Don't worry, Larry. His being your friend is not a problem. The background information you gave me convinced me he was right for the job." Daniel nodded to Larry.

"Detective, let me assure you that we want this crime solved." Daniel faced Wes. "From what we've learned so far, the dollars are big enough to make us mad, but not big enough to hurt our company. We will survive it. What I'm saying is, we want to cooperate fully. We'll keep Brian working on this for our needs, and you're more than welcome to oversee his work in as much detail as you need. I'm much more concerned about our people's safety than the embezzlement of a couple million dollars."

"Thank you. We really appreciate that attitude. It'll really help solve this case sooner." Wes said sincerely. He gained added respect for this CEO. "Rest assured. We want to find the bad guy, not delve into your financial picture. And, I'm sure we can work out Brian's salary."

"I'm sure we can." Daniel agreed. "Sounds as if Brian has your respect for his work, as well as having ours."

Brian felt a warm current of modesty pass through him.

"Detective Makelin, we have some concerns about confidentiality and proprietary information. We ask receivers of this information to sign confidentiality agreements." Stan had regained some of his confrontational posture.

"We don't sign those." Debra spoke with finality and looked Stan directly in the eye. "We investigate whatever we need to in order to solve the case."

"That's okay with us." Daniel intervened. He appreciated Stan's protectionism, but this situation was different. His people came first.

"Could we talk about what you've learned so far?" Wes asked. "Brian, I guess it's your turn."

Brian pulled his three page summary sheet from his briefcase. Larry dialed Liz on the intercom and asked her to make copies. After a few minutes, Brian explained his document, without too much technical detail, and answered questions.

TWENTY SIX

Friday Night, April 8
Manhattan Beach, California

Sitting at his desk, the man who thought of himself as the alpha male looked across his living room to the Pacific Ocean. Actually, he could only peek at the ocean. Two near-by high-rise buildings blocked most of his view. Nevertheless, he paid several thousand dollars more for the limited view. He used the second bedroom as an office and had removed the wall between it and the living room to enjoy the view. He also had upgraded the condo with hardwoods and travertine floors, granite countertops, and special lighting for his artwork. He lived on the fifth floor of a six-story building. Someday he would live in a penthouse.

From his condo, he could walk a few short blocks to popular restaurants, shopping, and a near-by park that overlooked the ocean.

He enjoyed collecting art, his primary extravagance. He owned a small Andy Warhol original and hung it in the living room under dimmer control recessed lighting. He also owned a Jackson sandstone sculpture of a native American Indian, which sat on a simple pedestal in the entryway with its own lighting.

His building and a few others, including the offending view-blocking buildings near-by, nearly reached the height limit for buildings in Manhattan Beach. Residents liked the city's height limits, which assured them that developers would not build higher ones.

Besides, tall buildings and Southern California earthquakes did not mix well. Except for the Northridge quake in the nineties, the LA basin had not had a major earthquake for many years. Minor earthquakes, many not felt, occurred daily in the LA area. Occasional media reports reminded people about earthquakes, otherwise they thought little about them. Experts encouraged people to prepare disaster kits for the coming 'big one'. A few responded, but most ignored the advice and continued with their lives.

The sun had begun to set in the horizon. Dark purples, reds, and oranges crowded the western sky. He thought to pour himself a glass of merlot and enjoy the sunset before he called his partner. Southern Californians often bragged about the sunsets, but few enjoyed them. They rarely had the time, or took them for granted.

He canceled the idea of the wine, and pulled a disposable phone from his desk drawer. He would call his partner, his action-man, and finish business first, and then he would enjoy the wine.

Unfortunately, his partner's recent display of obstinacy and bull-headedness could prove difficult. He needed to control this guy. He understood that the investigation into their joint venture was progressing, and not to their advantage.

He had planned this venture in minute detail. It involved complicated steps, multiple bank accounts, and technical access to computer databases. Elimination of computer trails and records required equally detailed planning. He had to work fast because of the current investigation.

He could not allow his action-man to become a problem, so frequent contact was necessary. Except for the clandestine meetings in obscure bars, they never met at the same place twice.

They used disposable phones. He had bought them in a questionably safe area of town and had paid cash. They would use the phones solely for this project and nothing else. No calling friends, no business calls, not even to order a pizza. This behavior would remove as much data/cyber trail as possible. When the project ended, they would destroy them, probably throwing them into the ocean.

They would talk with the disposable phones tonight.

Before he called, the alpha man jotted his thoughts on a white legal pad. He preferred the white pads. The yellow variety seemed too common, too pedestrian. White pads were crisper, cleaner, even if they were less environmentally friendly. Although he had an excellent memory and could keep most topics in his head, he preferred his lists, his pads. He kept all of the documents locked in a safe when not in use. At the end of the venture, he would shred them.

He would check each point on the list as he discussed it. He believed this practice freed his mind to think creatively, to analyze details, and to remember all of his points.

He also liked using wireless headphones. They allowed him to doodle, take notes, work his computer, or move about the room. Pacing also freed his mind to think clearly. He followed this behavior at work and at home.

He plugged his headphones into the disposable phone, and sat in his leather chair. He dialed his partner's number. He flexed and relaxed the muscles in his arms a couple times to reduce the little tension that had built in him. The phone rang five times. His partner was supposed to expect the call. Anger joined the tension he felt. He turned the phone to push the end button when he heard his partner answer. Loud music played in the background.

"Hello, there." The voice was upbeat, almost friendly.

"Hello. Is now a good time to talk?" *Of course it is. They had agreed to talk at this time.*

"Yeah, sure. Let me turn down the music." His voice still sounded friendly.

The loud music morphed into the low, background type.

In this conversation, neither man would identify himself or use the other's name, or anyone's name for that matter. They shared a dose of paranoia, but called it caution.

In their joint venture, they evolved into an uncomfortable, but symbiotic relationship. On any other level, they would not likely be friends. They did not share the same friends, or attend the same social events.

"Just wanted to talk with you. Be sure we're still on the same page."

"What. Don't trust me?" His voice less friendly.

"That's not it. It's just that I understand the investigation is progressing, but not to our advantage."

"But you're cleaning up the records. Right?"

"Yes. But that takes time." The alpha man did not like being on the defensive with this guy. He continued, "As you know there have been some developments that could interfere with our little project. This new consultant seems to know a lot about digging into computer data."

"That's not good."

"No. No, it's not. I need a little more time to change files and the security system to eliminate any kind of data trail." He changed his tactic. "I understand the police have also become involved."

"Yeah. I heard. There's no hiding anything from the company grapevine." The partner responded.

The alpha man chose his words carefully and spoke slowly. "About that idea you had, about eliminating someone else."

"Oh, so you are coming around to my way of thinking." The partner's voice reflected his grin. He liked this change in roles.

"Maybe so. I was wondering. What if we just eliminated one other person? Maybe this new guy."

"I'm open. Go on."

"It'd have to look like an accident. It can't have any of the tell-tale signs of drugs, like the last one."

"Okay." The partner let the idea move around in his mind. "Accident. Sure. Accidents happen every day in LA. LA's a big place. Most deaths aren't even reported in the papers."

"True." Alpha man continued, "I understand he lives alone. No one knows him where he's working. He could disappear quickly."

"Yeah. Out of site, out of mind." The action-man thought aloud. "I'd need to work quickly, learn where he lives, what his habits are, what are the risks in his neighborhood, and so on."

"Let's not do anything just yet." He cautioned, but liked his action-man's cooperation. "Let's think about it. Come up with some ideas. I'll keep working at cleaning the data trails. We can talk in a couple days. Use each other as a sounding board."

"That should work. I kinda like the idea."

"Remember, it really has to look like an accident. The police are already involved. They might call one death an accident, but two, in the same company, in the same department. Not a coincidence they'd easily accept."

"Don't worry. Don't worry. I'll work out the details. It'll look like an accident." The partner's voice was not as friendly as it was when they started talking.

"Good. Now just promise me, you won't do anything, until we talk some more."

"I promise." The partner agreed, but could not resist adding, "You know that guy isn't the only one working on this project. Maybe a couple people need to be eliminated."

"Now, I really hope you're kidding." The alpha man began to worry again. Almost demanding, "Don't get carried away here. Let's just take things slow."

"Just kidding." As much as he was the last time. "We can talk in a couple days."

They ended their conversation.

Alpha man removed his headphones, locked his disposable phone in the safe in the closet. He took a deep breath. He felt satisfied, in control again. He felt smug that his partner, *his fall guy,* would do one last task for him, and then he would *fall.*

The sun had set. The clouds had changed to a single dark color. Lights on several of the buildings, including the two view-offending buildings, had turned on. Not a bad view in itself. He decided he would pour that glass of merlot.

TWENTY SEVEN

Saturday morning, April 9
Long Beach, California

Lying face down, his head buried into his pillow, Brian opened one eye, then the other, and squinted to see the bedside clock. It read five-forty-four. Soon, the clock would play music. He would wait. He closed his eyes, but his mind had started analyzing the embezzlement, as if it worked during the night. Maybe it had. For the last few days, his mind, whenever conscious, worked on this project.

He smiled. He remembered today was Saturday. He would drive to Palm Springs to Larry and Peter's party. He worked late last night, so he would connect through the Internet to check the results from home this morning. No drive to Santa Monica. He looked forward to the drive to Palm Springs. The drive should be easy, light traffic, and require half the time it would have yesterday.

Music burst from the clock radio, startling him. He tossed off his covers, stepped into his slippers, and into his robe. Still April, still cool. He shuffled to the kitchen to begin his usual ritual, and started the coffee.

While it brewed, he retrieved the morning paper outside his door. The paperboy, assuming he was a boy, Brian had never seen him, probably lived in the building. With over two hundred units in the building, he probably had all the customers he needed.

185

Before reading the paper, Brian poured himself a mug that he had bought after a *Lord of the Dance* performance. He sat in his swivel rocker, near the glass wall, and stared at the city of Long Beach. The glass façades of the General Bank and Insurance building, hi-rise hotels, and other buildings shimmered in the morning sunlight.

Careful not to burn his hands, he held the mug close to his face to feel its warmth and smell the aroma that rose from the coffee. Following this slow, wake-up process, he felt ready to manage his world. After a few sips, his awareness elevated, he could hear the faint sounds of the Gran Prix outside.

Racecar engines roared from early morning to late evening. This was the weekend of the big race. When he stood to refill his mug, he could see that thousands of visitors already crowding the downtown streets. On one level, he enjoyed living in the middle of this activity. On another, he was glad to escape the noise and congestion.

Brian had packed what he needed last night. The suitcase sat near the front door. He would take his laptop computer with him. He only needed wi-fi access. The motel was supposed to have one.

Last night, he parked his car in the parking garage a few miles away at the Willow Street station of the Blue Line light rail system. He rode the Blue Line home. The downtown station was only a few blocks from where he lived. He reasoned that this tactic would save time this morning. Leaving the garage today would be very difficult, even if he could. And maneuvering the downtown streets would be a traffic nightmare. He would take the Blue Line to his car

When the coffee began its waking affect on his body, Brian inhaled deeply, refilled his mug, and decided he would only shower this morning. He would shave and shower before the dinner party. He looked forward to the weekend.

As expected, freeway traffic was light. He traveled the speed limit on the Interstate through Riverside and connected to the 10 Freeway that would lead to Palm Springs. He selected his favorite playlist on his I-pod and plugged it into his car's speaker unit. He turned the volume to a comfortable level. He liked a variety of music, so the playlist contained a mix of country, pop, and crossover.

After a couple hours, he turned off the Interstate onto Highway 111 that leads into Palm Springs. He pulled onto the side of the road and lowered the top of his convertible. He felt an immediate sense of relaxation wash over him. Something about the desert appealed to him, the sand, the dry air, the bright sunshine. Except for the distant sound of freeway traffic, and the idling motor of his Mustang, he heard little. The quiet soothed him. The sun felt warm. He leaned against his car, closed his eyes, and tilted his head up to feel the sun's rays, on his face, through his clothes. He could enjoy living here. After a moment, he climbed into his car to continue his trip.

In a few miles, Palm Springs grew out of the desert sand. Along the brown, bare, rocky mountains, the small city replaced the sand, the scrub mesquite, and tumbleweeds. Stately palm trees lined Palm Canyon Drive, the main avenue, one-way South, through the city. The wide sidewalks, small boutique shops, and dozens of restaurants with outside dining enchanted its visitors and locals.

Driving slowly down this street with his convertible top down, he reveled in the atmosphere. He drove the short distance to his hotel in the south end of the city. After check-in he would return to Palm Canyon, park, and join the others strolling the street. He would enjoy his lunch in one of the sidewalk cafes.

Brian had made reservations in an inexpensive hotel. He enjoyed the pampered treatment a five star hotel could give, but he needed to watch his spending. As long as the hotel provided a clean room, a comfortable bed, and hot shower, he could be satisfied. Function first, then pampering.

He left his briefcase, and laptop in the car's trunk, before checking into the hotel. For some unexplained reason, he felt they were safer in the car than in the hotel room. The Bombay gin that he would give to Larry and Peter this evening sat in the corner of the trunk. He unpacked his clothes, and hung his slacks and silk shirt in the closet.

Now, he felt hungry, ready for lunch. He drove Indian Canyon North a few blocks and at Frances Stevens Park, reconnected to Palm Canyon to again enjoy the drive through town, and to select a restaurant. The parking gods smiled on him, he found a parking space in front of a Mexican restaurant with its old looking brick and stucco arches covered in thick green vines. Spanish music played from unseen speakers. He ordered a frozen margarita, just plain, no salt. His server offered the jumbo size, but Brian ordered the regular. He wanted to enjoy tonight's party. He could no longer handle the booze like he could when he was younger.

Before ordering his food, he sipped his margarita and watched people strolling the crowded sidewalks. Young couples, multigenerational families, senior citizens. Women wearing colorful shorts and blouses. Men wearing cargo shorts with pockets full, wallets, cameras, and souvenirs. Brian enjoyed being a part of this afternoon in Palm Springs. Tonight's party would add an upscale side to his day. He liked Palm Springs.

He ordered a taco salad, and for a couple of hours, he pushed the worries of his financial state and the challenges of this new job onto the back porch of his mind.

TWENTY EIGHT

Saturday afternoon, April 9
Palm Springs, California

In two hours, the party would start. Since he skipped shaving this morning, Brian shaved his five-o'clock-shadow, and took a quick shower. He dried himself with two hotel towels. One lightweight motel-type towel was not enough to dry a man's body. He dressed for the party, lightweight beige slacks and a colorful, Hawaiian silk shirt, hanging outside the slacks. After buttoning the shirt, he shook it a few times to keep the body sweat to a minimum.

He expected to enjoy the few miles drive to Larry's place in Rancho Mirage, less than ten miles away. He drove East Palm Canyon slowly to Frank Sinatra Drive. His GPS system would guide him the rest of the way.

The temperature on the car's dashboard read eighty-two degrees. In his rear view mirror, he could see the sun begin to set behind the tall, San Jacinto Mountains in the West. The desert air felt warm and so very comfortable. Moments like this gave Palm Springs its reputation as a desert paradise. Those early movie stars who discovered this place knew pleasure.

He would arrive only a few minutes late, fashionably late as they say, although fashion was never a big concern for him. He just wanted to enjoy driving with the top down. In LA, he usually kept the top up, too crowded and noisy to simply enjoy a drive, unless he drove on Pacific Coast Highway, along the coast.

After reaching Frank Sinatra, his GPS identified the streets, many named after celebrities, Frank Sinatra, Dinah Shore, Gerald Ford, Bob Hope. Most communities on these streets were gated and required codes for entry. Larry's place was no exception. He passed the famed Mission Hills Country Club, where golfers played in major televised tournaments.

Larry had told him that he would have to park on the outside street and walk into the Los Pasos development where he lived. He had given Brian the gate pass code. Without difficulty, Brian saw the grand, expansive entry for Los Pasos, its two sets of giant bronze doors. Huge boulders lay on the sides and in the center median. He saw several cars already parked along the street, Lexus, Infinity, a couple Jaguars, even a Rolls Royce with a few Chevrolets and Fords parked in the mix. His Mustang would be in good company.

Brian took a deep breath before stepping out of his car. He wished that he did not feel any intimidation, but sometimes, on some small level, he felt insecure with people his age, who had achieved the success and financial comfort that he had not. Of course, he would never admit this fact to anyone.

He retrieved the Bombay gin from the trunk with a congratulations card taped to the box. Just ahead of him, two men were keying the pass-code into the gate control box. The taller man appeared to be in his seventies, the shorter his early sixties.

Thinking he could simply walk in with these two would be good, save an extra push on the electronic buttons.

"Hello" The younger man extended his hand to Brian. "I'm Frank. And this is Joe"

"Brian, here." He shook Frank's hand and reached to greet Joe who turned after keying the pass-code. The gates slowly swung open.

Recognition immediately showed on Brian's and Joe's faces. The broad smiles of long unseen friends shone on their faces. Their extended handshake became a hug.

"My god, it's been a long, long time." Joe spoke first.

"It has. It has. How long has it been? Fifteen years?"

"At least. It has been so long. Wow. I'm almost speechless. Where do I start? What have you been up to? Where have you been? I have a hundred questions." Joe asked.

"I still live in LA, a few different places since I last saw you. I'm speechless too." Brian felt excited. "Where have you been? Is this your partner?

"Yes. Yes. This is Frank. Frank, Brian. Brian and I worked together many years ago. Before he came out. I knew he was one of us."

"Hi Brian." Frank greeted a second time. "Nice to meet you. I bet you two have a lot to catch up on. We'd better get through the gate, before it closes." Frank pulled Joe's arm. The gate had started to close.

Joe and Brian continued talking as they walked through the gate. Joe, in animated conversation, frequently touched Brian's arm as he asked his hundred questions. Brian grinned as wide as his face could allow, he even hugged Joe a couple times. He genuinely liked Joe, always had. Frank seemed happy for the two friends.

As the men approached the house, huge ten-foot glass double doors stood before them. The high glass walls on both sides of the doors extended the drama of the house's entry. Inside they could see the large living space, the expansive furniture, the art on the walls, the freestanding sculptures. Talk about living in a glass house.

Before Frank could ring the doorbell, a bald man in his mid-fifties opened the door and welcomed them. He said for the moment he was the self-appointed door greeter. He said the person closest to the door had the responsibility to welcome newcomers. He too wore the casual dress that many people from Palm Springs wore, colorful Hawaiian shirts in blues, reds, and greens. This greeter's shirt hung outside his white, linen pants.

Seeing the gifts carried by the newcomers, he pointed to a nearby table that was already filled with anniversary gifts. He told the newcomers that their hosts, Larry and Peter, were probably on the patio nodding his head over his left shoulder. The men introduced themselves, turned the conversation immediately to the house, its travertine floors, fourteen-foot ceilings, expensive sculptures and paintings that gave the feel of an upscale art gallery. Huge leafy green plants added color and softened the hardscape of stone flooring and glass walls.

Brian set his bottle of Bombay gin on the table, next to a few other bottles of Bombay. Obviously others knew that Larry liked Bombay. Brian grimaced, he needed to think more originally.

The bald man said people were giving themselves self-guided tours of the house. He pointed to a wing on one side, and then to the other side to another wing. He led them to the nearest bar just outside the living area, and pointed to another one near the pool. The patio functioned as an extension of the already large living rooms, just outdoors, almost as expensively furnished. The patio chairs and couches were better than Brian's living room furniture.

Folding glass doors against the nearby walls, opened the entire living room to the patio. Only the flooring change from travertine to slate separated the house from the patio.

Holding a martini, Larry stood near the bar chatting with a small group. He wore beach casual, a lightweight blue cotton shirt and white cotton trousers. When he saw Brian, he excused himself from the small group, and approached the newcomers. "Welcome, welcome, you guys. I'm so glad you could come." Larry embraced Joe and Frank, welcomed them, and then hugged Brian. Larry pushed aside twenty years, animated, the same as his younger self after a couple martinis.

Larry was ebullient. This was his day. Well, his and Peter's. His face filled with happiness, he laughed, talked faster than usual, and his voice, maybe a bit higher pitched than usual. He and his partner had hired excellent caterers. So each could enjoy the party and not worry about the hosting details. It was their anniversary.

"I know we need to talk a little shop sometime while you're here, but it'll have to be later, I'm having way too much fun. Maybe we can talk tomorrow morning. Ok? So no talking business for awhile. Ok? The bar is right here." Larry pulled Brian to order a drink.

"Ok. Sounds good to me. No business until later. Just celebration. I'm all for that. I think I still know how to party." Brian grinned. Larry's animated mood was infectious. Brian liked seeing his friend happy. "Where's Peter, I want to say hello. Oh, and I brought you guys your favorite gin, Bombay. It's on the table in there, with the other hundred bottles of Bombay."

"Great, great. As you know, I love Bombay gin. Oh, and Peter is…" Larry paused and scanned the pool side. Spotting Peter, "There he is," at the other side of the pool. He's wearing a blue cotton shirt, just like this one. See him?" Larry pointed to where Peter was standing.

"I see him."

"Excuse me. I see I'm needed in the kitchen." Larry trotted toward the kitchen, grinning and talking to everyone on his way.

Brian reached his turn at the bar, and ordered his drink, "Chivas and water, please." He felt in a party mood, which called for a good scotch. He would order his usual beer another night.

Forty, or fifty people milled throughout the area, more were arriving. Larry had told him that a hundred people had been invited. Brian had expected the place would be overcrowded. But now he was here, the place could easily accommodate the crowd. Larry had been modest about his house.

Brian moved about the patio area, greeting the friends he recognized, and meeting new ones. They seemed as happy to see him, as he was to see them. He, like most others talked in small groups of three, four, or five people. They spoke in laughing voices, talking almost at the same time, often teasing, and using animated gestures. Un-offended by interruptions from newcomers, they shifted greetings and topics mid-sentence. This was a gathering of old friends, of long-since-seen friends.

Even the mention of the death of a friend, a partner resulted in a sincere, genuine expression of sympathy, a hug. But then just as quickly, the conversation returned to more pleasant topics. As new people joined the groups, others split to join other groups, or to refresh their drinks. Conversations shifted from the jovial to detailed, serious topics. Very few people stood alone, nursing their drinks, watching the crowd, or the sunset.

Consciously, or unconsciously people congregated on the patio to enjoy the sunset with its view of the setting sun with its reds and yellows. The few clouds in the sky were hanging around the snow-covered tops of the western mountains. The still, comfortable air added to the good feel of the party. An added benefit, no mosquitoes or other insects bothered these partygoers. Such was life in the desert.

Brian's anxiety of attending a large, somewhat formal, even if casual dress, party subsided. He would have a good time tonight.

Several people away, Brian saw Larry talking with an attractive woman, probably in her fifties. She wore a muted yellow sleeveless sundress and a light airy designer scarf tied around her neck, casual but with a definite upscale look. Older, less confident women probably would not, or could not, wear such a dress. But this woman could and looked smart, stylish. She and Larry both wore serious expressions on their faces. Larry caught Brian's eye and beckoned him to join them.

Brian excused himself from his conversational group, and walked around the pool to join them.

"Brian, I'd like you to meet a good friend of mine. This is Karen Coffman. Karen has written two, successful detective books. But of course I met her before she became somebody." Winking at Karen, Larry teased. "Karen, this is Brian Wells, a friend from many years ago."

"It's a pleasure to meet you." Karen offered her hand.

"The pleasure is mine, I assure you." Brian took her hand. "I'm a little embarrassed. I don't recognize your name even though I read a few novels a year."

"Don't apologize. It's okay. My books aren't quite as successful as Larry says. But at risk of a little immodesty, my readership is growing. Maybe I can win you too."

"After tonight, I will definitely look for your work.

"Brian, we three have something in common which may surprise you. Karen and I were just discussing Greg's death and the embezzlement at Leonard. Karen discovered Greg's body when she was going to LA from The Valley."

"That sounds unpleasant."

"I didn't see the body, actually. The paramedics wouldn't let me see it."

"Oh."

"We had talked after she made the connection to me – working at Leonard." Larry resumed talking about the embezzlement. "Brian, don't worry. We can trust Karen completely. She has really good investigative, analytical skills. She was saying that Detective Makelin was a fan of hers." To Karen, Larry continued, "Brian and I plan to meet in the morning to discuss the status of the work. I'd like you to join us if you can. No discussion of business allowed tonight. Although I think I just violated that rule."

"Sure I'll be here."

"Do you want to set a time?" Brian hoped his surprise did not show on his face. Perhaps Larry had had one too many martinis' that could have affected his judgment.

"Let's shoot for ten. Is that OK? Larry looked to both Brian, and then to Karen.

"Sure." Both agreed.

Larry looked at his watch, and excused himself. "Time for dinner."

Larry found Peter and together they passed among the guests telling them that dinner would be served shortly, and to please be seated. As the word spread, people moved in a slow, uneven wave toward the tables that surrounded the side and one end of the pool. A few moved in an opposite direction to the two bars to refill their drinks before seating. Conversations continued but were quieter.

Floor length, white tablecloths covered the tables. Flowers, two large blue carnations, and a large dark blue candle sat in the center of each table. Flickering votive candles reflected on the shining flatware lying on the blue placemats. Folded napkins squeezed inside crystal wine glasses, and matching water glasses sat at the top edge of the placemats. Each table also contained two small, framed pictures of their hosts. Two very young men, boys almost, looking very different from the men they are today. Larry and Peter knew how to produce an elegant dinner party.

Darkness settled over the valley as if on queue, someone turned down the lights. A gentle breeze, typical of the early spring desert evenings, began to blow. People took their seats. Elegance was definitely the ambience of the evening. Discussion of the embezzlement would have to wait until tomorrow.

TWENTY NINE

Saturday evening, April 9
Palm Springs, California

"Mind if we sit together?" Karen asked Brian as people selected their seats.

"No, not at all. It would be my pleasure. We can get to know each other better." Brian hoped he did not sound too eager. She was a celebrity after all. Brian had thought he would sit with Joe and Frank, but saw their table was full. Better satisfying, Karen and he could watch the sun disappear behind the San Jacinto Mountains at the table they selected. The giant silhouette of the mountains, against the reds and oranges in the sky, provided backdrop. The patio and landscape lighting added an artistic quality to the plants and boulders that surrounded the lawn and pool. Three life size bronze dolphins stood sentinel on the back side of the pool with small streams of water arching from their mouths. The backyard obviously reflected a talented designer's touch. In addition to the view, the dry desert air soothed the skin. A perfect desert evening.

Brian and Karen selected two chairs at a table on the outside perimeter of the closely grouped tables, near the end of the pool. From their seats, they could see most of the guests.

As they seated themselves, Brian worried that she would want to discuss the Leonard Construction embezzlement. If anyone overheard, the sensitive and confidential nature of the project could embarrass

196

Larry. Brian would not do that. Besides, Larry had jokingly instructed *no business* discussions this evening. Brian would teasingly remind her. Fortunately, she never mentioned the subject.

After a few minutes of small talk, Brian quickly warmed to Karen. Her easy conversational style embodied a nice mixture of intelligence and humor. She had an easy laugh, and her eyes twinkled when she smiled.

Other guests joined them. Brian did not know anyone else at their table. Fortunately, in his past, he had attended similar, quasi-formal social events, and could arouse his dormant charm on command. With a little effort, he could become a friendly, affable person. One of the few advantages of aging, a senior often acquired some mastery in social small talk. Would he always have this skill available or would he resign himself to watching television and eating on a TV tray.

He smiled warmly at his fellow guests and introduced himself. Half rising from his chair, he reached to shake hands with those he could. And nodded at those farthest from him. He introduced Karen. Half the table already knew each other. They exchanged names, usually with only the first name. He would try to remember their names, but remembering names always challenged him.

The guests continued their small talk. Naturally, they praised the party, the home, the table setting, and the sunset. A couple seated on the opposite side of the table turned to see it. One teased Brian to trade seats. Brian laughed and remained seated.

After the praise fest, Brian slightly raised the volume of his voice and asked the group a question that people in new social settings usually liked. How did they meet their hosts, Larry and Peter? Everyone around the table took delight in answering the question. A few, in addition to Brian, had known the couple for the entire length of their relationship. Who says gay relationships do not last.

When the table guests learned Karen wrote suspense novels, the conversation shifted full attention to her. She modestly downplayed her success. She thanked them for their attention, and maybe at another venue, she would be happy to talk about herself. But tonight was Larry and Peter's night in the limelight. She asked for their understanding.

As in most groups, conversations involving the entire group splintered into discussions between two or three people.

Like a small, quiet wave, waiters swept quietly, professionally among the tables offering chardonnay or merlot wine. They wore modified tuxedos, white shirts, black bow ties, and black trousers. They carried salads and breads. Two salad dressings in bowls already sat on the table.

As most guests finished their salads, they continued chatting with their tablemates, and the caterers silently removed the plates. With equal efficiency, they brought the main course of chicken divan with asparagus, and rice pilaf. Several expressed their delight at the presentation and aroma of the food. As people ate, the conversations became only a little quieter. They focused on their conversations as much as on eating.

As the guests at Brian's table neared the end of their meals, Larry joined them. With his hands on Brian's shoulders, he welcomed them to the party, hoped they were having a good time. Brian felt good. He could see across the dining area that Larry's partner; Peter was at another table, probably giving the same welcome. After a few minutes, Larry moved to another table to welcome them.

Soon, a commotion of voices and movement rose on the other side of the seated guests. Voices rose, and many applauded as two waiters rolled a dining cart to the edge of the crowd. Atop the cart sat an especially large cake. Yellow and blue icing with the inscription 'Happy Anniversary Larry & Peter' covered the cake. Two candles, a giant three and a zero, sat on top.

"Happy Anniversary! Congratulations!" Almost in unison, many in the boisterous crowd congratulated Larry and Peter on their thirty years together. The applause became unanimous.

Hopefully the neighbors were out-of-town, or at least invited. Camera lights flashed from around the patio. Everyone felt upbeat, even noisy. This was a good party. Guests called for speeches from the hosts.

"No, no. No speeches." Larry held up his hands in mock protest. "This is a party, not a platform. And, as many of you know, I'm not shy about expressing my opinions."

The guests laughed. More calls, more teasing, more congratulations sounded from the guests. Larry pulled Peter to his side and put his arm around him. The banter between them and the audience continued for a while.

With a slight rise in his voice, Brian called to them to tell how they had met, that over a quarter of a century had passed. He emphasized the words, *quarter of a century*. Even though many present knew how they met, Larry and Peter told their story to the now rapt guests. Afterwards, they cut the cake and fed each other a piece, smearing the cake on the other's face to the delight of the audience. Meanwhile, the caterers swiftly served pieces of cake to the guests.

The guests felt another surge of social energy. The musician played more lively, a little Elton John, a little Sting. After another hour, the party began to wind down. After all, the average age registered over sixty. Guests milled about the patio and the manicured lawn, splintering into small groups. A few prepared to leave, and paid their respects to the hosts with lots of hand shaking, hugging, and cheek kissing. Many swore they would call, or have lunch sometime, which in reality may never happen.

Outside earshot of the others, Karen brought up the subject of the Leonard project. They spoke in hushed voices.

"Brian, I know we're leaving the subject of Leonard Construction until tomorrow. But, I just want you to know that I understand you have a dual responsibility to Larry and the sheriff's department. Your relationship is an official one, with both of them, as well as a personal one with Larry. Larry is also my friend. Detective Makelin is nice enough to involve me. Of course, neither of us knew that Larry would be in the picture." Karen touched Brian's arm. "I'd like you to know that I will respect anything you tell me. I just hope we can be friends through all this. I want to make you feel comfortable in talking with me."

"I'm sure I can feel comfortable talking with you about this case. I'm glad you'll respect my hesitance if the need arises. I know you're a good friend of Larry's. I've known him for more than thirty years. We haven't been in touch much during the last few years. But the friendship and respect is there." Brian leaned forward as he talked.

They hugged.

"Thanks, that makes me feel better. I'm glad we're having this conversation. On some level, I'm excited about this case. There is so much human interest here. I think it might inspire some drama for one of my stories." Karen liked Brian even more. "On another level, this whole situation is very sad, about Greg's death, that is. I didn't know him, but from Larry's description of him, especially about his young family. That's very sad."

"Yes, it is. I've learned more about Greg in the last few days from Larry and David, Greg's co-worker. Greg was only about ten years older than my son. More than once, I wondered what I'd do if it was my son? I'm not sure I could handle it." Feeling emotional, Brian looked away.

"Maybe we should talk about something else." Karen's eyes moistened.

"Yes, I agree. We can discuss the details tomorrow morning, when we meet with Larry."

"Yes, three heads together will help us know what we can share." Karen agreed.

"Agreed." Brian wanted to leave while he still felt in a party mood. "I see several others are leaving. I think I'll leave as well."

"Same here. I see Larry over there. I'll give him my good-byes."

"Peter is not far from him. We can give both of them our good-byes."

Brian and Karen approached Larry and Peter separately. They thanked the happy couple for their invitations. They congratulated them on their anniversary. Brian hugged Larry and then Peter.

Brian left feeling good. He had enjoyed a good party. He felt good, or maybe the scotch and the merlot contributed to his upbeat state. Maybe more party lay ahead of him. He would explore the Palm Springs nightlife a little before returning to the hotel.

THIRTY

Saturday Evening, April 9
Palm Springs, California

Brian's buzz from the earlier Chivas and merlot during the party had faded, but he still felt upbeat. He joined a few guests as they walked through the Los Pasos gates to their cars. His drinking habits had changed radically since his younger days. Then, he would drink three or four scotches and unwisely drive home. Often, after the bar closed, he stopped at an all night café, or greasy burger joint for something to eat. He rationalized the late night eating sobered him before going home.

He was wiser now. He drank very little during an evening on the town. He could not remember the last time he closed a bar. His nights out now consisted of joining a friend for dinner, or for a couple drinks at a bar. By eleven, he normally lay asleep in his bed. Tonight, he would stay out a little later. How often does one come to Palm Springs.

He climbed into his Mustang, started the engine, and carefully pulled onto the street in case his reactions were a little slow. The powerful engine gave a low roar as he pushed the gas pedal. Brian liked his Mustang. Occasionally, in limited freeway traffic, he would test the engine for a short distance, just to enjoy the power surge. He liked knowing the power was there when he needed it, or if he wanted it.

From the Los Pasos development, Brian drove west slowly on Gerald Ford Drive for a few miles. Cities in the Palm Springs area required elaborate landscaping along their streets, especially along newer developments. Extensive use of palm trees, oleanders, sage, and lantana lined the roadsides and the medians. Bougainvillea covered the stucco walls that enclosed the developments. Streetlights existed only at intersections or at lavish stacked stone entrances to the developments.

Unseen lights shone on the palm trees, mesquite, large shrubs, and giant boulders. The place said money, even on the city streets. No wonder, the area referred to itself as a desert paradise. With the Mustang's top down, the stars in the sky, and the almost-warm night air, Brian reveled in the drive into Palm Springs.

Brian turned left at Date Palm to connect to Highway 111, the scenic route, instead of the faster route of Dinah Shore Drive. After about ten miles of reverie about the party, he passed his motel and drove a few more blocks into downtown Palm Springs. He turned onto Arenas where a few bars, clothing shops, and restaurants catered to mostly gay clientele. He found a space on the street, and parked. By habit, he locked his car, even with the top down. He smiled at the irony.

On Arenas, large spaces filled the area between the buildings and the sidewalks. Wrought iron railings often outlined these spaces, and expanded the occupancy numbers for socializing, drinking, dining, and smoking. Most business had large tinted glass for their front exterior walls. During the day, the tinted glass restricted what could be seen inside and with misters, warded against the cruel, bright summer sun. At night, the inside space appeared opened to the outside world.

California law does not allow smoking inside bars and restaurants. Instead, smokers with drinks must sit in the iron railing defined areas. As inside, people filled these patios, talking, laughing, and a few smoking. Small groups sat around metal bistro tables, on park-like benches, or leaned against the railing. An occasional lone person sat to one side nursing a drink, watching the people. Several people, in shorts and polo shirts, or tank tops milled about the sidewalks and the street traveling from one bar or restaurant to another. The many conversations, the banter, were noisy, but fun.

A bar further down the block blasted rock, disco-techno dance music. The glass walls visually vibrated with the music. Any louder, the glass would probably break. When someone opened one of its doors, the music escaped, tripling the sound. A few diners remained in a couple of the restaurants, the tables filling with drinkers instead.

Brian entered the Rainbow Bar and Restaurant. He knew it catered to a mature, older crowd. He liked men his age, maybe a little older. He did not like that he grew older. But like it or not, he and his type were in the same age bracket as the Rainbow crowd. He had heard the unfair and unkind jokes about patrons using walkers, oxygen tanks, and wheelchairs. He would shake his head, never appreciating the humor.

The bar was crowded. Loud, indistinct voices filled the room. Some laughed or spoke above the others. Glasses clinked. A matre'd stood behind his podium waiting for stragglers wanting a late dinner. The nearly empty dining room extended beyond him, beyond the bar area. He had eaten here during past visits. The Rainbow served an excellent lemon chicken and a great tasting BLT.

A piano man sat at the grand piano alongside one wall playing and singing a Liza Minelli tune, Cabaret. A few men sat on high stools around the piano, a few lip-synching with him. Others sat at small tables, or stood in small groups.

Brian ordered a Chivas and water from the bartender, asking him to mix it weak. While waiting for his drink, he scanned the room searching for anyone he might know or would like to meet. People from Los Angeles often came here for the weekend. As expected, the crowd consisted mostly of older men, who were of all sizes, shapes, and weights. Tonight they seemed very jovial, matching his upbeat mood.

After paying for his drink, Brian found a spot next to the matre'd and leaned against the wall.

A few thirty-something men were mixed in the crowd. Brian looked past them. Men in their twenties or thirties usually went to one of the high energy dance bars with loud music, like the one with the vibrating windows down the street.

Many people engaged in animated conversation with exaggerated gestures, and speaking too loudly. A few wore stone quiet expressions. Several constantly scanned the crowded room, even while talking. Others nursed their drinks, absorbed in thought, or focused on the pianist, who was not a bad musician and vocalist. Brian lingered his eyes on one man, who caught him staring. Both smiled, and looked away. Over the next few minutes, they exchanged glances a few times.

The interesting looking man sported a close-cut, salt-and-pepper beard. He was about Brian's height, but trimmer. Brian needed to pay more attention to his body so he could look as good as he once did. The man wore his hair closely cropped probably to camouflage the gray hair and his balding head. Balding men have masculine looks, but seldom see themselves as intensely sexual as they are. Brian watched him move to the bartender's station where he re-ordered a beer. Similar to Brian, maybe he needed the liquid courage to meet someone new.

Brian continued to scan the room.

"Hi, how are you tonight?" The balding man, grinning, appeared to Brian's side. "I'm Phillip."

"Hi, right back to you. I'm Brian." Brian chuckled and faced him directly. "Good to meet you Phillip."

They tapped scotch glass to beer bottle.

"Likewise. I saw you when you entered the bar. When we exchanged glances, I thought I'd get the chance to meet you." Phillip's face still held its smile and his eyes never left Brian's.

"I was hoping to meet you. I just needed a little more courage." Brian lifted his drink glass. He felt nervous, and attempted small talk. "Looks like this crowd is in an upbeat mood. Is it always this festive?"

"Mostly on weekends." Phillip kept looking at Brian, enjoying that his attention apparently made Brian a little nervous. "Now that you're here, it's more festive."

"Yeah, right." Brian grinned, enjoying the flattery. He did not want to jump into how attracted he was to Phillip too quickly. But then, "Fuck it, you are one good looking man."

"Why thank you, sir." Enjoying the mutual attraction, Phillip inflected a little southern accent and false modesty into his words. "I thought the same about you when you came into the place."

"As you can tell I need to work on my small talk." Brian offered.

"Small talk, in general, is not a bad thing. That's how we get to know each other."

Brian recalled his first conversation with Larry. He had rattled a series of small talk questions when they first met.

"Ok. Here goes. How old are you? Where are you from? Do you live here full time? How do you like the desert? Please feel free to answer any, all, or none of those questions." Brian squarely faced Phillip and grinned.

"Answers are fifty-five, LA, yes, and …" Phillip held his head at an angle to read the imaginary list of questions. "…and yes, except summers. Your turn."

"Answers are fifty-nine, Long Beach, no, but would like to, and no I don't like summers here either, but I rarely come here during the summer." Reading from the same imaginary list, Brian gave his answers in quick, rote order, but began laughing as he finished. He liked this guy. They obviously shared the same sense of humor.

Both men laughed.

"With the small talk out of the way, we could get down to business." Phillip teased with the double entendre, phrasing the words more as a question than statement.

"I'd like that. But I'd like to drink a little more of my scotch. Besides you just bought your beer." Brian angled his head with a teasing grin. Brian loved the direction of this conversation, but wanted to savor the moment a little longer. He wanted to enjoy the banter a little more before *getting-down-to-business*.

"I was partially teasing, just taking advantage of the mood. In fact I like standing here just taking you in." Phillip leaned against Brian.

The two men talked more, some banter, some wit. They stood closer together, let their arms freely touch or whispered in the other's ear, never straying far from their attraction to each other. Feeling the face hair or stubble growth against a cheek. Even enjoying the clean smell of the other's cologne.

Brian leaned into Phillip, and put his mouth next to his ear. "Ready?"

"Ready."

They rested their nearly empty drinks on the narrow railing where they had spent the last thirty minutes. So focused on each other, they had become nearly oblivious of the others in the bar which had become more crowded. The jovial noise level had risen higher in the bar. It did not bother them.

Once outside, they noticed the street had become even busier than earlier.

"Why don't I drive?" Brian suggested since he had very little to drink, and Phillip had had three.

"Sounds good to me. Especially since I don't have a car, here that is." Phillip countered. He laughed and nodded his head toward the

West. "I only live 4 short blocks from here, just on the west side of Palm Canyon."

Brian liked Phillip. He pulled him close, nuzzled his neck, and guided him to his car. Phillip suggested his place. It would be more comfortable than the hotel. He had food, coffee, comfort, and other amenities that a hotel did not offer.

Brian parked in Phillip's driveway. Phillip suggested closing the Mustang's top, sometimes, the palm trees molt this time of year. Phillip waited at the doorway while Brian latched the canvas top on his car, and locked it. As Phillip inserted his key into the door lock, Brian wrapped his arms around Phillip's waist, and nuzzled against him. Phillip opened the door, and they walked lockstep inside the condo. Once inside, Philip turned, they embraced, hugged, kissed. Now doing what they've wanted for the last hour.

Phillip in obligatory politeness offered drinks, food, whatever. Neither wanted anything, except each other, as only males can want. With males, passion is multiplied. No, raw sex is multiplied.

Their passion involved a rawness that only men can achieve. But at times, their lovemaking became gentle, their lips barely touching, and almost not touching. They explored each other bodies. Looked into each other's eyes in the dim light. This felt like love as much as passion. Sometimes, a person has to grasp what love, or deep emotion that comes available, even if just for a few hours. Intense love for a few hours is better than not having any love at all.

Tonight felt special for both of them.

THIRTY ONE

Sunday morning, April 10
Palm Springs, California

Brian parked outside the Los Pasos development, near where he had parked last night. He approached the code box to enter the code to open the gates. He watched Karen pull her car behind his, so he waited. When she approached, he hugged her, and then entered the pass code.

"A little night life?" Karen teased. She could tell he was a little less functional, quieter, than when they parted last night.

"Just a little. I haven't been to Palm Springs for a while. So I'm moving a bit slower this morning." Brian smiled sheepishly. He hoped she would not ask for details.

Karen grinned as she shifted her gaze to the opening gates.

They walked the short distance from the gates to Larry's house. The time was five minutes before ten, Brian rang the doorbell. Through the glass doors, they saw Larry approaching carrying a coffee mug and wearing a bathrobe. He moved slowly, obviously with a hangover. Maybe they should postpone the meeting until tomorrow morning at the Leonard offices. Brian certainly would not mind the change. But work always came first. Fortunately, this time, no one had to be his sharpest.

Larry apologized for his condition and led them to the kitchen for coffee, or whatever they wanted. Karen was all smiles, cheerful. She carried the conversation for the three of them. Larry offered food. He was certain the refrigerator contained many leftovers. Each declined. They chatted briefly about last night's party. Larry thoroughly enjoyed the party, but acknowledged he now paid for it.

Brian offered to reschedule, but Larry would not hear of it. He would manage. He led them to his office. A note, taped to the closed office door, asked last night's guests to not enter. Larry pulled the note from the door, crumpled it, and tossed it into a wastebasket.

Inside the office, Brian noticed the heavy mahogany wood floors with cherry wood desk and floor-to-ceiling bookcases. Walls were painted a light taupe color. Two large camel-color leather chairs sat opposite the desk. Tall glass French doors opened to a small, secluded patio built with cobblestone. Two outdoor chairs, and a large terracotta pot with bright red geraniums filled the small space.

Brian and Karen sat in the two camel-color chairs.

The doorbell rang again. Larry grimaced at the too loud noise, and excused himself. He expected Anna, his housekeeper. She had agreed to clean up after last night's party. Larry and Peter liked a clean house, but did not like cleaning it. Fortunately, they could afford a housekeeper. Anna began her chores. Larry returned to Brian and Karen.

After a little more small talk, Larry stated, "Since you two sat next to each other, I assume you exchanged some information about the embezzlement…"

"Actually, we didn't talk about it." Brian responded. "We'd thought someone might overhear."

"We decided to wait until this morning." Karen added. "For this meeting."

"Good. This way we can all pretty much be on the same page." Larry did not like using a clichéd business metaphor in Karen's presence, but his mind was too fuzzy to create a new one.

"We sort of thought that too. We both feel that you should probably be the one who decides what different people can know. Since Karen and I have relationships to Detective Makelin as well as to you, I like having all our cards on the table, so to speak." Brian discovered his chair swiveled.

"Ah, the metaphors." Karen teased. And then, "Are you blushing?"

Both men smiled, wishing they could hide their reactions.

"Larry, you're my friend as well as my employer for this project. I want you, and Detective Makelin to know that friendship sort of trumps. Besides, I think we all want the guy caught."

"We do. And thanks Brian, I appreciate your loyalty."

"Larry, as you know, you're one of my best friends. And I wouldn't do anything to hurt our friendship. I have to admit that initially, the case really intrigued me. I'm sure my overactive imagination played a part in my suspicions that the accident could be a homicide. It's sad that the situation actually turned out that way." Karen felt the sadness from the last sentence.

"Yes it is." Larry spoke softly.

"I'm eager to persuade Detective Makelin to allow me to follow this case, and even assist with the investigation in some way." Karen continued. She swiveled to face Brian, smiled, and added. "Brian, I now want to consider you a good friend too."

"I'd like that." Brian returned her smile.

"I realize these relationships carry some risk in the situation we're in. But I like my friends." Larry smiled. "I think we're all on the same side here. Let's just deal with this situation one day at a time. As long as we're open with the detective, I think he'll be agreeable too. My god, I can only talk in clichés."

"That's ok. Most of us overuse expressions. That's how they become clichés. And, I like my friends too." Karen grinned and swiveled in her chair.

"From my standpoint, we could use all the brainpower we can get. We need a solution as quickly as possible. The embezzlement, and now a murder, we need results, fast. All of these police shows say that the first forty-eight hours are critical. We're past that, a week past." Brian worried. "Larry, you and I can focus on the embezzlement issue. And Karen, I understand you can help with the Internet searches."

"Yes, I can."

"Why don't we just tell each other what we know so far? Karen why don't you begin, since you discovered the accident?" Larry wished he had not used the word accident. But he had trouble accepting murder.

Karen described the events of Tuesday morning when she discovered the crash scene. She retold her conversations with the rescue team and the Sheriff's detective. Hours had passed before she remembered that Larry worked at Leonard. Naturally, she called him.

Karen added that Wes, the detective, was friendly and amenable to her participating in the case as a consultant. She liked her role, and that she was on a first name basis with him. She would research the Internet. Larry liked the idea, but wanted to know everything she learned. She thought that she could comply.

Brian felt some discomfort discussing sensitive business in front of an outsider, namely Karen. That legal eagle, Stan Brothers, expressed such concerns about protecting the proprietary rights of the company. But Larry would know what was proprietary and obviously trusted her, so Brian spoke freely.

Brian retold what he had learned, mostly the details from the last few days. He reassured Larry that he kept the Leonard information encrypted and password protected if anyone should steal his laptop, which was in his car's trunk.

Brian explained that he and David had discovered more overpayments to both acceptable and questionable vendors. Brian uncovered additional times that system security was turned off for small periods. Tomorrow, he would enlist Dean Horvath's help to identify the people accessing the relevant systems around those times. Also, he and David would track changes to the master files around those times.

Brian explained as much technical detail as Larry or Karen wanted. They were curious about how the date/time stamps on digital files worked. And wondered if someone could manipulate them. Surprisingly, Larry understood much of what Brian described. Karen also liked knowing technical computer details. She could use them in future novels, but without the technical jargon.

"Brian, sounds like we're making real progress." Larry stood, folded his arms across his chest, and paced a small path between his desk and the French doors. "So our next steps are, what?"

"I think we need to update Detective Makelin about our progress." Brian offered. "I can call him, or…"

"We both should call him. We can call him in the morning, first thing. I'll talk to him from a Leonard perspective. You can give him the technical details. He'll probably have you talk to that lady, Ms… What was her name, in their White Collar Crimes unit?"

"Debra Becken." Brian finished Larry's sentence.

"Yes. I'm sure you'll have several conversations with her."

"Maybe remind him of our relationships to each other, as well as to him." Karen added. "Hopefully, he'll understand that we all want to work together on this. I just hope he stays open to us, all of us."

"Good point. I'll make a point of that." Larry's rubbed his temples, and tried to grin. "I'm glad we had this meeting. I haven't had a headache from a hangover in a long time."

"I feel a little slow this morning too. I guess I just can't handle my liquor like I could when I was younger. But I only had a few drinks last night." Brian laughed.

"Well I feel fine. I only had a couple glasses of wine." Karen grinned in mock superiority.

"Well, I can't say what either of you said." Larry grinned at himself. "I drank entirely too many martinis. I liked the party."

"Me too."

"Yeah, me too."

"My headache's returning, so let's end this meeting. I think I'm going to lie down for an hour. I don't want to leave for LA too late. Anna is cleaning up the house. At least I don't have to worry about that. Besides, I think I hear Peter in the kitchen."

"I'm going to head back to LA in a few minutes." Brian rose from his chair. "My car's already packed, ready to go."

"Same here." Karen added.

All three hugged. Brian and Karen re-affirmed their pleasure at meeting each other. Brian added that he would definitely buy one of her books, so that the next time they met, he could ask her questions about the characters. She thanked him; a new reader was always welcomed.

Brian and Karen walked through the gates to their cars, said good-bye to each other and drove away.

For a moment Brian wondered why Larry expressed such concern about everyone being on the same page. He also wondered why Larry wanted Karen to know all the details. What if some of the details were really law enforcement issues? He dismissed these thoughts, after all the embezzlement directly affected Larry's area of responsibility. And the murder, well Greg was one of his people.

THIRTY TWO

Sunday evening, April 10
Santa Monica

David panted after his early evening run. He inserted his smart card from his camera into his computer. With a few clicks of the mouse, he reviewed the few pictures he had taken during his run. He liked one picture that captured the activities surrounding the Santa Monica pier, the rides, the boardwalk, the surfers, and the jog and bicycle path that ran north along the ocean. It even contained a section of Pacific Coast Highway, full of cars, which paralleled the jogging path.

With a few mouse clicks he saved the picture as his background picture on his computer monitor. He then selected a special effect icon and applied it to three selected areas in the picture. He tried different effects and settled on one that showed the setting sun shining special rays on selected areas.

David enjoyed digital photography. He had always liked photography, but digital produced results faster than older methods. Film required several steps and time before he could see the results. With digital, he could see the results of special effects almost within seconds of taking the pictures. His computer required only a corner of the room instead of a dark room. Trial and error efforts resulted in no waste, unlike developer basins, film, and paper.

David's condo was one of a small complex of six units, located in an older section of Santa Monica. He bought the small two-bedroom condo two years ago, just as prices began to rise, now fifty percent higher. David felt grateful for his parent's help with the down payment. He liked the location, and especially liked the investment.

The second bedroom was hardly big enough to qualify as a bedroom. So David modified it by removing a wall to create an alcove to the living area. It worked great as a home office and hobby area. Although he brought work home, he usually worked on his photography. He worked long hours at the office so felt little need to bring the work home.

His place was expensively furnished for an accountant, early in his career. His mother had great taste and often passed nice art pieces to him as she acquired more. Thanks to her, expensive signed prints hung on the walls, a Bragg bronze sculpture sat on a small pedestal near the front door, and a giant, bright red-green hand-blown glass bowl sat on the coffee table. His main purchase involved an expensive Bose stereo set. Some of the art was out of scale for the small place. But his mother liked it, so, he liked it.

When in high school, David had wanted to be a photographer, an artist. But his parents pushed him toward a business career. His dad wanted him to be a lawyer, but did not object when David declared an accounting major. Unlike most kids who resented their parents pushing their career choices, David reluctantly agreed to their wishes. In time he accepted his decision to follow their advice. On one level, he liked accounting. He could see the finished work. But, he still liked photography as a hobby. It was his first love. Right brain, left brain. After he finished with accounting, he might return to that first love.

He heard a knock at the door. The clock on his desk read eight. He did not expect anyone, and wondered who would visit on a Sunday night. Maybe a neighbor, or maybe Mrs. Grayson, their complex's mother hen, which he meant in a good way. He liked her. He clicked apply and save on the picture he had selected for his computer screen. He turned on the outside light, and after looking through the door's peephole, he recognized his visitor. Feeling a little surprised, he opened the door.

"Hi. Almost didn't recognize you. Don't usually see you in a baseball cap."

"Hi. I was just in the neighborhood. Hope you don't mind my stopping by. If you're busy I'll just move on." The visitor gave a friendly laugh. He knew David would be hospitable enough to invite him inside.

"No. No. Welcome. Come on in. I just got back from a jog, and was saving one of the photos I had taken as a screensaver. I've added a couple special effects to it."

"You carry a camera with you when you jog?"

"Yeah. Photography is kind of a hobby. Never know when you see something that you want a snapshot of."

"You're into photography? No, wait. I remember. You had told me before. I'd just forgotten."

"Yeah. Let me show you. Oh, would you like a drink, a soda, or...?"

"No. No thanks. I just had a couple drinks." He lied.

David led the way to his computer desk in the alcove and leaned over the keyboard.

"With this package, I simply use the cursor to draw a line around the area where I want to apply a special effect." He pointed to the special effect on the picture. "Then, I select an icon from the palette of choices of special effects. Click Apply. And voila, I have a nice picture, with animation."

David straightened upright and faced his visitor.

His face reflected the confusion and shock that swept through him. His visitor held a knife, and wore a menacing grin. He obviously was not interested in David's computer screen. Before David could react, the visitor plunged the knife deep into his solar plexus. David felt intense pain. Fortunately, fear and anger immediately replaced his shock. His athletic good condition served him well. Ignoring his wound and with all the force he could command, he shoved away his attacker, with his knife still in his grip.

David slammed him against the wall with a loud thud, knocking over a nearby dining chair, an end table and breaking an expensive ceramic lamp his mother had given him. The attacker bounced against the wall, knocking a painting off its hook, and sank to the floor, dazed. His breath knocked out of him. He lost his grip on the knife.

Trying to catch his breath, David grabbed his phone and dialed 911. The dispatcher answered. Distracted with the dispatcher's questions, David, for a moment, took his eyes off his attacker. In that moment, his attacker revived, retrieved the knife and lunged toward David, striking him in the chest. Both fell against the wall breaking a mirror that hung there. Breathing heavy and holding David against the wall, he plunged the knife into David's abdomen again, thrusting upward and twisting it. This time, David became quiet, still. His energy to fight, his will, all ceased. He dropped the phone. Darkness entombed him. The dispatcher's voice still asking questions. David never answered any of them.

The attacker drew a deep breath and cursed the sequence of events. The attack did not go well, but he did complete it. He heard the dispatcher's tinny voice on the phone, grabbed it, and pressed the *end* button. Maybe he should have told him there was no problem, that the call was just a mistake, everything was ok. But he probably heard the commotion and would not believe him anyway. Now was too late.

He knew he had to hurry. He had planned a quiet, unhurried killing. According to the plan he would have plenty of time to clean the area, to stage the scene. No one would have heard anything, or have seen anything. He had worn long sleeves, a mock turtle neck shirt and black pants that do not shed fibers. Now, everything had changed. The dispatcher would send the police. Some neighbor probably heard the commotion. It was not a quiet event. He hoped the neighbors were watching TV or not at home.

But he felt he could still control the situation. He slipped on a pair of gloves he had in his rear pocket. He pulled a cloth from another pocket, and wiped everything he could remember touching. The doorknob, the fallen end table he used to pull himself upright after being shoved into the wall. He wiped the corner of the desk where laid his hand while looking at David's computer monitor.

He saw a small eco-friendly canvass bag and decided it would be good for the burglary-gone-bad part of his plan. He looked about the room. Seeing a small bronze statue on a credenza, and a crystal block with an etching of the twin towers from the 9/11 tragedy, he added those to his bag. Then, he scoped the bedroom where he took David's wallet and loose bills lying on a dresser. He bagged those too. Enough. He had to hurry.

He had not accepted David's offer for a drink; so had no worry about prints or DNA on a glass or can. Again, maybe he was paranoid from watching too many episodes of CSI on television. Even if the police found some evidence of his being there, he could say that they had visited each other on occasion. After all, they both live in the same city.

He knew he had delayed too long. The police could arrive soon, if they followed their standard procedure to respond to a 911 call even if the caller was non-responsive. Or the caller could not convince the dispatcher that the call was truly a mistake and everything was ok. He wrapped the wiping cloth around the knife and stuck it securely in a pocket of his jacket. He slipped his baseball cap on his head.

He paused briefly, tried to relax, and reviewed his mental checklist, which he had to alter considerably. He turned off both the inside and the outside lights before opening the door. He wanted to leave as quietly as possible, and as unobtrusively as possible. After closing the door behind him, he looked for others in the small courtyard. He wanted to run, but did not dare. He did not want to attract any attention from the neighbors, other visitors, or people on the street.

He walked down the street with his head bent down, looking at the sidewalk. He tried to walk no faster than the few others out for a stroll, in this pleasant, but cool Sunday evening. As he rounded the corner to his car, a police car turned onto the street from the other direction and pulled in front of the small condo complex he had just left. He paused to watch the police, as did a few of the other strollers. It was difficult to walk slowly with his system pumping with adrenalin. He continued to his car.

The two policemen, responding to the non-responsive 911 call, rang David's doorbell. Sometimes a non-responsive call was a misdial of a 411-information call, a kid playing with the phone, a distracted person who hangs up, or simply a glitch in the phone system. But to be on the safe side, most police departments responded to these calls, just in case of a real need. No one answered the door. They rang the bell again.

"Hello officers, is something wrong?" A gray haired lady wearing a long house robe and a colorful scarf tied around her neck. With the door slightly ajar and her hand on the doorknob, she stood on her stoop across the courtyard. A soft light cascaded onto the courtyard from her doorway.

"No ma'am. Just checking a call. The resident doesn't seem to be home. Do you know if anyone is home?" The taller officer asked as the other rang the doorbell again.

"Yes, I'm pretty sure he's home. I saw him earlier here in the courtyard. He'd been out jogging, about twenty minutes ago. David's a very avid jogger. I saw his light on earlier. I see his drapes are closed. But most of us close our drapes in the evening." The lady pulled her robe closer about herself and continued talking as she stepped toward the officers. "I'm Ellen Grayson. I'm sort of the mother hen for this complex. Most of my residents like it that I'm a little nosey. They know I mean well."

"We're not getting a response." The shorter officer stepped closer.

"Something's gotta be wrong. I'm almost certain he's home. I have a key." She switched into her mother-hen mode and turned to retrieve her keys.

"Thanks."

"David? David, is every thing alright?" Ellen asked as she unlocked and opened the door a few inches.

No answer.

She started to enter, but one of the officers touched her arm gesturing to allow them to enter and for her to wait at the door. Both officers entered. Ellen's maternal instincts forced her to follow, disobeying the officer's orders. The first officer who entered switched on the lights.

All three saw the mess of the furniture and almost as quickly saw David's body slumped against the wall, obviously dead. Ellen, again responding to her mother's instinct wanted to rush to him, to help him, to make everything all right.

The shorter officer took her by the shoulders to gently guide her outside. He told her she should go home, and wait while he and his partner secured the place. He would come to her as soon as he could. He would have more questions. She agreed, held back her tears, and tried to regain her composure. The officer returned inside.

Search of the small condo required only a few minutes. The taller officer called in the homicide. He requested the services of the crime scene forensics unit, detectives, and the county coroner. Santa Monica usually did not experience crime like this. Inner city Los Angeles, yes, but Santa Monica, no.

217

THIRTY THREE

Monday morning, April 11
Santa Monica, California

As usual, Liz arrived to work an hour early. The others, David, Greg, and Larry, would arrive within fifteen minutes. Of course this morning, Greg would not. She fished her keys from the bottom of her Beatles tribute souvenir mug, filled with pens and pencils, along with the keys to her desk, filing cabinets, and Larry's office. Not the best of hiding places, but functional. Besides, a security guard sat on the other side of the glass wall.

Liz unlocked her desk, the frequently-used file cabinets, and Larry's office. She locked her purse in a seldom-used lower cabinet drawer, booted her computer, and carrying her mug, headed for the break-room. She drank tea. Nice person she was, she prepared the first pot of coffee.

During the quiet time before the others arrived, Liz checked her e-mails, and other first-of-the-day tasks. Her phone rang two quick rings, indicating an outside call. Probably Larry. He would likely arrive late today, since his big party in Palm Springs Saturday night. She had to deal with her invalid mother over the weekend and could not attend.

"Accounting, Liz Bowden here." She announced to the caller.

"Hello, I'm Ellen Grayson. I'm calling about David Frazer. I live across the courtyard from him." The caller sounded alarmed.

"Hello, Mrs. Grayson. David has talked about you. How are you?" Liz sensed uneasiness in the caller's voice. Maybe David would be late this morning, Liz thought, but he usually called himself. Maybe he was sick, with Greg's death and working overtime lately.

"I'm fine, thanks." Mrs. Grayson responded too quickly. "Actually, I'm not fine. I feel very sad. I don't know how to tell you this, but David… This is very difficult... I'm very sorry to have to tell you… David was killed last night."

Liz's mind went numb. A fugue state, like an immense waterfall, cascaded over her. She felt removed, far down a tunnel, and could no longer hear Ellen Grayson's words. "I, I'm sorry but did you say David is dead, was killed?" Liz stammered.

"Yes, yes. He was killed. I know this is a shock. It's a shock for us here in the complex. David had given me this number as a contact, if anything was wrong.

"Oh my god, I…" Liz, still in shock, could not think, her speech confused. Questions crowded in her mind, but were unable to take voice. Absorbing this news drained the blood from her head. She felt faint.

"I thought you would want to know. He has talked about how much he liked the people where he worked." Mrs. Grayson continued to talk. "I'm sure the Santa Monica police will call you this morning. I hope you don't mind but I gave them your number when I talked with them last night."

"Yes, of course, we'll deal with them, whatever is necessary." Liz regained some of here ability to speak. "Please forgive me. I'm just having trouble believing this, I mean accepting this."

"I understand. I was in shock myself last night. I couldn't sleep. Of course the police didn't finish until around three. I'm just now getting my wits about me. Thought I'd better call you. I was sure you'd want to know." Mrs. Grayson's voice became soft, motherly.

"Yes, we do want to know. I appreciate your calling." Liz felt a semblance of control returning. She needed to tell the others. "Do you know if the police have contacted David's parents yet?"

"I don't know. I'm sure they will. I haven't called them yet. Probably better if you did. I only met his mother a couple of times."

Sadness showed in Mrs. Grayson voice. "Let me give you my number if I can help in any way. We're a small complex, here and we love... loved David."

"Sure. No, actually we have your number; David had given it to us." Liz remembered. "Thank you. Thank you for calling, Mrs. Grayson. I'll call his parents in a few minutes. I agree it would be better if they heard it from us. In fact, one of us should go over there. They live just south of here, in Torrance." Liz thought aloud.

"I'll let you go. I'm sure you'll want to talk to the others there."

"Yes. I need to do that. And, uh, Mrs. Grayson, thank you for telling us." Liz hung up her phone.

Sadness swept over her again. Unable to move, her elbows on her desk, her face in her hands, she started to cry. Two of her friends were dead. Two people she loved. She loved her mother deeply, but her senility had disabled her from loving Liz in return. Her office co-workers had become her family. They spent a lot of time together, and Liz was the person who provided the glue, the support that held them together.

Larry walked in, looking tired from the weekend, but had a positive air about him, probably from his successful anniversary party.

"Good morning Liz. It was a great party. I..." Larry spoke, but quickly realized something was wrong, as Liz, with tears in her eyes, looked up at him.

He laid his brief case beside her desk, walked around it to her. She rose from her chair, and laid her hands and head on his chest. He embraced her. Tears started to well in his eyes, even though he did not know what was wrong. He just knew that someone he cared for was hurting. He wanted to comfort her.

"David was killed last night." She sobbed the words, tears flowing.

Still holding her, Larry held his head back to face her, not comprehending, or perhaps emotionally denying, what she had said. "David was killed last night." Liz repeated, understanding the shock.

"No, no. What? How?" Larry's mind filled with disbelief, questions, shock.

"I just got off the phone with Mrs. Grayson... from David's condo complex. She said David was killed last night. It was horrible. Someone had gone into his unit, and killed him. Mrs. Grayson said they must have fought, the place was wrecked." Liz regained some composure, grief still filling her voice.

"My god. David's dead. On top of Greg's death last week. I... I just can't believe it..." Larry stuttered, unable to wrap his mind around this news. "Let's step inside my office."

Soon other admin people and secretaries would arrive. With his arm around her, he guided her into his office. He pulled a chair from the small conference table for her to sit. He sat in the next chair, facing her. He held her hands, trying to comfort her, needing comfort himself.

"What all did Mrs. Grayson tell you? This is so shocking. I don't know what to do, what to think." Larry was unable to believe what he had just heard.

"She said the police had arrived about eight-thirty in the evening, and were knocking on David's door. She saw them from her window and after a minute, went outside to ask them if anything was wrong. David had told me before that she was sort of the mother hen of the complex. The police said they were responding to a 911 call." Liz tried to smile as she recounted what Mrs. Grayson had told her. She wiped tears from her eyes.

Larry nodded his head, but could say little.

"David didn't answer his door. Mrs. Grayson has duplicate keys for just about everyone in the complex. She retrieved David's and opened his door. The police went inside and discovered the body. They wouldn't let Mrs. Grayson inside so she didn't see much, just the furniture tossed around, and David's body slumped against a wall. The police called the situation into the station, and cordoned the front entrance with that yellow police tape. Police technicians were there until three this morning."

"Has anyone called David's parents?" Larry asked.

"I told Mrs. Grayson that I'd call them. I think it'd be better they heard from one of us."

"I agree. One of us should. I know the police will tell them officially. They try to notify relatives within a reasonable time." Larry thought aloud.

"Maybe one of us should be with them? David was their only son. I bet their anguish will be unbearable. I'll talk with them first. David was like my little brother. He was such a sweet young man." Liz would summon the strength she needed for this difficult task.

"Liz, you've been through enough. I can handle this."

"No. I need to do this. I don't know where I'll get the strength. But I need to do this." Liz insisted.

"I understand. I'll take care of the rest of the staff. I think it will help, your contacting his parents." Larry felt numb. He appreciated Liz's strength. Then he felt a surge of responsibility. "First, I'll call Erica. She and Brian need to come up here. Let's tell them, then I'll tell the others."

Larry called Erica. He and Liz comforted each other while they waited. A light knock on the door, Erica and Brian stood there, immediately sensing the emotional heaviness in the room. They saw the sadness in Larry's eyes, the tears in Liz's. Erica bent over Liz and put an arm around her, and felt near tears herself. Brian closed the door. Larry asked them both to sit in the two remaining chairs around the conference table.

"We just received some very sad news. On top of the news of Greg's death last week...." Larry spoke in an almost monotone voice. Disbelief filled his voice as he spoke the difficult words. "We just learned that David was killed last night."

Erica started to cry. She had no questions; her grief was immediate. She wore her emotions as a chain around her neck, immediate, obvious. She always had a ready smile, an easy laugh. But now tears followed the sadness that overcame her. She covered her face with her hands, unable to hold back her tears. If she shielded her eyes, maybe the grief would go away, maybe what she just heard was not true. This time, Liz rose and put her arms around Erica, beginning to cry again herself.

Brian sat quietly. He too could not believe what he had heard. In the past week, he had gained a fondness and respect for David. He was a good kid. Brian felt a sense of loss sharing the sadness the other three showed. He and Erica listened as Larry and Liz re-told what they knew, what Mrs. Grayson had told Liz, and that the police would arrive this morning to ask their questions.

They sat there, talking quietly, absorbing the tragic news. They searched for words to comfort each other, to understand this tragedy, these events that had invaded their normal, quiet lives. They looked at each other, and tried to smile. They stared out the window. The views they often enjoyed, now felt empty, blank.

"Liz, Erica, if you two want some time to yourselves, you're welcome to take it." Larry broke the silence. "You're welcome to use Donna's office next door if you'd like. Brian and I need to talk."

"Yes, I think that'd be a good idea." Liz took a deep breath. Her tears subsided somewhat. Then, to Erica, she asked, "Would you like to join me? I think we both could use a quiet moment to absorb this."

"In a few minutes, Liz, would you notify the rest of the department to meet in the accounting conference room? So we can tell them." Larry asked. "After telling everyone about Greg's death last week, this is going to be especially hard."

"Sure." Liz nodded.

Erica mouthed *thank you* between her sobs. She and David were nearly the same age and they had become close friends. She had confided in him many times. Losing him, she truly lost a brother. She and Liz rose to leave.

This morning, even though Larry was tired, he had felt good. His anniversary party was a success. Old friends visited, laughed, talked. His emotional roller coaster life had reached a high point after last week's crash. But this morning, it had crashed again. His world had turned upside down. He felt a deep personal pain, grief beyond words. Greg's death was painful, but somehow, in the back of his mind, he rationalized his death as some horrible accident. He knew differently, but... But now his grief had sunk to some immeasurable depth. David was gone too. This just cannot be, he insisted to himself.

"Larry, would you like some time alone as well?" Brian offered, understanding the grief that his friend must feel.

"Later, later." Larry wiped away the tears that had gathered in his eyes. "There are things we have to do." A wave of anger swept over him. Someone had invaded their lives. "We have to solve this embezzlement. And someone has killed two of my family. On some level I just want to go into a dark room and block out all that's happened this past week. I know it sounds clichéd, but those two boys were the sons I never had."

"I understand." Brian wished he could say more to comfort his friend.

"Two of my people are dead, murdered. Both Greg's and David's deaths are related. I just know it. And, there's the real possibility that others in this department could be in danger. You included." Larry began to pace in front of the window.

"And both, both deaths have to be related to this embezzlement. You could be at risk, too, Larry." Brian countered. "Everyone associated with this embezzlement could be at risk."

"God, this could mean that everyone in the department is at risk. I've got to tell Daniel so we can decide how to protect our people" Larry sat in his chair, and lifted the phone's receiver. Before dialing, he added, ""But first I need to call Detective Makelin. He may not even know about David's death, since it happened just last night, in another city. Brian, please stay so we can discuss what we'll do next. Then I need to meet with my staff."

Larry pulled the detective's business card. Before he could press the numbers, his phone rang two quick rings, indicating an outside call.

Larry identified himself. The caller was Detective Argos, from the Santa Monica Police Department. In a somber tone, he asked to speak with David Frazer's supervisor.

"I'm David's supervisor, Larry Davis, head of General Accounting." Larry answered. Before the detective could respond, "Detective Argos, we were expecting your call. My assistant and I just learned a few minutes ago about David's death."

Larry recounted with the detective what Mrs. Grayson had told them.

"What can you tell us? We were shocked to hear the news." Larry had many questions.

"If you don't mind, I'll answer your questions when I come to your office. I need to ask you some questions regarding this case. I should be there in the hour." Detective Argos stated.

"Detective Argos, I need to tell you something. We had another member of our staff die last week. The LA County Sheriff's department is handling that case. They think it was a homicide as well. Our minds are reeling from both of these deaths. The Sheriff's investigator is Detective Wesley Makelin. Do you want his number?"

"Yes. Definitely. I'll contact him before I come to your office. We'll work out the jurisdiction issues." Detective Argos' voice showed surprise, then a little empathy. "Oh, and Mr. Davis, I am sorry for your loss. It can be tough to lose a co-worker."

"Thank you." Larry still had Detective Makelin's card in his hand. He read the number for Detective Argos.

Next, he called Detective Makelin's cell number. He wanted to talk with him as soon as possible. Wes answered on the second ring.

Larry kicked into business mode, otherwise he would emotionally collapse and cry. He relayed the information about David's death. He relayed his conversation with Detective Argos from the Santa Monica Police Department, and that he had given Wes' number to him. Unfortunately, Larry had failed to ask for Detective Argos' phone number.

Wes expressed his sorrow about David's death. He had learned quickly that the department was a close-knit group. He said he knew Detective Argos, not well, but knew him, and would call him to coordinate their work. There was no need to cover the same ground twice. Wes added that he had planned to come to Santa Monica this morning, as well. He and Detective Argos would handle the jurisdiction issues. He would call Larry back with a time.

THIRTY FOUR

Monday morning, April 11
Santa Monica, California

Brian returned to his office on the eleventh floor. For privacy, he closed the door, leaving a small crack. He needed a few minutes to absorb what had happened to David. Naturally, he did not feel the sadness to the extent the others did, but definitely felt a loss. He liked David, a respectable, hard working young man, much like his son.

In nearly sixty years, Brian had experienced the deaths of a few people he loved, a couple close friends, and his father a few years ago. But, he had never experienced the murder of someone he knew. Like many people, he had read about murder in newspapers, or heard on the evening news. After all he lived in LA, one of the murder capitals of the nation.

He would miss David, not just his work, but their growing friendship.

He stared out the large office window. The view that had impressed him a week ago, now it appeared like an old picture post card. He saw it, but felt no sense of appreciation for it. David's death quashed that pleasant sense. Also, the work on the embezzlement for the last week had required so much of his time and attention that he thought of little else.

He shook his head to shake the cobwebs of sadness from his mind. He and David had worked many hours together. They had become a team, but as of today, part of that team was gone. Now, he would work alone.

After arranging the reports and files on the small conference table, he reviewed his action plan and searched for David's name in the *Responsibility* column. He felt odd drawing a line through David's name and writing his own over it. He knew Larry would help with some tasks, but computer analysis was Brian's strength. His sense of IT mastery returned. He stood taller, filled with purpose.

Brian logged into the computer system and saw that some of his reports were ready. He had worked yesterday from home after returning from Palm Springs. He had submitted more computer jobs, which should have processed overnight.

Brian sucked in a deep lungful of air to relieve the tension. Maybe coffee would help. He started for the break room when the phone rang.

"Brian? This is Dean, downstairs in IT."

"Yeah. Hi Dean. How are you?"

"Good. I assume you've heard about David."

"Yes. I was upstairs with Larry and Liz a few minutes ago. That was really sad news. I just can't believe someone killed him." Brian's voice was genuine. The reality behind the words bothered him.

"We just can't believe it down here either. It's all over the department, probably all over the company." Dean's voice contained a mixture of disbelief and sadness. "We really liked David. He was good man, and a good friend."

"I was very sorry to hear about it. The short time I knew David, I came to like him. He's a good kid." Brian wished he had not used the word kid, but the word was out. Changing it now would be awkward.

Brian hesitated switching the subject to business, but did. "I assume you're calling about giving me access to David's files."

"Yes. It's done. I was in my boss' office when Larry called." Dean wanted to hide his emotions about David's death. He also switched his voice to a business tone. "You can do just about anything David can do, err… could do, except change things. Like your last request, just access to read, not change."

"Thanks. Oh, Dean, before I let you go. Any ideas on how someone could have stolen the Security Administrator's password?"

"Not really. That would be hard for anyone to steal. Only Ralph and I have that kind of capability. And we change our passwords every month." Dean responded quickly. "Oh, there is another Administrator-like id and password locked in Rob Carter's safe. It hasn't been changed in a few months. And I haven't seen any use of that user-id in probably over a year. Locking the id and password in his safe is part of our backup plan. It'd only be used if something happened to Ralph or me."

"Is it possible that someone, someone smart, could have looked over your shoulder?" Brian asked.

"We're pretty careful about not letting anyone look over our shoulders while we work. But I suppose it would be possible. Normally, we do that administrator type stuff in our offices, down here. Rarely, do we use it while in someone else's office, where maybe someone could have a key-tracker on their computer."

"Ok. Thanks."

"Call me if you need anything else. I sure hope you find this guy." Dean's youthful eagerness had returned.

"Me, too. And thanks."

Neither man spoke about what both now knew that Brian was not merely auditing the systems.

Leaving for the break room, Brian saw that Erica had returned to her desk, her eyes puffy from crying. She blotted her eyes with tissue. Feeling concern for her, Brian stopped at her desk, and sat in the side chair.

"Erica, how are you doing? Is there anything I can do?"

"I'm okay, I think." She tried to smile.

"I'm so sorry about all this. David had told me that you and he were close friends."

"Yes, sometimes I think he was probably my best friend." Erica's sobs subsided. She spoke more freely, more evenly. "Except for a couple girl friends I have, I could always count on him. He helped me with projects at home. He even fixed a plumbing problem once when I couldn't really afford it."

"I wish there was something I could do to help. I've lost friends in the past and I know it can really hurt. I'm sure Larry wouldn't mind if you took some time off."

"He offered. He's sweet that way." Erica pulled another tissue from its box and wiped her eyes. "I may go home a little later. But for now I just want to be here. With my friends. Stay busy."

"I understand. Again, if there is anything I can do." Brian laid his hand on her arm. He wanted to give her a hug. But maybe he should not, proper office protocol and all. Instead, he squeezed her arm and gave her a fatherly smile.

"Thanks. Thanks. But I'll be alright."

"Can I get you some coffee, or a soda?" Lifting his coffee mug, Brian offered.

Erica pointed to her mug with a tea bag floating in it. "Thanks, but I already have some tea."

After Brian returned from the break room, he stood at his desk and sipped the coffee. He ordered his thoughts, rearranging the reports and files lying on the table. His mind began its work. He appreciated the good mind his parents had genetically given him. Again, he used his skill of holding several thoughts in his mind at one time. He could see relationships and patterns. He sat and wrote more notes on his legal pad.

Using the codes that Dean had given him, Brian logged into the system. First, he changed the password. Next he explored David's files. David had used a good system of file naming conventions, the sign of an organized individual. He reviewed David's e-mails, word processing memos, letters, and spreadsheet files. Thanks to prior experience with Bill Gates' Microsoft products, Brian would not have any technical issues with this work.

David had received more than two-dozen new e-mails. Many were from the nine companies in David's list, related to the embezzlement. Each e-mail contained amounts that the companies had received into their bank accounts. Brian would compare this information with the reports that he and David created from Leonard's files. The difference would likely be the embezzled amounts that went to the *unauthorized* accounts. Hopefully, the Sheriff's Department could act quickly to obtain a court order to identify the owners of those accounts.

Other e-mails were internal, requesting information from other Leonard staff. Art Dexter in Construction Projects had sent two e-mails. His answers were vague, or too general. Most respondents had answered David's requests with specific information. A few e-mails appeared personal, casual, meeting a friend for dinner, where is a good place to buy a bike, and the like.

David's e-mail files were clean, a good business practice. Too many people keep e-mails indefinitely, cluttering their files. Most companies developed policies to delete old e-mails, not only to save storage space, but for legal reasons. People often write very candid e-mails. Such information has, on occasion, been used against the company. Companies want their systems used for business purposes only. But, people being people, will use e-mails for personal use, often thinking they are private, which they are not.

Brian reviewed David's digital document files and found two folders that looked promising. One contained David's daily logs that related to the embezzlement project. The second folder contained spreadsheets of David's work. Pleased, Brian would not need to recreate these spreadsheets. He would add the new information from the e-mails.

David was organized. Thank you, David. Brian wished he was alive to thank him.

Eureka! Brian thought. The updated spreadsheets further confirmed what they suspected of the unauthorized accounts, and the dollars that went to those accounts over a two-year period. Maybe with the Sheriff's detectives, and a court order, they could identify the owner of those accounts. Meaning, the one who embezzled the money, and likely the one who killed Greg and David.

Brian heard a knock at the door, and lifted his head to see Larry walk into the room.

"Looks like you're really absorbed in your work." Larry said. "I stood there for just a moment, before I knocked."

"I am." Brian smiled. "And I have some good news. Let me show you."

"Great." Larry took the adjacent visitor chair.

Brian clicked the print button at the top of the screen. They waited a couple minutes for the pages to print.

"I called Dean about giving you access to David's files. Did he…"

"Yes. We talked a few minutes ago." Brian answered as he retrieved his print file.

"Oh, and I talked with Detective Makelin again. He said he and Detective Argos would be here just before noon." Larry said.

The laser printer finished its printer noises. Brian leaned toward it and removed the spreadsheets, set them on the table, in front of Larry. He scanned the information for a couple minutes.

"This is good information. Good work." Larry understood the information, and his face brightened.

"Yes. It is good. But, I wish David was here. He deserves a lot of the credit."

"David was a good young man. We're going to miss him." Then, Larry tapped the spreadsheet document. "This is good. It covers two years. Right?"

"Right. So far. Now that we know these accounts we can expand time periods and determine how long this has been going on." Brian continued. "I don't think the number of accounts will increase. Because monitoring several accounts would be a nightmare for anyone, including the embezzler. He already uses a pretty complicated scheme."

"Right. Right." Larry agreed. "I had planned to help you, but Daniel wants me to develop a plan to keep our employees safe. We've had two murders. I know that information is traveling like wildfire among the employees. We need to protect our people."

"That's okay, Larry. I can handle it. I'll keep you informed as I learn anything." Brian tried to reassure Larry. "The next big thing involves finding out who bypassed the security system. These spreadsheets tell what the culprit did, but not how, or who he is."

"Another concern, I understand the media has called different people in the company. Fortunately, most are good at referring them to our Public Relations Department. Daniel also wants me to work with Jesse Dietz. I think you met him. He's the head of our PR department. They cannot keep telling the media that they're working on a comment." Larry inhaled deeply, stretched, and rose to leave. "So, I'm going back upstairs. Brian, I have to depend on you for a lot of this. I know you can handle it."

"I will. Thanks for you confidence. I will get results." Brian leaned back in his chair.

"Can I keep this?" Larry gestured to the spreadsheet he held.

"Sure. I'll print another." Brian moved his mouse and clicked the left key of his mouse to print another spreadsheet.

Larry reached for the door handle. Liz knocked, entered, almost bumping into Larry.

"Oh, Larry, I'm sorry. And, I'm sorry for interrupting, but Jesse just called. Also, I needed to deliver some of these admin documents to Brian. Jesse said a TV reporter from Channel Six is downstairs. He would like you to join him, the sooner, the better. Carla has the media people waiting in the public room next to the lobby."

"Very well then. When it rains…" Larry did not finish the overworked metaphor.

"And if this isn't enough, law enforcement from two separate agencies will be here soon." Larry massaged his temple with his fingers. His head already ached. "Brian, it'll probably be very difficult for us to meet before the detectives arrive. Would you please have a summary ready for that meeting? Maybe I can scan it before they walk into my office."

"Sure, Larry. Including these spreadsheets?"

"Including the spreadsheets."

"I'll have them and a summary ready, with copies for all of us."

THIRTY FIVE

Monday morning, April 11
Santa Monica, California

"Hello, Carla. Remember me from last week?" Wes smiled and laid his hand on her desk counter in the Leonard building lobby.

"Hello, Detective Makelin. Yes, I certainly do remember you. Welcome." Carla responded, turning the visitor register for him to sign, and added, "Liz called a few minutes ago that you would be here this morning. Also, she said a Detective Argos would join you. You're the first to arrive. Do you want to wait for him, or would you rather go on upstairs?"

"He should be here any minute. I'll just wait for him, if that's all right?" Wes signed the register.

"Yes, certainly. I don't see Detective Hadley. Will she join you this morning?" Carla handed Wes a visitor's badge. Her voice more formal than usual, masking her grief for Greg and David.

"No, she had other obligations. I'm alone this time."

In his peripheral vision, Wes saw the giant glass lobby doors open and a barrel of a man in tan stepped inside. In his early fifties, he dressed casually, a large tan blazer, probably an attempt to hide a beer gut, beige button-down oxford shirt sans a tie, khaki slacks, and brown loafers. A Santa Monica police badge dangled from a military style neck chain. Detective Argos, no doubt.

233

When they had talked briefly on the phone a couple hours ago, their conversation focused on David's death and they agreed to meet at Leonard Construction to discuss the case further. Now Wes remembered the man. They had attended a criminal profiling seminar last year. Wes remembered him as pleasant, even jovial. They had planned to connect socially, but time, distance, and busy schedules worked against them.

"Detective Argos. Now I remember you." Wes offered his hand.

"Yeah. Same here. I thought I knew you from our phone conversation this morning." Argos grinned and shook Wes' hand vigorously.

"Good to see you again."

"Same here."

Wes gestured to Carla, as if to introduce her.

"Are you Detective Argos?" She asked.

"Yes, Yes, I am." He lifted his badge for her to read.

"Welcome. Would you please sign in?"

As Argos signed the Visitor's Register, Carla dialed Liz's number.

The detectives chatted briefly while they waited for Liz. They avoided discussing their cases until they settled into a private office. They wanted the privacy. Wes explained the company gave them a very plush office to use, small but plush. It would allow them to work quietly and in the background, a good setup for them as well as for the company. Employees would not see police presence any more than necessary.

The elevator doors opened with their usual chime and swoosh. Liz exited and approached the detectives. She recognized Wes, and presumed the newcomer, with a badge hanging from his neck, was Detective Argos. She had talked with him earlier about David's death. Liz maintained her polite demeanor, but grief clearly showed on her face. She led them to the elevators.

"I was very sorry to hear about David this morning. He was such a good young man. I only met him last week, but I could tell what kind of person he was. All of this must be very hard on you, and the others." Wes said softly as they rode the elevator to the Executive floor.

"Yes. To lose David and Greg, it's just unbearable." If she said more, she would cry.

Wes wanted to put his arm around her, to comfort her, but propriety forbade any such behavior on his part.

Changing the topic to business could help. Wes asked Liz if he and Argos could use the small conference room again for a while to update each other on the cases before meeting with Larry and the others. Certainly, they were welcome to use it. When they were ready, she would call the others as needed.

Before they entered the office side of the executive floor, she asked if either wanted coffee, soda, or use the restrooms. They started to decline, but then said yes.

"Liz, do you have to escort us each time? If we can help ourselves, then we wouldn't have to bother you. If that's all right?"

"Yes, you're welcome to help yourselves. I'll tell Ron, here, to buzz you in to give you access as you need it." She stepped near the security guard and spoke to him. He nodded yes. "Ron will buzz you in whenever you want."

"Thanks." Wes and Argos responded.

"If you don't mind, I'm going back to my desk, now. Just call me if you need anything." Liz forced a smile trying to hide the quiver in her chin. "Simply push the button next to my name on the phone."

"Will do. Thanks." Wes wanted to say more, but no adequate words came to him.

Wes acted as host to Argos. He poured coffee for the both of them, black, no cream, no sugar. Argos opened the refrigerator and scanned its contents. He selected a nutrition bar, read the back cover, and returned it to its box. It probably was not a good substitute for a candy bar.

When the detectives were ready, the security guard saw them approach the glass door, and buzzed the doors unlocked. Juggling his briefcase and a mug of coffee, Wes nodded to Liz as he pushed conference room door open with his shoulder. Inside, they sat in adjoining chairs.

"I know we talked on the phone, but I thought we could catch up on each other's case, just so we'd be on the same page. More than ever, I know they're related to this embezzlement." Wes opened his brief case and laid two brown binders with elastic ropes around them on the table, one folder much thicker than the other. "I know the cases are related. And I'm sure you will too, once you hear what I have to tell you."

"From what you've told me already, I'm sure I'll agree. So, go ahead." Argos nodded. "Do we start with the embezzlement?"

"Let me talk about where we became involved. Then I think the details of the embezzlement will make more sense."

"Sure."

"Initially, last Tuesday, we thought it was another car accident caused by heavy rain. A tragic accident, but a closed case. A car went over the side into a ravine on Topanga Road." Wes opened the larger brown binder, removed its contents, and positioned them for both to review. "We had some thoughts that it might have been a suicide, but have since learned that it was more likely a homicide."

Wes recounted the details of the accident, the interviews with the victim's family, and his colleagues at Leonard Construction. He explained that the employees at Leonard have been very cooperative. Except perhaps for the Legal guy, Stan Brothers.

Throughout telling his case, Wes pointed to the specific related documents. Argos was welcomed to review its contents and ask questions. The smaller folder contained overviews and copies for Argos' files. Since Argos asked few questions, Wes must have presented his case thoroughly.

Argos recounted the few details he had on the Frazer case, since only fourteen hours had passed since the killing. He also had two folders, both thin ones, one for Wes' files, and the other his. The contents included only the report from the policemen who answered the 911 call, a few pictures, and his report.

The reports from the forensics unit, results from the labs, and the autopsy report should be ready in a few days. Obviously, there was no question that the Frazer death was a homicide. Argos needed only fifteen minutes to describe his case.

For a few minutes, each detective familiarized himself with the other's case. They read the summaries, scanned the reports, the photographs, and searched for details that might tie the two cases together. They asked a few questions of each other. Naturally, Wes took less time for his review.

Wes sensed a slight confrontational attitude from Argos. He seemed different, more all business, and maybe more judgmental, than the jovial, friendly guy he remembered from the seminar. Wes chose to think of it as Argos' version of being a professional. Argos did have a lot of information to absorb.

"If I seem a too intense, or thorough, it's because my boss sometimes micro-manages my cases. I need to answer a lot of detailed questions. He's already given this case high priority. We don't have many homicides here. So, we'd like to clean up this case as soon as possible. Obviously, it's a much larger case than it at first seems." Argos smiled but spoke intently.

"Yes, we have a high priority on our homicide cases as well. But fortunately, my boss doesn't micro-manage, however, he does demand results." Wes understood Argos' position and tried to explain his own.

"I understand. But my boss has a strong sense of protectionism for our city. My first obligation is to him. I hope you understand."

"I do understand. I think you'll agree that these cases are related. I hope that we can cooperate effectively for both our jurisdictions." Wes leaned back, trying to insure that his body language was friendly, non-confrontational.

"We will. I'll make sure my boss understands that and cooperates." Argos smiled. His friendly persona had returned.

"I think as long as we cooperate and keep both our bosses informed; we'll be ok. And, of course, solving these cases quickly will help" Wes finished and turned back to the documents in front of them. "Now, the embezzlement."

Wes told Argos about the company investigating the embezzlement on their own. They had hired a computer forensics expert, a Brian Latimer.

The Sheriff's White Collar Crimes unit knew about Brian and would probably have hired him in the near future anyway. With agreement from the company, he will work with us, more specifically with the WCC unit.

Both victims were involved in the internal investigation of the embezzlement. One, Larkin, discovered the scheme, the other, Frazer, assisted in the research. Wes was convinced both deaths related to the embezzlement, even though the killer's methods differed in both cases. One involved drugs that caused a fatal accident; the other involved downright physical violence.

Wes also explained that the people involved with Greg Larkin genuinely felt hurt and saddened by his death. Learning that his death was probably related to the embezzlement frightened them for their own safety. Now with David Frazer's death, they will really become afraid.

Argos questioned that using Latimer might create a conflict of interest on his part. Wes reassured him that Debra Becken, head of the

WCC, micro-manages her cases. She will check his procedures and results very closely. Argos seemed satisfied with Wes' answer. He understood micro-management.

"Is there anything more that we need to discuss before we meet with these people? I'm sure they will resent answering the same questions multiple times. But I have to ask my own questions."

"Understood. And that'll be ok. I'm sure you'll find them cooperative." Wes reassured him. "My advice. Let's talk with Larry Davis first. Both our victims reported to him. You can see from my notes the organization of the people here. You'll probably want to talk with some of the same people we've talked with."

"I agree. In fact, I don't have a problem with our interviewing people together." Argos stated more than asked.

"Not a problem, I think we can complement our efforts. I'll call Liz." Wes swiveled his chair to the credenza behind him, and pressed Liz's call button. "Hi Liz. I believe we're ready to meet with the others. Could we start with Larry?"

"Very well. I'll tell him. Oh, Detective Makelin, Larry would like Brian Latimer to join in the meeting since he's closest to the details. Why don't I bring you to Larry's office, when he's ready?"

"Sure, that'll be fine. Thanks." Wes hung the receiver in its cradle.

THIRTY SIX

Monday morning, April 11
Santa Monica, California

Moments later, Liz brought the detectives into Larry's office. Brian and Larry stood as they entered. Wes introduced Detective Argos to the others. They sat around a small conference table in Larry's office.

"Thanks, Liz." Larry said. "On second thought why don't you join us? You're just as important as any of the rest of us. Uh… If that's alright with you detectives?"

"Not a problem." Wes deferred. They could meet privately with Larry another time.

She sat next to Brian.

"I want you to know how sorry we are about David's death. In this past week, I've come to appreciate what a close-knit group you are." Wes looked at those in the room, his voice genuine. "Coupled with Greg's death, this has to be especially hard on you. I know our being here seems like an imposition. But we have to solve these cases. I hope you understand. Detective Argos, here, needs to ask you some questions, and can probably answer some of your questions. We think the cases are related, that's why we're both here."

"Thank you. We understand you have your jobs to do. I think we're all still in shock about David's death. We only heard about it a few hours ago. We haven't had enough time to absorb this... this situation." Larry drew a deep breath, bracing himself for the work ahead, but at the moment he felt only sadness, his mind felt numb. Almost to himself, he said, "If there ever is enough time to absorb something like this."

Detective Argos sat forward in his chair. He looked from Larry to Liz, to Brian, and back trying to read their body language, facial expressions. He switched from his earlier confrontational, all-business attitude to a genuine, sympathetic one. Wes might have to rethink his opinion of him. Maybe, through experience, Argos adapted to the situation it demanded. Of course, it begs the question of which persona is his real one.

"This has to be tough on you. I'm very sorry. I wish there was some way we could help. But as Detective Makelin said we want to solve these cases as quickly as possible." Argos returned to his all-business persona.

A knock at the door. It opened, and Stan Brothers walked into the room.

"Gentlemen." The newcomer nodded to Larry, and sat in the remaining empty chair.

"Detectives, this is Stan Brothers. He heads our Legal Staff." Larry introduced him and Detective Argos.

"Sorry to interrupt, but our CEO and I feel I should be present in these meetings. Hope you don't mind." He would still attend even if they minded.

"Not a problem." Wes responded, bothered, but knew he could not restrict legal reps from attending.

"First, I'd like to thank you for giving me a heads up about Mr. Larkin's death and giving me Detective Makelin's number." Argos leaned back in his chair. He wanted to establish a rapport with them. "After talking with you, I called Detective Makelin, here, so we could be on the same page. As you know we talked in the small conference room a couple doors down. His work will really help. And he tells me your people have been very cooperative."

"Detective Argos and I agree the cases are very likely connected. So we plan to work together with a minimum of overlap. Maybe we can solve them faster."

"Can you tell us anything about David? About how he died?" Liz looked directly at Detective Argos, her voice quivering.

"Yes. I suppose so." Argos spoke haltingly. Usually, he asked his questions, but helping ease their grief, could help. He would ask his questions later.

"Well, the dispatcher received a 911 call around eight pm, but the caller did not say anything. The dispatcher heard loud noises in the background, things breaking, people yelling. Nothing sounded like a television program. Then, the line went dead. Our standard procedures involve responding to these types of calls. Caller ID identified the address."

"A Mrs. Grayson had a key and gave the police officers access. Naturally, they wouldn't allow her to go inside the condo once they saw the scene and determined it to be a crime scene. Of course she could see some of it from where she stood in the doorway before the officers closed the door and cordoned the area.

We couldn't tell her much, and unfortunately, we can't tell you much either. I hope you understand." Argos' sympathetic persona spoke for him.

Heads nodded they understood.

"I can tell you however, that David fought his attacker. Furniture was overturned, broken, scattered about the living room. Artwork knocked off walls. It was probably during the struggle that David tried to call 911. So we know the time of the attack." Argos paused a moment before the last word.

"How did he die?" Larry could barely ask the question that the others could only ask in their minds.

"The attacker used a knife. Multiple stab wounds." Argos hesitated but answered directly.

For a moment, the brutality of David's death again overcame them. Silence. No one could speak for a moment.

"I'm sorry. I'm so sorry." Liz sobbed the words. She raised her hands to her face, and cried. She rose from her chair, "I need a few minutes. Please excuse me."

Detective Argos started to speak, but did not. He respected the grief she obviously felt. He could ask her more questions later.

After a moment's pause, Argos turned to Brian and Larry to ask more questions. Standard police questions. Similar questions that Wes had asked about Greg Larkin. Did David have any enemies? Did they know of anyone who would want to hurt him? Where were they last night around eight? The responses were very similar.

241

Brian and Larry explained that they returned from Palm Springs last night. Brian around eight. Larry around ten. Neither could give the name of anyone who could collaborate the times since each was alone for the night. Brian did remember that he used his card-key for access to the parking garage. The system supposedly recorded the card number and the time. He would find the phone number of his building's security people and give it to the detectives.

Larry thought that his house security system kept a track record the codes entered to turn off and turn on the system. He would have to check with the company that provides the system.

Wes and Argos listened closely. The answers regarding David provided no new clues. Argos learned what Wes already knew. Like Greg, David had no known enemies. He led a clean life, no drug habits, or any negative behaviors that could lead to his death.

The methods of Greg's and David's deaths certainly differed. One was poisoned, usually a coward's way to kill. The other death was physical, violent. Could the same person have killed both men? Not likely.

Neither of the victims led dangerous lives. The profile of someone who uses poison to kill usually involved a quieter, peaceful appearing person. Someone who stabs his victim was usually confrontational, with flares of temper, and physically violent. Factor the embezzlement into the scenario; a third profile presented itself, an educated, professional type, such as an accountant, or a technology person.

The detectives strongly believed a connection existed among the three crimes. They did not believe in coincidence. Two or more people were involved, or the person was a complete psychotic.

"I know this is difficult for you. But can we discuss the embezzlement a little further?" Wes leaned forward and shifted his note pad, with his questions, in front of him. His voice became more intent. He guessed that he and Argos were alike after all. Each became what the situation required. "I understand you've had some progress in that investigation…"

A knock at the door interrupted everyone's attention.

"I'm sorry to interrupt, but Liz wasn't at her desk." Dean Horvath opened the door just enough to allow him to lean into the room. "Brian, you said you wanted to know about system accesses just as soon as I had it, before this meeting if possible."

"Larry, why don't you and I step outside for just a moment?" Brian looked to Larry and the detectives.

The detectives nodded their approval.

They excused themselves, stepped outside, and closed the door.

"What did you learn?" Brian asked.

"While I can't tell you who the person is, I can tell you that two different administrator passwords were created about two years ago, but became more active in the last three months. David had said that his results showed that's when the embezzlement activity began." Dean continued, "Somehow that person got the administrator password, created another userid, gave the same full access power as the primary administrator. In turn, he created two more userid's with full power. To try to eliminate the audit trail, he deleted the first userid."

Dean used mostly technical jargon. But Brian understood and nodded as Dean talked. Larry smiled as he watched the two animated technical geeks talk in an almost foreign language, sprinkled with occasional words of English.

"Freeze that userid." Brian directed. "He probably already knows we're investigating the situation. We don't want him returning to the system to delete any tracks he might have left."

"Ok. I'll do that now. That's why I interrupted the meeting. I didn't know whether you wanted me to freeze the access or allow it to continue, and monitor his activity." Dean explained. "We can reload the history files for the last five years if you like. Those files are offsite. We can have them here in two hours. We'll load them into the system as soon as they get here. When you're ready, we can run job queries to identify every situation where that userid was used."

"And we can relate those situations to specific embezzlement activity that we've identified so far. Scan security files. Scan accounting files. I'm sure this meeting will finish in a few minutes." Brian felt excited. This was good progress.

"Will do." Dean shared Brian's excitement.

"Any thing else?"

"That's it for now."

"Thanks. You did good work Dean." Brian turned to Larry, "We're closer to identifying the person or persons who defeated the security system."

"Maybe you can explain a little further, later. In English." Larry teased.

"Sure. Be glad to. Shall we go back in?" Brian grinned and opened the door to the conference room. He liked seeing the brief lift from depression in his friend.

"Anything we should know about?" Wes asked not wanting to let any information bypass him.

"Yes. All of it. But first I think I need to tell you the results of the weekend's research so far, for background. I'll include these new details where they fit. If that's ok?" Brian took charge of the meeting.

"Sure."

Brian summarized from the beginning of the investigation for Argos' benefit. He updated everyone with the results of the last few days, and what Dean had just told him. He spoke in laymen's terms, and struggled not to sound like a technical auditor presenting a technical report. He expanded on his explanations if he saw confusion on someone's face. Brian's skills included a talent for presentation as well as analysis and computer forensics.

Brian handed copies of the spreadsheet he had showed Larry earlier. Brian pointed to the affected accounts on the spreadsheet. Another column listed the related bank account numbers. They could easily see the large dollar amounts involved. Brian asked Wes if his people, Debra specifically, could get search warrants on those accounts.

Wes pulled the spreadsheet closer to him so he could check those accounts against the list he had been given a few days ago. Some information was new, especially larger dollar amounts. He said he would call Debra. Maybe Brian could e-mail the numbers to her. Brian said no problem. With this information, Debra could probably have results by tomorrow.

Brian, in a softer voice, told them that David's work has been key to achieving these results. He added that although he had only known David for a week, he had come to like and appreciate him. He would miss David.

Liz returned, and quietly stepped into the room. She had used the empty nearby conference room for some quiet time. Her eyes were puffy from crying, but otherwise she appeared composed. She approached Larry and whispered in his ear.

"Excuse me, detectives." Larry sat upright in his chair. "Are we at a point where I can excuse myself for a few minutes?"

"We can meet more later if needed." Wes looked to Argos for agreement.

"Thanks. Liz just informed me that two different TV reporters and their cameramen are downstairs. Jesse Dietz, our Public Relations Department needs to talk with them, and wants Stan and me to join him downstairs." Larry and Stan both rose to leave the room.

Looking directly at the detectives, Larry added, "I'm sure Brian can answer most of your questions, anyway. We'll finish the media situation as quickly as we can, and I'll call you."

Larry and Stan left the room. Liz followed. They chatted briefly in the executive floor lobby; then Liz turned to go to her desk, while the other two went to the elevators.

"Reporters. I hate dealing with reporters." Argos said as if speaking to friends. His friendly demeanor had returned.

"Reporters can be annoying, but sometimes they provide interesting information." Brian rested his elbows on his chair arms and clasped his hands in his lap. "I want to review more of David's work, and develop more specific conclusions. Dean, the IT guy you just saw, should have more information for me within a few hours."

Brian realized he sat alone with the detectives. He worried a little that no company people, or legal people were present. He preferred their involvement, just to be sure. After all, they were technically his employer. Meanwhile, he would conduct himself as professionally as he could. He would tell Larry later about any final comments.

"Brian thanks again for your help. I think we're finished here for now." Wes looked to Argos for agreement.

"I'm ok." Argos shrugged his shoulders.

"You're welcome." Brian rose from his chair.

"Could I have your number, please? I'm sure I'll have more questions later." Argos asked.

"Sure." Brian wrote the number he used at Leonard on the back of his personal business card, and gave it to Argos.

"Next, I'd like to talk with this Art Dexter and Chas Erickson." Argos stored his notepad in his briefcase.

"I thought they would be next on your list." Wes grinned and stuffed his folders into his briefcase. "I have a few more questions for them too, especially Art."

THIRTY SEVEN

Monday Afternoon, April 11
Santa Monica, California

Jesse Dietz, Leonard's PR Director and his assistant Patricia O'Connell waited in the elevator area for Larry and Stan. Larry motioned for Liz to join them. Patricia gave the newcomers copies of Jesse's prepared statement.

Jesse stood tall, his back straight, an inch under six feet. Every day, he wore a dark blue, or pinstripe suit, with a bright, but sophisticated tie, usually red or green and a matching kerchief tucked in the breast pocket. When outside his office, he always wore the jacket. Image and public presence were always important. In his early fifties, he looked forty.

Patricia his assistant, and feminine counterpart, wore a dark suit jacket and skirt. And she wore a robin's egg silk blouse that fastened around her neck. She had ambitions to become head of a Public Relations Department, someday, somewhere.

Liz and Patricia stood close and listened for any instructions as their bosses discussed the prepared statement.

"I really wish we had more time to think about this and discuss it together before we met with the media." Larry said as he finished reading the statement. "Actually, I wish we didn't have to meet with the media at all."

"That's kinda what we're doing now." Jesse responded with a bit of sarcasm, and ignored the second half of his statement. "I spoke with Daniel about this. He's also agreeable. I plan to keep close to the script. Either of you is welcome to speak."

"Larry, at least you should say something. It'll give us a solid front." Stan added as he scanned the release. "I don't see any problems here. There's no comment about the embezzlement. I agree that we keep it quiet for as long as we can."

"I don't know how long we'll be able to do that. I'm certain this news is spreading like wildfire among the employees." Larry added. "Besides, the police and, I'm sure, a few others know about it."

"After this media interview, we need to get a statement on our internal website as soon as we can. Both about the deaths and the embezzlement. For our employees." Jesse advised. "Are we in agreement on this statement?" Jesse asked.

"Ok with me." Stan replied.

"Same here." Larry agreed.

In the lobby, Carla asked the reporters to sign the visitor' register, but she did not give them badges. Jesse had directed her to ask them to sign the register and to wait in the lobby's public room across from her desk. He wanted a list of who actually attended the news conference. After they signed the register, including the cameramen, she asked the security guard standing to escort them to the public room. He complied, and escorted them with their equipment. She also whispered to the guard for them to move their vans from the circle drive, preferably around the back of the building. The circle drive was a fire lane. Actually they wanted the vans out of site from public view.

Leonard Corp designed the lobby conference room to impress visitors, while retaining multi-purpose function. The dark granite floor tiles in the lobby continued into the room. Enlarged photos of Leonard Construction work sites around the world hung on the walls. The chairs were padded, comfortable, but inexpensive. The room could easily hold an audience of thirty people.

The room's purpose was to house people who would otherwise congest the lobby, or people the company just did not want in easy view. Impressive, but spartan compared to the luxurious main presentation room on the floor above.

Although chairs were available, no one sat. The media crew chatted quietly while waiting for the Leonard group to arrive.

Shortly, the Leonard group entered the meeting room. Jesse raised his hand, smiled, and asked the reporters to hold their questions until he delivered his prepared statement. He stepped onto the small stage at the front of the room.

The cameramen hoisted their bulky cameras onto their shoulders.

"First, I'd like to introduce myself. I'm Jesse Dietz, the Public Relations VP, here at Leonard. On my left here is Larry Davis, our Executive VP over Accounting. On my right is Stan Brothers, our Chief Legal Counsel. To his left..." He nodded to Patricia and Liz. "Are Patricia O'Connell, my assistant, and Liz Bowden, Larry's chief Administrative Assistant."

Jesse spoke formally, but with a friendly tone, his voice engaging. He used his public speaking voice even though the group was small. He possessed obvious above average speaking skills.

"The news of David Frazer's death has saddened all of us here at Leonard." Jesse spoke virtually word-for-word from his statement with frequent eye contact with the reporters. "Especially when coupled with the loss of another member of the accounting department, our friend and colleague, Greg Larkin, who was killed in a car accident going over Topanga Canyon Road..."

"Wasn't that also a homicide?" An over-eager female reporter interrupted.

Without losing a beat, Jesse looked her in the eye and answered, "The Sheriff's Department is investigating that. You'd probably be better off asking them that question. We don't want to state anything that might be wrong or in conflict with their work."

Jesse smiled at her and continued speaking. "We here at Leonard feel a terrific sense of loss for these two employees, these two members of our corporate family. Leonard will cooperate fully with the law enforcement agencies."

"Two homicides in the same department, or rather one homicide and one questionable death. What's happening at Leonard that could contribute to this? Something that Leonard doesn't want the public to know?" A second reporter asked. Cameras still rolled. "Surely you don't believe they are a coincidence."

"We are concerned. Very concerned. But we don't see any connection between the two deaths. As I said, we want to allow law enforcement to do their work, and we will help where we can. But until they find results, we must not jump to unfounded conclusions. We ask you to do the same. We don't want to say anything that that would impede their investigation, or start rumors." Jesse remained unflustered. He had experienced confrontational reporters in the past. He would not let them frustrate him now.

Stan stepped forward and laid a hand on Jesse's shoulder. "Leonard Construction has not experienced any problems beyond what companies its size experience. Our records clearly indicate that we're in good shape as a company. We project a good future, and our employees are satisfied."

"What about the safety of other employees in the company? Are they at risk?" The first reporter asked.

"We don't believe anyone in the company is at risk. However, we will still take precautions, such as increased security. Daniel Post, our CEO, Larry, Stan, and I..." Jesse nodded to Larry and Stan. "We will address that issue this afternoon and post that information on our internal website for our people."

It was Larry's turn to comment. He leaned toward the mike. "You must remember that we, here, have lost not only two employees, but have lost two very good friends. We need to grieve... We are grieving through this... People in my department are devastated. It will be awhile before we can resume a business-as-usual operation."

Jesse appreciated the other's comments; it gave a united front to the reporters. Perhaps even gained a sympathy vote.

"I can assure you, we will do all we can to insure the safety of our employees." Jesse answered.

"What can you tell us about David Frazer? Was he married? Children?"

"No. David was not married and had no children. David is from this area. He grew up in the LA area. Earned his degree from UCLA."

"What about his parents?"

"I'm sorry, but we really can't tell you more about him. We want to protect his family's privacy. Please respect this wish. Next question."

"Greg Larkin. Could we have some information on him?"

"Greg graduated from Cal Poly in San Luis Obispo. He had worked here at Leonard for just over six years. Again, we want to protect his family's privacy. We hope you will understand."

Jesse was accustomed to answering questions quickly. He rarely had an afterthought of wishing he had answered differently. His answers appeared spontaneous, but had a prepared quality. He almost never stuttered, or at a loss for words.

The reporters asked more questions. Jesse answered most, but deferred a few to Larry, or Stan. As the questions subsided, Jesse asked that if they had additional questions, to contact his office. He nodded to Patricia to give business cards to each of them. He further requested that they respect the privacy of Greg's and David's families.

After the interview, the cameramen turned off their cameras. One of them noticed Detective Argos and another man at the receptionist's desk. He nudged his reporter counterpart, nodded toward the receptionist, and whispered that the detective from last night's murder in Santa Monica was standing there. The others overheard. As a group, they rushed into the lobby.

Larry and Jesse felt relieved, even a little abandoned, at the abrupt departure. Stan headed for the elevators. Larry worried that the detectives might tell about the embezzlement that he and Jesse had specifically avoided. Naturally that would arouse the suspicions of the reporters. And few people in life are more bothersome than suspicious reporters. They and their assistants waited on the sidelines in the lobby to listen to the encounter between the media and the detectives.

The detectives entered their departure time on the visitor log and gave Carla their badges. Fortunately, the detectives provided little information to the reporters' questions. They only identified themselves, said something about their departments working together, and would comment further when they learned more. The detectives left the lobby, and returned to their cars.

Erica waited nervously at Liz's desk when she and Larry returned. She was biting her nails, her common nervous habit. She was obviously stressed. She had regained most of her composure from earlier, but her eyes were puffy.

"Liz, Larry, I'm really sorry to bother you. But the news about David's death has really spread through the company. Several people have come by my office to offer their condolences, and to talk. They're really saddened by David's death, and by Greg's. But a lot of people are really concerned about their own safety. Most had thought that Greg's death was an accident. But now, with Greg and David gone.

Some of us are really worried, even scared. I'd said I'd come up here and talk with you."

"Why don't we go in here to talk.?" Larry touched Erica's elbow and gently guided her into his office. "Liz, if you would, please join us."

"Larry, just as you asked, I've been very careful to not tell anyone about the police's visits, or even that Brian is here on this embezzlement project." Erica's face was filled with worry. She did not want Larry to think she had been disloyal to his instructions.

"Erica, please don't worry. I completely trust you. I know you're very loyal to me, and to this department. This kind of information cannot be kept quiet. Especially in light of what's happened in the past week. I want you both to know that Jesse and I are meeting with Daniel in a few minutes. Jesse and I will have a statement, a plan ready for Daniel. We'll address the safety concerns of everybody. We'll post it to the company website by late afternoon. You can tell anyone who asks, to read it before they leave work. We'll also send emails to all employees to visit our website. Does that sound ok?" Larry tried to comfort her.

"Yes. Yes, I'll do that. Thanks, Larry. Thanks, Liz." Erica turned to leave.

THIRTY EIGHT

Monday Evening, April 11
Manhattan Beach, California

The alpha male and his partner had agreed to meet at Greely's, a small sports bar located in Manhattan Beach. This area, a long, uphill block from the beach, had little street parking, free but limited to one hour, assuming a driver could find a space. To enforce the parking rules, a meter maid rode a small golf cart, and marked each car's back tire with a chalk stick. They followed their tedious routes every hour and wrote tickets for people who overstayed the limit.

To alleviate the parking problem, the city built a small two level parking structure on one corner. The structure was one block from Greely's. The alpha male parked in the last space available. He plugged two dollars worth of quarters into the meter for the two-hour limit. He wanted plenty of time to talk with his partner. A ticket would create a paper trail, and he wanted these meetings untraceable.

He crossed the busy intersection, and walked the few storefronts to Greely's. He was not likely to encounter anyone he knew.

He had to regain control over his so-called partner. This partner had acted without consulting him, creating a problem, a big one. His anger toward his partner had escalated in the last twelve hours. He must control his own anger first. Then, he would reestablish control over his associate. In the beginning his associate cooperated, behaved as told. Now, he acted on his own, far too rashly, and out-of-control. He had to be brought back under control.

The alpha male entered Greely's through its glass and wood doors. Like many small sports bars in LA, a few small tables sat in the center of the dining room. Booths flanked the walls. Televisions, one or two mounted on each wall, gave patrons a view from nearly any seat in the place. A different game played on each TV. Weathered, plank boards covered the walls and floors, with a thin layer of sawdust and peanut shells scattered on the floor. LA bars must have a fetish for plank wood. Photos of popular athletes and past sporting events filled the wall space among the televisions.

Unlike many LA sports bars, Greely's had opened its doors more than thirty years ago, giving it an authenticity that the others struggled to replicate. Along one wall, six stools faced a combination bar-kitchen area. Greely's served a limited menu of comfort food. Generous sized portions of hamburgers, pork sandwiches, fries, and onion rings. They served mixed drinks, and of course, beer, by the mug, or the pitcher, mostly domestic. A few of the trendy, micro-brews were available.

The partner sat in the rear of the room, in the last booth along the wall, predictable. A nearly full, frosted mug of beer sat in front of him, so he had not waited long unless this was a second beer. He faced the front, which forced the alpha male to sit with his back to the room. No worry. He would still control the situation. The alpha male preferred sitting against a back wall facing the room. This position allowed him to watch people enter and leave. Knowing the activities around him added to his sense of control.

"Hello…" He spoke calmly and did not use his associate's name. He sat in the padded booth.

"Hello." The partner greeted with a slight nod of his head. "Before you start, I know you're upset about the way things went. That they didn't go as planned."

"Eliminating him was not part of any plan." He clenched and released his fists in an effort to release the tension he felt. No small talk in this conversation. "I really hope you have good reasons for doing what you did."

"We had decided to eliminate the one guy…"

"We had decided to plan, to talk about eliminating the one guy." The alpha felt his anger rising again. No, he would control himself.

More calmly, he said, "Just to plan and talk about the job, before we actually did anything."

"I know."

"Yeah, you know. But…"

"Now wait, hear me out." The partner held up his hand to stop him.

The alpha male clenched his fist and wanted to strike him, hard.

The waitress approached them, after taking an order at a nearby table. The alpha man took in a deep breath and ordered a draught beer, keeping the atmosphere ordinary. She asked if they wanted food. Both men declined, almost unfriendly at the interruption. She left.

"Listen, I talked with him a couple of times. I learned that he knew more than anyone else, including the cops, about what was going on. So, I decided a change in plans was necessary, and needed to do something quick. By eliminating him, the investigation would lose its primary source of information. Simple as that."

"But we still should have talked before you did anything." The alpha shook his head in frustration. This would not be an easy conversation.

"We had talked about eliminating the obstacles, and I said I could take care of things." He talked slowly, emphatically, and gulped more beer from his mug. The frost on the mug had melted and saturated the coaster. "I just didn't figure he could be as difficult a he was."

"Do you realize the problems you've created?

"I don't see the problems." He wore a smug expression on his face. "Besides, both events happened in different cities, different law enforcement departments. Can you imagine the jurisdictional nightmares they will have?"

"Do you really think they won't talk to each other? They share a lot of the same technical experts. Do you think you can outsmart those technical experts?" The alpha male could not believe the ignorant thinking his partner used.

The alpha took a breath. This guy was unbelievable. He continued, "I work my butt off to clean the audit trails and remove the transactions from the files and databases. And you shoot from the hip to fix the problem as you see it. Unbelievable."

"I don't agree." The partner shook his head, dismissively, defiantly.

"You do realize that it's not a big leap to connecting the deaths to our little joint venture?" The alpha man tried reasoning again. "If they haven't already."

No answer. Silence for a few moments.

"Don't worry. I didn't leave any prints. No fibers, nothing. I just don't see how they can trace anything to us." He continued his defense. "I made it look like a home invasion robbery that went bad. I took his wallet, and a couple small art pieces that looked expensive."

"But you killed him." *Such a simpleton. Why couldn't he see what a moron he worked with before now?* He shook his head in disbelief. "And what did you do with those items?"

"I have ways to get rid of them."

"How?"

Sensing the contempt, the partner slammed his mug on the table, a little too hard.

Nearby patrons halted their conversations mid-stream and looked at them. He grimaced with mock embarrassment, acting as if it was an accident. The others resumed their conversations, and watched the games on TV.

The alpha male calmed himself and tried reasoning again. "Our little project has netted us some good money. I'm sure you've bought some things, including your expensive car, and have had some fun experiences. But with all of the things that have happened, we have to stop. No choice. I have to clean up the records and modify the files so that the evidence points to someone else." He leaned on the table.

Was he pleading with his partner? He groped for the right words. He would rather just give orders and action-boy here would just do as he is told. *Where is fiefdom when you need it?* But tact was needed. He would treat him as a *respectable adult*, which of course he was not.

The waitress returned with the draught beer. He gave her a ten, and she counted his change. He laid two dollars on her tray for a tip, not too big so she would not likely remember him.

"It's true. I like the money. I like spending it. Not having it won't be any fun." Crossing his arms, the partner spoke more calmly and leaned back in his seat. "Would we be able to restart the venture, later?"

"That's just it. We need to clean up the current mess first. We need solutions." He liked seeing this new cooperation. "And solutions take time and thought." He controlled the conversation again. Against his desire, his treatment of his partner as a true partner worked. "We've got to control this situation again." *Amazing how effective words could be.*

They continued to talk, partner to partner. The alpha male tried explaining the technical details of computer systems, accounting, and security. The words went to the front door of his partner's ears, but could not enter. A little like vampires, they have to be invited in.

Tired of pretending he understood, the partner said, "Ok. Ok. I know this stuff is very technical. You can handle them better than me. Just how much time do you need? Is there anything I can do?"

"I'm not sure, probably a couple weeks. All of this attention has to go away. If we point the evidence toward someone else successfully, then we're home free. Or if the police cannot solve the crimes, they become cold cases. The police will then go on to new cases. LA has a very big crime quotient."

He continued, "As far as the company is concerned, if nothing new happens, they will lose interest, especially with a short staff. When everything is quiet, we can talk about a new venture. We just have to be careful for a while." He drew a deep breath and sat back in his seat. Maybe he had extracted an agreement from his partner after all. He began to relax.

Too soon. Another bombshell.

"What about eliminating this consultant guy?"

"What? You've got to be kidding." The alpha male asked, incredulous, trying to keep his voice low. There was no controlling this guy.

"No, no. We'd already talked about eliminating this consultant guy. Maybe, maybe, then we can get everything back under control." The associate gulped more of his beer. "You know that everything moves fast at the company. They're making a lot of money and everybody's too busy to miss small amounts. Or spend the time to research any missing money."

Control had fled the room again.

"And the police will still play dumb?" Sarcasm dripped from the alpha's voice. He could not believe what he had heard.

"The consultant lives in another city. More jurisdictional bureaucracy."

More stupidity.

"You can't be serious. The police are not that dumb. We don't have any idea how much they have learned already. And the company, they're wising up. That's why they hired this consultant in the first place. And the money, yes, they have plenty of money but not so much they would ignore the missing money. They will hire the resources they need to find the missing money. If for no other reason than to save the embarrassment. More importantly, two well-liked people are dead. That only makes *them* afraid and very angry. *Them* have very deep pockets, and *them* can do just about anything *them* wants."

He continued, "Besides, this consultant seems pretty sharp. I know he's accessing a lot of data, and running a lot of query programs. He knows a lot that the super-techies in IT know." He leaned forward and glared directly into his associate's eyes. "We just have to cool it. So don't do any more stupid shit."

"I don't do stupid. I get results. I think the obvious next thing to do is to eliminate this consultant. And I won't make any mistakes." Angry, the partner was in full defiance. His voice rose, but the bar noise was higher.

"Please, just wait. Give me some time to erase the digital trails. And point the blame to someone else. Just wait until we can plan our next step. Ok?" He turned up his palms. *Pleading again?*

"As I said; I don't do stupid. But I'll think about it. We can talk again in a couple days. That'll give you a chance to do your techie magic." He gulped the last of his beer, set the mug on the table, and left. "Later."

The alpha started to demand cooperation, but thought better of it. He watched his partner storm out of the bar, without looking back. He waited five minutes, set his half full mug of draught on the table, and left. He had to decide how he would fix this problem, his partner.

In the last hour, the booths and tables had filled with patrons. The noise level was high with loud, drunken voices and television volumes set on high. The TVs all now turned to one channel. He remembered that this was Monday, Monday night basketball. The game had started. Outside, a few people walked the sidewalks, looking in windows, entering and exiting other restaurants.

THIRTY NINE

Tuesday Night, April 12
Long Beach, California

Brian hated freeway traffic. But it was the price he paid to live in LA. Living somewhere else would require finding a job in *somewhere else*. And at his age, that would be almost impossible. Recruiters did not call as they did in the earlier years of his career. He wrote a good resume, filled it with good experience. He left out his age and some of his earlier work experience. Not to mislead, but the experience was more than a quarter of a century ago, and would not apply in today's computer environment.

He left Leonard Corp's offices early, six pm, and expected heavy traffic. Tonight, he had special plans to enjoy dinner with his son. He exited the 405 Freeway onto the 710 to downtown Long Beach. He shared this stretch of the 710 with dozens of trucks going to the Ports of Long Beach and Los Angeles where ships brought their massive loads of imports from the Pacific Rim to the United States, cars, clothes, plastics.

He dreaded this section of the 710. His Mustang seemed so David-like among these Goliath trucks. He liked the section where the trucks split away to the ports, and the freeway became Shoreline Drive, which swept around the south side of downtown Long Beach with its panoramic views of the hi-rise buildings, the convention center, and the marina. Day or night this short drive always lifted his spirits.

He was amazed that the Gran Prix organizers could remove blockades, fencing, and seating so quickly. Only tire rubber marks remained on the street where high speeding cars turned sharp corners in their races.

This time of year, darkness settled early, and the many lights in the hi-rises showed Long Beach at its best. This view was one of the reasons he liked living here. He could see some of this view from his condo, at least the hi-rises, but not the marina. However, he had an equally terrific view of the lights of Los Angeles.

After driving into The Spire's terrazzo portico, Brian circled to the underground garage. At its entrance, he pushed the transmitter button and waited the few seconds for the gate to open. Over the years, he had become accustomed to the narrow circular drive that descended to the parking floors. He drove slowly and watched for other moving cars and people.

Because his work was important to him, Brian worked long hours, especially on this embezzlement project. However, his son was far more important. As always, he looked forward to spending time with his son, Jimbo. Jimbo lived with his mother most of his growing-up years. Although she had custody, they both shared responsibility for him. Even now, Brian and his ex-wife were friendly, not close, but friendly. They both shared Jimbo's best interests.

During Jimbo's high school years, he seemed embarrassed about his father being gay. However, in college, he rediscovered his father and liked him.

Brian and his son had become close during the last few years. Part of that time, Jimbo lived with Brian to cut costs in his senior year at Long Beach State. They were crowded in the small condo, but got along most of the time. After graduation, Jimbo found a job, in Long Beach, to Brian's immense satisfaction.

Every couple of weeks, they met for dinner, a ball game at the nearby arena, or a movie at the theater complex downtown. Their favorite restaurant was a little Creole restaurant about a mile east on Ocean Boulevard.

He saw Jimbo's car in one of his two parking spaces Parking spaces were a premium luxury in urban, high-rise condos in most LA area cities, including Long Beach. Many of Brian's over two hundred fellow residents had only one parking space. He was fortunate, he had two. Visitors parked in one of only a dozen visitor spaces, or on the street. Guests attending residents' parties parked on the street. Some residents rented parking spaces from one of the nearby hotels.

Brian parked his Mustang and inserted his elevator key in the *call* box and pressed the button. He normally stopped at the main floor lobby to check his mailbox, but figured Jimbo had done that. The elevator stopped at the lobby anyway, and a few other residents joined him.

Riding the now crowded elevator, Brian felt a little hungry. He and Jimbo had agreed on Chinese carryout instead of going to a restaurant. They had bantered about who would pay, then dropped the topic. Like many parents, Brian felt the need to pay, even though his son probably earned as much, or more than he did, now.

Brian loved his son, more than he had ever loved anyone else. He may not have done his best to show it, but he felt it. Brian felt innately that providing food, clothes, and shelter was a primary responsibility of a father. He could not switch gears just because his son was now an adult. Another lifetime would have to pass before his parent mode would change, if then.

Knowing Jimbo waited inside, Brian felt a surge of pride as he inserted the key into the door lock. Hearing the door open, Jimbo pushed the TV's mute button, and greeted his Dad.

"Hello, there, Jimbo. It's good to see you." Brian laid his briefcase and jacket on the dining table and hugged his son.

Jimbo was short, five foot, six inches. He hated being short, but had adjusted, as long as no one talked about it. He had taken after his mother. He had her hazel eyes and dark brown hair, a full head of hair. But he had his father's square jaw. And he was bright, brighter than either of his parents. Seemingly with little effort, he maintained a four-point-o in high school and just under that in college.

"Hi Dad. It's good to see you, too. I hope you're hungry. I sure am." Jimmy stepped into the kitchen and opened the food bag. "I picked up some food from Wang's. I got you, your favorite, Kung Pao Chicken, and Mongolian beef for me."

"Sounds good. Let me give you some money." Brian reached into his pocket as he followed Jimbo into the kitchen.

"No, Dad. I make my own money now. I think I can afford some carryout food." Jimbo insisted, and changed the subject. "Oh, your mail is on the counter there. And a box from Amazon. I see you're still ordering books. What ones did you order?" Jimbo removed plates from the cabinets and set them next to the boxes of food.

"I don't remember ordering any. I must've just forgotten." Brian said, a little puzzled. He retrieved a knife from a drawer and handed it to Jimbo. "Here, you open it. I'll check my other mail."

Like his father, Jimbo liked books. He took the knife and slid it along the taped edges of the box. As soon as he cut the last tape, the flaps burst open, styrofoam peanuts overflowed from inside. Something moved. Something was alive.

An angry snake shot its head through the peanut styrofoam, and squirmed to free itself from its trap. Seeing the coiling snake, Jimbo's phobia of snakes billowed inside him. His heart pounded with fear. He jumped back, shoving the box away from himself. The angry snake slithered and squirmed out of its cardboard prison and onto the counter, falling into the sink.

Brian jumped out of the small kitchen into the entry hallway. He looked for something to kill the snake. The angry, writhing snake squirmed out of the sink, and fell onto the floor, trapping Jimbo in the closed end of the small galley kitchen. With nowhere to go, and overcome with fear, Jimbo tried to jump onto the counter, slipped, jumped again, slipped. Another reason being short sucked.

Still in attack mode, the snake sensed Jimbo's movement nearby and struck, two, three times. Jimbo screamed and tried again to jump onto the counter. He succeeded. But the snake had already bitten him.

Seeing the enraged snake strike at his son, Brian cursed it and grabbed a liquor bottle sitting on a small cart near the door. He threw it at the snake. The bottle shattered against the granite floor. The snake recoiled to strike again.

Sensing movement elsewhere, the snake turned, and headed toward Brian. He grabbed another bottle. This time, his aim was better. More shattering on the granite floor. The snake lay still, unmoving. Brain, still feeling the surge of adrenaline, pulled a large walking stick from an Asian umbrella jar. He beat the unmoving snake, repeatedly striking it until its head was flattened and bloody. He felt such fear, such anger that this animal, this thing would try to hurt his kid.

"Are you alright?" Trying to catch his breath, Brian jumped past the snake to Jimbo.

261

Jimbo started to say something. But his eyes rolled backwards in their sockets. He slumped and started to fall from the counter. Ignoring his fear of the dead snake, Brian moved to catch his son. He now knew that Jimbo had been bitten. He controlled his breathing, or his heart would burst in his chest. Brian helped his son to the couch in the living room. The fear and hatred of the snake immediately changed to fear for his son's life.

Brian laid Jimbo on the couch, and pushed his pant legs up, first the right leg, nothing, and then the left. He saw the two puncture marks bleeding slightly. Fear and numbness engulfed him. He must not let that happen. His parent mode switched into high gear. He would react to the event later. First, he must save his son.

He struggled to remember the treatments for snakebite. Earthquakes, employment were his life's worries, not snakebite. Tie a tourniquet above the bite, slit the bite mark, and suck the poison from it. Were those the steps? He would do what he remembered.

He remembered he had a rubber exercise piece that he had used after back surgery a few years ago. Actually it resembled a large, very wide rubber band. He would use it as a tourniquet. He found it in the lower right hand drawer of his dresser. Brian had a good practice of putting everything in its place. This practice helped him now.

He went to the kitchen for a knife. He grabbed the one on the counter that Jimmy had used to open the box. The snake lay in the same spot, still, with its bloody, smashed head. The liquor bottles, shattered, lying around the snake gave an overwhelming pungent smell of red wine and malt scotch. The walking stick lay broken beside the mess. Worry about his son's life replaced his fear of the snake, which now seemed so small, so unimportant.

Jimmy moaned. Brian told him to hang in there. Everything would be all right. Brian said soothing words to his little boy. Like most parents, he would make everything all right. But in the back of his mind, Brian worried, no feared he could not help. He shook his head. He would not think that way.

He tied the tourniquet. He slit the bite-marks. The blood oozed from the wound. He sucked the poison from the wound a few times and spit onto the carpet. He felt frantic, but kept his emotions under control.

Brian grabbed the phone, and dialed 911. He spoke clearly and deliberately to the dispatcher who said she would call the paramedics and notify the police. On TV news, 911 calls from frantic people required the dispatcher to calm them and answer obvious, annoying questions. Brian knew that an emotional, unclear call would delay the ambulance. Brian would maintain his control. Only later, would he allow his emotions to affect him. Right now, his son needed him.

Still in control mode, Brian called the security desk downstairs to tell them an ambulance would be there in a few minutes. A snake had bitten his son. The security man assured Brian that they would do everything to help. He would give the paramedics immediate access. He would over-ride the freight elevator and hold it for them.

He wiped his now groggy son's forehead, and remembered that an icepack on the bite mark could help slow the progression of the venom. He went to the kitchen, removed ice cubes from the freezer, stuffed them into a plastic bag, and wrapped it in a kitchen towel. He again saw, but ignored, the mangled snake and broken glass lying on the floor. He propped open the front door so the paramedics could notice it and enter when they arrived.

He heard the wail of an ambulance's siren. Living in the city, he often heard police and ambulance sirens. He hoped this one was the one coming to help. The sound grew louder as it approached. And shut off at its loudest. It had arrived.

The few moments seemed several minutes.

The intense fear of losing his son forced its way into Brian's mind again. He felt the grief, the intense worry return. He would not allow himself to think these thoughts now. He had to focus on his son's needs. By sheer will, he retook control of his mind. He spoke to his son, asked him questions to keep him alert and talking. He held the icepack with one hand and wiped the sweat from his son's forehead with his other hand.

When will the paramedics get up here?

FORTY

Tuesday night, April 12
Long Beach, California

The Condo security guard escorted the paramedics, carrying a gurney, to the freight elevator and used the over-ride key for a non-stop ride to Brian's floor. The guard led the paramedics directly to Brian's open door. The paramedics rushed inside, and immediately began their work. With few words, each performed his tasks swiftly.

The older paramedic with gray hair removed the icepack that Brian held to the wound. He unraveled a suction device and covered the bite marks with it. He turned on the suction machine and removed the tourniquet. Then, he put an oxygen mask on Jimbo's face.

The other paramedic wrapped an armband around Jimbo's upper arm, and checked his blood pressure. Then using a stethoscope, he checked the heartbeat.

The first paramedic pressed a button on his radiophone attached to his shoulder. He called Long Beach Memorial's emergency room to update them with the status and vitals, and ask for instructions. He pressed the mute button and asked Brian if he knew the kind of snake it was. Brian did not know, but could show him.

"It's pretty mangled. It's about two feet long. It's dark, almost black with a few darker stripes if you look closely." Brian tried to describe the snake as he led the paramedic to the kitchen. "It's definitely not a rattlesnake. We never heard it."

The paramedic followed Brian, and bent over to look closely at the dead snake. "A cottonmouth? I'm not sure what kind it is. They're certainly not native to this part of the country." He pulled a small smart phone from his pocket and snapped a picture of the snake. He transmitted the picture to the hospital as he resumed his conversation with the doctor in the emergency room. With Brian following, the older paramedic returned to Jimbo's side.

He relayed the information from the doctor to his partner, who opened another tray of the medical bag and selected a syringe and a small vial of clear liquid, anti-venom. After he rubbed a cotton swab saturated in alcohol on a spot on Jimbo's leg, he inserted the needle.

"Ok. Let's get you to the hospital. You're going to be fine. Your leg will swell to twice its size, and will feel very sore for a few days. You're not out of the woods yet, but you'll be fine." The gray haired paramedic said to a groggy Jimbo. He smiled and patted Jimbo on his head.

His partner adjusted the legs on the gurney for transport and pulled it beside Jimbo. Both, on the count of three, lifted him onto the gurney.

Brian stepped close and laid an affectionate hand on his son's head. He bent over and kissed his little boy's forehead. He felt so relieved, yet exhausted. So much had happened. His worry, his feverish work to save his son, the flow of adrenaline began to subside. Intense tiredness began to replace the worry.

"Mr. Latimer." The gray haired paramedic looked to Brian. "You're welcome to ride with him if you want."

"I want." As if he could be prevented.

"I suggest you bring his wallet, also the insurance information if it's handy. The technical stuff." He shrugged his shoulders on delivering the verbal fine print.

"Can do." Brian pulled the wallet out of his son's hip pocket, and easily found the insurance card. He slipped his son's class ring from his finger, and put it in his own pocket.

The security guard waited at the doorway, partly curious, partly concerned. The retired couple from next door stood with him. They had returned from an early dinner and asked if Brian was ok. The guard had told them about the snakebite, and added the little information he had overheard.

As the paramedics wheeled Jimbo to the front door, two Long Beach Policemen arrived. The shorter officer asked the security guard about what was happening. The guard gestured to the activity inside, and stepped aside. He told them that the older gentleman, Mr. Latimer owned the condo and had called 911 and the paramedics.

"Mr. Latimer?" The shorter officer approached Brain.

"Yes." Following the paramedics, Brian stopped to face them.

"Mr. Latimer, I'm Officer Crane. This is Officer Cruz. We'd like to ask you a few questions." The older of the two took a pad and pen from his pocket.

"Well, sure." Brian paused. Confusion spread across his face. Why were they here so quickly? Did he tell the dispatcher that someone sent the snake to him? "I don't know where the snake came from…"

"Wait, wait. We're here to investigate the snakebite, so can you tell us what happened? From the beginning" Officer Crane interrupted.

"My son was bitten by a poisonous snake." Brian wanted to get his son to the hospital. He did not have time to recount the whole story. "We have to get him to the hospital."

"I understand. But I need just a minute. Was it an accident, a pet, what?" Officer Crane insisted. "You know that it's illegal to own a poisonous snake in the city of Long Beach, don't you?"

"It was not a pet, it was not an accident. Someone sent that damn snake to me." His frustration with the officer began to rise. Realization that someone sent the snake to him, a deliberate attempt to kill him, invaded his mind.

The package was sent to him. During the crisis, he needed to help his son. He had forgotten the detail that someone had sent the package. As he thought about it, he felt more anger, more rage, that his son had been bitten. The sender tried to kill his son.

Coming out of a fog, Brian added, "I'll be damned. Someone sent that snake to me. Officer, someone tried to kill my son with that snake."

"The dispatcher informed us that a snake had bitten someone at this address. Naturally, we thought of the illegal nature of owning a poisonous snake."

"Someone sent it to me. Thinking it was a book that I'd ordered from Amazon, Jimbo, my son, opened the box and the snake jumped out of it. Nearly scared us to death. We tried get away from it. Then it bit Jimbo." Brian paused. Then almost thinking aloud, "My god, I think someone wanted to kill me."

"You received it in the mail?" Officer Crane now gave Brian his full attention. "Well, tell me what happened." He nodded for Brian to step aside with him and allow the paramedics to pass."

"I'm sorry, but I have to go with my son. You've got to understand. I'll answer any questions later." Brian pleaded. "Please, let me go with him to the hospital."

"We really need to get this guy to the hospital, Long Beach Memorial." The paramedic interrupted. To help Brian, he added, "His father should come along."

"Ok. I understand. But we need to secure this as a crime scene." The officer looked to Brian and the paramedics.

"Thank you, officer." Brian sensed relief. His son came first. "You're welcome to look around all you want. You can see the dead snake on the floor. And the package it came in is on the counter there." Brian pointed to the cardboard package.

"You say you're taking him to Long Beach Memorial?"

"Right."

As they passed the security guard and the retired couple expressed their genuine concern to Brian. They asked if there was anything they could do. Brian thanked them. But there was nothing they could do.

Officer Crane called his station for a detective, and the forensics unit. He stood guard at the door, smelling the unpleasant aromas of Kung Pao chicken and splattered red wine and scotch. Officer Cruz went to the car for yellow crime scene tape.

As Brian's worry subsided, he thought more about someone sending the package to him. He knew it had to relate to what was happening at Leonard. Greg's and David's deaths. He would call Larry and Detective Makelin later.

FORTY ONE

Tuesday night, April 12
Long Beach, California

The paramedics loaded Jimbo into the ambulance and locked the gurney into place. Brian sat next to the paramedic monitoring Jimbo. After everyone strapped themselves in their seats, the driver turned on the siren, maneuvered through the fencing left from the weekend's Gran Prix race, onto Ocean Boulevard and raced, sirens blaring, nearly non-stop to Long Beach Memorial. After fifteen minutes, the driver squealed to a stop at the Emergency Room entrance.

Before the paramedics could unlock the back door, two ER staff joined them.

The paramedic monitoring Jimbo's vitals stored his equipment in the van's cabinets, and released the braces that held the gurney in place. The double glass doors to the ER opened with a swooshing sound while another nurse in scrubs and a flowing smock rushed to help them. Brian tried to stay close, to hold his son's hand. The nurse in the smock took charge, giving instructions to the other nurses and paramedics as they rolled Jimbo into the ER.

"You'll have to let us take over here, sir. I know you want to be with him, but we have work to do. You can join him shortly." She spoke politely, but forcefully. She nodded for Brian to step aside.

"I want to be with him." Brian protested, but realized he could do nothing more and stepped aside.

"Sir, Sir. I need some information." The nurse at the admissions' station half rose from her chair and called to Brian. When he turned, she added, "I'm sorry sir, but I need some information."

Brian paused; he wanted to go with his son as they wheeled Jimbo into an area just past the admissions station.

The admissions nurse kept asking questions. He remembered that the paramedic told him to bring Jimmy's identification and medical insurance card. He pulled them from his pocket. He tried to focus and answer the nurse's questions, but could only think about Jimbo. He watched the frenetic activity that surrounded Jimbo in the next room.

Brian's frustration increased when a nurse slid the hospital curtain around the gurney. As a matter of practice, it was better that family members and friends not watch and possibly interfere with their life saving activities. After they completed their work, the family members could then visit their loved ones.

The doctor standing over a patient a few beds away turned his attention to Jimbo. He assumed control from the nurse in charge, and gave more instructions to the staff. He listened to Jimbo's heartbeat. He directed another nurse to insert an IV of saline solution, and another to take blood samples.

Outside the ER activity, the admissions and waiting area was quiet. The few, who waited spoke in hushed tones, read magazines, coughed, or watched a TV with the sound turned low. This was Tuesday night, not a weekend night when the ER is busiest. A middle-aged woman with a bad cold used several tissues. Another patient, an infant, suffering from a fever, squirmed in his mother's lap.

Brian tried to focus and answered the admissions nurse's questions. She told him he could join his son when the doctor and the nurses finished their work. She asked him to sit in the waiting area.

Brian worried about his son. Brian knew he must let the doctors work, but he could not simply sit. He had not been this worried about his son's well being since he was nine years old. Brian paced as he remembered that day.

Riding his bike then, Jimbo hit a rock in the street and hit his head on the curb, knocking him unconscious. His young friends could not revive him and ran to Brian's house. Brian ran to Jimbo's side, and yelled for a neighbor to call an ambulance.

The paramedics arrived in minutes, but could not immediately revive him. On the way to the emergency room, he regained consciousness. Brian felt the most fear in his life then. Until now. This time, his fear felt greater. Losing a child, at any age, is a parent's greatest pain.

Ten minutes passed. It seemed like an hour. The nurse in the smock approached him.

"Mr. Latimer?"

"Is he alright? Is he going to be alright?" Brian rose from his chair and walked to her.

"Yes, yes he is. You did the right things. Although your techniques are a little dated, but they worked." She smiled, and placed a comforting hand on his arm. "The paramedics gave the right anti-venom, and got him here in time. We're going to keep him here for another hour; then, we'll move him to a room upstairs. We don't want to send him home just yet. We'd like to keep him here for at least twenty-four hours. Just to make sure everything is ok. We don't get many snakebites, here. He'll be very sore for a few days, and experience considerable swelling, but that should go down in a couple weeks. He'll be just fine."

"Thank you. Thank you." He wanted to hug her. He closed his eyes and felt a wave of relief sweep over him. "Can I see him, please?"

"Sure, but just for a moment. We still have other cases here. When he gets up to his room, you can stay as long as you'd like." She smiled and returned to the other ER patients.

Brian followed her. She held the curtain aside, and Brian approached Jimbo's bedside. He could see he was awake, but groggy.

"I was so worried." He hugged his son letting the feeling of everything-is-going-to-be-alright course through him.

"Man, that was something. Something I never want to experience again. That snake nearly scared the crap out of me. You'd think I'd have done a better job of jumping up on the counter, to get away from it. I kept slipping. Then after that, everything became cloudy. Did I pass out?" Jimbo could hardly speak. His tongue felt thick, his mind cloudy. The sedative drugs would require time to wear off. But he needed the pain medication.

"Almost. After that snake bit you, you were out-of-it for a while. I'm so glad you're going to be OK, son. I was so worried." Brian held his son's hand and looked him in the eyes. He wiped Jimbo's hair from his eyes. "They said I could only stay a minute. They're going to move you upstairs, and then I can join you."

They talked briefly. Jimbo became sleepy and his part in the conversation dissolved into sleep.

Brian returned to the waiting area. He leaned against a wall, and inhaled a few deep breaths. He felt such relief. Now, he could sit. He saw a man in his early fifties standing at the admissions' desk. The nurse who had asked all the questions pointed toward Brian. The man nodded to the nurse and walked toward Brian.

He wore brown, a brown jacket, dark brown slacks, a beige shirt, probably short sleeves, since no cuffs hung below the jacket sleeves. His body was square, bulldog or fireplug shape some would say. He wore his salt-n-pepper hair in a crew cut.

"Mr. Latimer?"

"Yes."

"I'm Detective Philip Kaminski, from the Long Beach Police Department. I understand you had a little excitement at your place."

"To put it mildly." Brian answered. "I thought the policemen would be here."

"They're securing the scene. They called me. I stopped there first, looked at the scene. They'd thought at first, it was snakebite from a pet. Of course, as you may or may not know, having a poisonous snake in the city of Long Beach is against city ordinance. Anyway as you told them, and from what we've seen, we're calling it a crime. The forensics unit was there when I arrived. They've bagged the package that was on your counter to check for fingerprints, and other tests."

"I can assure you it was not a pet. I hate snakes. So does my son."

"By the way, how is your son? I'm sorry about his being bitten. Sometimes, I focus on the work too closely."

"The doctor said 'he'll be fine'. I was just in there with him. He's groggy from the anti-venom and the pain killers. They're going to move him to a room in an hour, then I can join him."

"Good." Detective Kaminski returned to his questions.

Brian recounted everything from coming home, to getting away from the snake, to killing it. After he killed it, he realized his son had been bitten, so he called the ambulance and the paramedics rushed his son to the ER.

While Brian told the story, he again felt some of the fear of losing his son. But now knowing that he would be ok, his worries subsided.

Now he thought more about someone sending a poisonous snake to him; someone wanted to kill him.

His thoughts switched to the murders at Leonard Construction.

"Detective Kaminski, I need to tell you about two recent murders at Leonard Construction where I'm doing some consulting work." Brian took a deep breath. This would not be simple to explain. He still struggled to comprehend the situation himself. He definitely would not worry about holding back on possible proprietary facts.

Brian recounted the events of the past week, the embezzlement, Greg's accident turned murder, David's murder, and now this attempt. He gave him Sheriff's Detective Wesley Makelin's phone number.

Kaminski could not write in his notepad fast enough. He knew this was a far bigger case than it first appeared. Kaminski motioned to a couple chairs away from the others in the waiting room. He asked some questions, but mostly listened.

Brian now felt a new and different kind of fear, not as great as the losing-his-son fear, but fear for his own life. He would add his name on the list of people who are in danger.

"You probably won't be able to re-enter your condo for a few hours. You probably should make arrangements to spend the night somewhere else. I'll have the forensics team call you when they finish. Could I have your cell number please?"

"I'll be here until I'm sure my son is completely ok. I have a couple neighbors in the building where I can spend the night, if necessary." Brian thought of the older couple who lived next door to him. They had a spare bedroom. He gave the Detective his cell number.

After Detective Kaminski left, Brian called Larry, and then he called Detective Makelin. The case had become more deadly, in addition to Greg's and David's deaths.

He saw two orderlies pulling Jimbo's gurney from the ER to take him upstairs to a room. Brian joined them. He held his son's hand the whole trip.

FORTY TWO

Wednesday morning, April 13
Santa Monica, California

Following her usual morning practice, Liz locked her purse in a file drawer. She turned on her computer to read her emails, when she saw Larry approach. He looked ragged, his face filled with worry.

"Larry, my goodness, you don't look well. Are you alright?" Concerned, Liz stopped, and looked directly at him.

"No, actually, I'm not. I got some very disturbing news last night. Brian called around ten. His son was bitten by a snake."

"What? How did that happen? How on earth…" Liz's voice filled with alarm.

"At Brian's condo. His son opened a package with a snake inside, a cottonmouth, if you can believe it, and it bit him." Larry's voice shook as he thought about it. "The disturbing part is the package was intended for Brian."

"I don't understand. Intended for Brian? How is a snake *intended* for someone?" Liz puzzled, asked.

"Someone sent it to Brian. Through the mail." Larry realized he was not completely clear. He added, "Thinking it contained books his son opened the package, while Brian looked at his other mail. Of course, the snake escaped, and bit James, Brian's son. The ambulance took him to Long Beach Memorial."

"Oh my god." Liz could not believe what she heard. Her legs felt weak. She nearly collapsed in her chair.

"I talked with Brian a few minutes ago. He said his son was doing much better this morning." Larry added. "He also called Detective Makelin, and told him. I expect a call from him and from a Detective Kaminski from the Long Beach Police Department."

Larry gave Liz more details about the snake, killing it, the package, and the trip to the emergency room.

"I need a meeting with Daniel and Jesse as soon as possible. I'll call Daniel. You call Jesse." Larry directed.

"Of course. Of course." Liz picked up her phone and pressed Jesse's speed dial.

Larry turned to go into his office. "I'd like you to join us. I'll explain further when we meet with the others. Also, ask Brian to join us when he arrives. He said he was coming in this morning. I told him to not worry about it, but he's more determined than ever to finish this project, to find out who is behind it."

"Will do." So many questions filled Liz's mind as she dialed the numbers.

"And, please add Stan to your list."

Larry called Daniel. When he answered, Larry described the attempt on Brian's life.

A few minutes later, everyone except Brian sat around Daniel's conference table in his large, corner office. A few wore puzzled looks wondering why they needed to meet. They gave their attention to Larry.

After everyone was seated, Daniel nodded to Larry.

"Liz, is Brian on his way?" Larry asked.

"Yes, he is. I just talked with him on his cell. He had just left the hospital. He'll join us as soon as he gets here, probably a half hour."

"Thanks. Brian has good reason to run late. As if Greg's and David's deaths weren't traumatic enough, there has been another event that's very alarming." Larry looked around the room to emphasize his next statement. "Brian's son opened a small box. Inside it, a poisonous snake escaped and bit him. But what makes it alarming is the snake was intended for Brian. I know it's related to this embezzlement, just like Greg's and David's."

Gasps of alarm spread through the room. Larry gave them the details he had given Liz. When Brian would arrive, he could tell them more.

"Is his son alright?" Daniel asked looking at Larry.

"He's doing well, out of the danger zone." Liz answered for Larry since she had just spoken with Brian. "Brian's son will stay in the hospital another day or two."

"Every parent's nightmare, losing a kid." Daniel said, and continued, "Larry and I are really worried that other company people who work in the areas related to this embezzlement are in real danger." Daniel took a deep breath and leaned on one elbow on his chair arm.

Larry added. "Brian told the Long Beach Police about Greg's and David's deaths. The Sheriff's detectives should be here around noon. Detective Kaminski from the Long Beach Police Department will be here sometime today. That makes three law enforcement agencies involved, the Sheriff's Department, the Santa Monica Police, and now the Long Beach Police." He looked Stan in the eye. "Stan, our intent to keep the details of the embezzlement out of the investigation is now impossible. Too many people know, and the connection is pretty damn obvious."

"I agree. I don't think we have a choice." Stan acquiesced.

"We still need to use my department as central point of information, especially with the media." Jesse Dietz from Public Relations added.

"And for the employees." Stan added.

"Agreed." Daniel spoke for the group. "Jesse, how is the statement for the employees coming?"

"We updated our internal website Monday afternoon with information about David's and Greg's deaths. Now, do we need to update it again with last night's event?" Jesse asked.

"Let's wait another day. I think we need more information." Stan directed.

Daniel shook his head in agreement.

"Larry, I suggest you meet with your accounting people, since they are closest to the investigation." Stan added.

"I plan to arrange one as soon as we finish here." Larry responded. "Jesse, why don't you join us?"

"I will."

"And I want total cooperation with the law enforcement people." Daniel spoke. "We have to find this guy. Whoever it is. Sadly, and I can't believe it, but it could be one of our own people."

Daniel's admin assistant saw Brian approach Larry's empty office and motioned for him to come to Daniel's office.

"Brian, hello. How are you? How is your son?" Larry greeted Brian at the door, and shook his hand, held it actually.

"Jimbo's fine. He's very sore. His leg is very swollen. He's medicated. I actually slept at the hospital. I'm tired, very tired. That was really a scare." Brian appreciated his friend's concern.

"I know it had to be. I'm really sorry that it happened."

"Thanks."

"Take a seat. A part of me wants to tell you to take time for yourself. But I know you want this situation resolved as much as we do. We definitely need your help on this investigation." Larry gestured to an empty chair.

"More than ever, now. I want to find the guy who did this. It's personal now, very personal."

Brian sat in the remaining chair. In sympathy, others reached across the table to shake Brian's hand. Brian recounted the events of the evening.

"Brian, you know, you and a few of us may still be in danger. Were the police able to tell you anything about who sent that damn thing to you?" Larry asked.

"Not much. I understand their forensics people were there until well into the morning hours. Even though I was sure my son would be ok, I stayed there. Detective Kaminski, from Long Beach, was supposed to talk with Detective Makelin this morning. I understand that both Makelin and Kaminski will be here later this morning." Brian looked around the table. "Now that the crisis with Jimbo is over, I'm also worried that more of us may be at risk."

"We had just started to discuss that." Larry's voice turned all business. "In addition to the work to solve the embezzlement, we need to come up with some ideas to protect our people, especially those associated with work on the embezzlement."

"Can't the police provide us some protection?" Jesse asked as he looked around the table.

"I doubt it. They probably don't have the staffing to give five, six, or more of us twenty-four hour protection." Daniel responded. "But we're not going to let that stop us from doing something for ourselves. We can check into security services. Maybe our security company that we use can give us more protection, at least some direction."

Others suggested ideas such as sequestering key employees for a few days. But what about their families, another asked. The group discussed several ideas, but they were unable to identify clear workable ones.

"I'm certain these new developments will panic some our employees, and rightly so. You know they'll find out about the attempt on Brian's life last night." Jesse cleared his throat. "And, I'm sure the media has already picked up on it. It's not every day that someone receives a poisonous snake in the mail. I'll prepare another statement for them. Some will start to ask if they're next."

"Just a thought. None of the deaths, or this attempt, happened here at work. Two were at home, and the other was on the way home. I wonder if that's worth thinking about." Brian rested one arm on the table.

"So maybe the extra security, at work at least, isn't the answer." Larry tapped his fingers on the table. "Does that mean it's someone outside the company?"

"No. That person has to know what's going on here, and know who is involved." Brian sat up straight in his chair.

"But we've got to do something." Stan leaned on the table with both elbows.

"Larry, Jesse, work on some specifics. Provide some concrete steps that we can take to protect our people. Develop statements for our people, and for the media. And of course, continue with the embezzlement work. Can you have something for me later this afternoon?" Daniel's question sounded more like a directive. He swiveled his chair as he looked around the room. "I guess that's all we can do in this meeting. Anything else? And let's not forget to help the detectives all we can."

"Sure. We'll get right on it." Larry responded and Jesse nodded agreement.

"Liz, thanks for taking notes. Please send me a copy." Daniel smiled at her.

"Sure." Liz nodded.

FORTY THREE

Wednesday morning, April 13
Santa Monica, California

Wes drove swiftly, but with caution over the winding Topanga Canyon road through the mountains to Santa Monica. Earlier he and Phyllis completed some needed deskwork at the stationhouse for a couple of hours. The delay gave them the side benefit of missing early commuter traffic before they headed for the Leonard Construction offices.

On the way, they planned a brief stop at Art Dexter's apartment complex while he was at work. They would interview his neighbors, observe his lifestyle, and develop a clearer profile of him.

"I can't stop thinking about Brian's encounter with that poisonous snake last night. We know all of these cases are related, but…" Wes shook his head in disbelief. "I almost couldn't believe what Detective Kaminski told me when he called me last night. Right after I talked with him, Brian called me."

"I can't believe it either. This is the big city, for crying out loud." Phyllis shuttered. "Murders, gang wars, robberies, car hijackings, but snakes!"

"Our suspect, or suspects are all over the map. There has to be more than one person involved. No MO is the same." Wes' stomach tightened. His *gut technique* did not seem to work.

279

"There have to be at least two people, maybe three. There's enough money embezzled for a group." Phyllis agreed. "A bank heist wouldn't get them any more money."

"Detective Kaminski said he'd keep me posted as soon as he gets any details from his forensics people." Shaking his head, Wes continued. "He'd interviewed the security people in Brian's building. They'd had a shift change, so Kaminski called the guy at his home, at midnight. The guy on duty said the delivery person looked like someone from the regular carriers. He remembered brown. He remembered young. He didn't even have to sign for the package, so he stacked it with the others, and went about his work. He wasn't very clear at all about what the guy looked like."

"They probably receive a lot of packages for their residents. So associating a specific person with a package probably wouldn't be easy." Phyllis said.

"I'm sure they do. I understand the building contains more than two hundred residences. It's a thirty plus stories, round building, right downtown." Wes glanced at Phyllis. "I grew up in Long Beach. My parents still live there."

"Oh so you know the area."

"Yeah. Quite a bit." Wes answered. "Went to school down there, including Long Beach State.

"That's right. I'd forgotten you went there."

Wes kept discussing what he'd learned from Kaminisky and Brian. "The sender used an old Amazon book box, but all of the bar codes and other identifying marks had been torn off. The Long Beach forensics people took the box along with the snake to their lab."

"I hope they get some readable fingerprints. Maybe some code stamps, bar codes. Anything would probably help us." Phyllis wrote a note in her binder. She suppressed a grin. "Although might be hard to get fingerprints from a dead snake."

"I'm sure the sender wore rubber gloves." Wes grinned.

"I'm sure some people in LA have snakes, but it just doesn't fit. Too uncommon. I've never had a case that involved a snake as a weapon." Phyllis shuddered again. She did not like snakes. Does anyone?

"I wonder if Art has access to snakes." Wes pressed his brakes as he maneuvered Topanga's curves. "Since he's sort of floated to the top of our *persons of interest* list. He was the last to see Greg alive. They had stopped for a drink. He could easily have put that drug in Larkin's drink."

"How does someone source a drug like that?" Phyllis wrote another entry in her notes.

"I'm not sure. I'll give Harold at the ME's office a call. Still wrapping my mind around these cases. Killing one person by a drug, then stabbing another in a brutal attack, and now an attempt to kill with a poisonous snake."

"This guy has got to be some kind of sociopath." Phyllis shook her head in disbelief.

"There are such people. He could have had an accomplice." Wes took a breath. "Let's learn what we can today, and when we get back to the office, we'll chalkboard it."

"When is Argos supposed to call with the forensics results from the Frazer crime scene?" Phyllis changed the subject.

"He said yesterday that he should have something this afternoon. He also wanted us to give him feedback on our visit to Art's neighborhood. I don't want to jump to conclusions, but if anything ties him to the Frazer case, then I'm convinced he's our man." Wes paused. "We'll have to work on the snake angle."

"When we talked with Dexter on Monday, he said he was alone Sunday night. But of course most single people are alone the nights before a workday." Phyllis wrote another note on her pad. "It'd be fishy if he had a good alibi for the evening."

They drove for a few minutes in silence and slowed as they approached the signal light where Topanga Canyon met the PCH. The huge Pacific Ocean lay ahead in beautiful, stark contrast to the scrub and rock covered mountains they just exited.

"I know I've said it before, but I still love this ocean. As soon as I see it, I immediately begin to relax." Wes slowed to a stop at the signal light. It turned green, he turned south onto PCH.

"Same here." Phyllis looked out her car window and stared at the ocean.

Wes sneaked glances at the ocean, but kept his eyes on the road. An accident would put a real crimp in their day.

The ocean continued west as far as they could see. To their left, the sun hung high in the eastern sky, and its rays reflected off the water. Small waves lapped the shoreline in their unending, rhythmic pattern. Inside the car with its windows up, they could not hear the sounds of the waves, but the visuals were perfect. Phyllis pushed the window button on her armrest to roll it down to savor the experience.

A few dedicated, or maybe obsessed surfers, fishermen, and joggers enjoyed the un-crowded beach this weekday morning. Since the month was April, the water was likely cold. Only the very dedicated played in it today. When summer approaches and the sun warms the water, cars will fill all the available parking spaces along the roadside. Visitors will pack the beaches, leaving little room for the regulars, the fishermen and the surfers.

Except for a few restaurants and other commercial buildings, this stretch of beach was a public park. Nearer Santa Monica, and in Malibu in the other direction, very expensive private homes packed the space between the water's edge and PCH.

"Keep your eyes on the road, please. I'll drive next time and you can look at the view." Phyllis grinned, watching Wes sneak glances of the ocean.

"I'm a very good driver, thank you very much." Wes teased in self-defense.

She looked for Art's address in her case file and entered it into the GPS system. Only a few miles to the exit into the hillside streets that led to Art's place.

"Take a left on West Channel Road and go about three blocks then a couple lefts to Art's apartment complex." Phyllis played the role of navigator.

"Will do."

Wes turned as directed and drove the few blocks. The small complex sat on small rise of land from the street. An unkempt row of ten mail boxes stood guard at the street. Two variations of ice plant sparsely covered the shallow space of land. Small drifts of beach sand lay against the vegetation, hindering its growth. Beach communities often contend with sand in their yards, on their streets, and in their houses. Maintaining clean houses probably frustrated to no end the obsessively clean types.

A narrow driveway at the side of the property led to the backside of the small collection of duplexes that surrounded a small courtyard. Overgrown ferns, camellias, bird of paradise, and other plants gave the courtyard an intimate, but crowded ambiance.

Not yet summer, Wes had no trouble finding a parking space on the street. In summer, parked cars would fill the side streets this near the beach. Some beach city neighborhoods required stickers on cars for their residents to force beach goers to find other parking. Wes laid an Official Sheriff's business placard on the dashboard.

He and Phyllis walked up the few steps that led to the courtyard. Wes knocked on the door of apartment A. No one was home, the same for apartment B. They went to the next duplex. The drapes were closed in apartment C, Art's apartment; otherwise they would have peeked inside. They approached apartment D, next door.

"We can guess the kind of person this neighbor is." Wes knocked on the door, and pointed to a sticker in the window. It read 'Legalize Pot, California proposition 21a".

The drapes were open. They could see a sparsely furnished living room. The back of a television sat against the window. An old lumpy couch with a sheet loosely serving as a slipcover sat against the opposite wall. A cheap veneer brown coffee table and end table with an amber glass lamp flanked the couch. Two orange beanbag chairs sat along another wall in front of two empty aquariums. A surfboard leaned against the wall in a far corner.

"I hear somebody inside." Phyllis tilted her head toward the door listening.

After a second knock, the door opened. An apparent refugee from a sixties hippie commune stood before them. His balding head grew hair only around the sides and back of his head. The long, gray-white hair was tied into a ponytail with a rubber band. He wore bifocal glasses with brown horned-rim frames. Probably sixty years of age, he wore loose fitting clothes, a pair of faded jeans and a worn floral Hawaiian shirt with holes. They were not dirty, but also not clean. He wore rubber flip-flops, which had seen better days. Pale white skin with a few white chest hairs poked through the holes in the shirt.

"Good morning. What can I do for you this morning?" The guy was surprisingly friendly for an LA person with law enforcement standing on his front stoop.

"Good morning, sir. We're with the LA County Sheriff's Department. I'm Detective Makelin, and this is Detective Hadley." Wes nodded toward Phyllis.

Both detectives held their badges forward for the man. Squinting, he appeared to read them and then resumed eye contact. The detectives returned their badges to their belts. Wes placed his hands on his hips in relaxed friendly gesture. "We want to ask you a few questions about your neighbor, Arthur Dexter. If you don't mind."

"Well sure." The man stepped onto the front stoop, pulling the door behind almost closed behind him.

Although his answer and behavior implied that he did mind, Wes asked his questions anyway. Most people answer the *do you mind* question with a yes, when they mean no.

Wes shifted giving the man room to share the small stoop.

" How long have you lived next to Mr. Dexter?"

"About four years." The neighbor looked upward as if the answer was there.

"How well do you know him?" Wes liked open-ended questions to encourage a person to talk.

"Well, so-so. Close enough, but not too close. He's a pretty good dude." Mr. Harvill's dipped his head to the right and stretched it as if to relieve a crick in his neck.

Maybe open-ended questions weren't sufficient.

"Do you know any of his friends? Any that he might see on a regular basis. Does he have a girlfriend?"

"I know a couple of the dudes that he surfs with. I don't know them very well, like I don't know their last names. Sometimes they come over and grill some burgers. They invite me to join them since we share our backyard together. And I do the same for them."

"Them?"

"Yeah, the two dudes like I just said. I don't know the others. They come and go. Sometimes, they invite me along to surf, but I just can't, like I used to. I have this bum leg. Guess I'm getting old." The neighbor again dipped his head to the right and stretched his neck.

"Does Mr. Dexter live pretty basic, or like someone who has a lot of money?"

"Yeah, dude. Everyone here lives pretty basic. It's hard to find a place close to the beach any more, without paying an arm and a leg. Only reason most of us can afford it is rent control." The neighbor stood straighter, his voice contained some pride. "When he moved in a couple years ago, I think he was related to the person who lived there. So his place is rent controlled too."

"Anyway," The neighbor continued, "I think he makes more money now. He bought a really nice Porche a few months ago. He always seems to have money. He certainly knows how to entertain the girls. He has enough of them."

"The girls? He doesn't have a special one?"

"No, seems like a different one every weekend." He did the head-dip-neck-stretch thing again.

"Would you know if he was home last Sunday night?" Wes slipped in a specific question into the conversation.

"You know. I don't think so, if you mean after dark that is." He held his head at an angle as if he had some difficulty remembering three days ago.

"I took some garbage out around ten. Mondays are our trash days. His place was dark. His car wasn't in its place." He did the head-dip-stretch thing again.

"Why do you remember the car, in particular?" Phyllis asked.

"That car. It's a Porche. Hot looking car. I never could afford something like that. Take a look at it pretty regular."

Wes saw movement in Mr. Harvill's shirt pocket. A small snake slipped its head through one of the holes. It looked at the outside world, its little tongue testing the air. Wes stepped back, almost slipped off the stoop, but realized it was a simple garden snake.

"A pet?"

"Yes. She's one of them. This is Carrie. You know. After that Carrie in the Stephen King movie, Carrie." He pulled the snake through the hole and let it wrap around two of his fingers.

"You said 'one of them'. You have more?" Phyllis stopped taking notes.

"Yeah, just a few. I keep them in a couple aquariums. They're fun to keep around. Easy to take care of, you know."

"Any poisonous kind?"

"Err, no. No poisonous kind. Them being illegal and all. Besides, I like to let 'em out occasionally. Let 'em loose in the house. Get some exercise. Have to keep the windows and doors closed so they can't get out. Some neighbors get picky, might kill the little guys."

"Mind if we see them." Wes asked.

"I, ah, maybe another time. They're napping now. I'd hate to upset them. You understand."

"Sure." Wes did not press the issue. Maybe a warrant would be necessary later. He wanted to develop a stronger connection to Art.

"Did you know a Gregory Larkin, or a David Frazer?" Wes pulled photos from his inside jacket pocket.

"No. Can't say that I do. Should I?" He squinted his eyes again to focus on the pictures.

"No. No. We just wondered if you knew them."

"May we have your name please?"

"Ken. Ken Harvill." The neighbor said with pride in his voice.

Phyllis wrote the man's name in her notepad.

Well Mr. Harvill, you've been very helpful. Thank you. Let me give you my card." Wes pulled his card from his shirt pocket.

"Please call us if you think of anything else about Mr. Dexter." Phyllis gave him her card too. "I don't know what that'd be. I've answered your questions. But if I think of something important, I'll call." He did that head-dip-stretch thing again.

"Maybe you could just not mention to him that we talked?" Wes added, but did not care if Harvill told Dexter or not. Maybe it would worry Dexter, and he would make a mistake.

Wes and Phyllis thanked him again, and moved to the next two duplexes. No one was home in any of them, including the one with the manager sign beside the door. They returned to their car for the short trip to the Leonard Construction offices.

"Did you notice how many times he used the words 'dude' and 'you know'?" Phyllis laughed as she buckled her seat belt.

"Yeah. He's a little old to use the surfer dude language. Seems like he should live in Topanga or Fernwood. I understand a lot of hippies from the sixties and seventies still live up there." Wes laughed too.

"But how could he be a surfer dude if he lived up there. The beach is too far away." Phyllis teased.

"Yeah. Right."

They rode in silence as they returned to the PCH.

"We learned a few things about Art Dexter. One, his alibi for Sunday night doesn't hold water." Wes felt a little smug that his gut technique was working again.

"That's right. And point two. He spends money, probably more than his salary, a new Porche, entertain the girls." Phyllis wrote more notes on her notepad.

"And three, that snake. Maybe Senior Dude has poisonous snakes. Just didn't want to admit it to us."

"Or for us to come inside. *'them being illegal and all'.*" Wes mocked Senior Dude's gravelly accent.

"Even if he doesn't have the poisonous variety, I'm sure he knows others who have access to them. A little background check on our Dude Senior might uncover some valuable information." Wes continued listing his points. "And that would tie Dexter to the attempt on Brian's life."

"That it would." Phyllis shared Wes' enthusiasm.

"I hope Argos has more information this afternoon. If any of it links to Dexter, I think we have our man." Wes felt good. They very possibly were going to solve the case soon.

"And maybe Brian has more information that can help us." Phyllis thought about the case, and ignored the ocean outside her window.

They approached the tunnel where PCH turned east and became the Santa Monica Freeway.

FORTY FOUR

Wednesday noon, April 13
Santa Monica, California

"Hi Brian, Detectives Makelin and Hadley have arrived." Liz asked. "Can you join Larry and them in his office?"

"Sure. Be right there." Brian replaced the phone handset in its cradle. He logged off his computer, locked his files and notes in his desk, and grabbed a couple folders with reports and documents.

As Brian locked his office door, He relished his new role working with law enforcement. He had become a part of a bona fide criminal investigative team, not just an employee working with systems and databases. Even more compelling, this case had become very personal for him.

"Hello. Wes, Phyllis." Brian half-smiled and nodded to Larry and Liz as he joined the small meeting. "How are you?"

"Good." Wes replied. Others nodded. Wes added. "Last night really had to be scary for you."

"That's for sure. I've calmed down some. Just very exhausted." Brian smiled, only because his worry about his son had subsided a little.

"I bet. I know we talked on the phone last night. But tell us about what happened." Wes tapped his pencil on the notepad that lay before him, and swiveled his chair to face Brian. "But first, how is your son?"

"He's doing okay. I talked with him about an hour ago. He's stabilized but still groggy from the sedatives the nurse has given him. He'll stay in the hospital for another day, just for observation. He says he's ready to come home now. He's a pretty tough young man."

"That's good to hear. I'm not a parent, but that had to be really scary for you." Wes' face showed his concern.

"I have a daughter, and I can't imagine going through something like that." Phyllis added.

"Thanks for saying that. I've had a few scary events in my life. But this was the worst. Being in the same room with a snake is scary enough. I hate snakes. But when I realized it had bitten Jimbo, and he had begun to pass out, I really became scared. I thought he was dying. Helping him came first, nothing else mattered. It's amazing how the parent instinct takes over and you do what you have to do to help your kid. Even with a snake on the floor."

For a few minutes, Brian recounted what he had told Larry and the others earlier.

"And on top of all that, to realize that someone actually *sent* the snake to you, someone was trying to kill you." Larry gripped his hands together and twisted them back and forth to relieve some of the tension he felt.

When Brian finished talking, Wes told them about his conversation with Long Beach Detective Kaminisky about what their forensics team had learned.

Wes further told them that there were no new developments from the Santa Monica Police Department about David's case. He also explained that both the Long Beach and Santa Monica Police departments would work with the Sheriff's department to reduce duplication of effort. Wes also reminded them that detective work involved investigating the victims as part of the process. Most often the victim knows the assailant.

"So, Brian, you should expect some investigation into your life, especially looking for people who have something against you." Wes looked at Larry. "Just as we asked questions about Mr. Larkin and Mr. Frazer."

Brian and Larry nodded that they understood.

"And I think, it goes almost without saying, that there's a connection between this snakebite incident, and David's and Greg's deaths. Namely, the embezzlement being the connection." Larry unclasped his hands and drummed his fingers on his desktop.

"I agree." Wes looked directly at Larry, and then at Brian. "Brian, you should be aware that you're probably still in danger. He's tried it once, and he'll probably try it again. I suggest your son stay in the hospital a little longer."

"I hadn't thought of that with everything that I have on my mind. Everything has happened so fast." Brian took a deep breath.

"The Long Beach Police might be able to provide you some protection, but probably not much because of their current caseloads. Kaminski said he would alert your building's security people. He did say that they had a pretty good reputation in Long Beach." Wes tried to reassure Brian.

"On the subject of safety," Larry shifted the conversation. "Our upper management wants to meet with you to discuss protection for company employees. They are very concerned about employee safety, especially those working in the Accounting and Construction Projects departments. We want to know what law enforcement can provide and what we can do on our own. As in most companies, our grapevine is alive and well. And a lot of people are scared."

"We understand. How soon do you want to meet?" Wes looked to Phyllis who nodded agreement. "And who will be in this meeting?"

"How about an hour from now?" Larry straightened in his chair. "Besides us, Daniel Post, Jesses Dietz, and Stan Brothers will be there. I believe you met them last week."

"Yes, I remember them." Wes nodded. "Maybe, you should add whoever is in charge of your security, as well."

"Good idea. Meanwhile, Detectives, I'm sure you need some time with Brian. If you want, you can use the small office he uses, if that's alright." Larry swiveled his chair to face Brian. "Will you show them where your office is?"

"Sure. I have more materials there so it should be easier to talk."

"Good. Liz will call everyone to coordinate the meeting."

Brian, Wes, and Phyllis gathered their materials and left for the eleventh floor. After they laid their materials on the conference table, Brian showed them where the restrooms and the break-room were.

Once settled around the small conference table, Wes laid his notepad in front of him and asked Brian. "OK. Are we ready to go over the details in this case? Brian, why don't you update us with what you've learned in the last couple days?"

Wes thought of Brian as part of his investigative team, and wanted a free flow of information among them. However, he was always conscious that Brian worked for the company under investigation. He, Phyllis, and Debra would talk frequently about Brian's results, just to be thorough. Further, he and Phyllis had agreed to not discuss their visit to Art Dexter's apartment complex, especially the part about the snakes, just yet.

Brian gave copies of his worksheets to Wes and Phyllis. He explained that the names on his short list remained the same. He explained more about the method the perpetrator used to embezzle, and how he circumvented the computer's security system, without using too many technical terms.

Brian answered questions as they arose. The detectives seemed to understand the process. Brian reassured them that he had updated Debra with the technical details yesterday afternoon.

Next, they turned to Brian's list of possible suspects. Unknown Hacker appeared at the top of the list, twice. One, a hacker - Inside the Company, the second, a hacker - Outside the Company. Wes felt impatient and wanted to skip these two names. Too vague. According to his *gut technique*, he preferred specific names, but he kept quiet and let Brian describe how a hacker could access and change the system. He was sure Debra would appreciate this part of the discussion more than he did.

"As part of this project, I asked the IT guys about the skill levels of the people on this list."

"You didn't discuss this list, as suspects, with them did you?" Wes interrupted.

"No. No. Definitely not from a suspect perspective. Just their IT skill levels. Actually the skill levels of about everyone in these departments." Brian reassured them.

"Good."

Brian continued. "They said that Greg, David, and Larry probably were the most knowledgeable. But Art and Chas probably know a lot, but harder to determine. They seldom call the IT Help Desk for assistance, which indicates they can solve most of their IT problems themselves. Meaning they understand IT to some level greater than the average person."

"Looking at the company organization chart, I notice that a Donna Gerardi heads up the Construction Projects group. She and Larry report to the CEO." Wes pulled the chart from a folder, as he checked the names on Brian's short list. "Should we consider her and the CEO?" Wes felt he knew they could be eliminated, but wanted agreement from Brian and Phyllis.

"I would eliminate them as suspects." Brian responded. "Donna Gerardi requires IT help, she calls the Help Desk pretty often. Or at least she gets her admin assistant to call. She doesn't get into the computer details. She even has her assistant print her emails and directs her to actually respond to the emails. I don't believe she has the computer skills required to carry out this embezzlement."

"I would agree. I talked with her on the phone. She's strictly, a *big picture* person." Phyllis laughed, adding her opinion.

"And as for Daniel Post. He owns most of the company, more than fifty percent of the shares. Why would he embezzle? He could simply write himself a check, or give himself a bonus. It'd be a lot easier than devising a complex computer scheme." Brian answered.

"So, that leaves us with Chas, Art, and Larry. Of course, there's no way Larry could do this. He's just not the kind of person who would embezzle. And especially not the kind of person who could kill someone." Brian paused knowing his logic was flawed, but convinced of his friend's innocence.

Brian did not know that Art had moved to the top of Wes's suspect list, at least as the killer.

"Let's compare notes on what we've learned about these people. Let's talk motive, then opportunity. Brian, in your experience what motivates embezzlers?" Wes asked. He wanted Brian to think like law enforcement.

"Well, money?" Brian rested his elbows on his chair arms and splayed the palms of his hands. *Wouldn't that be obvious?* After a little thought, he added. "Embezzlers steal for a variety of reasons. Greed, they just want more money. Some financial need could arise, like major medical bills. Or, they may simply feel the company owes them the money for some unfair treatment, at least in their minds."

Wes nodded in agreement.

"Next, they must have the opportunity to steal. And they must have the skills necessary to commit the crime. It can be low tech, such as stealing from petty cash, or high tech, such as in this case. With motivation, they see an opportunity and take the money. Generally, these people are in a position of confidence and responsibility over the area where they commit their crime."

Brian still felt uncomfortable with the idea that someone he knew could be the criminal.

"I asked because I just wanted to be sure that we're on the same page as far as understanding cause, opportunity, and motive." Wes rested his elbows on the table. "But before we talk about each of these people in those terms. I'd like to phone conference someone who has done some research on a couple of these people. And she knows a lot about psychological makeup of people. She's a writer, a very good one in my opinion. I believe you know her, Karen Coffman."

"Yeah. Yeah, I know her. Met her at Larry's party this past weekend." Brian smiled, but felt unsure of involving her.

"Let's call her." Wes pulled her business card from his wallet.

FORTY FIVE

Wednesday afternoon, April 13
Santa Monica, California

When Karen answered her phone, Wes almost said Ms., but caught himself as he leaned toward the speakerphone. "Hello Karen. Wes Makelin here."

"Hello Wes. How are you today?"

"Great. Thanks. Yourself?"

"I'm doing great too."

"Karen, Phyllis Hadley and I are here at the Leonard Construction offices. We're working with Brian Latimer building profiles on the cases here. I believe you two know each other."

"Yes. Yes, I know Brian. We met last weekend. Nice guy. Hi Brian."

"Hi Karen. Good to talk with you again."

"Same here." Karen continued. "And Phyllis it's nice to actually talk with you, almost in person. Wes has talked about you."

"Nice to meet you, Karen." Phyllis responded. "I feel like I know you. Wes has told me about you and your books. He is without doubt one of your biggest fans."

"That's good to hear. Thanks, Wes."

"Phyllis is right, you know." Wes grinned. "Okay. Business. Karen, as I was saying, we're building a profile on the suspect, or suspects as the case may be, and trying to determine who might fit the profile. You and I talked yesterday about the unfortunate death of David Frazer. And since you think outside-the-box, so to speak, you might help us build a picture of our suspect guy. Brian has learned a lot about the systems and the people here. He also has a good understanding of the motives of an embezzler. Maybe together the four of us can get our minds around these cases a little better."

"I'm more than glad to help. I appreciate your involving me."

"Good." Wes looked at Brian. "Oh, before we begin. On top of all that's happened, Brian had a very scary experience last night. His son was bitten by a poisonous snake."

"My god, what happened?" Karen's voice filled with alarm. She knew Brian was very proud of his son. "Is he alright?"

"Brian why don't you tell Karen what happened?" Wes leaned back in his chair and nodded to Brian.

"Sure. Well, fortunately the crisis has mostly passed, so I can breathe easier. Jimbo's in the hospital and is doing okay. He came to my place for diner last night. We were opening my mail, including a small package that looked like an order of books. I frequently order books from a couple of the on-line book websites. My son opened the box, and an enraged snake thrashed itself free from its cramped space. Slithering on the counter, it then fell onto the floor. It bit my son before he could get away from it. I killed the damn thing with a couple of liquor bottles and a walking stick. Fortunately, the ambulance came quickly and rushed him to the hospital." Brian's adrenalin rose just recounting the events of last evening.

"Oh my god, Brian. That had to be scary. You say he's okay, now?"

"Yeah. He's going to be okay, just a very swollen and painful leg. The doctors have given him some painkillers. I expect to bring him home tomorrow" Brian's heart beat faster.

"And if that experience wasn't scary enough, realizing that someone sent the snake to Brian, with the intent to kill him, doubles the danger factor in this case." Wes added the shocker behind the event.

"Oh, my god. Someone is getting desperate." Karen thought aloud as alarm surged through her.

"This attempt to murder Brian just emphasizes that we must solve these cases, and quickly. Phyllis scolds me sometimes for using my *gut technique*, but I find it pretty reliable." Wes winked at Phyllis. Then he said, "I'm convinced these four crimes are related."

"I think we're all convinced now." Phyllis added.

Wes knew that Brian, Karen, and Larry had discussed some of the embezzlement details in Palm Springs. He felt a little uncomfortable that the people close to the case were talking freely among themselves. Normally he preferred keeping people separated so they could not synchronize their stories, just in case. He trusted his instincts about these people, but would keep his guard in check anyway.

"What I'd appreciate from you two is an analysis of the kind of person who would commit these crimes, a little profiling if you will." Wes leaned back in his chair. "A while ago, Brian started describing what motivates an embezzler. Brian, maybe you could start over."

Brian had read about a few embezzlers in his experience as a computer forensics professional. He explained that embezzlers often live beyond their means. They buy expensive houses, cars, or other expensive toys that they could not afford on their salaries. They could have costly drug addictions, or take exotic vacations. Or high medical bills. They would likely continue the embezzlement even after the perceived need no longer exists.

Brian further explained that embezzlers often do not feel moral guilt for their actions. They feel they deserve the money. Another possibility, they may experience mood swings or feel depressed, and the money elevates their moods.

Karen added that Brian's definitions also describe a psychopath, or sociopath in some cases. And such a person could have committed the two murders, and the attempted murder of Brian. The embezzlement is of course a white-collar crime and usually does not involve violence. So these cases could involve accomplices, or a very complex intelligent person, a sociopath.

Brian talked further about his experiences, and Karen talked about her understanding of character behavior. Wes and Phyllis occasionally asked questions, nodded, or murmured they understood. Most of what they heard confirmed much of what they already knew. The shared knowledge would add to their shared effectiveness.

When they finished, Wes asked Karen to tell them anything more that she had learned from the Internet.

"Most of the searches retrieved standard information that we discussed a few days ago. Brian, I found an article you wrote for the Information Technology Journal a couple years ago."

"Tried to enhance my career." Brian said modestly. "Did you read it?"

"Yes. Yes, I did. But I'm sorry, it was little beyond my knowledge base. I'm afraid I'm not much of a 'techie'. I think the Journal is written for techie types."

"Yes, it is. But thanks for reading it anyway."

"Most of the other information I encountered was factual, standard. The kind that employee personnel files contain."

"Wes and I reviewed the personnel files for several people. We didn't find much there that would help us with these cases." Phyllis added.

"I did learn that some of these people have money. Leonard Construction is a very profitable company. Daniel Post and Donna Girardi own a lot of company stock, especially Daniel Post." Karen emphasized the last sentence.

"Money can always motivate bad behavior, namely greed. But I guess that's the definition of embezzlement." Wes wished he hadn't stated the obvious, and moved the conversation forward. "Let's talk about some of the people we know who are close to the case. We can start with management. As you said, Daniel Post owns most of the stock. And as Brian pointed out, it's very unlikely that he would use a complicated computer scheme to embezzle his own money. How about this Donna Girardi?"

"She's been with the company a long time. She runs the most profitable division in the company." Karen answered. Her Internet search had helped.

"She's not very IT savvy. She delegates most of her computer related work to her admin assistant who actually handles most of her emails. She would definitely need an accomplice." Brian added.

"Both Mr. Post and Ms. Girardi are worth millions, many millions. Post is probably worth about a hundred, Ms. Girardi, about fifty. We could do more research into their finances. Actually Wes, Phyllis, you would have more access to that kind of information than I would." Karen's voice sounded a little tinny from the speakerphone.

"We're examining their financial records. I think we can eliminate them as 'persons of interest'." Wes preferred greed as the more reasonable motive.

"I do have another piece of information that might be interesting." Karen's voice from the speakerphone sounded distant. "Charles Erickson. Apparently he has money, or at least his family does. His father was a big real estate tycoon in the Los Angeles area. From the articles I've read, his father is in his seventies. Again, we're talking multi-millionaire category, here. I don't know if Charles shares that money now, or stands to inherit it."

Wes revealed that Chas' bank records only indicated good income, consistent deposits, no unusual deposits or expenditures. Other financial records indicated a few stocks, a comfortable life, but no high net worth. Karen's comments about his family money could help.

"Chas has been very cooperative in my work here. He's probably the best resource for information about his division, and he knows the accounting side of the business. I haven't sensed any indication that he's hiding anything." Brian continued, "As far as technology capabilities, he can run computer queries against databases, understands all the reports, and the like. I haven't been able to determine if he can circumvent the internal computer security system yet."

Almost an afterthought, Brian added, "However, he's been very helpful, and seems very interested in the details of my work. But I think that it's just his eagerness to understand everything that's going on around him. David told me that Chas is ambitious, very focused on climbing the corporate ladder. I guess I could add he drives a BMW, and lives in an upscale condo here in Santa Monica."

"Are we going to exclude everyone who has money? I'll admit I'm the first who thinks money is the usual motive for embezzling and a strong reason to kill someone. But, maybe we should consider other motives? It's reasonable to ask, why steal a couple million when you already have many millions?'" Wes let the question hang in the air. Or, maybe his *gut technique* was not always reliable.

A brief silence ensued while they considered Wes' words.

Wes looked at the next name on their list, *Larry Davis*. He could not just ignore it because he was a friend to both Brian and Karen. Besides, either of them could know useful information about Larry.

This time, Wes had to walk the fine line between interviewing them as witnesses and treating them as members of the investigation team.

"Brian, Karen, I know Larry Davis is a close friend of yours. But we have to consider all possibilities, understand all the players. I hope you understand. All we need is some defense attorney asking if we looked at all possible candidates." Wes chose his words carefully.

"Sure. I understand." Brian felt uncomfortable talking about his friend fitting a possible suspect profile. And he liked being part of the investigation team, so he would maintain his loyalty to Larry and be honest with Wes, somehow. "There is no way that I could believe that Larry is capable of something like this. He doesn't need the money. He is the most self-sufficient person I know when it comes to finances. He wants to retire in a few more years, and is in a good position to do so. I wish I were as financially well-off and as self-disciplined as he is."

Brian continued. "Larry obviously has the necessary accounting knowledge and has strong abilities with the computer. But I really don't believe he has the in-depth IT knowledge to hack the security system. I believe the IT guys will support me in that statement. Now Greg was interested in understanding technology to that level." As he spoke, Brian's confidence in Larry grew.

"Naturally, Greg can't appear on a suspect list." Phyllis stated the obvious.

"I know its opinion and not fact, but I want to add something." Brian took a deep breath. "Larry doesn't have a cruel bone in him. He couldn't hurt Greg and David. They were like his sons. He was very proud of them. From talking with David, he felt like Larry was almost a second parent. I put Larry on this list only because he has access to the systems. In fact, all of the names were put here because of their access levels."

"Brian, I understand how you feel about Larry. He's your friend. I appreciate that. I agree with you about him. I just needed to hear all pertinent information." Wes sensed Brian's discomfort and switched tactics for the moment.

"I understand your position. I didn't mean to get emotional." Brian shook his head and took a deep breath to calm himself.

"Brian, it's okay to support your friend." Wes gave Brian a supportive smile.

"I've known Larry for about five years now." Karen wanted to alleviate some of the tension. "I know he earns a high salary at

Leonard, and owns real estate here in LA and in Palm Springs, without mortgages. And his…" she paused, but continued, "partner of thirty years has a lot of money. He made a lot of money in LA real estate. So I think Larry would also fit into the 'has money' category."

"I could add that Peter, Larry's partner, has a much older sister. She's infirm and lives in an upscale nursing home in Palm Springs. So Larry would inherit a boatload of money." Brian interjected although he did not actually know the terms of Peter's will.

"Karen. Yes, we know that Larry is gay. That's not an issue. Believe it or not, most of us in law enforcement are in tune with the times." Wes' smile carried in his voice.

"I just didn't want to out someone without their permission." Karen added, "While I agree that having a lot of money probably precludes any need to embezzle. I try to give my characters motivations other than greed or financial need. For example, I like using psychopathic or sociopathic characters. They're more interesting, and more difficult for my hero to capture or overcome. Psychopathic characters usually fit in with the world around them, but have a sinister need or aspect to their lives that's not very obvious."

"I agree. From a fictional point-of-view, a book is more interesting if the villain is complex. But in my experience, most crimes are pretty basic, greed, anger, passion, retribution, and the like. Most criminals fit the standard profiles more often than not." Wes tried to keep the focus to the basics.

"But sometimes, reality imitates art. Or, is that the other way around, art reflects reality?" Brian scratched his head and leaned on the table.

"Ok. Let's explore that area for a minute. Maybe I can learn something." Wes allowed the conversation to follow a tangent.

"Great. As I said, a psychopath fits very nicely in the world around him." Karen continued. "But it's all an act. He may appear friendly, helpful, but he's really manipulative. He may seem sympathetic to someone, but he doesn't really feel any true emotion. He could manipulate you in small ways without you realizing it. When he causes someone pain, he does not feel any sympathy, or guilt. For example, he could stab you with a knife, but later act if nothing had happened. And he can be very convincing."

"That's interesting. I wonder if one of the people we're discussing would fit this description. Or anyone outside this group. Maybe we need to add more names to this list." Wes asked.

"And that will be hard to determine, because he, assuming the killer is a he, is very practiced in 'fitting in'." Karen continued.

Wes scratched his jaw stubble as he thought. It felt more like short wire bristle than sandpaper.

"One last thing on Larry, in the phone records, I noticed a few calls between him and Art Dexter in the evenings. What was their relationship?" Phyllis asked.

"I've not heard Larry mention Art, other than to identify him and his role here at Leonard. Sometimes there was tension around month-end, Art would provide numbers for reports late, or was slow to reconcile the reports. That sort of thing. What time of the month were the calls?" Brian interlaced his fingers and laid his hands on his lap.

"Various times. No pattern. Just trying to get a picture of the people." Wes shook his head. "How about Art Dexter?"

Wes did not volunteer any information that he already knew about Art, or that he suspected Art.

Karen answered first. "Very little, unfortunately. He wasn't listed on the Leonard company website. After you gave me his name, I searched my favorite websites. I only found that he graduated from Cal State in Carson five years ago."

"I worked with Chas mostly. He knew Art's job in detail, so I didn't have to spend much time with Art." Brian stifled a yawn. The lack of sleep over the last twenty-four hours began to show.

Wes still did not volunteer his information about Art.

"Karen, thanks for your help. You've given us a lot to think about." Wes leaned into the speakerphone, making eye contact with Brian and then Phyllis. "I think we can wrap up this meeting for now. Any more questions or comments?"

"I appreciate your including me. And if I learn more, I'll call you. Again I'll keep everything we discuss private. Nice talking with you again Brian. Nice meeting you, Phyllis."

"Same here." Brian and Phyllis chimed together.

"Bye." Karen pressed the disconnect button on her phone.

The phone line went quiet. Wes pressed the speakerphone's end button.

"I think what Karen has told us is useful. From reading-a-novel perspective, I like complex villains. But as I said, I work easier with the specific, basic evidence in a case. As they say, 'just the facts ma'am'. We unfortunately don't have time to call in psychiatrists to psycho-analyze all of these people, even if they agreed to meet with the psychiatrists."

"I liked what Karen said about psychopaths, that they can hide in plain sight. Besides, I think we've done a pretty good job developing a profile here on our own." Phyllis leaned on her chair arm.

"I agree." Wes tapped his pencil on his notepad.

"On the financial records side, Debra told me earlier that she's having trouble identifying the owners of the accounts in question on our list. Of course people often setup offshore accounts so that they're difficult to trace." Phyllis leaned back in her chair. "Debra's also looking at additional financial and personal records. Bank, phone, public, not so public. It's amazing how much info is out there."

"So we move on." Wes did not want Brian to know that Art was his primary suspect. So, they would discuss Art last.

Wes would use a cautious approach when dealing with Brian. After all, he worked for Leonard Construction, and was a longtime friend to someone on the short list of possible suspects. And the bigger issue, at least for Brian, if he knew that Art may have sent the snake to him, it could drive him to do something rash. If Wes had a kid, and someone put his kid in danger, he'd probably take justice in his own hands. And he was law enforcement, sworn to uphold and such.

"Now, what about Art Dexter?" Wes hoped his voice did not belie his feeling that Art was his chief suspect. "Brian, you go first."

"Ok. As expected, he knows his work responsibilities very well. Although, he doesn't seem particularly ambitious, he does his job well, even though only at a minimum. He is Chas' right hand man. So he must do something right. Chas is such a driver when it comes to work. On the technology side, I don't see Art as a super-skilled individual."

"Could he just hide his abilities?" Phyllis asked.

"He could, but I think when someone has computer skills, they usually show, especially to IT savvy guys." Brian responded. "However, he drives a Porche, a pretty expensive lifestyle item. But of course many young men his age buy expensive cars and sacrifice in other areas, like he lives in a cheap apartment."

"His financial records don't show a lot of activity." Phyllis added.

"But if he lives on a cash basis…" Wes said.

"Right. Cash would not necessarily show in his financial records. However, his bank records do show his car payments. Actually they're more than his rent."

"But if he embezzled a couple million dollars, it'd have to show somewhere? That amount of money would make a pretty big wad of cash in anyone's pants." Brian grinned as he swiveled his chair back and forth.

The phone rang. Brian answered. Liz was on the other end of the line.

Brian swiveled to face the Detectives. "Sorry. I don't mean to interrupt our session, but that was Liz. Our meeting with Mr. Post, Larry, and the others is in about ten minutes."

"Ok. Let's wrap this up. After we finish meeting with them, Phyllis and I want to talk more with Chas, Art, and possibly Larry." Wes collected his papers into folders and slipped them into his brief case.

"Do you want me to join you when you talk with them?"

"Nah, that won't be necessary. We just have a few questions. We need to get back to the station. We still need to review the new reports that Debra has for us. Phyllis and I need to discuss search warrants after we review those reports." Wes looked to Phyllis for agreement.

"We'll be fine." Phyllis responded.

Other thoughts emerged from the back of Brian's mind; his suspicions about the people at Leonard began to grow. The people at Leonard were likable people, including the ones on his list. But with the events of the last week, two murders and especially Jimbo's snakebite. It was not an accident, by any means. He could have lost his son, the most important person in the world to him. Someone, probably someone on his list, was evil, very evil.

His suspicion slowly changed to anger, and a vengeful rage stood just outside the door of his consciousness. He worried if he could maintain an objective, professional attitude with these people as he continued to research this embezzlement.

He forced these thoughts out of his mind. He had to. Self-control was important. Right now, he wanted to go to Long Beach Memorial to check on his son.

FORTY SIX

Wednesday Night, April 13
Santa Monica, California

The alpha man parked two blocks from his partner's apartment. He wanted this visit unannounced, unexpected. In the past, they met in out-of-the-way places, different each time. This meeting would be their last one. They had talked earlier, his partner would be home, alone tonight.

A dozen broken concrete steps with a shaky handrail in the center led to a small collection of stucco duplexes surrounding a small courtyard. The light blue colored buildings with white window trim desperately needed paint. Poorly maintained tropical plants crowded the small courtyard. Several stand-alone pots containing a variety of plants in various stages of life and death sat on the front stoops. He approached the front door of apartment C, stepping around a broken terra cotta pot with an almost dead areca palm in its dry soil. He sarcastically thought a real plant lover lived here.

He wondered why his so-called partner chose to live in such cheap surroundings. He earned enough money to afford better. And their joint venture certainly gave him more spending money.

Of course, no place this near the beach was exactly cheap. Although, city rent controls kept the rents low. However, it provided little incentive for owners to maintain their properties in top condition.

This owner probably waited for the right time to sell the property to some developer, who would clear the land and build expensive, million dollar condos.

He pressed the button on the attached doorbell unit, just below the peephole. The cheap battery-operated unit sounded tinny, but loud. The small paper insert that should identify the resident was blank. That did not matter, he knew the resident.

He pressed the button again. The door opened.

"Hey, wasn't expecting you." He opened the door wider to allow his visitor to enter.

"Hey, right back at you. I just thought maybe we could catch up on things." He lifted a six-pack of Budweiser as an offering. Sweat had formed on the cold bottles.

"Sure. Come in. Always like a cold Bud. But thought you preferred those micro-brews."

"Not always. A Bud can be good too." The alpha man stepped inside the room.

"I know you're worried about things happening too fast." The partner spoke defensively. "I'm doing what I do best, what I think is best."

"I know. I know. I don't want to argue. Let's just relax for a while. Enjoy our beers. I've been thinking. Maybe your methods aren't all bad. Maybe, even pretty good." *He lied*. He pulled a beer from the carton, and handed the carton to his host. He twisted off the bottle cap. "If that's alright with you?"

"Sure." The partner tilted his head, smiled, and took a cold one for himself. "I'll put these in the fridge to keep them cold." He turned and headed for the kitchen. Maybe his controlling partner wasn't such a bad guy after all. "Just lay your jacket there." He nodded to the stand beside the door.

The guest removed his jacket and cap, laid them on the small wood stand, and sat in the overstuffed chair alongside the matching couch. He scanned the room, a rectangular living area with a small dining area at the opposite end. A blonde wood dining table with three matching chairs dominated that space. A computer, monitor, and keyboard sat on a small folding table against the wall. A fourth dining chair faced the monitor. Two surfboards leaned against the wall in the other corner near the door to the kitchen.

A blue-green plaid couch and matching chair filled most of the remaining space in the room. A couple surfer magazines lay on top of the small glass top coffee table. A large oil painting of a western sunset, probably bought from an unknown artist on the beach, hung above the couch. Opposite the couch, a large window opened to the outside courtyard, and a large flat-screen television sat in front of it. As much as possible, he sat with his back turned to the open window so passers-by could not see him clearly.

When the host returned, he slouched into the far end of the couch, and faced his guest. He took a few gulps of the cold beer, and appeared to relax, even self-assured, cocky. He acted as if he was in control. *He would learn better.*

"Must be nice living this close to the beach. How long did you say that you've lived here?" The alpha man asked.

"Just over four years. I like it. I get to surf most days. Except when I have to work late. I can literally take my board, walk down the block, cross PCH, and surf. Mostly on weekends." He nodded toward the surfboards in the corner behind him.

They talked more about beach life, surfing, and living in California. The partner finished his beer, said he wanted another, and rose from the couch to get it. He asked if his guest was ready for another. Yeah, sure was the response. He returned with two beers, and handed one to his guest.

"Cheers." The alpha man twisted off the top, wiped the bottle top with his hand, and raised the bottle in a toast.

"Cheers." The partner twisted off the top, and gulped some of his beer. He slouched further into the couch.

"Well, what do you want to talk about?" The partner asked when the conversation entered a lull. He looked his guest directly in the eyes. He began to feel tired. "Or have we had enough small talk? I've never thought of you much for small talk, anyway."

"That's true. Sure. Let's talk." The alpha man set his bottle on the table and crossed one leg over the other. "I thought we had agreed to talk about what we would do, each step of the way."

"We had, to a degree. We agreed that you'd handle the technical stuff, the complex stuff. And I would handle the physical stuff. We agreed our primary problem, namely Greg, needed to be disabled. He just ended up killing himself in an accident. Everyone believes it was an accident. "

"I agree. Then we talked about eliminating the consultant. But, before we decided, you eliminated David. And now the attempt on the consultant. We needed to talk about these things first. I really wish we had talked."

"David just knew too much. And the consultant, well…" The partner became defensive.

"But the snake bite didn't work. Did it?" The alpha man rested his elbow on his chair and scratched his chin with his index finger. "How can I solve the technical stuff if you keep eliminating people?" He paused before continuing, "How are we going to solve all of this? Are we going to work together, or not?"

"I know, I know. But I had to act fast. Maybe a little too fast. But, the job is done." His voice contained no apology. "You'll just have to point the blame at someone else. You'd said you had a good idea."

"Actually, I was thinking of the consultant and maybe another person, one of the finance people. But you've complicated that possibility." The alpha picked up his beer and sipped it. "As I told you, it will take time to change all the records and files. And leave enough evidence to point to a new person. But if you keep eliminating people, I won't have anyone to blame. Do you understand me?"

"Yeah, but you can still point the blame at someone else. Right? There are several financial and IT people with access to the databases."

"I think so." The alpha man was in control again. Maybe. "But with all you've done, in this age of DNA, latent fingerprints, and all that forensics stuff. You've made my job a lot more difficult."

"For that, I'm sorry."

Did he apologize? A little late. The alpha man sarcastically thought.

"Besides, look at that cop guy in Illinois. He may have gotten away with killing two of his wives. The law moves slow." The partner inhaled a deep breath to relax. "Even OJ got off."

"True." The guest agreed. "But OJ isn't exactly living a comfortable life."

"I know you like being in control. But I needed to act quickly. I did. And I know what I'm doing. I'm very careful to not leave fingerprints, DNA."

Apology retracted.

The alpha man did not respond. He began to tire of this argument. Besides, he argued only to agitate his partner. Like a cat plays with its captured mouse.

The alpha man changed his tactic "On some level, I'm coming around to your way of thinking. Even though I'd like for us to talk about all the steps we take, I've been thinking. Just because I have a different approach to dealing with problems, doesn't mean that your methods won't work. I have to admit your methods get the job done." He played to his partner's ego.

"Good." The host grinned, even felt relaxed, and settled deeper into the couch's cushions.

"What do you think went wrong with the attempt on the consultant? Using a snake was creative. Unfortunately, it didn't work. It bit his son, who I understand is going to survive just fine. The consultant met with the Sheriff's detectives today. He didn't stay away for long." He taunted his host.

"I'm sorry that didn't work. Sometimes things don't work out as planned." He missed the taunt. "I'll have to plan better next time. But thanks, it was creative, wasn't it."

"I'm curious, what do you plan next?" The alpha man smiled, allowing his partner to think he was in control.

"I'm still thinking about that." His words slowed, slurred.

"We have to be careful. If we kill off everyone, we won't have anyone to point the blame to. Everything will just point to us." He noticed his partner's slowed reaction. "Talking about pointing the blame to someone else, who do you think that should be? Any suggestions?"

The partner sat there. His thoughts moved slowly. He heard the unclear question, as if someone in another room had asked it. He set his beer on the coffee table, next to the empty one. He stared straight ahead, engulfed in a mental fog, his eyes focused on a small tear on the corner of the label of his nearly empty bottle. Then he noticed the empty bottle next to it, had a small tear in the same position on the label.

He felt sleepy, groggy. Wait a minute, he thought, he doesn't feel this sleepy at nine in the evening. Not with only two beers. His mind sensed something was wrong, very wrong.

FORTY SEVEN

PRESENT DAY And TIME
Wednesday night, April 13
Santa Monica, California

The guest proceeded to the next step.

So far, everything had gone according to plan. He pulled a tissue from deeper in the jacket's pocket, and wiped the syringe clean of possible fingerprints. He positioned his host's fingers around the syringe, and squeezed them in a couple positions, leaving clear, full fingerprints. He laid the syringe on the coffee table, just as a user would. He removed a foil containing a disposable hand wipe, and cleaned everything he remembered touching. He had purposely kept his hands to himself this evening.

He retrieved the carton of unused beer that he had brought from the refrigerator. He returned the empty ones from the coffee table to the carton, and put them in the plastic grocery bag that he had brought. A guest carrying a carton of beer from a house he visited might be noticeable. He added the used tissue, the used hand wipe and its foil package.

Next he canvassed the apartment, looking for items he could use to further stage his scene. Curiosity also played a part of his search. He had never been to his host's apartment before tonight.

He moved to the bedroom. In a middle drawer of a dresser, he found a small metal box that contained a small bag of pot, a well-used pipe and a lighter. In the same drawer, he moved well-worn underwear aside and almost missed a small, half full vial of what appeared to be cocaine. He expected to find more, since he knew his host sold the stuff.

Never mind. What he had would work just fine. He was careful to leave any existing fingerprints on the goods he selected. He laid the metal box opened, and the coke, alongside the syringe on the coffee table.

The setting would appear to be a small party with everyone leaving after their host 'fell asleep'. The partiers would likely have used a variety of recreational drugs and alcohol.

He found empty beer cans in the trash and added them to the other items on the coffee table. They would probably have fingerprints of other people, which could help with the someone-else-did-it defense, in case the *overdose* theory did not work. He moved two dining chairs around couch, turned facing the television.

When he finished, he reviewed his staging. He had completed what he thought was a good scene of some dudes watching TV and having a drug party. His planned use of putting the drug in four beer bottles worked well. He smiled, self-satisfied at his genius for his little scheme of tears on the labels.

He slipped on his jacket and baseball cap. He took off one of the latex gloves, placed it in the plastic bag with its other contents, opened the door, and pressed the self-locking button on the handle. He stepped outside, and closed the door as he removed the second glove.

"How are you this evening?" A gravelly, but friendly voice behind him asked.

Startled, he jumped. His heart skipped a beat. He almost dropped the plastic bag with its contents. He curled the second glove in his fist, and tried to keep the beer bottles from clinking. He didn't face the man directly.

"Sorry, didn't mean to scare you."

"No. No. Just a little startled. I'm fine. Just deep in thought." He quickly regained his control and turned on his charm. "I'm great. How are you this evening?" He tilted his head to not look at the man directly. He hoped this newcomer did not see him remove the latex glove.

"I'm doing good. Thanks. Have a good night." The newcomer shifted his grocery bag, and inserted a key into the lock.

"Thanks. I will. You too." The visitor said, sounding cheerful.

He kept his face turned from the newcomer and exited the opposite end of the stoop shared by the two apartments. He heard the newcomer shut his door and saw the light come on. This was good. This meant no one was home while he was there. He walked down the steps through the courtyard to the street. His fast heartbeat slowed a little. He felt pleased with himself; all went according to his plan, as it should. He liked being in control.

FORTY EIGHT

Thursday morning, April 14
Santa Monica, California

Wes and Phyllis drove through Leonard Construction's small visitor's parking area. The wipers in intermittent mode squeaked as they pushed the light rain off the windshield. With no space available, Phyllis suggested parking in the employee structure in back. They could leave a Sheriff's placard on the dash. They found an unreserved space on the second floor.

A few people wearing employee badges walked to the northeast corner of the parking structure where a small bridge connected it to the main building. Wes and Phyllis joined them through the employee's entrance, smaller, and less grand than the main lobby on the front side of the building.

Two uniformed guards sat behind a chest high desk-bar unit, just inside the glass doors, and checked employee badges as people entered. With a nod, or a smile, they greeted the people. Visitors rarely entered through this entrance. The guards saw the same people every morning, the early arrivers, the stragglers, the friendly, the pretty, and the older. Over time, *strangers* narrowed to the few, the visitors, temps, or consultants.

Wes and Phyllis showed their badges as they approached the security desk. The guard standing almost stood at attention. The one sitting stood. Security guards often think of themselves as law enforcement, have goals to become police, or at least respect law enforcement. Wes liked the respect, and sometimes took advantage of it. Security staff often answered questions, or gave access that others would deny.

Wes introduced himself and Phyllis. He said they had an appointment with Brian Latimer. The smaller security guard could not find Brian's name in the employee roster. Wes added that Brian was a consultant in the accounting department. The second guard found Brian's name and phone number on a supplemental sheet. He dialed the number, as he asked Wes and Phyllis to sign the visitor's log. He handed them visitor badges.

After a couple minutes, Brian exited the elevator doors and greeted them. He thanked the guards, and escorted the detectives upstairs.

"Brian, how is your son this morning?" Wes asked as they waited for an elevator.

"He's doing very well. Thanks. They're letting me bring him home this afternoon, at least to my place. He'll stay with me a few days." Brian smiled at Wes and Phyllis. He stroked his chest as if straightening an imaginary tie, an old habit. "He's still in some pain, soreness, swelling, that sort of thing. The doctor told us that was to be expected, at least for a couple weeks. They have him on some mild painkillers."

"I bet he's glad about getting to go home." Phyllis said.

"He is." Brian added. "Larry asked that I take you to the small conference room near my office. I hope that's okay."

"I sort of liked the plush on the executive floor." Wes teased. "The room near you is just fine."

The elevator bell rang. They had reached Brian's floor.

"I talked with Detective Kaminski this morning." Wes said as they stepped out of the elevator.

"Oh. Did he have anything new to say? I talked with him late yesterday. He didn't have much news for me. The toxicology and forensics reports weren't ready yet." Brian led them to the small conference room.

Erica saw them approach, and stood. With the same politeness as others had shown, she asked if they wanted coffee or sodas. Brian told her not to worry, that he would take them to the break room. He wanted a soda, anyway.

Brian plugged a dollar into the vending machine, and selected a Diet Coke. Wes and Phyllis poured themselves coffee. Wes took his black. Phyllis added two packets of artificial sweetener to hers.

Wes and Phyllis noticed that this break room was the homely cousin of the plush break room on the top floor. Vending machines replaced the free options, except for the coffee. The refrigerator contained lunch bags and bottles of varying contents with clearly marked owners' names. A mix-match of mugs sat on the counter instead of the matching mugs with company logos in the cherry wood cabinets upstairs.

As they returned to the conference room, Brian excused himself for a minute to retrieve his files from his office. When he rejoined them, he closed the door and took a chair opposite Wes and Phyllis.

Wes spoke first. "As I mentioned a while ago, I talked with Detective Kaminski about your case. He has talked with the security people who were on shift when that package with the snake came in. That guard had no clear memory of the delivery person, except he was a youngish white guy, blond hair, dark brown uniform, and a matching baseball cap. Overall, not very helpful."

"Lobby security receives bunches of packages for the residents. They probably don't pay much attention to the delivery people. But they usually have to sign for them." Brian added. "Even if the guard signed something, I'm sure the delivery guy would have destroyed it."

Wes leaned back in his chair, scratching his head. "It'll still be a couple more days before Long Beach Forensics finishes with the package. Wine logged as it was, they found some latent fingerprints, very likely they would belong to the security people and of course, your son. The perp probably wore gloves. They're even analyzing the snake's remains. Apparently, identifying the stomach contents can help determine where the snake may have come from."

"I sure hope you catch this guy soon. Talk about feeling disillusioned. Until a couple days ago, I wouldn't have believed that I actually know someone who could kill another person." Brian's face tightened with anger.

"I understand. That's really a pretty common reaction. Don't beat yourself up. I don't want to jump to conclusions, but…" Changing the subject, Wes grinned and nodded to Phyllis.

"Yeah. Right." Phyllis rolled her eyes at the understatement.

"Phyllis is used to me." Wes continued. I've developed a pretty effective gut instinct. We call it my GAT, my *gut analysis technique.*"

"We try to keep the concept to ourselves." Phyllis cautioned.

"Brian, do you have anything new, since yesterday?"

"Sure." Brian retrieved his summary sheet and laid it on the table.

Brian reminded them how systems administrator passwords work. Only an administrator can shut down and restart system security. With the help of Dean Horvath, the IT network techie, Brian had discovered that this had happened seven times in the last four months. And he has traced those times to suspicious activities in the accounting system.

When in *on* mode, the systems security records huge amounts of data, showing all access activity on the computer. For those seven times, the activity log was blank, as if no one did anything on the computer, a very unlikely scenario. But things happened in the accounting system. Fake accounts were created, and payments were paid. Actually, the payments were split between what the company really owed and another account. Brian gave details and answered questions.

He continued to explain that only a few people in the IT technical staff, like Dean Horvath or Ralph Chung, should have or know such powerful security access codes. Wes asked if they should add Dean's, or other IT staff names to the list. They added three new names to the list.

"Can you tell me anything new about Art?" Wes asked sounding anxious.

Brian said he also learned from Dean that he shared a limited social life with Art. He had surfed with him and his friends a couple times, and had joined them for beers other times. Art had expensive surfing boards, and often paid the bar tab. The girls seemed to like him. He always seemed to have money. He's not that good looking but something sure appealed to the girls.

Wes was eager to discuss the Art Dexter topic.

"I hope I'm not jumping to conclusions. Didn't I just say that a moment ago?" He looked at Phyllis and grinned.

"Yes you did." Phyllis smiled at Wes' consistency, knowing where he headed the conversation.

"Ok. Anyway, I think that everything points to Art. He was the last to see Greg alive. He spends more money than he earns, and has no debt." Wes did not stop. "He has given us inconsistent information. His alibi for the night David Fraser died doesn't hold water. He drives a late model Porche, almost paid for." Wes scanned Brian's face for his reaction. "However, as we talked yesterday, I'd like to know the reasons for the few after work-hours phone calls between him and Larry."

"I don't know. I've not heard Larry talk about Art, except as it relates to work. I'd assume that the calls would still be about work." Brian shook his head.

Wes' words had begun to raise the brightness level in Brian's mind.

"We'll need to find out. Now, Brian, this next information might upset you. But I think you need to know this. You're part of this team. We have to solve this case, and we need your help." Wes was on a roll.

"Ok. I'll try." Brian felt anxious and braced himself.

"Please don't just try. All of us have to be in full self-control, here. Now, the big thing. Yesterday we canvassed Art's neighborhood, his apartment complex really. He lives in a small collection of duplexes, with a central courtyard. One of his neighbors, actually his next door neighbor, an aging hippie type has pet snakes. He claims they're non-poisonous, but he could have poisonous ones that he won't admit to. He wouldn't let us inside to see them. We suspect, at a minimum, he has sources to the poisonous variety." Wes folded his hands and rested his elbows on the table. "It can't just be a coincidence that someone sent a snake to you, and Art's neighbor has snakes."

Brian's face flushed, showing the rage rising in him. But he resolved to control his anger, and sucked in a deep breath. He would control himself and work with Wes to catch this guy. No, not *this guy*, Art.

"We just have to connect the dots, build the evidence." Wes continued to watch Brian's reactions.

"And he has blonde hair. So he could be that delivery guy." Phyllis added.

"I can't believe this. I don't want to believe this. But my son could have died." Brian's voice tightened as his anger surged through him again.

"Brian, I understand. I really do. You've just been through a major traumatic event. I can only imagine how you feel. I don't have kids, but I have a couple nephews. I love those boys and I know how my brother loves them." Wes looked directly at Brian. He needed his full cooperation.

"Because of our jobs, we focus on finding the bad guy and bringing him to justice, as corny as that may sound. It may seem that we don't care about the people, the victims." Phyllis added. "But we do care. We work very hard to get justice for the victim."

"We have to solve this crime, and that means 'going by the book'. And we need your help." Wes put his hand on Brian's shoulder and looked him directly in the eye.

All three were silent for a moment while Brian regained his composure.

"I understand. Forgive me. I am normally very self-controlled. And I will be this time. It's just that this snakebite, Jimbo's near death weighs heavy on me. When I feel this intensely angry, I want to strike back." Brian spoke, his face tight.

Brian began to relax, his self-control returning. He almost smiled. "I'll be alright. This is probably one of the few situations where a victim gets to help catch the asshole. This is personal. But I will stay in control."

"Thanks, Brian. We understand. You're our technical guy. You're the best guy to sift through all of these computer details. We're the detectives. We work together. We are going to catch this guy. But we have to do it by the book to make it stick. Ok?"

"Ok. I'm ok." Brian took a deep breath. Actually he felt encouraged.

"Ok." Wes also took a deep breath. He shared Brian's anger. "Phyllis will you call the DA's office? Get us a search warrant for Art's apartment? And Brian will you ask your secretary, ah..."

"Erica."

"Yes, Erica, to call Art here to the conference room. Let's just keep it at the interview level, general, so we have all of our ducks in a row, so to speak."

Phyllis pulled her cell phone from her briefcase and rolled her chair to the side of the small room. Brian excused himself to talk with Erica. Two minutes later, he returned.

"Wes, Phyllis. Erica just told me that Art didn't come into work today."

"Not a good sign." Wes angled his head, suspicious. He swiveled in his chair to face Phyllis.

"Debra heard from the DA's office, said she should have our search warrant in about a half hour." Phyllis could almost read Wes' mind. "All it needs is the judge's signature."

"Does that mean you'll have to drive back to the valley for it?" Brian asked.

"Hey, we have some of the modern technologies. We have a printer in the car. Debra just has to fax it to us, and we're in business. We'll have the physical copy in our hands by the time we get to Art's apartment." Wes grinned, his adrenaline raced through his veins.

Wes and Phyllis collected their files and notes and stuffed them into their briefcases. Outside the window, the rain clouds had parted, allowing the Southern California sunshine to return.

"Now, Brian. Continue what you're working on. Don't tell anyone what we're doing." Wes took another deep breath. "Phyllis, let's confront Mr. Arthur Dexter. With the search warrant, we'll search his house and probably arrest him."

Brian and Phyllis nodded their heads in solidarity.

"Let's roll."

FORTY NINE

Thursday morning, April 14
Santa Monica, California

Rather than drive surface streets, Wes chose the freeway to Art's apartment, faster, fewer signal lights. As they exited the tunnel where the I-10 morphs into the PCH, the small printer on the console between them beeped. Paper rolled from the small thermal platen. Gripping the corner of the document, Phyllis tore it from the printer. She scanned it for correctness, and legibility. It was.

"Looks like we're in business." Phyllis smiled and pushed the *print ok* button to acknowledge successful transmission.

Wes slowed as he approached West Channel Road. He turned right. After a couple turns, he parked a couple houses past Art's complex. Wes wanted out of the line of sight from Art's apartment. He did not want Art to see their approach; otherwise, he might run.

Wes and Phyllis unsnapped their holsters as they walked cautiously to Art's apartment. The drapes were closed. Next door, the drapes to Senior Dude's apartment were opened wide.

Wes rapped on the door with his knuckles. "Arthur Dexter, LA County Sheriff's Department. We have a warrant." No answer. He paused a few seconds, knocked again, louder. Still no answer.

Wes rested his right hand on his gun. He stepped to the large picture window to see through the small gap where the drapes met in the center of the window. He could not see anything.

"Mr. Dexter. We're with the LA County Sheriff's Department. Open the door." Phyllis demanded, resting her hand on her gun.

"Officers, I think he's at work." The senior dude neighbor poked his head out his front door. Recognizing the detectives, he stepped onto the front stoop, "you're the two detectives I met yesterday, aren't you?"

"Yes, Mr. Harvill. We are." Wes removed his hand from his holster. His jacket fell in place and hid his gun. "We were just at his place of business. They said he didn't come into work today."

"I saw him last night. Actually, early in the evening, but haven't seen him since." He looked back to the parking area and pointed to the parking structure. "Wait, I see his car, still in his parking space."

"He doesn't seem to be home. Any idea where he could be?" Phyllis asked.

"Not really. But you can check with Don Emerson, if you like. He's the manager, unit F." Harvill gestured with his hand to the apartment across the courtyard.

"Thanks. We'll check with him." Wes answered.

"Mr. Harvill, please wait in your apartment?" Phyllis instructed while she waited at Art's door.

Mr. Harvill stepped back inside, closed his door partly, and stood at his large picture window to watch the activities.

Wes walked across the courtyard to unit F. He knocked. After a minute, a stooped man, probably in his seventies, opened the door. He wore an athletic shirt, the underwear variety, and dark polyester trousers. His obese torso stretched the shirt to its limits. Sparse white body hair covered his visible pale skin. Heavy dark eyebrows, the size of large furry worms, shaded his bloodshot eyes. For someone living close to the beach, he spent no time in the sun.

"Hello, can I help you?" He grunted his voice gravelly. His breath smelled of cigarettes.

"Hello, Mr. Emerson?" Wes showed his badge to the man.

"Yeah." Another grunt.

"I'm detective Makelin from the LA County Sheriff's Department." Wes identified himself. "We need access to unit C, Mr. Dexter's apartment. We have a search warrant. Can you give us access?"

Emerson hesitated for a moment. "Sure, I guess so" Leaving the door open, he turned to retrieve the keys from a nearby rack.

Wes followed Mr. Emerson to Art's door. Phyllis introduced herself and offered the warrant for him to read, but he waved it away, and opened the door.

Wes pulled his gun from its holster, and told the manager to step back. Wes nudged the door open wider and entered first. Phyllis removed her gun and followed him inside.

The apartment door opened into a large living room. The mid-day light flooded the white painted room, even with the drapes closed. Art lay awkwardly on the couch, his head propped on a pillow, one arm lay across his stomach, and the other dangled to the floor. One leg stretched along the couch, the other with the foot resting on the floor. Wes and Phyllis had seen enough bodies in their years of law enforcement to know Art was dead.

The two detectives proceeded to clear the area. With guns still drawn, they covered each other as they determined that the four rooms were clear, and they were safe to proceed. Once satisfied, they holstered their guns, and returned to where the body lay.

They saw Harvill and Emerson standing at the doorway, gawking. They too could tell that Art was dead. Wes approached them, and insisted that they return to their apartments. He also told them not to leave, that he would have questions later. He closed the door.

Harvill and Emerson returned to the manager's apartment. His front window gave them a better view of the activities.

Wes and Phyllis examined the body, careful not to disturb anything until the Medical Examiner and the crime forensics unit completed their work. Wes wanted to open the drapes, but decided against it. He wanted to preserve the crime scene. He did turn on the overhead lights.

They noticed an empty syringe on the coffee table and beer cans. A pot bong and a half empty vial of coke sat on the end table. Before examining the crime scene further, they followed necessary protocol. Closing the door, they stepped outside to call the necessary units.

They called Detective Argos since this crime was in his jurisdiction. Argos answered. He was en-route. Wes suggested Argos call his department for the necessary units. No ambulance would be needed, since the body had been dead for several hours. They would need uniforms to secure the crime scene and for crowd control. Also, they required crime scene forensics people to process the scene. Wes told him that Phyllis was calling the ME.

"This case just got a lot more complicated." Wes looked at Phyllis and shook his head in frustration. "There definitely is another person involved."

"That there is." Phyllis agreed with the obvious.

"This means of course that the others on our short list move up the list." Wes thought aloud. "Art could have been the inside guy. Was his partner the killer, or did they share? Does the other guy have the IT skills? More questions that need answers."

"Yeah. Art certainly didn't seem the IT type. We just need to rethink the whole situation." Phyllis turned to leave. "I'll get some poly gloves and cotton booties from the car."

"Okay. Meanwhile, I'll talk with the manager, and Mr. Harvill."

The two were watching from the manager's large front window. Wes raised his hand to knock on the manager's door. It opened. Mr. Emerson invited Wes inside, and gestured to sit on the dark worn couch against one wall. Mr. Harvill sat on the other end. Mr. Emerson sat in a lumpy swivel rocker that shared an end table with the couch and a TV tray on the other side. All furniture faced a small TV across the room, near the front door.

"Mr. Harvill, you said you saw Mr. Dexter early last evening. Tell me more about what you saw."

"Yes. I didn't talk to him. He passed by my front window, carrying what I thought were groceries." Harvill answered. "Haven't seen him today at all. Now we know why."

"How about you, Mr. Emerson?" Wes asked.

"I saw him yesterday early evening, probably about the same time as Ken here. Looked like he was carrying some groceries from his car. I was coming back from putting out some trash." Emerson mumbled through his smoke damaged voice. "We said 'hello', 'nice evening', that sort of thing."

"Mr. Harvill, Did you tell him that we had stopped by?" Wes asked.

"No, like I said I never talked to him. I just saw him walk by the window." Harvill raised his hand and tapped the side of his head. "Wait, I just remembered, someone was leaving his place last night, early evening. I'd come back from the store. Had to get some groceries for myself."

"About what time was that?"

"Oh, I'd say eight-thirty, nine."

"What'd he look like?"

"Oh, average size. Baseball cap, windbreaker."

"How about some more information? Young? Old?" Wes pulled a notepad from his pocket, and wrote in it.

"Young, I guess. No gray hair."

Five minutes had passed. Wes tried prompting Harvill for more description than just young, average. Wes could see out the front window that Phyllis had returned to the stoop of Art's apartment and was slipping on the latex gloves and shoe covers. Police sirens sounded a few blocks away.

"We're going to need to talk with you two more. So, please don't leave the area." Wes instructed them, and re-joined Phyllis.

In a few seconds, a Santa Monica Police squad car arrived, lights flashing, sirens wailing. It squealed to a stop in front of the apartment complex. The lights shut off, and the sirens died. Two officers exited the car and approached the detectives. The officers reflected the common police department pairing of the experienced with the new hire.

Officer Shick, showing his age, represented the experience side. Probably in his late forties, his heavy paunch stretched his uniform shirt. Heavy breathing or a big meal could pop its buttons. He stood just less than six feet tall, and wore his salt-and-pepper hair in a crew cut style. His face displayed a permanent pissed-off expression.

His counterpart, Officer Jesson, twenty-something, lanky frame, a little shorter than Officer Shick, wore his head shaved. It gave him an intense, tough look that his young boyish face would otherwise give. Or perhaps by shaving his head, he simply attempted to hide a pronounced bald spot.

Seeing Wes and Phyllis standing on the stoop at Art's apartment, the officers climbed the few steps to join them. The officers, Wes, and Phyllis introduced themselves

Wes told the officers that Detective Argos from their department would arrive shortly. Wes updated them on the crime scene and asked them to secure the area,

Officer Jesson returned to his squad car and retrieved two rolls of yellow crime scene tape from the trunk. Wes outlined the areas to cordon, the crime scene, namely the apartment, Art's car in the carport, space on the street for police and crime scene vehicles that would arrive shortly.

After the officers cordoned those areas, Officer Shick stayed at Art's stoop, and Officer Jesson remained street side for crowd control and waited for forensics units to arrive. A small crowd of neighbors collected to watch the commotion.

The crime scene forensics team arrived, followed by the County Coroner in a Crown Victoria and his two assistants in a black windowless van. Both the Crown Vic and the black van displayed the County Coroner logo. Officer Jesson lifted the yellow tape to allow them to park inside the cordoned area. Moments later, Detective Argos arrived.

Those who could fit in the space gathered on the stoop. Others stood nearby within hearing distance. Wes and Phyllis updated them on the sequence of events. Wes opened the door for them to see the body on the couch. Detective Argos, the coroner, and the forensics lead looked inside, but did not enter. Wes explained that the crime scene had not been disturbed except for securing the area.

Wes explained that the body was that of Arthur Dexter, a primary suspect related to two other murders. Wes believed that Dexter's death was homicide, although it could have been a suicide. But highly unlikely.

The three detectives agreed they would tag team with the coroner and the forensics people. After the newcomers asked a few questions, and Wes had answered them, everyone slipped on latex gloves and sterile shoe covers. The coroner and the forensics people reminded the detectives to not touch or move anything until they finished their work. Protocol must be followed.

As a group, they entered the apartment. They shared the investigative duties, observing, commenting, while allowing the coroner and the forensics guys to lead. After an initial look at the scene, and with permission, Wes closed the door and turned on the lights. He left the drapes closed.

Members of the forensics team and the coroner's staff worked the crime scene with practiced efficiency. They examined the body, and the apartment in minute detail. One forensic member worked Art's car. No one interfered with another's efforts. They placed numbered yellow plastic placards beside several items and at several locations throughout the apartment. The photographer took pictures, lots of pictures. He responded to several requests to photograph objects in different rooms.

The teams collected skin scrapings, samples of suspicious dust from the coffee table and end table, and fingerprints from furniture. They bagged the empty syringe, the coke bottle, and the bong. The detectives hovered around the technical people, lifting some items with a pen, and pointing to others for forensics to not miss, or to take a picture. They wrote in their notepads.

The coroner took the body temperature to establish a time of death. Rigor was in its early stages. He concluded that twelve to sixteen hours had passed. He turned the body looking for cause of death, if possible. Seeing the syringe on the coffee table, he examined the body for puncture wounds. After some effort, he found a single puncture between the toes. His initial thought was that an overdose had caused the death. But the lack of other puncture wounds puzzled him. Most habitual users have several needle track marks, regardless how they try to hide them. He now agreed with the detectives that this was likely a homicide, but would not give a firm conclusion until after the autopsy.

For the next hour, they worked steadily, purposefully, and thoroughly. They knew their jobs, and did not rush. With the coroner and the forensics unit, the detectives continued to examine the apartment, searching for other evidence and clues.

In a closet, behind some boxes, Wes found a loose wallboard that covered the plumbing connections in the adjoining bathroom. Wes moved the boxes and the loose board. He found a small box.

"Hey, photo man, forensics guy. Would you come here please?" Wes called, excited about what he had found.

The box contained a small bag of white stuff, probably cocaine, a small grinder, and a few gram size empty bottles. The photographer took pictures of the box, contents, and its hiding place. The forensics guy bagged the box with its contents.

In the bathroom, Phyllis opened the medicine cabinet. She saw the usual, shaving equipment, toothpaste, aspirin, and the like. On the top shelf sat a roll of duct tape.

"Now why does a man have a roll of duct tape in his medicine cabinet?" She asked herself aloud, suspicious.

"Men normally don't." Wes joined her in the bathroom. He looked knowingly at her. "Look in the toilet basin, under the lid."

"Well, well, well." Phyllis smiled at the discovery. "Not a very original hiding place."

Taped inside the lid, with the duct tape, was a small notebook. After the photographer took pictures, Phyllis opened the notebook with her gloved hands. It contained several lines of codes, initials, and numbers.

"Maybe he was more creative with his record keeping than his hiding place." Wes read from over her shoulder. "Besides, why didn't he use his computer? Why is such a young man so old school?"

They would study the notebook later. Meanwhile, the forensics guy bagged this item also. They searched the apartment further, but found no new evidence or clues. They would allow the forensics team to finish their work.

The coroner's assistants lifted Dexter's body into a black body bag and zipped it closed. Then, they lifted it onto a gurney and rolled it down the steps to their van for transport to the morgue. With the door open, the noise from the outside swept into the room. It had escalated, not to the level of chaos, but loud. More neighbors had gathered. A reporter and cameraman had also arrived. The Santa Monica officer kept them behind the yellow tape.

"What can you tell us about the deceased?" The reporter yelled to the assistants as they loaded the body into their van.

"Sorry, you'll have to talk to the detectives, or the coroner." One answered.

"Any comments? What kind of shape is the body in?" The reporter persisted.

"The man said you'd have to talk with the detectives. He's not allowed to comment. You know the drill." Officer Jesson warned as he kept them behind the cordoned area.

A reporter with her cameraman from another TV station arrived and elbowed her way through the crowd to the front.

The detectives and the coroner huddled on Art's front stoop to discuss the case. They spoke quietly so no one could overhear them. Inside, the other technical people finished their work. The detectives removed their protective gloves and the no-longer sterile cotton booties. A forensics assistant returned with a plastic bag to collect the discarded items.

The coroner explained his group had done what they could and would call the detectives about scheduling an autopsy. He asked the detectives if they would like to attend the autopsy. Wes and Argos both answered yes. The coroner left, walking down the steps to his assistants waiting at the van. He instructed them to return to the morgue with the body. He would follow.

The reporters yelled their questions to the coroner and the detectives. The coroner ignored them. The detectives looked to each other as if to decide who should talk to the reporters, if at all.

"It's your jurisdiction." Wes grinned as he looked to Argos.

"Humph. I guess you're right." Argos grumbled. "But it'd probably be better if we both were there."

"Yeah, I guess so." Wes acquiesced. "Besides, we need to talk with Dexter's neighbor. I think you'll find him very interesting."

Argos grunted. Both men walked to answer some of the reporters' questions. Civic responsibility.

FIFTY

Thursday, Early Afternoon, April 14
Santa Monica

Several neighbors and spectators gathered street side to watch the excitement. Their collective voices raised the noise level especially as the detectives approached them. Passing cars slowed as they maneuvered through the limited space left on the street. The drivers and passengers rubbernecked to see the commotion. In front of the crowd, TV and radio reporters, including two cameramen jostled for position, stretching the yellow police tape, and drawing stern warnings from Officer Jesson.

Wes and Argos approached the swarm of people. They saw the small red lights on the cameras in the *on* positions. The reporters stretched their arms full length so their microphones could capture the detectives' comments. They shouted their questions simultaneously. As if on cue, the spectators shushed one another and quieted.

Reporters as a group never seemed satisfied with the answers. Journalism schools probably give required courses in keep-asking-questions, regardless how dumb they sounded. Although to law enforcement, reporters were a pain-the-butt, they sometimes provided useful information to the public. Over time, Wes developed the attitude that reporters were a necessary, although trying part of the investigative process.

The reporters asked a barrage of questions.

"Was Art Dexter's death a homicide?" "Was there only one death?" How did it happen?" "When did he die?"

Wes and Argos looked at each other. Wes smiled and nodded to Argos. It was his jurisdiction. Argos stepped closer to the microphones.

"I'm Detective James Argos with the Santa Monica Police Department. This is Sheriff's Detective Wes Makelin with the LA County Sheriff's Department." Argos faced the crowd. "Mr. Dexter was the only body in the apartment. The Coroner's preliminary estimate is that Mr. Dexter died last night around nine pm. We do not know the cause of death. So, we cannot declare his death a homicide until the coroner and the forensics units finish their work. They should have their results in a few days. You can contact the Public Relations Department of the Santa Monica Police for any information."

"How was Dexter killed?" A reporter persisted. Homicides make a more interesting read.

"As I said, you'll have to wait for the coroner's results. We're just beginning the investigation. I'm sorry but we just can't comment on what we don't yet know. So please don't jump to any conclusions." Argos sounded genuine, believable. "Give us a chance to do our work. If anyone of you has any information that might help this investigation, please contact one of us, or one of the officers. If you think of something later, please call the Santa Monica Police Department, or the LA County Sheriff's Department."

The crowd scene, although a little noisy, seemed less chaotic than in larger groups that Wes had experienced in the past. Their questions continued, but less loud, more controlled, almost fact gathering. They asked name, age, home invasion, where he worked. Argos answered a few questions, the basics. Argos showed his amiable side. His relationship with the public seemed positive. Wes stepped back. This crime scene was in Argos' jurisdiction.

Then, one question elevated the interview to a different level.

"I understand Mr. Dexter worked at Leonard Construction, here in Santa Monica. Does his death have anything to do with the two other deaths of Leonard Construction employees that happened in the last week?" The reporter asked.

This reporter obviously knew more than the others. He knew he had lead story material for the six o'clock news, not a story that would be lost on the newsroom floor. For a brief moment, silence settled over everyone.

"There was another death in Santa Monica a few days ago, a home invasion robbery." Argos spoke haltingly, groping for the right words. "And yes, the victim was also an employee of Leonard Construction, a company headquartered here in Santa Monica. We are investigating that burglary-homicide. We expect the autopsy and other forensics results in another day or two." Argos then emphasized, "We have no evidence that the two events are related, other than they both work for the same company. Again, you'll have to contact our PR department."

Argos looked to Wes who stepped forward.

"As far as the death of the third Leonard employee, we, in the Sheriff's Department, are investigating it. Right now, it's classified as an accident. During a rainstorm, a week ago, a car went over the railing over Topanga Canyon road into a deep ravine. In the crash, a Mr. Larkin, an employee of Leonard's, was killed. His death occurred in the jurisdiction of the County Sheriff's Department."

Wes continued. "The coroner's results for that case aren't finished yet. When they finish, the Sheriff's PR Department can give you the information." Wes chose his words carefully. He nodded to Argos. "We're cooperating with the Santa Monica Police Department. Both units are investigating all possible links in these deaths. We hope you'll cooperate by not jumping to any conclusions, until we finish our investigations."

As expected, chaos swept through the crowd. Like sharks tasting blood, the reporters escalated their questions, sensing a larger story, a very newsworthy story. The reporter who asked the pivotal question dissolved into the crowd, and allowed the others to attack the detectives with their questions. He had his lead story.

Both detectives fielded more questions, but were unable to satisfy the blood-thirst that had developed. They specifically avoided discussing the embezzlement at Leonard Construction, probably the central connection of the three deaths. And they also avoided discussing last night's snakebite attempt on Brian Latimer. Both apologized that they could not answer more questions and needed to return to their work. They turned and walked the steps to rejoin Phyllis standing on Dexter's front stoop.

A couple reporters turned to find the one who asked the question about the multiple deaths to learn what he knew. He had disappeared, probably to write his story.

While, the detectives crossed the courtyard to the manager's apartment, Wes gave Argos a quick synopsis of their past contacts with the two men.

Through his front window, Emerson saw them coming, and opened the door to invite them inside.

"Thanks for keeping yourselves available." Wes started. "I'd like to introduce Detective Argos from the Santa Monica Police Department. I believe you both know my partner Detective Hadley."

The stench of cigarette smoke assaulted them when they entered the room.

Argos shook hands with both men. Again, he showed his amiable side. Phyllis smiled and nodded. Emerson invited them to sit. Wes and Argos sat on the small couch. Emerson sat again in his swivel rocker, obviously his favorite chair, and the best seat for watching television. Harvill sat in a frilly padded Boston rocker a few feet away, facing the group. Perhaps Emerson had a wife at one time who sat there. Otherwise, the apartment showed no signs that a woman had ever lived there. Phyllis stood almost gaging from the cigarette smoke.

The detectives asked their usual questions about the last time the two men saw the deceased, any involvement in drugs, who his friends and acquaintances were, and did they know of any enemies that Mr. Dexter might have had. Most of their answers provided no new information. Wes asked Harvill to describe last night's visitor again. Maybe he would reveal more, or different information

They talked for several minutes. The detectives were pleasantly surprised with the cooperative attitude of both senior men, considering their peculiar mannerisms.

The questions subsided. Wes and Phyllis had agreed to save the best topic for last. Phyllis accepted the honors.

"Mr. Harvill. One more question. I remember, from when we talked before, that you have a small snake collection. The non-poisonous variety, right?" Phyllis looked directly at Harvill.

"Right. A small collection, non-poisonous. It's illegal to have poisonous ones'" Harvill's voice sounded a little defensive. He repeated his neck stretch-and-dip tic. He looked at Emerson. "I've told you about my collection."

"Un-huh." Emerson grunted.

"But if someone wanted a poisonous type, sort of off-the-radar type purchase, where could he buy one?" Phyllis spoke casually. Otherwise, Mr. Harvill may not cooperate.

"It's illegal to buy or own poisonous snakes, and I don't do anything illegal." Harvill felt accused, and defended himself. Again, his neck-stretch-head-dip thing. He began rocking.

"Mr. Harvill, we're not trying to accuse you of anything. We just have a case, in another city that has us a little confused. It's hard to find anyone who can give us information on owning snakes."

"Well, I guess there could be a way someone could buy an exotic pet that could be illegal to own, such as a poisonous snake." Harvill paused, rocked in his chair more slowly. His voice's tone returned to one of cooperation.

"Go on." Wes encouraged him.

"There are a couple of guys who might have access to illegal exotic pets. I don't know them, personally. I've just heard about them. Maybe I might have met them once, or twice. I don't think they're listed in the phone book. At least not for that service." Harvill stopped rocking, crossed one leg over the other, and glanced at the floor.

"We need their names." Argos politely demanded.

"Ok. Ok. But you can't tell them where you got their names. Or I, I could get into a lot of trouble."

"I think we can keep your name out of it." Wes reassured him. Law Enforcement can keep their sources quiet, as long as they aren't part of a crime.

Harvill gave the two names he knew. He did not have their phone numbers.

The detectives searched their notes for more questions, but decided they had all they needed to for now.

"If we're about finished here, when can I have my apartment back?" Emerson asked with his smoke damaged voice.

"Probably in a week. Two weeks at most." Argos answered. "We have to finish analyzing the evidence as much as we can. You understand."

"That's not too long. Dexter had paid through the end of the month." Emerson relaxed. A grin crept quickly across his heavy face, and just as quickly disappeared. He did not tell that his income increased as rents increased. Instead, he said, "Actually, the owner will be pleased to hear this. He can raise the rent; probably double it, or more."

The detectives thanked the two men for their cooperation. They asked them to watch Dexter's apartment and to call them if they saw anyone prowling around.

They returned to Art Dexter's apartment for one last go-through. Officer Jesson had removed the crime scene tape from the stoop, and started to tape over Dexter's doorway.

"Hold off on that for a couple minutes, officer." Argos spoke to the young officer. "We want to go through it another time, now that everyone is gone."

"Sure thing, sir."

"Thanks."

Wes and Phyllis followed Argos through the door. Phyllis closed the door. They summarized what each had learned or observed during the earlier search. They thought it odd that Art lived so spartan. Except for the Porche, his home life did not show much extravagance. His salary alone would give him a better lifestyle than what they saw. If he was a drug dealer, and was involved in the embezzlement, he would have had more money, much more.

Wes reminded them that Art liked being a big spender, entertaining girls, eating in restaurants, and paying the bar tab. Maybe he did not value how he lived in his house; maybe he simply lacked good taste.

Their biggest frustration rested on the belief that Art had committed the Larkin and Frazer murders. If they had arrested him, they would have solved the two murders and probably the attempt on Brian's life.

Were they back to ground zero? Was Art part of a duo? If he had an accomplice, was that person on their short list? Should they expand the short list? So many unanswered questions.

They left the apartment, checked that the door was locked, and Argos instructed the officers to seal the apartment with the yellow crime scene tape.

"Why don't we meet at that restaurant down the street, just off PCH?" Argos suggested. "It's past lunchtime, and I'm hungry. After all this excitement, we need a quiet place to go over this case."

FIFTY ONE

Thursday afternoon, April 14
Santa Monica, California

Wes and Phyllis left for the restaurant, the Golden Bull, a few blocks away, near PCH. Argos needed to update his boss and would follow in a few minutes. As he neared PCH, Wes saw the restaurant on the left, switched on his blinker and waited for oncoming traffic to clear. He pulled into the small parking area, and maneuvered carefully around a red Chrysler convertible leaving the lot.

Typical of restaurants in LA, parking was limited. Patrons often parked on the street, and walked. The lunch crowd had thinned leaving several spaces. Wes self-parked the car. Carrying their briefcases, Wes and Phyllis would wait for Argos inside.

The restaurant building occupied more than half of the property, leaving the small parking lot. Weathered, unpainted planks covered the exterior. Street-side, a single large dark tinted window broke the continuous board exterior. Etched in the window was *Golden Bull*, sub-titled, *A Steakhouse*. A small valet kiosk, now closed, sat near the entrance, and faced the parking lot.

The restaurant, odd for beach restaurants, had no outside patio dining. Of course, with its location, a block from the beach, east of PCH, any ocean view would be very small and further reduce the already limited parking.

Once inside, their eyes required a minute to adjust to the darkness. They then noticed that the restaurant typified small, older steakhouses. A long wooden counter with faux leather bar stools divided the otherwise square room. Small, dark tables and chairs filled the center, and a bank of red faux-leather booths sat along the wall.

The back of the bar contained glass shelves with soft under-lighting and filled with a colorful display of liquor bottles. Behind the bar area, the main dining room completed the layout. A dozen high back, red faux-leather booths filled the room.

During evening hours, a full contingent of staff, bartenders, hostess, half dozen waiters, and cooks served the dinner crowd. But during the day, only a single bartender, two waiters, and a cook handled the lunch crowd, and the few who ate liquid lunches.

"Welcome to the Golden Bull. What can we do for you?" Wearing a black tank top, the well-built, hairy, bearded bartender looked at them and smiled as he continued washing the drink glasses.

Phyllis felt a slight shiver pass through her as she looked at the male eye-candy.

The bartender noticed their badges. He set the glasses in the drain rack, the glasses clinking against metal. To give the detectives better attention, he dried his hands on the towel tucked in his belt and leaned on the bar as he faced them.

"We're just here for lunch." Phyllis smiled, acknowledging the bartender's attention hoping her stare at his torso was not too obvious. But before he could respond, she added, "Some place in the back so we can talk would be nice."

"Sure. There are several empty booths in back. Take your pick. A waiter will be with you in a minute." The bartender grinned appreciating her stare. He nodded over his tattooed right shoulder and resumed washing the glassware.

Wes and Phyllis chose a horseshoe shaped booth in the back of the room. The large booth would easily allow room for open briefcases and shared papers. As they sat, Detective Argos entered the restaurant. He saw Wes and Phyllis removing their jackets and sitting at their table in the back. He gestured to the bartender that he was joining them. The bartender nodded he understood and continued washing glasses. A waiter followed Argos to the booth and handed each a laminated lunch menu.

"Would you like something to drink while you decide"?

Wes ordered an iced tea, Phyllis a Diet Coke.

"I'll have a Pepsi, a regular Pepsi. Thanks." Argos ordered as he sat. "What do you think of our little steakhouse?"

"Very Dark." Wes grinned as his eyes continued to adjust.

"How's the food?" Phyllis asked.

"You'll like it. Trust me." Argos answered.

"Okay. I'll trust you." Phyllis scanned the menu.

"I'm surprised Phyllis isn't taking her food at the bar." Wes teased.

Phyllis elbowed him and tried to suppress her grin.

"What?" Argos missed the inside joke at first, and then grinned.

"Well, it's turned out to be quite a day. Looks like things are getting complicated. We have very few murders here in Santa Monica. I had one on Sunday, now three days later, another one." Argos changed the direction of their conversation.

"Definitely has gotten more complicated. Just when we thought we were about to close in on our best suspect, he turns up dead." Wes agreed and added with a little sarcasm. "And it wasn't an accidental drug overdose, and I don't think he killed himself."

"Not with all the other stuff you've been telling me about." Argos scanned the menu. "This just might be a long lunch. I have a feeling we have a lot to discuss."

"Yes. Yes, we do." Wes decided on a club sandwich, and laid the menu on the table.

"I believe Dexter murdered Greg Larkin and David Frazer. I know you don't have toxicology results on Frazer back yet. But considering everything else, especially how all of it relates to the embezzlement, Dexter was our guy." Phyllis refused to believe the case had returned to square one. She leaned on the table and massaged her temples with her fingers.

"But his death does throw a big wrench in our machinery. Who killed him?" Wes asked. "And let's not forget, I was sure he had something to do with sending the snake to Brian Latimer."

"I agree with you guys. But," Argos interlaced his fingers and leaned on the table. "But let me play devil's advocate here. What if, what if Dexter is a victim in all of this. He was after all murdered, which makes him technically a victim. At least of someone." He sat silent for a moment while they absorbed his comment. "Maybe someone used him as a scapegoat."

"But they would need Dexter alive for us to capture." Wes countered.

Feeling frustrated, Wes and Phyllis both inhaled deeply. They had reviewed and discussed the evidence until they were exhausted. They had already asked themselves all of these questions. They just needed to review it again, in detail, this time for Argos. Wes and Phyllis gave each other a forced smile. Relying on her sense of organization, Phyllis retrieved a summary sheet from her briefcase, and gave a copy to Argos. Wes knew it by memory.

The waiter returned with their drinks. Phyllis and Argos quickly returned to their menus while Wes ordered his club sandwich. Phyllis ordered a Philly cheese-steak with fries. Both men looked at her with mock criticism on their faces.

"What? I'm hungry. I jog four miles every morning. Cut me some slack." Phyllis smiled as she defended herself.

Argos ordered a chef's salad with ranch dressing on the side. The others faced him with the same teasing expressions given to Phyllis.

"So. What? A big guy can't order a salad? Since when is a salad girl's food? No offense, Phyllis. Besides, my doctor wants me to control my tri-glycerides. This is one way I do that." Argos grinned at his tablemates and handed his menu to the waiter.

The waiter wrote their lunch orders on his pad and left.

The light banter brought some needed levity. They relaxed. Argos' devil's advocate routine played a normal part of good detective work. Their work often involved a lot of stress. But they worked on the same side of the law. Their bosses might have jurisdictional concerns, but these detectives wanted these cases solved.

"Before we begin, I just need to say that my gut tells me now, stronger than ever, that Dexter had a partner. And Dexter was the junior partner. From the beginning, I questioned that he had the smarts to commit the embezzlement." Wes unrolled his flatware from his napkin, which he laid on his lap. Just like his mother had taught him. He grinned, and added, "With that said, Phyllis will you begin, from the beginning, for our devil's advocate, here."

Wes pulled his notepad from his shirt pocket. Phyllis positioned her summary sheet squarely in front of her and held her pen to check the points as she discussed them. Wes liked her sense of organization. She complemented his GAT instincts. They were a good team.

337

Phyllis began by describing the Larkin crash scene. She and Wes tag-teamed the details through what they had learned about the Larkin death, the embezzlement, and Frazer's death.

Phyllis saw two waiters approach with their food, and stopped speaking. She moved her papers to the seat beside her. Wes and Argos followed her lead and moved their papers onto their seats. The food smelled good and looked appetizing, especially to three hungry detectives. The waiters asked if they needed anything, hearing no, they left.

For a few minutes, they ate their food. They shared small talk about each other, their careers, and their caseloads, with some discussion on similar open cases.

After the detectives finished eating, a waiter returned, removed the dishes, and refilled their drinks. He asked if they wanted desert.

"They have a terrific coconut cream pie, best in all of LA." Argos grinned.

Wes and Phyllis shook their heads no.

"I guess not, this time." Detective Argos told the waiter.

The waiter apparently sensed the detectives wanted to talk longer, so he joined two co-workers in a booth across the room.

Phyllis returned to her presentation at the last check mark on her summary sheet. Again, she and Wes shared the details regarding the snakebite of Brian's son, and finished with Art Dexter's death. Argos wrote in his notepad and asked a few questions. He also added more information on the Frazer death.

"That's a very good summary. You guys are good. I'm sorry about the devil's advocate routine." Argos leaned against the seatback.

"Not a problem. It doesn't hurt to revisit the details, especially if it helps everyone get on the same page." Wes downplayed the issue.

"But, my bosses." Argos added. "With this second murder in a week in our little seaside town, they want results, quick results. Two murders in a week may not be unusual in south Central LA, but here, we're really concerned. I think we're going to see a lot of each other in the next few weeks."

"Understood. I think, working together, we might solve these cases faster." Wes looked to Argos, and then to Phyllis. "Actually working together should eliminate duplication of effort. Witnesses don't like being asked the same questions twice."

Wes and Argos nodded agreement.

They brainstormed the partnership idea for a few minutes. If Dexter was the murderer, the muscle, it's likely the partner, the brain, had developed his own muscle for some reason. He killed Dexter. It still begged the question, was the partner in the company, or an outsider, maybe even a hacker as Brian had suggested. Regardless, he and Dexter obviously knew each other.

Phyllis offered. "Well, we know the people that he associated with at work. Some of those people are already on our list."

"We just continue investigating the same people. We already look for IT and accounting knowledge, we just add capable-of-murder to the criteria." Wes shrugged his shoulders. "Brian has already identified people with the IT and accounting knowledge."

"Sounds like a plan." Argos smiled. He looked at his watch. "It's nearly five; most people there are probably ready to head home. Maybe we should start in the morning. Besides, I need to get my head around all of this information anyway."

"Yeah they probably are." Phyllis said. "Although a lot of people there work late."

"I'd like to get back to Leonard, to talk to Brian, see if he has any new information since this morning. He's our best bet identifying the possible suspects." Wes tapped the table and look to Phyllis. "Let's meet with him before we head back to the Valley. He's only a few miles away. I'm sure he's working late."

"Normally, I'd bet that he works late, but he may want to head back to Long Beach to be with his son." Phyllis responded. "I'll call him."

"Okay."

Argos drew a deep breath. "I'll follow up on the poisonous snake trail. I have some local informants who might help. Maybe I can tie Dexter to buying a poisonous snake. I have Kaminski's number. I'll work with him as well as with you. And I still have to work on the Frazer case."

"Why don't we reconvene tomorrow morning at the Leonard offices? They have offices we can use." Wes said.

"Better yet, why don't we meet in my office? It's more private, more secure." Argos suggested.

"A better idea. How's nine?" Wes suggested.

"Sounds good. Why don't we phone conference in Detective Kaminski?" Argos rubbed his chin. "I'll take care of that."

"Well, I guess we're finished here. We have our work cut out for us. We can add names to our suspect list. But I think its best to focus on our short list of names. Namely, Chas Erickson and Larry Davis." Wes snapped his briefcase closed.

The waiter saw movement at the detectives' table, and brought the check.

"Oh, we'll pick up the tab, here." Wes pulled the check to himself and scanned it.

"I was going to suggest that." Argos grinned.

FIFTY TWO

Thursday early evening, April 14
Santa Monica, California

The detectives left the restaurant. Their eyes had adjusted to the dark interior. Outside, the afternoon sun had begun its descent in the western sky. They cupped their hands over their eyes, to shield them from the sun's glare. The parking valet had opened his kiosk with its rows of key hooks, ready for the early dinner crowd. He asked if they needed assistance.

The detectives shook their heads and said 'no thanks' as they walked to their cars. They continued their small talk, 'drive safely', 'talk with you in the morning'.

Argos sucked in his stomach and hitched his pants up around his belly, which pushed the pants back down as soon as he released his hands. Only weight loss would leave his pants around his waistline. He unlocked the door to his department-supplied Taurus, settled into the seat, and drove away with a wave to Wes and Phyllis.

Phyllis called Brian a she stood beside the passenger door. Phyllis told him about finding Art dead, but he already knew. The company grapevine worked at full throttle.

Wes pressed the unlock button on his key fob twice to unlock the car's doors.

"Brian says he's getting ready to leave. He wants to check on his son. But he's willing to stay if we want." Phyllis held her hand over the mouthpiece of her phone.

"Why don't we just call him at his place, after we arrive at the station? If that's all right?" Wes suggested.

Phyllis relayed the message. Brian agreed with the idea. They would talk around seven. They would give him more details about Art's death, then. Also, Brian would have time to prepare dinner for his son and himself. Phyllis snapped shut her phone.

"Did he say how his son is doing?"

"Yes. He said his son has improved a lot. He's on medication so he doesn't feel much pain."

Wes maneuvered the car slowly out of the small lot and joined the cars heading west to PCH.

After work commuter traffic had increased on PCH, especially north bound. Even so, the waves, and the huge expanse of the blue Pacific uplifted their senses, even if only for a few minutes. The view sent any preoccupation of other thoughts to the back of their minds.

After a few miles riding in silence, Wes switched on his car's blinkers to exit PCH onto Topanga Road.

"Why is it that white collar crimes are more complicated, more difficult to solve than the violent, physical stuff?" Phyllis wondered aloud, breaking the silence. "With physical crimes, we have so much technology to help. We identify evidence more easily. Guns, shell casings, DNA, fingerprints, lots of things."

"True, but that's our world. Technology has evolved to help us with the physical stuff. And people like Debra, and even Brian." Wes worked his steering wheel as he rounded the many curves in Topanga Road. "Maybe we just don't know enough about the white collar crime world. But there are sciences that try to understand psychology and other mind motivations."

"True. As we learn more about the workings of the mind, we get more insight." Phyllis looked out the car's window. "Like you new friend, Karen Coffman. She seems to understand motivations, people behaviors. I have to admit that does help us understand that kind of criminal."

"True."

"I guess I'm just tired. When I think about it, I can understand some of the art of catching the white collar criminal." Phyllis gave a half smile to Wes.

More than an hour had passed as Wes pulled into the Sheriff's Malibu Station. He and Phyllis appropriated a small interrogation room, near their desks. After a few minutes organizing their thoughts and papers, he pulled a starfish shaped speakerphone near him, and dialed Brian's home number.

"Hello."

"Hello Brian. You already know the big news, that Arthur Dexter is dead." Wes jumped into the work topics as he leaned back in his chair.

"Yes, probably everyone at Leonard knows by now. I'm not sure who told, but within two hours after you left, I heard it from Erica." Brian said, his voice a little shaky. He, like many others at Leonard struggled to adjust to the news. He worried because another murder had occurred.

"A neighbor called, or someone heard it on the news. The media got to the scene awfully fast. I bet the media will be at the Leonard's front door first thing tomorrow. So if I were you, I'd go in the back way." Wes straightened in his chair and pulled some files and a notepad from his briefcase.

"I'm sure many of the employees there are frightened, with three people killed in the last two weeks." Phyllis added. "And the attack on you and your son."

Wes and Phyllis relayed a few details of Art's murder. How he was found, the syringe and other drug paraphernalia, the puncture between the toes. Wes admitted he did not have proof that it was murder, but he just did not believe it was suicide or an accidental overdose. His GAT operated at full throttle.

Wes reminded Brian that as part of the team, he would have to keep these details, all of them, to himself. Not tell Karen or Larry. The Sheriff's PR department would handle the information releases to the media and public. They don't reveal all details. And it would not be a good thing if certain details were leaked from their little group, even unintentionally.

Brian understood, although he felt conflicted. He now knew information that he could not tell anyone at Leonard, including Larry. He decided to deal with each situation as he encountered it.

Wes also described the scene in Art's apartment; that it appeared like an attempt to create a party turned bad, or a drug overdose situation.

Regarding David Frazer's death, Detective Argos said the autopsy revealed the expected, death by stabbing with a knife, with a six-inch blade. Frazer had fought with his attacker. He had defensive wounds, and had skin beneath his fingernails. DNA results will help, but that'll take a few days.

Frazer probably knew his attacker, no signs of breaking and entering, and no fingerprints, other than Frazer's. The attacker probably wore gloves. Again, toxicology results should be available in a few days.

Wes decided to tell Brian that they believed Dexter killed both Greg Larkin and David Frazer. They had suspected an accomplice before, but believed stronger now that Art had an accomplice, probably the embezzler. And for some reason that partner killed Art. They needed more facts, more evidence to identify this person. And for that, they needed Brian's help.

Brian felt frustrated that his work had not progressed much beyond their conversation this morning. He had reviewed the names of all the people in the two departments. He also reviewed a list of ex-employees from the last two years. His special access to the online HR files expedited the research. For three hours, he reviewed the personnel files of those people.

Three names emerged from his review. Robert Crocker, Jennifer Pounds, and Ann Douglas. Crocker and Pounds still worked at Leonard, but Douglas left the company a year and a half ago. Brian told Wes and Phyllis what he had learned from their files, but had not had time to interview them. Wes said it would be better if he and Phyllis interviewed them.

Wes vaguely remembered that Art and Robert Crocker shared something in common. He looked through his notes, but could not find the connection. He added a note to ask Crocker tomorrow.

"So far, we've thought the embezzler has to have accounting and IT knowledge. And now we add the capability to commit premeditated murder. Art's death was definitely planned, and executed with calculated coldness."

"I think we're talking about Karen's psychopath now." Phyllis offered. "So, who do we focus on?"

"The only names left from the original list are Larry Davis and Chas Erickson. This morning, we added a couple of the IT guys to the list, and now Crocker, Pounds, and Douglas." Brian hoped his voice did not carry the worry he felt.

For a moment, silence.

"From what we know, Chas and Larry fit similar profiles. Neither seems a likely candidate to embezzle. By the way, Debra is collecting information on the IT guys now. We'll call her with these new names." Wes interlaced his fingers behind his head and leaned back in his chair. "Well I think we've done about as much as we can for now. Besides, I'm tired. We'll talk again in the morning. You'll be at Leonard, right?"

"Yes. I'll be there. I'm tired too."

"Sorry, I forgot to ask. How is your son doing?" Wes leaned forward, genuinely interested.

"Much better. Much better. The crisis is over, at least so he says. His drugs keep him in a relaxed and upbeat mood. The doctors said otherwise he would have quite a bit of pain."

"Good to hear. Talk to you later. Bye."

"Bye."

Wes pressed the end button on the phone. To Phyllis he said. "I didn't want to say this in front of Brian, but we have no choice but to focus on Davis, and Erickson. If these new names don't reveal anything, and we eliminate Davis and Erickson, we'll really be at square one."

Davis and Erickson were at the top of their list, and now the focus of their investigation.

FIFTY THREE

Thursday Night, April 14
Studio City, California

"Hello, sir. I'm glad you're here." Nurse Faye wore a worried expression on her face as she opened the door.

"Hello. Faye? How's he doing?" He saw her concern and stepped inside.

"He's resting better now."

He headed to his father's bedroom/den. This time he ignored the family photos hanging on the wall.

"He was very uncomfortable earlier this afternoon, weak, coughing, irregular heartbeat, not resting at all well. His breathing was very labored. I was going to call an ambulance after we talked, but he settled down and has been sleeping ok since. I was going to wait a few more minutes to call you so you wouldn't have to hurry." Nurse Faye followed him to his father's bedside.

The heart monitor and the oxygen machine emitted their rhythmic beeping and pumping sounds. The TV, normally blaring, was turned off. Half listening, he watched his father sleep, as Nurse Faye quietly described his condition. He hesitated, but then laid his hand gently on his father's shoulder.

He had warm feelings for his father, sometimes. He hesitated to call it love, but they shared a bond. Unfortunately, this bond contained a deep level of resentment within the son. He wondered if all sons felt this love-resentment conflict with their fathers.

His father's favoritism for his oldest son continued after his death. Unfortunately, death of the favored often elevates them to a level of sainthood that the living can never achieve. Consequently, the relationships with those still living become unbalanced, unfair.

Like so many sons, he wanted his father's approval. No academic or business success ever sufficed. Even now, as a grown man, he wanted, but could not earn his father's approval. He would not admit it to anyone, and did not like admitting it to himself that he felt these internal conflicts.

His mother had insisted he enter therapy to adjust to his brother's death. His father refused to attend, even the family sessions. The son's therapy lasted for two years, and did not resolve his internal conflicts.

His father jerked and trembled. His breathing became spasmodic, labored. He coughed and gasped for air. Almost as quickly, he settled his thrashing, and stopped coughing. He resumed breathing normally. He squinted his eyes trying to open them and after a moment, he recognized his son at his side.

"Hello, there boy." He spoke as if with a throat full of gravel. He cleared his throat of mucous, and tried to smile.

"Hello, Dad. I understand you've had a rough afternoon." He removed his hand from his dad's shoulder, and nodded toward Nurse Faye standing on the other side of the bed.

Nurse Faye wiped the mucous from her patient's lips with a tissue. She poured water into a plastic cup and held it for him to drink. He sipped a little. She dabbed the few drops of water from his lips and set the cup on the hospital tray.

After a few minutes, she decided that he was okay. "I'll leave you two alone. I'll be just outside if you need me." She left the room.

The son nodded.

Nurse Faye pulled the door near closed, sat in the comfortable chair in the alcove, and opened a magazine.

"Can I get you any thing? Some more water?" He asked his father.

"No, thanks, I'm alright." He mumbled, his voice still sounding full of gravel. "On second thought, maybe some water."

The son emptied the cup into a bowl, and poured fresh ice water into it from a plastic pitcher coated in condensation. He held the cup to his father's lips. After his father drank a couple sips, he returned the cup to the bedside tray.

"How was practice today?" His father asked.

He entered a fugue state.

He hesitated answering. "Fine." He wanted to correct his father. To tell him he wasn't Jeff. That Jeff had died many years ago.

Are the fugue states becoming more frequent? But it should pass in a minute.

"How's your work?" His father asked. He had returned to the present.

"It's fine." He thought to brag, wanting to impress his father. *Why does he bother?*

"When's your next big game?" His father asked.

Back to the fugue state. Low level anger rose inside the son again. Sometimes, he felt little patience for the old man. Knowing dementia as a disease did not always eliminate the emotional reactions. *Why couldn't his father just stay with reality? Why couldn't he accept that he was just as important as his dead brother?*

He was probably more successful than his brother ever would have been. High School sports jocks seldom achieve high success. Yes, doors open for them, but usually close just as quickly. He felt guilty thinking these thoughts. He had liked his brother.

Sometimes he just wanted to shake his father. Other times he just wished the old man would die. End this turmoil. But he, consciously and unconsciously, wanted that approval, at least once.

"Next week." He played along. He regained his composure and waited for his father to return to a lucid state.

His father began coughing uncontrollably. The heart monitor on the nightstand beeped erratically.

"Nurse Faye!" The son called, jumping back to the present.

Hearing the heart monitor go wild, dropping the magazine, Nurse Faye jumped from her chair. She flung the door open and rushed to her patient's bedside, nudging the son aside. She propped her patient upright and cleared his throat of mucous. She placed the oxygen mask on his face so he could breathe easier. Using the bed control button, she positioned him more comfortably.

Both son and nurse sighed relief. In silence, they watched him for a couple minutes. Quiet settled over the room.

But then, the coughing and the erratic beeping of the heart monitor again broke the silence. Nurse Faye sprang into action again, repeating her resuscitation work, trying desperately to clear the air passageway. The patient began convulsing. The heart monitor blared its alarm. He became worse.

The heart monitor changed from its erratic beeping to the steady tone of an un-beating heart.

"Call 911." Nurse Faye commanded.

He grabbed the phone on the bedside stand and dialed 911.

Nurse Faye checked to insure the air passageway was clear, tilting his chin upwards. Using a plastic mouth device, she blew air into his mouth to fill his lungs with air, and alternated with chest compressions for five minutes.

No change. No heartbeat, no breathing on his own.

Determined to save her patient, Nurse Faye turned to the bedside cabinet and retrieved a home-use defibrillator. It lay on a lower shelf, already plugged into a power source, ready for an event as this. She switched the unit on. She instructed the son to open his father's shirt. He complied. She applied salve to one unit, rubbed them together, and laid them on her patient. She triggered the shock. His body jerked.

Nothing. Still no heartbeat. The monitor continued its steady tone. While the unit recharged, she upped the voltage to near the red zone. She applied more salve, rubbed the plates together, and applied another shock.

Again, no response. She repeated the procedure. Again, no response.

The son felt stunned, numb. He could not react. He admired Nurse Faye's take control behavior. She knew her job. As he watched her, he felt his awareness slowly return.

Nurse Faye, still determined to save her patient, performed her procedure again. She could not increase the voltage any higher, but tried again.

Still the same results.

"That's ok. Let's let him go." The son rested his hand on her arm. "He has said that he did not want to be resuscitated. No heroic measures."

"Are you sure sir?" She knew about the DNR, do not resuscitate, instructions, but her instincts always drove her to revive a dying patient.

"Yes. Yes, I'm sure." He said slowly.

She accepted his words. She laid the defibrillator on the cabinet and turned the unit off. She also turned off the heart monitor and oxygen machine. The room became quiet. She gently closed the dead patient's pajama top and buttoned one of the buttons. She softly touched his cheek, a small gesture of caring and respect for her patient of the last several months.

"I'll go into the next room to call the hospital and the medical examiner." She pulled the sheet up to the dead man's chin, but did not cover his face. "That'll give you some time alone with him."

"Thanks." The son understood that California laws were sometime complicated when someone died outside a hospital or absent a doctor.

When she left the room, she again pulled the door nearly closed to allow the son and his father some privacy.

He stepped closer to his father. He started to lay a hand on his shoulder, but hesitated. He felt confused. He was not accustomed to his father as a dead man. Except for the last few years, his father was always strong, always in charge, always the dominant person in a room. Now he was just a body, lying there, small, no action, no reaction.

It has been said that before people die their whole lives pass before them. In a few seconds, they remember important and unimportant events in their lives. Their minds flash through a checklist of sorts of each memory in no logical order. He wondered if his father saw such a slideshow in his mind.

This son saw his own video slideshow, of experiences where he and his father interacted during the last three decades. At first, the memories came sporadically, as if entering and then bouncing from side-to-side in his brain. Then his emotions joined the documentary flashes that played in his mind. Emotions ranged from fondness, to love, to resentment, to hate. He felt overwhelmed.

He inhaled a lungful of air and forced his mind to stop the slideshow and return to the present, to reality. He heard the front door bell ring.

Knowing the paramedics had probably arrived, Nurse Faye looked through the peephole anyway and opened the door. Leaving it open, she led them to her patient's bedside. The lead paramedic checked the body and agreed with the nurse that he was dead.

The lead called the hospital emergency room. To comply with California law, they would transport the body to the hospital for the official pronouncement of death. After some discussion with the hospital staff, the doctor on duty reminded the paramedic that if the nurse on duty was a registered nurse, that her pronouncement of death, along with the lead paramedic, would be sufficient. The body could be transported directly to the funeral home or to the county morgue.

Nurse Faye stated that she was a registered nurse and pulled her identification from her purse. She brought the son into the conversation. Although he usually was obsessive about controlling every activity, he had not thought much about his father's death and the subsequent details. Inheriting the money, yes, but not the funeral details.

Nurse Faye had dealt with dying patients and knew answers to many of the questions relatives asked. She maintained a notebook to help in these situations. She gave the son a short list of mortuaries in the Studio City area. He saw Ball's Mortuary on the list. He knew of it, and had driven by it many times to his father's house.

"I'll call them to pick up the body. If you want?" Nurse Faye volunteered.

"Yes. Thanks." He nodded approval.

The paramedics packed their equipment to leave. The lead paramedic pulled a document, a certificate of death, signed it, and obtained Nurse Faye's signature. The paramedics left quietly. Nurse Faye closed the door.

Nurse Faye returned to the bedroom to assist if she could. She touched the son's elbow to guide him into the living area. He resisted.

"I'd like to spend a little more time with him." He said.

"Sure. I'll just step outside to call the mortuary."

Silence. No beeping hospital equipment. No voices, except for Nurse Faye's quiet voice in the next room calling the mortuary. When she finished the call, she stood in the doorway a moment watching the son stand beside his father, his back to her. She walked inside the room.

"Is there anyone you'd like me to call?" She laid a soft hand on his arm. Even though she had been through this experience before, she still felt sympathy for her patient's family.

"No, no. We don't have a lot of family, a couple of distant cousins. I'll call them later." He faced her and tried to smile, and added, "His friends. Well, they sort of disappeared over the last few years."

"Let me get you some tea? Or coffee?" She asked, trying to comfort him.

"Some tea would be nice. Thanks." He looked at her, then, turned to face his father again.

After a few minutes, she returned with the tea and set it on the bedside nightstand. She said nothing, and left the room.

The doorbell rang. He joined her as she opened the door for the mortuary staff. He led them to the bedroom. An assistant pushing a gurney followed. The mortuary supervisor requested the death certificate and explained the process, giving the son another form to sign. Then, he and his assistant prepared the body for transport to the mortuary.

After they left, the son closed the door and faced it in silence. Nurse Faye watched him for a couple minutes. Then, the son turned to face her.

"Faye, there's no need for you to stay. I appreciate your being here. But I think I'd like to be alone for a while."

"Sure. I understand." She paused. "If you're sure you don't need me. I'd be happy to stay with you. Losing a loved one can be a difficult experience."

"Yes. Yes, it is. I appreciate your offer to stay, but I'll be fine."

Nurse Faye collected her things, her nurse's bag, her purse, and a few personal items. "I'll call the hospital supply company and set up a time to remove the medical equipment and other devices. I'll be here for that." She would handle the business side. "But please call me if you need anything. Anytime, day or night. I know Jenny feels the same way. We both loved your father. I'll call her. She'll be heartbroken."

"Thanks." He unfolded his arms and placed his hands on her shoulders. "I want you to know that I really appreciate all that you've done to help my father. And Jenny too. I know it's your job, but you've done far more than the expected. I know you didn't just take care of him. You spent time with him, talking with him. You gave him friendship. I can't thank you enough."

"I'm sorry your father died. He was a good man." With her free arm, she hugged him.

She did not know her patient as a father.

"Thanks. Take care of yourself, Faye."

"I will. You too." Carrying her bundle, Nurse Faye left the son alone.

He closed the door behind her. The room became quiet. He felt an odd sense of change surging inside him.

FIFTY FOUR

Thursday Night, April 14
Studio City, California

The son leaned his head against the door after Nurse Faye left. Strong, puzzling emotions surged inside him. Was this grief? Intense relief? Anger? His mind struggled to understand these feelings that demanded his attention. Did he need to control them? Were they precursors to emotional pain? He has never allowed his feelings to affect him negatively. He always controlled his feelings and his reactions to them. Could he savor this rush he felt? Maybe. As these thoughts filled his mind, he turned and leaned against the door, facing the room.

Then, he sat in one of the overstuffed chairs near the large front window in the living room, gripped its soft leather arms. He would think.

He chose to slow the emotional impact of what he felt. A self-control technique he had developed as a young man. He remembered how this room, this house felt, years ago. Then, his family filled this house with noise. He, his brother, and their friends laughed, yelled, and fought insignificant battles. They played after school, weekends, and holidays. He smiled at the memories.

He remembered hearing of his brother's death. He was a freshman in high school; his brother was a senior. His parents had called him downstairs. He sat in this same chair. They sat on the couch now opposite him. The world stopped.

A quiet pall settled over the house. His father became distant, working more hours. His mother remained affectionate to him, but rarely smiled. She would hug him and pat him on the cheek. But the frequent, broad smiles that filled her face were gone. The holidays, with the smell of Thanksgiving turkey and the colors and sounds of Christmas, the decorations and the music, became quiet dinners for three.

In his reverie and the quiet of the room, he ceased watching the events that bounded into his consciousness. Turning his head slightly, he could see into the den, with its family history wall. He went into the den, looked briefly at the now empty bed where his father had died. He turned to look at the pictures hanging on the wall with its empty spaces where his father had removed several of them. His eyes focused on the remaining family pictures hanging there. Almost with tunnel vision, he saw each picture, as his mind filled with the memories and thoughts each picture evoked.

As his eyes moved from one picture to the next, he remembered more. He remembered his father's distance, his favoritism for his brother. During the last few years of high school, his father often compared him unfavorably with his brother, his successes in basketball and football. Only his mother showed him that he was wanted, important, cared about. In fact, she called him her Good Son to compensate for her husband's obvious preference for the older, athletic son.

He moved about to examine each picture more closely. As he looked at them, the memories paraded through his mind, stronger, faster. Sometimes the memories seemed mechanical, factual, without emotive content. Other times, strong emotions such as anger, rage, or hurt engulfed him.

One picture showed his father with his two sons, around twelve and fourteen years old, after a soccer game. Even though his arms were around both sons, he smiled down on his oldest. His pride showed. His father rarely showed this kind of pride in him, even when he achieved top grades in college, or success in his work.

After several therapy sessions, he understood on some level that his career ambition was partly an effort to win his father's approval. He understood that on an intellectual level, but not on an emotional one.

He could parrot his condition verbally, as if reading from a psych textbook. But they were just words, without meaning.

Although he resented his father, he liked his brother. He shifted his focus to a picture of the two of them, ten and twelve, arms around each other. When his brother was alive, they were best friends. He envied his brother's athletic success, and his brother admired his academic success. They were a team. One had the physical prowess; the other had the brains.

As if compelled by some external force, his eyes returned to the pictures of them with their father. They glared back at him as he stood there, mocking him, especially, the one taken after the soccer game. As he looked at them, his resentment for his father grew. He wanted to strike his father as he had felt earlier in the evening.

With effort, he turned his head and moved his attention to other pictures on the wall. Pictures of his parents, his grandparents, and more of him and his brother.

The pictures stopped around the time of his brother's death, as if time had stopped. Only a few pictures containing him remained, one of him and his mother. Another at his college graduation. He stood between his parents, his mother proud, smiling, his father somber faced.

There were no pictures after his mother's death. But he had to admit to himself that his father had been sick in those years. And he certainly had no interest in maintaining the family history wall himself.

He returned to the picture after the soccer game, re-igniting his resentment. It surged inside him.

It exploded into rage. He struck his fist into the picture, shaking the wall. Its glass shattered and the frame broke. It fell to the floor. The nail had jarred loose. Another picture fell to the floor. Others precariously hung on the wall. He felt no pain in his hand. He ignored the blood that dripped from his knuckles.

Another nearby picture showed his father with Jeff alone. Again that same pride, that smirk taunted him. There were no pictures of him and his father. None showed that his father was proud of him. Even in the group pictures, his older brother was always at his father's side while he stood elsewhere. He slammed his fist against the wall again. Still feeling no pain, he tore more pictures from the wall and slammed them to the floor.

Soon, only one picture remained. He held it. It showed him and his parents at his college graduation. Her smile showed that immense motherly pride she felt in him. Her face beamed. She smiled as she had in the early years. He removed the picture from its frame. He folded his father from the scene, and tore an even tear, removing his father completely, throwing him to the floor. Then, he held it, of his mother and him, close to him, hugged it, a warm feeling swept over him. The feeling lasted for only a moment.

The pictures of his father smirked at him from the floor. He stomped the pictures lying there.

He took a few breaths to calm himself. He grinned an ironic grin and marveled that he was capable of such an outburst. He laid the picture of his mother and him onto the nearby credenza. He continued his deep breaths to regain his self-control.

He looked into the living room and was glad no one could see his outburst. He returned to the overstuffed chair he had sat in earlier. He slowed his hyperventilating and ran his fingers through his hair. He would sit until he felt comfortably in control again.

After a few minutes, he took his jacket from the guest closet beside the door.

Looking at the mess on the floor, he made a mental note to call Nurse Faye later to delay the removal of the medical equipment for a couple days. He would need a little time to clean the mess that resulted from his brief lapse in self-control.

He assured himself that it would never happen again. Once is enough.

He inhaled deeply again. He felt relief, and in control for the moment. He did not realize that his rage had only relaxed. It would lie dormant, fester, and consume him again.

FIFTY FIVE

Friday morning, April 15
Santa Monica, California

After a scenic, cool ride over Topanga Canyon Road and along the ocean on PCH, Wes and Phyllis passed through the tunnel that connected the PCH to the 10 Freeway. They exited at Fourth Street. They quickly located the Santa Monica Police Station. Argos had told them to park in the officer's lot, just show their badges to the attendant.

The Police Department occupied a large two-story complex with a couple basement levels. The landscape on the Olympic and Fourth streets included vibrant green tropical plants and colorful flowers. Santa Monica and other coastal locations fostered lush plant life year round. The other sides of the property, unseen by the public, maximized the functional use of the valuable real estate.

At the receptionist's desk, they asked for Detective Argos. After a couple minutes, he joined them and escorted them through a bullpen of partially private workstations similar to their stationhouse. He suggested that they visit the break room for coffee or sodas.

After the quick break, they settled in one of the interrogation rooms, removed files and writing materials from their briefcases and settled into business. They closed the door, so they could talk freely, pace around the room, or use the whiteboard. Phyllis agreed to serve as recording secretary. Although she was lowest ranking and would have been stuck with the task anyway, she was better organized than the other two.

"After more thought, I have to brag a little. From the beginning, I doubted Dexter had the knowledge of accounting and technology to carry off the embezzlement by himself. His death confirms, at least to me, that he had a partner, probably more intelligent than him." Wes turned sideways in his chair to face the other two and rested his elbow on the table.

"And you're concluding this without all of the autopsy and toxicology results on Larkin and Frazer." Argos challenged. Without announcing himself, Argos' alter ego, the devil's advocate had returned.

"I'm not saying I'm totally right, but the evidence so far supports what I'm saying." Wes defended himself. "Besides we have three more names. We talked to Brian last night. He uncovered more possibilities. One worked with Dexter."

"Wes has good instincts." Phyllis defended him as she tapped her pen on her writing pad. She smiled half-heartedly. "Wes likes the bragging rights when the evidence supports his gut analysis technique, or his GAT as we call it. However, we will wait for all of the results."

"Look at the summary sheet on Dexter that we discussed yesterday. Do you have any questions, or want to add anything to it?" Wes asked.

"No, I still agree with everything we've discussed. And, I agree that the evidence you have, without the toxicology, is enough to arrest Dexter. I would have done the same." Argos's nice persona returned.

"Now, let's talk about the names on our list. Brian gave us two IT names yesterday morning and two more last night. Our technical people are working on the background information, phone records, bank records, police records, and the like. They'll feed us the information over the next couple days. Meanwhile, we can focus on the Davis and Erickson." Wes pointed to the two names on the summary sheet, and pulled two folders from his briefcase. Both folders had grown in size over the last two weeks.

"Before we get started, let's conference in Detective Kaminski. Ok?" Phyllis suggested.

Wes and Argos agreed. Argos dialed from the speaker phone lying on the table. Kaminski's voice mail answered. Phyllis left a message with her cell phone number.

"Now, what about Mr. Lawrence Davis?" Wes sat straight in his chair. "I know he's the one that began the investigation. He called it to the attention of management, and hired Brian Latimer as a consultant."

"Actually, his employee Greg Larkin discovered the embezzlement. But of course, he's dead." Phyllis surprised herself correcting him. But she always paid close attention to the details.

"That's right." Wes grinned. He liked having Phyllis as his partner. She kept the details correct.

Phyllis opened the Davis file in front of her. She quickly scanned the documents, a summary sheet, contact information, job description, detailed notes from interviews, and phone and bank records. Phyllis explained that records were generally very clean. No negatives on DMV, or Department of Motor Vehicles, court documents, taxes, and the like.

They asked and answered questions of each other. They hypothesized about each fact that related to Larry Davis. They felt comfortable challenging each other. Would each fact support innocence or guilt?

Wes commented about Brian's assertion that Davis is totally innocent, in no way could he commit such a crime, embezzlement, or murder. They talked objectively because none had the personal connection to Davis as Brian had. In their experience, innocent appearing people sometimes were guilty.

"Maybe it's a good thing Latimer isn't here." Argos looked at the other two. "We can be more open with just ourselves."

"Maybe." For a moment, Wes mulled over the thought that Brian might be too close to the case. He would have to think about that possibility.

"What if Davis wanted to remove Larkin from the picture, since Larkin was the one who discovered the embezzlement." Argos pushed his point further. "Davis couldn't bring himself to eliminate Larkin. So, he enlisted, used Dexter to do the dirty work."

"There were those suspicious after work calls between Davis and Dexter." Phyllis scratched her temple with an index finger and looked at Wes.

"And Davis insisted that people working at Leonard Corp were *family*. A lot of companies give the impression of family to ingratiate the employees' loyalty. But they would fire them in a second to improve the bottom line." Wes speculated.

"Brian did say that for a couple weeks before all of this happened; everyone was worried about a big layoff." Phyllis added.

Argos proposed. "If Davis, probably the smarter of the two, engineered the embezzlement, and Dexter 'got out of hand' somehow, Davis eliminated him. You said they talked after work hours. So they may have had a non-work related relationship. We need to know if Davis has an alibi for Wednesday night."

Wes thought more about Argos' comments and entered a note on his to-do list. "It could be a possibility. Davis obviously knows accounting and could have hidden any IT knowledge he has. If you know how to commit a crime, you certainly don't tell people that you know how."

Could Davis be the embezzler, turned murderer? Silence settled over them for a moment while the thoughts exercised in their minds.

Wes explained that they had put Davis' name on the back burner in the beginning because he had money, and therefore no likely motive. Dexter had looked like the culprit. He just seemed to lack the IT knowledge to commit the embezzlement.

"Since we found cocaine in Dexter's apartment, maybe there was a drug connection between him and Davis. There was an L.D. in his notebook. Could it be that Dexter supplied Larry Davis?" Phyllis rested her arms on her chair and looked at the two men.

"That would show a negative relationship between the two." Wes nodded his head slowly.

More silence.

"Another possibility. Maybe Davis hired Brian Latimer to cover-up the embezzlement. What better way of hiding something than to have an *expert friend* deflect attention. Latimer worked for Davis. Surely Davis could control Brian's activities." Argos' devil's advocate has resurfaced.

Wes stiffened and moved into defensive mode. He and Phyllis had worked closely with Brian for nearly two weeks. He felt he was a good judge of character and Brian was one of the good guys.

"That is a possibility. However, even though Brian has strong convictions that Davis is innocent, Brian is the one who listed Davis as someone with high access capability. If he wanted to help Davis, he could have just not listed him. Or he could have simply downplayed Davis' IT knowledge." Wes just could not see Brian involved in any cover-up.

Wes continued. "The Sheriff's Department thoroughly investigates all consultants before using them. In fact, Debra Bowen, the Sheriff's WCC supervisor, monitors Brian's work very closely. She would easily spot any attempt to manipulate the technical information, the names of people, and accounts affected. It would be pretty close to impossible for anyone to deceive her."

"There were no phone conversations between Latimer and Davis until about two weeks ago. Most of Latimer' income for the last several months came from his retirement funds. If he received any money from the embezzlement, it did not show in his financial records." Phyllis sided with Wes on his gut instinct.

More silence.

"Well. This is enlightening." Wes cleared his throat. "More to think about. Feels like progress. I like it."

"Next on our list is Mr. Charles Erickson." Phyllis read the next name on the list. "What do we know about him?"

"Well, for the same basic reason, as Davis, we put Erickson on the back burner." Wes responded with curiosity in his voice.

"And those reasons were…" Argos spoke.

"He has very good income, and has family money." Wes answered. "His father has money, another fortune made in real estate. When Erickson has access to it, we don't know."

"We need to be in real estate." Argos wished aloud.

"That's for sure." Wes agreed.

"Records indicate a pretty clean background. No unusual deposits or expenses. A nice address in Manhattan Beach, but that could have come from family. His mortgage payments are low considering the neighborhood." Phyllis scanned the folder on Erickson.

"We expect more reports today or tomorrow. Our technical people can access all sorts of databases. Thanks to the internet." Wes added.

Of course, they worked closely together. Dexter reported to Erickson. So phone calls at anytime would not be unusual." Phyllis clicked her pen closed and opened repeatedly for a few seconds.

"Does Erickson have any money problems?" Argos asked. "Risky stocks, gambling, that kind of thing."

"Records don't show any." Phyllis answered. "Yet."

"He obviously has some of the same capabilities as Davis, accounting knowledge, probable IT knowledge to embezzle. Could he murder?" Argos inhaled deeply and settled into his chair.

"And, he would have the same reasons to eliminate Larkin and Frazer." Wes rested his hands on the table, and tapped it with his thumbs.

"And use Dexter as his muscle to do the dirty work." Argos said.

"And the snake attack on Brian's son." Phyllis pointed a finger at the ceiling. "And if Brian was involved, do you really think he would subject his son to a poisonous snakebite." Again defending Brian from the earlier conversation.

"A few days ago, we talked with Karen Coffman, who described psychopathic behavior. They had the ability to fit in. Her definition could fit both Davis and Erickson. They both seem nice enough, not likely to commit a crime. Of course, how often do we hear a neighbor say that the murderer seemed so nice." Wes thought aloud.

"You know. I really think we have enough for search warrants." Argos clasped his hands tightly, his knuckles turning white.

"On both Davis and Erickson?" Phyllis asked.

"Yeah. Both." Wes added.

"I can get the warrants, but…" Argos spoke.

"Maybe it'd be faster if we got them. Since Larkin's death was in LA County, and Frazer's and Dexter's deaths were in Santa Monica, as well as LA County. I wish this was simpler."

"It might be cleaner if you guys got the warrants." Argos agreed. "Especially since Davis and Erickson live in separate cities, Long Beach and Manhattan Beach."

"I'll call the DA." Phyllis retrieved her cell phone from her briefcase.

"Let's do it as quick as we can." Wes pushed.

"Shouldn't take more than a couple hours." Phyllis pressed her cell phone's keys, and held it to her ear. "I suggest we interview the new names on our list in the meantime."

"I'll call Detective Kaminski in Long Beach. Give him a 'heads up'" Wes pulled his cell phone from its case on his belt.

FIFTY SIX

Friday early afternoon, April 15
Santa Monica and Long Beach, California

"Ellie?" Larry answered his phone as a question. The caller-id listed his home number. Peter would not arrive from Palm Springs until tomorrow. So, it must be Ellie, his housekeeper. But, why would she call?

Elena Olvera, fiftyish, slim, and friendly, she had cleaned Larry's house for the last fifteen years. In their early forties, she and her husband Juan immigrated to the United States twenty years ago. Juan spoke limited English, but she spoke it well, except when she became excited. She had her own key, and rarely called him at work.

He always left cash on the kitchen counter for her, a practice they had followed for several years. Without keeping records, Larry rationalized that the amount he paid fell under the IRS limit to withhold taxes from her pay. He would never run for public office, so why worry.

"Mr. Larry." Ellie's voice anxious, elevated. She spoke rapidly, a mixture of English and Spanish, her accent more pronounced with each word. "Mr. Larry, the police are here. They showed me a piece of paper, and just walked in."

"What? What's happening? What did they tell you? Are you alright?" Larry struggled to keep his composure. Fear swelled in him like an early winter chill.

"Yes. Yes sir, I am. I don't read English very good, but… They say it's a search warrant. You, you come home, okay?" The anxiety in her voice increased to near tears.

"Ellie, just calm down, try to relax. Let me talk with whoever is in charge. I just can't believe this." Larry's heart pounded in his chest. His mind flooded with the problems at work. The embezzlement. The murders. Just when things could not seem worse, they now did.

"Mr. Davis? Detective Makelin, here, with the LA County Sheriff's Department."

"I know who you are." Larry's voice tightened.

Wes continued. "This search warrant is strictly in order. Detective Kaminski from the Long Beach Police Department is here as well."

"There's got be something wrong. Why on earth are you searching my house?" Larry worried. A giant boulder of panic rumbled toward him. He knew little of search warrants, only what he had learned from TV, episodes of Law and Order, and CSI. He had never experienced one in his life, until now.

"I've cooperated with you. I've answered all of your questions. I've helped in any way I could. Why are you doing this to me?" Like railing against a wall, Larry pleaded, almost shouting into the phone.

"I understand you're upset. And we appreciate your cooperation. But new evidence has come to light." Wes spoke calmly, officious.

"What, what evidence?" Larry demanded.

"I can't tell you that. What we're searching for is in the warrant. Your housekeeper has a copy. And as I said, everything is in order."

"I'll, I'll be right there. Give the phone back to my housekeeper."

"Suit yourself. We'll be here, conducting our search." Wes replied, still the official, and handed the phone to the housekeeper.

"Mr. Larry."

"Ellie, Ellie I'll be right there, as soon as I can."

"Please, Mr. Larry, hurry. I don't know what to do."

"Try to relax. You've not done anything wrong. I'll be there as quickly as I can." Larry breathed deep to regain his self-control. He hung the receiver in its cradle, snatched his briefcase from the side of the credenza, and grabbed his jacket.

He stopped by Liz's desk and whispered that he was leaving. The police were at his house with a search warrant. God only knows why. He knew he could trust her confidence. She drew a quick breath and covered her mouth with her hand as if to stifle a scream. Almost speechless, she whispered that she was sorry and asked if she could do anything. He said he would call her when he knew more. He almost ran to the elevators.

Larry slammed his car door shut. He drew another deep breath. He needed to call his attorney, Jim Osgood, and dialed his number. Jim, also a good friend, would take his call and move Larry's situation to the top of the list, unless he was in court.

Osgood's secretary answered. Hearing the anxiety in Larry's voice, she interrupted her boss. He came on the line almost immediately.

"Larry, old pal. What's up?" His voice was upbeat, glad to receive a call from a good friend, for any reason.

"Jim. I think I'm in some kind of trouble. I've told you about some of the troubles we're having here at Leonard. But the police are at my place with a search warrant. I'm on my way there now."

"Oh my god, Larry. Did they say what they're searching for?" Jim sat up straight in his chair. His voice switched into serious, attorney mode.

"I don't know. I talked with Detective Makelin from the LA County Sheriff's Department. He wasn't any help at all. Just a 'following procedures' 'everything in order' kind of guy."

"Try to relax, Larry. I know that's easier said than done. But they could be just fishing. From what little you've told me, they could be running out of suspects, or just very thorough. However they do need *probable cause*." Osgood tried to calm his friend, now his client. "I'll meet you at your place. Traffic shouldn't be too bad this time of day. I can leave in about five minutes."

Larry closed his cell phone, took another deep breath, and started his car. He told himself to calm down, to get control of himself. The boulder of panic did slow its onslaught.

Questions plagued Larry's mind. Why would they search his place? What were they after? Surely, they could not believe he had anything to do with the embezzlement. And the murders. God, he would never hurt Greg, or David, never. He had heard of Art's death.

Maybe they knew about his relationship to Art. That Art was his supplier. He tried to calm himself, tried to relax, to not panic.

Larry parked on the street. Two cars sat in his driveway, one a police car, the other a dark blue sedan with government tags. At least no flashing lights. A Long Beach policewoman stood outside his door on the front porch.

Larry and Peter had bought the two-story colonial soon after they met nearly thirty years ago. Six columns, two stories high, held the roof that sheltered a nice sized porch across the entire front of the house. They kept the color white with black shutters and trim. Traditional. Some would describe it boring, but he and Peter had considered it stately, elegant, now it was just home.

Larry rushed to the front door. The policewoman blocked his way into the house. He identified himself and showed her his driver's license.

She escorted him to Detective Kaminski in the living room. Kaminski introduced himself and offered his hand, but Larry refused to shake hands. Ellie rose from her seat on the couch. Kaminski gave him a copy of the search warrant. He tried reading it but was so upset that he could not understand it, just words, lots of words. His mind could not comprehend. That boulder of panic increased its speed toward him.

Larry tried to comfort Ellie. He stood away from her as he saw Detective Makelin enter from another room.

Wes saw the anger in Larry's eyes. They had become adversaries. Larry no longer was the cooperative, helpful individual from yesterday. Wes focused on standard procedure, on protocol, on covering all the bases. He now suspected Larry of crimes, but was not convinced. This confrontation would challenge his people skills. He would not shirk from this task.

Larry attacked first. "I don't understand. I've cooperated with you, with the authorities. I was the one who called you, remember? How can you even assume that I'd have anything to do with these crimes? Are you trying to connect me to the murders? I can't believe this. Those kids were like members of my own family." When he finished, he felt panic surge in him again. It tasted of bile. He wanted to vomit.

Detective Kaminski remained silent, but would assist if needed.

"Mr. Davis, I know you're upset. But this warrant is in order. If you read it, you'll see we're searching for any evidence that connects you to Art Dexter."

"I work with him. Of course, I'm connected with him." Larry defended the obvious. Calm returning, he added, "I understand you found him dead this morning."

"Yes. That's the third death in less than two weeks. As I've tried to tell you, we have to investigate all of the connections. I know this is difficult for you, but I'm going to have to insist that you wait outside."

Larry opened his mouth to say more, but decided against it. Instead he nodded to Ellie and asked, "Could Ellie at least go home?"

"Sure." Wes nodded to her.

Just then, the policewoman who stood at the front door returned escorting Jim Osgood. Osgood immediately took charge. He advised Larry to say nothing more. He took the search warrant and reviewed it for a moment. He told Wes that he wanted to speak with his client alone for a few minutes. He placed his hand on Larry's shoulder and guided him outside.

Osgood tried to calm Larry. He assured him that if the police had anything on him, they would have arrested him. If it was a 'fishing trip', they may simply be posturing. The warrant was in order, so they would just have to wade through the process.

Before Ellie left, Osgood asked her to join them. He asked what the police had asked her. She explained that she felt so nervous that she could not answer any of the questions.

Looking to Osgood for approval, Larry told her she could go home. He hugged her and said everything would be all right, doubting his own words.

Another half hour passed. Then another.

An officer in one of the bedrooms called the detectives that he had found something. Inside a dresser drawer, he had found a small, nearly empty bottle of cocaine. They bagged it, and continued searching the house.

The sheriff's deputies and city police officers filled two boxes with papers, and loaded them with Larry's home computer into the trunk of the dark blue sedan. Larry started to protest, but Osgood blocked his path with his arm. Osgood said they would give them a detailed list of the items they were taking. He assured Larry these were standard, legal procedures, unpleasant, but standard.

A half hour later, Detective Makelin gave Osgood the list of items taken. Then, the law enforcement people left. Osgood read the list.

"If they'd had anything incriminating, they would have arrested you." Osgood said. "Wait a minute, there's one item here that's a little worrisome."

"What?"

"They found a vial of coke, approximately a quarter gram. Larry, is there something I should know about?" Osgood looked Larry in the eye. "They could've arrested you for that, but... I guess they weren't too worried about it, since they left. Let's not worry about it yet. You'd probably get off with a slap on the wrist."

"I was a little worried about that. I thought it was hidden pretty well."

Osgood offered to buy Larry a drink, but needed to meet another client. Osgood advised him to try to relax. They would survive this. Osgood suggested Larry meet a friend, have a stiff drink. They would talk again tomorrow when they would have more information.

After Osgood left, Larry tried to relax. He thought about mixing himself a martini. His whole body shook. He went inside, surprisingly, the place was not in too big a mess. Not as clean, as Ellie would have left it, but ok. The search warrant and all that it implied upset him. For the moment, it was over.

His life seemed out of control. He wanted his quiet, controlled life back. Maybe Osgood was right. Maybe, he needed a stiff drink, and to talk with someone. He thought of Brian. Talking with him would help him cope with this situation.

He called Brian. He told him that the Sheriff's Department had served a search warrant on him. He asked if Brian could meet to talk. He needed to talk with a friend. Shocked, Brian would leave work immediately. They agreed to meet at Brian's condo. Larry would tell Brian everything that had happened.

FIFTY SEVEN

Friday afternoon, April 15
Long Beach, California

Brian sped along Shoreline Drive home. He liked this drive; it swept around downtown Long Beach, actually a quicker route to home.

Normally, Brian enjoyed this drive past the marina, Shoreline Park, and the waterfront restaurants. But today, his mind struggled to understand why the Sheriff's Department served a search warrant on Larry's place. He thought Wes and Phyllis agreed with him that Larry was not capable of the embezzlement, much less of the murders. Over the phone, Larry was obviously stressed. He would be too.

Brian pulled into The Spire's circular drive and saw Larry pacing under the entrance portico. He powered down the car's window and unlocked the door.

"Hi Larry. Jump in." Brian said.

Larry almost literally jumped inside. Brian could not remember ever seeing him this animated, this upset.

"I still can't believe this. I just can't believe this is happening to me. First, the embezzlement, then the murders of Greg and David. With what happened to you, or rather to your son. And then with Art." Larry talked rapidly, giving Brian little room to speak. Then he asked, "Brian do you know anything at all? You talk with the Detectives pretty often. What have they said? You've got to tell me."

"Larry, I've told you what I know. I talked with them last night." Brian felt conflicted, between his loyalties to the Detectives and his friend, his employer. "They didn't say anything about a search warrant. They told me a little about Art's death, but nothing about you. Did something happen last night? This morning?"

"Nothing that I know of. I just don't understand." Larry still visibly agitated blurted the words.

"Actually, Larry, I don't know everything they think. Our conversations usually deal only with the results of my analysis. I can tell you what I've told them. At least I think I can. At least, I will." Brian felt more conflict, but he also felt loyalty to his friend. "Larry you're my friend. They know that my friendship for you is very strong. I've told them that. I'm sure they don't tell me everything about the cases. Partly because of our friendship and that I also work for Leonard. They're probably just covering all bases."

Brian allowed his car to idle for a few minutes while waiting for the garage gate to open.

"Brian, I appreciate that, but I'm just so upset. I don't know whether it bothers me more that two of my friends were killed or that somehow I'm a suspect." Larry rubbed his face with both hands. "I'm sorry Brian, I know you're in a difficult position. Being my friend, working for law enforcement, and for Leonard. Can we just go upstairs and have a stiff drink. Ok?"

"Sure. Let's do that." Brian laid a friendly hand on Larry's shoulder.

Brian drove through the security gate and descended the circle drive to his parking space. They walked to the elevator, and joined another resident waiting. Brian suggested they talk more, after they were upstairs. They rode in silence. Even so, thoughts of the murders, the embezzlement, and now the search warrant saturated their minds.

Brian could not believe that Larry was guilty of any crime in any way. He did not care that he developed the short list. That list contained the names of who had access, not of who committed any crimes. He had used his best skills researching computer files, and interviewing people. Maybe detective work required more skills than he had. But in no way was his friend guilty. He would prove Larry's innocence.

The elevator stopped on the lobby floor. The elevator doors opened, Brian saw the mailman depositing the mail into the resident's boxes. He would return later for his mail. Two more residents joined them on the ride up. Except for neighborly greetings about having a nice day, little was said. The elevator stopped on two separate floors for the companion riders. Then, it stopped on Brian's floor.

"How about that drink? Martini?" Brian reached for the gin as he asked.

"Yes. A big one. Bombay if you have it. With a twist."

"I have it. Always keep it in stock. Ever since we were young guys. It always seemed the sophisticated thing to do. Although it's been replaced a few times." Brian grinned.

"Thanks."

Jimbo walked into the living room from his bedroom and greeted them. He vaguely remembered Larry from years ago. They shook hands. He tried to participate in small talk, but was too groggy. Brian explained that he and Larry had some things to discuss. Jimbo said that was fine because he wanted to sleep some more, probably from the drugs. He returned to the small bedroom.

Larry walked to the sliding glass doors with its views of the Los Angeles basin. He opened the sliders and stepped onto the balcony. He could see the endless housing spread before him, the surrounding mountains, the freeways, and the airplanes approaching LAX in the west. He had never seen Brian's condo. Actually, although he had lived in Long Beach for more than twenty-five years, he had never been inside the building since it was built thirty years ago.

Normally, he would consider it a treat to enjoy the views, but this time, he could not. The thoughts of today's events overwhelmed his mind.

Brian filled the shaker with a generous amount of gin and poured a little Chivas into a crystal tumbler for himself. He added ice to both. He took a small spritzer containing vermouth from the refrigerator, gave a quick spray to the shaker, and fit the lid on top. He shook it vigorously, and poured the gin into the martini glass where a thin sheet of ice formed on the gin. He cut a small twist from a lemon and added it to the martini. He added a little filtered water to his Chivas.

He joined Larry on the balcony. They clinked their glasses and toasted their friendship.

"Beautiful. The view." Larry sipped his drink and scanned the landscape.

"Yes. Yes it is. I still enjoy it. I've lived here four years now and still enjoy this view." Brian leaned on the railing.

They stood in silence for a moment, savoring the view, savoring their drinks. The moment lasted for less than a minute.

"I'm sorry but I can't think about anything else." Larry broke the silence.

"Try to relax. Just tell me what happened. Tell me every thing from the beginning. What did the search warrant say? You said your lawyer looked at it. What did he say? What did the police say?" Still leaning on the railing, Brian faced Larry.

As they talked, they sat in the two swivel patio chairs, which were clean but showed stains from exposure to the elements throughout the years. The narrow balcony had room for only two chairs and a small glass top table between them. They set their drinks on the table.

Larry recounted the details of the day's events. He started with the call from his housekeeper. He did not give the details in complete chronological order, and had to re-tell some of the details in their proper order. He recalled his conversation with his attorney, who had met him at the house.

Larry needed to vent, to pass the stages of fear, and anger. The anxiety consumed him, exhausted him.

"Brian, please tell me why they're doing this." Larry begged. "I know that search warrants require probable cause. They have to convince a judge before he will sign a search warrant."

"Larry, I haven't heard them say anything about a search warrant for you. Maybe I shouldn't tell you this, but the only search warrant I heard about was for Art's place. They went to his place to serve it, but as you know, they found him dead.

Brian continued, "As I said, I'm sure they don't tell me everything. I know their White Collar forensics unit monitors my work very closely. And I'm sure they talk among themselves, without telling me what's discussed." Brian knew he treaded on thin ice in this conversation. "What we have discussed - my information, their

373

research of phone records, bank accounts and the like - the information seemed to point to Art. They did not say specifically. But in the back of my mind, I thought they had found the culprit. If I'd made the connection between Art and the snakebite, I would have done something. Maybe that's why they kept me out of the loop. But of course with Art's death, I thought we were back to ground zero."

"Art was a suspect?" Larry seemed genuinely surprised.

"Yes. Yes he was. You have to realize that all of this has happened in the last couple days. Actually, everything has happened within less than two weeks."

"I know. I know. But today. This search warrant. I never once felt that I could be seen as a suspect. I don't commit crimes. I'm an accountant, for crying out loud." Larry stopped talking, took several deep breaths to keep from hyperventilating. "I can't breathe."

"Take a moment. Try to relax." Brian tried to comfort him.

"Why don't I call Wes? I know he has to be careful about what he says and does. After all, he is investigating the case. And whatever we say to him can affect anything legal." Brian started to rise from his chair to retrieve his phone.

"I don't want to talk with him." Larry exclaimed. "He just served a search warrant on me. It'd be too risky to talk with him. Don't you think? Besides my lawyer should be here, especially if we're talking with the police?"

"You're right. I guess I'm just in information gathering mode. I'm sorry. What was I thinking?" Brian shook his head at his lack of wisdom, and returned to his chair.

Brian's cell phone rang. He could barely hear it. He excused himself, stepped inside, and retrieved it from his briefcase. The caller id listed Wes Makelin's name.

"Hello." Brian answered.

"Hello, Brian. This is Wes Makelin."

"Hi Wes. Caller ID showed your name."

"Brian, I need to talk with you about some things. I have some sensitive information to go over with you." Wes started.

"Is it about the search warrant on Larry?" Brian already knew.

"Oh. Well I guess you already know about it. It's one of the things I'd like to discuss with you."

"Yeah. In fact Larry is here. He wanted someone to talk with."

"Brian, I realize this puts you in an awkward position. With him being your friend, and employer."

"Yes. But I'm really trying to keep my objectivity and loyalties in perspective." Brian groped for the right words. "Larry is my friend. I really didn't think he was a suspect."

"We decided to investigate everyone further. As we talked before, we thought Art was our man. But with his death, we have to dig a lot deeper. You need to realize that search warrants can also prove a person didn't have anything to do with a crime."

"I guess I still have a lot to learn."

"Brian, you're going to be ok. Just keep doing what you're doing. We'll get through this." Wes tried to encourage Brian. "I'm on my way to Long Beach to have dinner with my parents. I have an hour to make it by six. I hope I can make it. What time do you plan to leave work? I was wondering if I could come by your place."

"I'm sorry, when I said Larry was 'here', I meant here at my condo. I'm already home." Brian offered. "I left work about an hour ago. I don't know how long Larry plans to stay. But he's pretty upset. In any case, you're welcome to come by. What time do you think?

"Around seven. Would that be alright?"

"Sure."

Brian returned to the balcony. Larry was leaning on the balcony railing and scanning the view. He had finished his drink, and the empty glass sat on the small table.

"Can I fix you another drink?" Brian asked.

"Yes. Yes, thanks. I'm beginning to feel a little relaxed. Mostly, I feel exhausted." Larry turned, leaned his back against the railing, and faced Brian. "After a while, I think I'll go home and get some sleep."

"FYI. That was Wes Makelin on the phone. He wants to come by later."

"Well I'll leave before then. What time is he supposed to come?"

"You don't have to. You're more important. We're friends first." Brian leaned on the railing, enjoying the view as he spoke. "Although he might have more information that I could pass along to you."

"Probably worth while."

"We still have plenty of time. Why don't I fix those drinks?" Brian picked up the drink glasses and proceeded to the kitchen.

FIFTY EIGHT

Friday afternoon, April 15
Long Beach, California

Brian and Larry talked more about the search warrant and the events surrounding the embezzlement and the murders. Larry became less agitated as he vented his feelings, and his martinis took effect. He drank the second martini more slowly than the first. Brian refilled his glass, light on the Chivas, more water. He wanted full use of his mind when Wes arrived.

An hour passed.

"Ahh, look at the time. It's well after six. I've stayed longer than I had planned." Larry finished his drink and set the martini glass with its pewter stem on the table between them. "Thanks for listening. I guess I just needed to talk. I appreciate it. I feel some better. I haven't been this upset in a long time."

"You're welcome. It's always good to spend time with you. I'm sure there's nothing to worry about, Larry. We'll get through this." Brian took a sip of his drink, and nodded to Larry's empty glass. "How about another?"

"Thanks, but no thanks. I need to get on the road. Detective Makelin will probably arrive soon." Larry spoke more calmly now. "I really don't want to be here then. I'd probably get upset again. I think I'd rather have the information second hand, if you don't mind. Before this today, I had a positive opinion of law enforcement. Now I'm not so sure."

"I can understand that."

The sun began its descent, changing to dusk. Downtown building signage lights added color to the early evening. Street noises became louder. More cars. People leaving work. Returning to nearby homes, or leaving for the suburbs.

Both men rose from their chairs, stretched, and headed inside. Brian picked up Larry's glass. Larry offered to carry his, but Brian downplayed the task.

Inside the condo, the city noises slacked. Balancing both drink glasses, Brian closed the glass sliders. He slid the lock into place. He always locked his doors. Why, especially since he was twenty-six stories up? Brian carried the glasses to the kitchen, set them in the sink, and flipped on a couple lights.

The doorbell buzzed.

"Wes? He's early. It's not quite six-thirty, yet." He looked at Larry. "I guess he showed his badge downstairs to get into the building."

"I'll just excuse myself, and go. So it won't be too awkward.

Brian answered the door. It was not Wes.

"Chas, what a surprise." Brian stumbled with his words. He had worked with Chas over the last two weeks, but never thought they were close enough for him to visit Brian at home, especially unannounced. Almost stuttering, "Chas, come in. Come in. What brings you here?"

Chas wore a dark blue windbreaker jacket, jeans, and a black baseball cap. Brian almost had to look twice. He had seen Chas always wearing his signature dark suits, button-down shirts, and bold-colored silk ties.

"Hello, Brian. I was in the neighborhood and just wanted to chat." Chas stepped inside. Seeing Larry, and with a half smile and a little sarcasm, said, "Hello, Larry. I guess no one is at work. How will Leonard survive?"

"Can I offer you a drink?" Brian offered.

"Sure, a bottled water?" Chas asked, his smile still awkward.

"Yes, I have that. Or, if you want something stronger. Have a seat." Brian gestured to the couch.

Brian kept sodas, bottled water, and a few odd drinks for the occasional guest.

Chas and Larry remained standing.

"Water is fine." Chas answered. Looking at Larry, he added, "I don't want to interrupt anything." His voice sounded empty of emotion.

"Brian and I were discussing why the police were at my house today…" Larry spoke before he thought. He did not want anyone else, especially someone from work to know what he had been through. But the words came out of his mouth quickly. His mind could think about little else all afternoon.

Brian rejoined them with the bottle of water and a Diet Coke for himself. He handed the water to Chas.

"They were at my place too." Chas volunteered and took the water.

"They were? I wonder who else was served a search warrant. Have a seat." Brian again offered for them to sit. They declined. Brian leaned against the nearby dining table and opened his soda.

Brian asked Larry if he wanted something else to drink. He shook his head no.

Brian thought of the names on the short list of accesses that he developed. He did not feel free to discuss those names with Larry, and certainly not with Chas.

"They're probably looking at everyone with access to the systems." Brian tried to generalize the situation, to ease the conversation, hoping that no one would ask specific questions.

"Brian and I were discussing that point earlier. I thought they had to have 'probable cause' for a judge to sign it." Larry looked at Chas.

"That's what I understand too." Chas agreed. "That female detective, Hadley, served me mine. I was at home when she called. I wanted some time to myself, so I took the day off." Chas did not explain that his father had died last night.

"My housekeeper called me. She was nearly hysterical. I'm sure I broke a couple speed limits racing home." Larry crossed his arms, and sarcastically added, "Detective Makelin served me. And I thought they were such nice people too."

Each did not want to discuss the specifics of his situation. And Brian did not feel at liberty to discuss anything. He liked Chas, but did not feel comfortable telling him about his relationship with the detectives.

Silence hung over the room for a minute. Even attempts at small talk failed to fill the void. Brian felt the tension in the room rise. He wondered if something was about to happen. What did Chas want?

"I guess you're wondering why I'm here. In fact, it's probably good that you're both here." Chas broke the silence.

"I don't understand. Why?" Brian felt curious. The tension he felt earlier returned. "Is there something you want to tell us?"

"Over the last several hours, I've changed my thinking." Chas looked at one man then the other, then back. Almost as if reminiscing, he continued, "For most of my adult life, for most of my career, I've always planned ahead, always prepared for the possibilities. I always developed a plan A and a plan B. If A didn't work, then B would. I left little to chance. Usually plan A worked. My career has gone well. My investments have gone well. As for my personal life, well, little time has been left for a personal life. Oh, but I ramble."

"Chas, aren't you a little young to refer to your life in the past tense? You sound a little depressed." Brian responded. He tilted his head trying to understand what Chas was saying and the rising tension in the room.

"I'm beginning to think Art was right. Sometimes it's easier to just eliminate a problem rather than simply try to resolve it, or control it. A lot less effort. Extreme consequences, but less effort." Chas continued, as if remembering a prepared statement. "If you guys just hadn't kept trying to solve the money problem."

"I'm not sure I understand." Brain felt confused. He sensed something negative was about to happen. He could not infer the intent behind Chas' words. How were Chas and Art involved with each other, other than work?

"I had a good thing going. Most of the money Leonard earned, I earned. I made the projects profitable. I deserve a part of that money. Gerardi is old, unfortunately, not old enough. She needs to retire. I should have her job." Chas began to rant.

"Are you saying that you're responsible for the embezzlement?' Brian began to realize Chas's involvement. He remembered the earlier conversation with Karen about embezzlers feeling they *deserved* the money they stole.

The case was beginning to make sense. Chas had the knowledge and the brains to develop the intricate scheme. Maybe Art helped him.

"But I thought your family had money." Larry asked, tilting his head sideways.

"Having family money is different from getting it for yourself." Chas growled at Larry. "I had a selfish father who kept his own money. I was supposed to earn my own. And I did."

"You said *had a father*... Brian caught the past tense. This choice of words sounded important.

"The old fucker died last night, finally." Chas' face showed an evil grin. "Now I have money, real money."

"Did you embezzle the money from Leonard?" Brian asked Chas directly. "I know my work pointed to someone inside the company, but I just couldn't believe it was anybody I'd worked with."

"As I said, I deserved the money. It wasn't embezzlement." Chas answered.

"How did Art figure in all this?" Brian asked. "Why did you need him? Couldn't you have done the technical stuff without him?"

"You may know computers, but you don't know people, do you." Chas ridiculed rather than asked. "I needed a fall guy. As I said, plan B. In fact I have a couple fall guys."

"You know Art is dead, don't you?" Larry asked.

"Of course." Chas answered, smiling with a sense of accomplishment. He paused for a couple seconds and stepped away to face the two men. "I killed him."

"What?" Brian nearly dropped his soda, spilling some on the floor.

"What did you say?" Larry gasped. He could not believe what he had heard.

Chas set his water bottle on the sofa table, and stepped aside, facing the two men. He reached into his jacket, and pulled out a Glock 9mm pistol. He held it casually, not specifically pointing it at either man. Of course, he could point and fire it very easily before anyone could do anything.

For Brian and Larry, shock quickly turned to fear.

"I said that I eliminated Art. He became a problem. I had to admit that I couldn't control him anymore. So, I needed to eliminate him."

"And you killed Greg and David too?" Ever the analyst, Brian asked. Wes had convinced him that Art likely killed them.

"No, no I didn't kill Greg and David. They were ok guys, for accountants that is, not upscale, cream-of-the-crop types, but ok. For an analyst, your skills suck." Chas belittled Brian.

"If you didn't kill them, who did?" Larry asked with defiance.

"Art did, didn't he?" Brian said his thoughts aloud. He asked, "As you said, you used Art to handle the dirty work, didn't you?"

"Smart guy. Now you're catching on," Chas responded with a little less sarcasm. "Maybe there is hope for you yet. In the detective department, that is. Unfortunately, your smarts came too late. But you're right. I needed someone to handle the *dirty work*. For a few dollars, Art was the guy. He liked his drugs, the girls, and surfing. Always the surfing. He was easy to control in the beginning."

"But he wanted more, so he became difficult to control." Brian added and took a deep breath. His mind raced to find words to talk Chas out of what could happen. After all he held a gun. "So you had to eliminate him?"

"Correct again. But I think I just said that." A smirk played at the corners of Chas' mouth. "Now, ironically, I have to think a little more like Art and eliminate my other problems. I wanted simply to divert attention, to point to someone else for the police's attention. I put my little money scheme on hold for the last couple weeks. And it was such a clever scheme. What are a few million when company profits are in the billions?"

Chas continued. "To answer your earlier question, yes, Art killed both of them. Actually, he was supposed to only disable Greg. An accident. Cripple him for a few weeks. Enough time for me to clear the computer tracks. "

"Greg's the one who discovered my little scheme. And it was such a small scheme. The dollars didn't even pass the allowable limits. It could have stayed under the radar for a few more years. Anyway, I really thought with Greg's *accidental* death, everyone would be too sad and too busy to follow-up. But I was wrong." Chas looked at Larry, and lathered more sarcasm. "But no. You had to hire a technology expert."

"Looks like I got results." Larry challenged.

"Don't push it." Chas's face filled with savage anger.

"Sounds like Art did become a problem." Brian redirected Chas' attention. He wanted to keep him calm. Brian worried about Jimbo in the next room. *Please stay asleep, son. And Wes, please get here.*

"Ah, Art. He had to do things the tough way. He put too much drug in Greg's drink. And as for poor David, Art just had to be the tough guy. David was just helping pick up where Greg left off. On his own, Art had to eliminate 'the problem'."

"I can't believe I'm telling you all this. I'm actually solving your case for you. You'd have all the answers for the Sheriff's detectives. But..." He paused for dramatic effect. "But, you two won't be telling anybody anything. Actually, you won't leave here today, alive that is."

"Chas, please put the gun away. Let's talk about this." Brian pleaded, without begging. "I have to grant you that your little system was pretty sophisticated. You must know a lot about computer systems, including the very technical stuff."

Brian realized that although Chas did not kill Greg and David. He did kill Art, and therefore capable of killing him and Larry. He wanted to keep Chas talking, to keep him busy until Wes could arrive. He pleaded in his mind. *Wes, come on, we need you here. Save-the-day sort of thing.*

"Thank you. I thought so." Chas smiled and bowed his head mockingly at the flattery.

Larry stood there, still in shock, almost unable to speak. Brian's mind rushed to keep Chas talking.

"Actually, the evidence, at least what I was aware of, pointed to Art. But we thought he didn't have the accounting or technical know-how to orchestrate the embezzlement. He had to have an accomplice. We even thought it could be an outside hacker." Brian talked, hoping Chas would participate. Anything to give more time for Wes to arrive.

"Accomplice. He was the accomplice." Chas snapped, insulted. "The guy was a lamebrain. Give him some money, some drugs, and a surfboard, he would stay happy. But let a little problem come up, he'd go off the deep end. He was strictly strong arm stuff."

"But enough about him. Now, I have to do the strong-arm stuff myself. I have to eliminate my two biggest problems. And both problems are right here. Nice." Chas took a breath, tired of talking. "Besides, it really isn't that hard to eliminate someone. A little pre-thought, some staging, including those legal dramas on TV help more than you'd realize. Sometimes cleaning up someone else' mess requires a little more work."

"Chas, Detective Makelin is on his way here, right now." Brian tried another tactic.

He wanted to prevent Chas from *eliminating* his problems, specifically eliminating Larry and him. Worse, he knew Chas would probably kill Jimbo sleeping in the next room. He could not let that happen.

"Yeah, sure. You, an amateur detective with questionable analytical skills. And now apparently with poor lying skills. You'd best stick with computers, Brian." Again sarcasm soaked every word. "Or are you getting too old to keep up with technology, with its constant changes."

"I do ok in the technology department." Brian defended himself. He wanted to add that he had discovered the evidence that pointed to Chas too. But he did not want to provoke Chas further. He had to keep the conversation going until Wes arrived.

"Chas, I'm serious, Detective Makelin is on his way. So please don't do anything irrational. You won't get away with it." Brian started to remind Chas that murder has far more serious consequences than embezzlement, but he remembered that Chas had just confessed to killing Art.

"Yeah, sure. As I said, you really need to work on your lying skills." Chas waved his gun, pointing at Brian, then at Larry. "So, I guess I'd better get on with this. Oh, I almost forgot. Brian. You haven't asked the important question."

"What's that?"

"Oh come on, think."

In less than a second, a light bulb went on in Brian's head, actually, it exploded.

"The snake! You sent the snake here." Rage surged in Brian. His fists clenched, he bounded toward Chas.

"Uh-unh. That was Art." Chas held the Glock in Brian's face, three inches from the middle of his eyes.

Brian froze. He had to regain control. Jimbo was in the next room. No words came to him, just primeval rage toward the man with the gun.

"Now, which one of you makes the best victim? I think a murder-suicide might just work here. Larry, you be the murderer. They'll think that Brian had learned too much, so you had to eliminate him. Then you felt such remorse for killing your friend, that you committed suicide."

"Chas, that's weak."

"Not really. Since, I've directed some of the evidence to point to you. The 'probable cause' for the search warrant. I planted it."

"What probable cause?" Larry had wondered since the search on his place this morning.

"Your relationship with Art."

"What relationship with Art?" Larry asked with worry in his voice.

"The coke. He was your supplier. Don't you see the connection? Both of you druggies. Easy for law enforcement to connect. A druggie killed his supplier. Wouldn't that work? And now you're going to kill your own investigator." Chas was on another rant.

"Larry? What does he mean?" Brian felt a little self-control returning.

"Art supplied me some. Just on occasion. I needed a pick-me-up occasionally. Not a big deal." Larry defended himself.

"It could be a big deal. At the restaurant, I thought you had a pickup of energy a couple times." Brian worried for his friend.

Detective Makelin, where are you? Brian thought.

384

FIFTY NINE

Friday early evening, April 15
Long Beach, California

"Enough talk already. You couldn't do anything with the information anyway. As I was saying, this is going to be a nice, little murder-suicide. Probably won't even make the papers. Not very original, I admit. But I don't have a lot of time for thorough planning." Chas' sarcasm shifted to cold-blooded intent. He straightened his back, stood taller with an evil sense of self-satisfaction and control.

Chas continued, "Larry, as I said, I'm thinking you should be the murderer since the police are already looking at you as a possible suspect, the search warrant and all. You suspected Brian here was uncovering too much, so you decided to eliminate him. Simple."

Chas did not know of Brian's and Larry's close friendship, so such a plan working was probably very remote.

Chas pointed the Glock at Brian. At that moment, Larry reached for the small, but heavy Bragg bronze statue of Pan, sitting on a nearby pedestal. He flung it at Chas. Chas tried to dodge the small statue which grazed his head. He stumbled backward, but jerked his pistol toward Larry, and pulled the trigger. The pistol issued a loud crack. Larry clutched his chest, moaned, and crumpled to the floor. Blood oozed from his chest between his fingers.

385

As Chas tried to regain his footing, Brian rushed him. Struggling, they fell on the coffee table, breaking the glass top, and knocking candlesticks, a glass dolphin, and magazines onto the floor.

Chas kept his grip on the gun, trying to point it at Brian for a good shot. Chas was twenty years younger, stronger, but about the same height. He knew he could handle this old man. He fired twice but the old man would not stop fighting. He cursed Brian. He kept enough of his senses to know that he needed to shoot Brian in the temple or mouth to make it look like a suicide. Since he shot Larry first, then Brian had to be the murderer turned suicide. A small change of plans. It could work.

Brian refused to accept defeat. He had to win this fight. His son was in the next room, and Chas would kill him too. In no way, would Brian let that happen.

Just then, Jimbo opened the door from his bedroom, still groggy from the drugs to help him sleep. This distracted Chas for just a moment. Brian struck Chas one more time, hard, with his fist. He rushed to Jimbo, pushing and yelling for him to get back into his bedroom.

Chas fired again. His aim was bad, the bullet whizzed past Brian's head. With Brian pushing, Jimbo fell onto his bed. Brian slammed and locked the door to the small bedroom. He knew he had little time. The door was the thin, hollow type. It wouldn't hold long. He had to think fast. Another shot rang and whizzed through the door.

Chas, determined to follow his murder-suicide plan, would eliminate his problems. He had eliminated one, Larry. Now he would eliminate Brian. And the new guy from the bedroom, well he would just be collateral damage. *More bad logic.*

"We've got to get out of here." Brian commanded his son in a loud whisper. He had to protect him. He lifted Jimbo and half-dragged him to the sliding glass door that led to the balcony. Jimmy's grogginess began to lift. The sound of gunfire can wake most anyone.

"You might as well let me in. There's no way you can escape. You're more than twenty stories above the street." Chas taunted, unaware the nearby glass sliders in the living room opened to the same balcony. He stood at the door, tapped quietly for entry. He had cornered his prey, as a cat would play with its trapped mouse.

"Hurry, climb around the divider. I know it's scary, son. But hang onto the railing and to the divider. You can do it. Get the neighbor's attention and call the police. If the neighbor isn't there, go on to the next one. I'm right behind you." Brian helped Jimbo climb over the four-foot wrought iron railing and around the metal divider. Jimbo was awake now. He tried to convince his father to go first. But Brian would not hear of it. His father mode was in over-drive. He would protect his son.

Chas waited a moment. Impatient, he stepped back a couple steps, and fired his pistol again. With a loud crack, the bullet busted the door handle and lock mechanism. He slammed open the door and stepped inside the dark bedroom. Through the glass sliders, he saw the two men struggle to climb over the balcony railing.

Solid metal dividers separated the condo owner's balconies. The balcony circled the entire building. Without the dividers, someone could walk literally around the entire building, on each floor. Because of the building's round structure, they would find protection because Chas would not have a direct shot at them.

After Jimmy dropped onto the neighbor's balcony, Brian started to follow. Hearing the glass slider open, he looked back and saw Chas aiming his gun at Brian. Another shot whizzed by Brian. He wondered for a second why Chas did not shoot him. Chas certainly had a clear, easy shot, from just a few feet away.

Brian remembered Chas' planned murder-suicide scenario. He guessed that he had become the *murderer* in Chas's little drama since Larry was shot first. Chas would need to shoot from a very close distance for Brian's death to look like a suicide. How could Chas think so coldly in such a crises. The word sociopath came to mind, then left as quickly as it came.

Worse, Chas would kill Jimbo regardless of how the drama played. Brian would not let that happen. Brian felt better that Jimbo was safer on the other side of the metal divider. Hopefully the neighbors were home and had heard the gun shots. The residents in the Spire were accustomed to street noises, but not nearby gun shots. They had offered to help Tuesday night after the snakebite. They could really help now. Just take Jimbo inside and call the police.

As Chas approached, Brian rushed Chas and grabbed his wrist with both hands to keep him from firing the gun, and to wrestle it from him. Chas stumbled backward knocking over the patio chairs and breaking the small glass table. Chas still would not release his gun and with his free hand tried to fight Brian off him. Brian held onto Chas' gun hand fiercely. He would not let go, using the weight of his body to block Chas' other hand.

Chas tried to regain his footing so he could control the situation. He would not allow this old guy to defeat him. They fell against the giant glass doors, nearly knocking the breath out of both of them. The glass doors gave but did not break; however, huge cracks spread like a spider web from the point of their impact.

Locked in combat, they rebounded and fell against the railing. It gave, bending slightly from the force of their combined weight. Brian grunted from the excruciating pain in his ribs. They nearly toppled over the side. Brian had to prevail. He could not let Chas kill them.

Chas still wanted to control how Brian would die. He wanted his murder-suicide drama to work. He pulled back.

This move gave Brian enough leverage to turn and push Chas against the railing. Brian's strength began to fade. He could barely manage to control Chas' gun arm, much less defend himself from the beating from Chas' other fist. Brian had to act quickly with the little strength he had left.

If Chas wanted a suicide, Brian would give it to him. But he would take Chas with him. They both would die. But Jimmy would live. That worked for Brian. Brian freed one hand and gripped Chas in a bear hug and leaned both of them over the railing.

Both began to fall, almost in slow motion. Amazing how the mind processes critical events. As they fell, Brian released one hand from around Chas and grabbed the top railing. A last subconscious attempt to live, to survive.

Chas refused to drop the gun. He tried to grab onto Brian with his other hand, clutching only his shirt. Brian's shirt did not hold. The shirt tore off. Chas held it in one hand and the gun in the other as he fell to the street below. He did not scream. He did not flail his arms and legs. Resigned to the obvious outcome.

Brian held onto the railing, his fist locked around the wrought iron. His adrenalin pumped. Sirens sounded on Ocean Boulevard below. He heard the noise from the crowd gathering below. Exhaustion overcame him. He wondered if he could hang onto the railing, or ever loosen his grip. He swung his left arm around and gripped the railing.

He did not think he had the strength to pull himself over the railing. He vowed he would get into shape. He was just too old for situations like this.

He looked up. Wes was standing there reaching for Brian's arms to pull him onto the balcony. Once on the balcony side, Wes helped Brian pry his fingers free from the railing.

During the commotion, no one heard Wes fire his revolver into Brian's front door. He had used his badge, to gain access into the building downstairs. He started to knock on Brian's door, but heard gunfire inside the unit. He knew something was very wrong.

"Larry's been shot."

"I know, I saw him lying on the floor."

"You check him. I need to check on Jimbo." Brian went to the metal divider to see if he was there. Brian called to him. No answer. Brian felt new fear. Could one of the stray bullets have struck him? He rushed inside the condo. Jimbo walked in the front door with the neighbor man close behind. He rushed to his dad, grateful that he was ok. Father and son held each other in silence for a moment. Brian kissed his son on the cheek even though he was a foot taller. The new fear left, calm returned to Brian.

"Dad, I called 911. The neighbors were home."

"Good son. You did good. I'm just glad you're ok."

"I'm glad you're ok too, Dad." Jimbo sounded ready to cry, or to laugh. He hugged his dad again.

Happy that Jimbo was ok, Brian turned his attention to Larry. Wes had checked Larry's breathing. He was alive. Wes looked at the wound. It was serious but the bullet appeared to miss key organs. Wes pulled his cell phone from his jacket and called 911 to send paramedics to the condo. He then called Long Beach Detective Kaminski.

After only seconds, more sirens sounded on Ocean Boulevard. The Long Beach Police Department was located only a few blocks away, so they had responded quickly. The police received several 911 calls that night. Other neighbors heard gunfire and called 911. People on the street saw the fighting on the balcony and called 911.

SIXTY

Sunday morning, April 17
Long Beach, California

Brian sat quietly on his balcony, drinking coffee. Sunday mid-morning felt almost normal again, especially considering the scare from two nights ago. His body still hurt, his wrist and ribs hurt. The ambulance had taken him to the hospital. They treated him, and gave him prescriptions for his pains. He had a couple cracked ribs, and some serious bruising on his right wrist, but he would survive.

But now he enjoyed these moments, the morning sunshine, the street noises, and his hot coffee. The Long Beach Telegram paper lay on a wooden TV tray, beside him. It contained an article of Friday night's events on page one. He would read it later. He sat away from the bent balcony railing. The small glass table, missing its glass top, sat in the corner. On Saturday, after the Long Beach forensics group finished, he and Jimbo attempted to clean the house of broken glass and other debris.

Brian's mind wandered through the events of the last two weeks. In the beginning, he felt excited about the promising, well paying job at Leonard. It gave his consulting practice a good start after several months of unemployment. But a simple case of tracking missing money quickly led to three murders, and the near deaths of him and his son. But now it was over. The murders were solved, and he and his son would be ok.

He could again enjoy the sun, the quiet, and the slow start of a weekend morning. Jimbo was asleep in his room.

Brian heard a soft knock at the door. He carried his 'Evita' coffee mug with him. He expected Karen. They had talked earlier. She had called from Larry's hospital room in Long Beach Memorial.

Brian liked Karen. He hoped they would become good friends, not because she was an up-and-coming writer. But she had a good sense of humor with an infectious laugh, and she could enjoy the nuances of words. He enjoyed her company, and she appeared to enjoy his.

Brian unlocked the door chain. "Good morning, Karen. Welcome. Come in, please."

They hugged. A warm hug between friends.

"Good morning, Brian. I'm so glad you're alright." Karen's words were genuine. She looked at the door's absence of a locking mechanism and handle. "What happened here?"

"When Wes arrived Friday night, he heard gunfire. So he shot off the lock." Brian explained. "Good thing he did. A classic case of arriving in the nick of time. If he hadn't, I might not have been able to climb back onto the balcony."

Brian explained that he had scheduled a locksmith to come Monday. Until then, the chain lock would have to suffice.

"You know, I have to hear the whole story. But first, tell me how you feel. The truth." Like a big sister, Karen held Brian by his shoulders and looked directly at him, demanding honesty.

"I'm fine. A couple ribs hurt, and my wrist is extremely sore from the gymnastics on the balcony. But I'm sure it'll be fine in a few days." Brian set his coffee mug on the counter and massaged the weakened wrist.

"Gymnastics. That's a good word for it. Harrowing, nearly killed are words that come to my mind." Karen expressed mock surprise at the understated word.

"I'm having some coffee. How about some?" Brian offered, enjoying her use of words.

"Yes, I would like some. Thanks."

"Cream and sugar?" Brian asked.

"No. Black. Thanks. No additives."

Brian retrieved a mug from the cabinet. He selected a white one with a 'Brigadoon' green imprint. He had taken Jimbo to see the vintage musical. He was polite and called it interesting, without further commitment. Maybe it was generational. Brian poured coffee for Karen and refreshed his mug.

"You're all over the news this morning. You, Wes, Larry, Leonard Construction. I saw a clip of a reporter interviewing Wes. He always seems in control, unfazed by the events. He's such a professional." Karen took her coffee, careful not to spill it. She sipped the coffee, testing the hotness.

"He is a professional. But, I guess he's captured bad guys before, so he has developed that detached, objective attitude. I like working with him." Brian agreed. "But when his evidence pointed to Larry, and they searched his house, I worried that maybe we couldn't work together. I just knew that Larry was in no way guilty of any of this."

"Yes. Larry told me about the search warrant, and how you defended him. I'm with you. I know Larry." Karen joined in Larry's defense.

"Let's sit on the balcony." Brian picked up his coffee and guided Karen outside.

"Wow, that looks unsafe. Is that where the drama happened?" Karen reacted to the bent railing.

"Yes. Yes, it is. I'll have to tell you about it."

"And, what a view. You can see forever. Is that the Hollywood sign?" Karen stood at the railing, away from the section that bent outward, enjoying the view of Long Beach, Los Angeles, and the mountains beyond.

"Yes it is the Hollywood sign. Of course, you need a good pair of binoculars to read it. But you can see it." Brian used his chamber of commerce voice. In a singsong voice, he added with an obvious reference to Barbara Streisand. "And on a clear day…"

They both laughed at his weak pun.

Brian leaned on the railing, and faced Karen. "I talked with Wes for a couple of hours yesterday. He had more information about the search warrants, Art, Larry, and Chas. Apparently Chas designed his scheme to point to Art and Larry. And he pushed Art to involve Larry in drugs." Brian took a sip of his coffee. "Wes also told me they found some coke in Greg's car, but he didn't have any in his system. The vial of coke didn't have any prints on it, so they figured Art planted it. Since he had cocaine in his apartment."

"It's unfortunate that drugs became a problem for Larry in the last few years. It's very sad." Karen continued. "I didn't know about it until Larry told me this morning. He said if he can't resolve it on his own, he'll enter rehab."

"He told me that yesterday too. I understand that Art sold him the coke which accounts for the phone calls between them." Brian added. "We'd had dinner a week ago, and I suspected he might have been a user. But I know he'll overcome the addiction. He's strong that way."

"For somebody who had been shot, he seemed pretty upbeat. I half expected him to be in a coma." Karen shifted the subject.

"That's what I thought. Friday night, I really thought he was dead. After Wes helped pull me back over the railing, he checked Larry, and he was breathing. The paramedics said he was seriously hurt, but would live."

Jimbo joined them on the balcony, carrying a Diet Coke. He had dressed in jeans and a wrinkled Long Beach State long sleeved t-shirt.

"Karen, I don't think you and my son have met. Jimbo this is Karen Coffman, my friend, the writer. I'm sure you remember my talking about her."

"Yes, yes I do. Hello Ms. Coffman." Jimbo offered his hand.

"Karen. Call me Karen, please." Karen stood, grasped his hand, and pulled him close to her for a hug. "I hear you've been through your own high drama the last few days. How are you doing? I see you're using a cane."

"I'm doing pretty good, considering. Still sore from the snakebite, but every day is a little better. Friday night, of course, was really scary. But I'm sure everything will be back to normal in a few days."

"Jimbo, there is a folding chair in the closet outside your bedroom." Brian nodded to the hallway closet.

"No that's ok, Dad. I was just getting ready to leave. Remember, I haven't been home for nearly a week. And before you ask, I feel much better. I'm a big boy. I can take care of myself." He paused, "Unless you need me."

"No son, that's alright. I just like having you around."

"Nice to meet you Ms., err, Karen."

"Nice to meet you, too."

Brian escorted Jimbo to the front door. They hugged.

"Love you Son."

"Love you too, Dad."

393

Jimbo left, carrying his gym bag and Diet Coke. Brian rejoined Karen on the balcony.

"Now, you've got to tell me everything. Assuming you feel up to it." Karen commanded. "I talked with Wes yesterday, but he's too busy closing the case, or I should say, cases. He has to update the Santa Monica and Long Beach Police Departments. And, Larry gave me more information this morning. But he was groggy from his painkillers, so we didn't talk long."

"Well, in a nutshell, Chas and Art were our guys. The criminals. As of yesterday morning, I only knew that we had a short list of people with access to the systems. Chas, Larry, and a few other names. And I was convinced that neither Larry nor Chas could be guilty. So I began researching the others."

"Did any evidence point to the new people on the list?" Karen asked.

"Not really. But then things happened too fast. Wes and Phyllis of course knew more than I did, and they suspected Art. They served a search warrant on him, but found him dead. With a dead body, they can pretty well search all they want." Brian added. "They found drugs and a few other things. But of course the big thing, another murder had been committed. They didn't believe suicide or coincidence."

"Wes told me they found him dead Thursday morning, but nothing else. As I said he was too busy the last couple days." Karen took another sip of her coffee.

"That was Thursday. So, Wes and Phyllis focused on the next names on the list, namely Larry and Chas. Those search warrants were served on Friday." Brian shifted in his chair, his ribs protested. "Ouch. Of course that upset Larry. It'd upset me too. Then he came here after the police finished their search."

"I didn't know about Chas's search warrant."

"I didn't either until Friday night. Well, that must have driven Chas over the deep end. That, and the death of his father. A whole different person showed up at my door around six. The conversation started with small talk, and then Chas drew a gun. He talked about a murder-suicide. He had developed this drama where Larry would shoot me, and then killed himself. He said the police would think Art killed Greg and David, which he did. And then connect Art to Larry, and to me. Obviously, he didn't think the whole thing through. I just couldn't believe we were talking to the same man I'd worked with for the last two weeks."

"Really sounds like Chas was a true sociopath. It's not surprising that he was able to befriend you. A sociopath can fool the people around him into thinking he's normal. He manipulates them without any attached feelings." Karen faced Brian.

"Well, that fits Chas. He certainly had me fooled. He was cooperative, helpful." Brian held his coffee with both hands and sipped it.

"But Chas probably reached a breaking point. He just blew up. I wonder what triggered him." Karen looked toward the mountains. "And why did he embezzle? He earned good money at Leonard, ambitious, fast promotions. I understand his father was very wealthy, and he was an only son."

"I'm not sure why he embezzled. But Chas said his father died. 'Old fucker' were his exact words. That may have been the trigger." Brian answered her last question, first.

Brian continued, "A nurse who worked for the elder Erickson called Wes yesterday. She had seen the news about what happened here Friday night. She told Wes that the elder Erickson had been sick for some time and died a couple days ago. She needed to pick up some of her things; she still had her key. The place was in shambles. She thought Wes would want to see it."

"According to Wes, a wall of family photographs was ripped from the wall and smashed. Interesting enough, the pictures were mostly of an older son, who had died in high school. The nurse said the dead son was the father's favorite since he talked mostly about him. She thought Chas probably felt a lot of resentment growing up."

Wes also said the elder Erickson took lots of medicines, which could have been the source for the drugs in Greg's system, and in Art's system. Naturally, the father's place has become a crime scene. After all it's likely related to three murders."

"What you're describing certainly fits the definition of a sociopath. The father favored the older brother. The younger son, Chas, probably spent his life trying to win his father's approval through professional success and money. I'll corner Wes another time to learn more about that family. It would be a good story, if it was only a story. Unfortunately, it is so tragically real." Karen's voice filled with sadness.

Karen thought how difficult it must have been for a teenage boy to feel rejected by his father. She wanted to think about the story elements because she did not know Chas, so she could keep her emotions in check. But she knew the other people involved, so keeping her emotions detached may not be easy.

"And according to what Chas said Friday night, he involved Art in case he needed to deflect the blame, and to do the dirty work. Chas said Art was cheap muscle, until he became uncontrollable. So Chas killed him. Chas had planned only to disable Greg, but Art put too much drug in his drink. And Art decided, on his own, to kill David."

"Chas admitted that to you?" Karen asked in disbelief.

"Yes. I guess he just felt confident that he'd eliminate Larry and me." Brian sipped more coffee. It had become cool. "I want more coffee. How about you?"

"Sure I'll have a little."

Karen followed Brian into the kitchen.

"We could probably analyze Chas all afternoon. But tell me about Friday night's drama. You, Larry, and your son had to be scared to death." Karen quizzed Brian for more details. "That's a long way to the street to hang from a railing this high up."

Brian summarized in digest form, as they returned to the balcony.

He and Larry were talking about the search warrants. Wes called and asked if it would be ok for him to stop by later. Naturally, I said yes. So, Larry planned to leave before Wes would arrive. But then Chas arrived, pulled a gun, and shot Larry. Brian knew Chas would kill him, but feared that Chas would also kill Jimbo. So he and Chas fought. They fell over the balcony, but Brian was able to hang onto the railing. Chas hung onto Brian's leg, but slowly slipped until he fell.

Karen begged for more specifics. Brian relented and answered her questions.

"I'd also like to add a personal observation, about myself. My attitude has changed. My vocabulary has changed. Even my opinion of people has changed. Until recently, I called my work *research* now of course it's an *investigation. Employee fraud* in now a *criminal act,* and a *murderer* may actually be somebody I know, or knew." Brian set his coffee mug on the TV tray between them. "And I'm probably a little more skeptical about human nature than I was before."

"Well, going through what you did would change anyone." Karen sympathized. "But I'm sure any changes were positive in a way, character building, as some say."

"I hope so."

They talked for another hour.

Brain changed the subject.

"Larry talked with Daniel Post this morning." Seeing a question on Karen's face, Brian added, "Daniel Post is Leonard's CEO. He and Larry offered me more work in Larry's department for a few months. At least until Larry recovers and rebuilds his department."

"That has to relieve your mind. When we first met, you worried about building you consulting practice. You'd said that this so-called retirement was more a burden than a blessing."

"Yes it does relieve my mind a little. I can worry a little less about my mother in the nursing home." Brian said. "Oh, another thing that I like, Wes said their WCC Division liked my work. They plan to use me in the future." Brian smiled, and sat a little straighter. "I think I could get used to consulting with law enforcement. Even though I still work with data and computer systems, it can be very interesting, lots of pressure, but interesting. Many older people don't have these options."

"That's good. Just be careful. Well, I need to run some errands and you, Brian, need to get some rest." Karen played her big sister role. "Let's stay in touch. Oh, just in case there are more sociopaths out there, you, go the other direction."

"I will, I promise."

Both laughed. Brian closed the door; his phone rang.

"Brian? What's this drama I'm hearing about you on the television?" A disbelieving voice asked.

"Phillip, good to hear from you. Yes, we've had our drama here." Brian felt good hearing the caller's voice. A warm, pleasurable feeling washed over him. Last Saturday night was a good night.

"So it's all true? Are you all right? Are you hurt? There I go with the questions. But really, are you alright?"

"It's really good to hear your voice." Brian sat in a nearby chair. He would answer questions in a moment. He wanted to enjoy this feeling a while longer.

Phillip sensed the same warm feeling. "It's good to hear your voice too."

They shared a quiet moment. Then they talked, asked and answered questions, and reminisced.

ACKNOWLEDGEMENTS

I appreciate the help and encouragement of certain people in my writing journey of Tenth Boomer. I very much want to thank Marcia Bouey, Tootsie Panayotou, John Sommers, and Mark Taylor.

I also want to thank Richard N. Crauthers for his contribution to the cover design.

www.ingramcontent.com/pod-product-compliance
Lightning Source LLC
Chambersburg PA
CBHW060812030726
47503CB00002B/452

* 9 7 8 0 6 1 5 3 2 6 8 3 2 *